SIMON & SCHUSTER CHILDREN'S PUBLISHING
ADVANCE READER'S COPY

TITLE: Coldwire

AUTHOR: Chloe Gong

IMPRINT: Margaret K. McElderry Books

ON-SALE DATE: 11.04.25

ISBN: 9781665960137

FORMAT: hardcover

PRICE: $21.99

AGES: 14 up

PAGES: 496

Do not quote for publication until verified with finished books. This advance uncorrected reader's proof is the property of Simon & Schuster. It is being loaned for promotional purposes and review by the recipient and may not be used for any other purpose or transferred to any third party. Simon & Schuster reserves the right to cancel the loan and recall possession of the proof at any time. Any duplication, sale, or distribution to the public is a violation of law.

Please send any review or mention of this book to
ChildrensPublicity@simonandschuster.com.

Aladdin • Atheneum Books for Young Readers
Beach Lane Books • Beyond Words • Boynton Bookworks
Caitlyn Dlouhy Books • Denene Millner Books
Libros para niños • Little Simon • Margaret K. McElderry Books
MTV Books • Paula Wiseman Books • Salaam Reads
Sarah Barley Books • Simon & Schuster Books for Young Readers
Simon Pulse • Simon Spotlight

COLDWIRE

COLD

ALSO BY CHLOE GONG

These Violent Delights
Our Violent Ends
Foul Lady Fortune
Last Violent Call
Foul Heart Huntsman

WIRE

CHLOE GONG

MARGARET K. McELDERRY BOOKS
NEW YORK   AMSTERDAM/ANTWERP   LONDON
TORONTO   SYDNEY/MELBOURNE   NEW DELHI

MARGARET K. McELDERRY BOOKS

An imprint of Simon & Schuster Children's Publishing Division

1230 Avenue of the Americas, New York, New York 10020

For more than 100 years, Simon & Schuster has championed authors and the stories they create. By respecting the copyright of an author's intellectual property, you enable Simon & Schuster and the author to continue publishing exceptional books for years to come. We thank you for supporting the author's copyright by purchasing an authorized edition of this book.

No amount of this book may be reproduced or stored in any format, nor may it be uploaded to any website, database, language-learning model, or other repository, retrieval, or artificial intelligence system without express permission.

All rights reserved. Inquiries may be directed to Simon & Schuster, 1230 Avenue of the Americas, New York, NY 10020 or permissions@simonandschuster.com.

This book is a work of fiction. Any references to historical events, real people, or real places are used fictitiously. Other names, characters, places, and events are products of the author's imagination, and any resemblance to actual events or places or persons, living or dead, is entirely coincidental.

Text © 2025 by Chloe Gong

Jacket photo-illustration © 2025 by Sean & Eve

All rights reserved, including the right of reproduction in whole or in part in any form.

MARGARET K. McELDERRY BOOKS is a trademark of Simon & Schuster, LLC.

For information about special discounts for bulk purchases, please contact Simon & Schuster Special Sales at 1-866-506-1949 or business@simonandschuster.com.

The Simon & Schuster Speakers Bureau can bring authors to your live event. For more information or to book an event, contact the Simon & Schuster Speakers Bureau at 1-866-248-3049 or visit our website at www.simonspeakers.com.

The text for this book was set in EB Garamond.

Manufactured in the United States of America

First Edition

10 9 8 7 6 5 4 3 2 1

CIP data for this book is available from the Library of Congress.

ISBN 9781665960137

ISBN 9781665960151 (ebook)

For Owen,

Because "this cyberpunk novel idea I have" sparked such conversation on our first date

and because of every conversation since then. I love you!

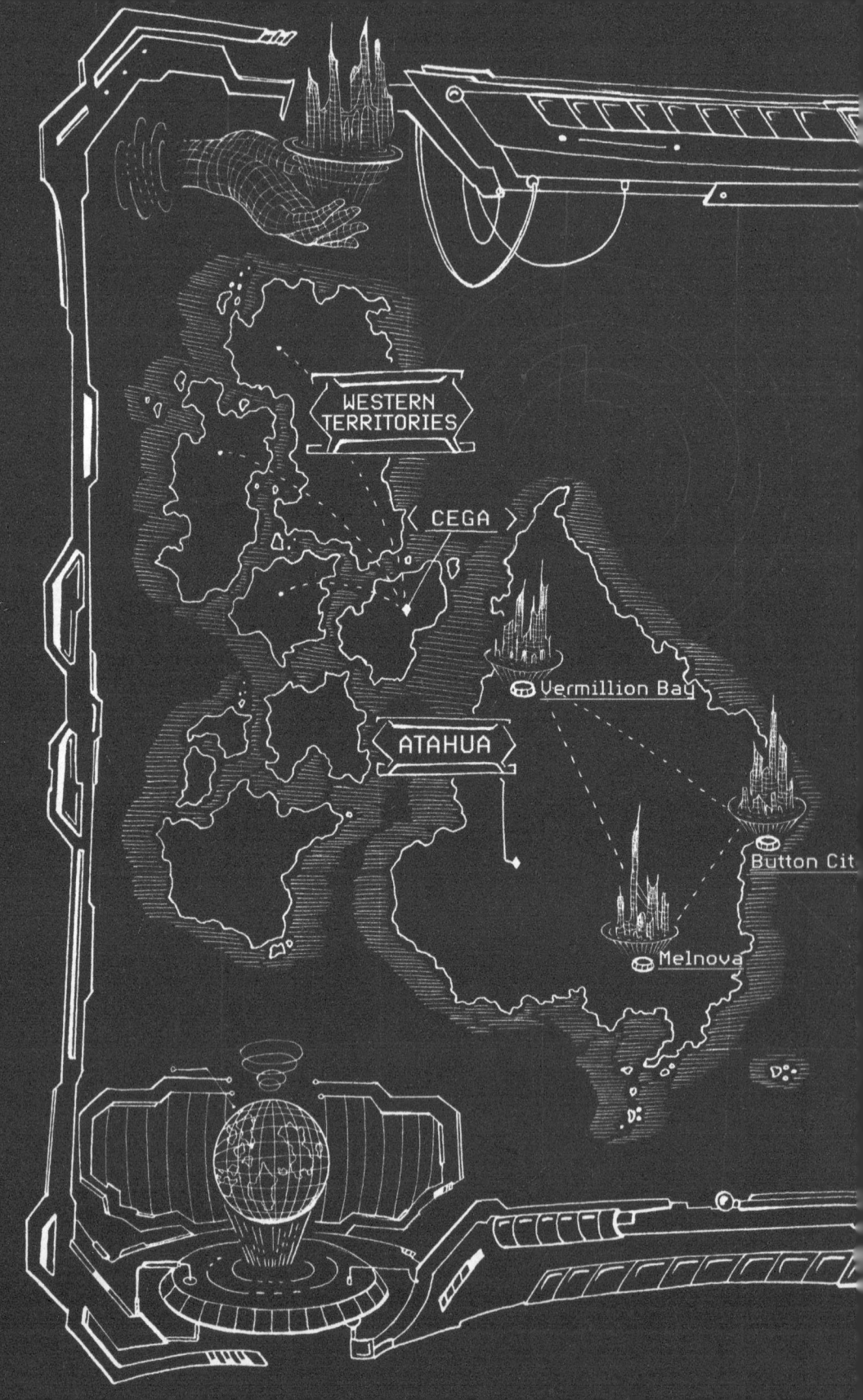

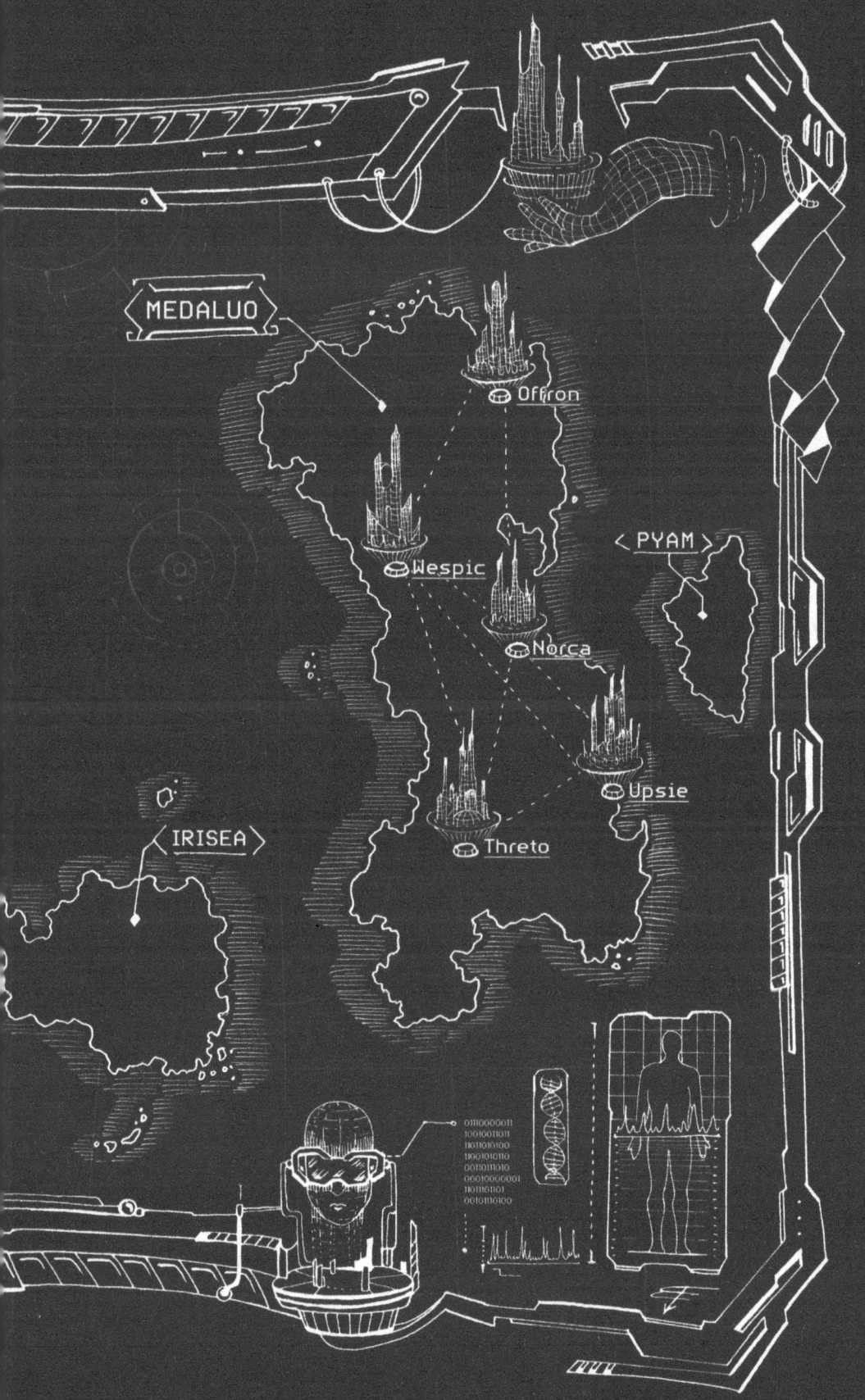

1

EIRALE

At ten minutes to midnight, the riot bots detonate around the block.

Our ropes tremble, each suspended harness bracing against the shock waves slithering up the skyscraper's exterior, but we stay put patiently, twenty floors overhead. By the time the protesters run in our direction, the tear gas will have dispersed fully from the explosions, exactly as we outlined at the base. They won't see us.

"Capture unit, get ready."

Anti-NileCorp protests are a common sight along Button City's main avenues. When they get too unwieldy, NileCorp rolls in their riot bots on behalf of the Atahuan government, always faster on the scene than local police. Button City has more NileCorp warehouses per square foot than anywhere in the world. There's going to be something at the ready no matter what sort of trouble disrupts.

I test my line. The hold loosens enough for me to take two careful steps down the vertical glass before glancing over my shoulder, tracking the panicked figures running below. There's faint yelling, maybe. Hard to tell. My suit helmet does its best to block out nonessential noise.

"Mint, keep eyes on surveillance." My earpiece continues to feed through. "Eirale, proceed to ground floor."

Tonight's demonstration is made up of truckers. They cobbled together their signs when a new line of NileCorp's autonomous semis put tens of thousands out of work, and then NileCorp's data scraping smoothly deposited their plans onto our radar. There's a process to shutting down a protest quickly, efficiently. Riot bots steer the dissidents all to one side of the road. Tear gas explodes from the canisters and takes out their vision for a few hours—or a few days, with the unrulier troublemakers who try to tackle the bots. Before long the street will clear, and their resistance symbols copied off the internet will be nothing more than soggy signs disintegrating in the sidewalk puddles. Usually, there's no need for the corporate soldiers, the units like us, to get involved.

We're reserved for high-level hire. Such as capturing anarchists.

"All right," Teryn declares, satisfied with the coverage we have. "Let's go."

I unlatch my carabiner, let the rope run slack. My suit screams a warning that I'm going too fast, that I'm going to hit the concrete and I should consider rappelling properly. The screen before my eyes flares red, trying to calculate the damage upon impact.

I turn the line taut suddenly. My harness seizes tight; I jolt to a stop just before my boots touch the ground. I haven't been a NileCorp contractor for long. They assigned me to the Button City base six months ago. While everyone else in my grade who went the route of NileCorp private forces was posted directly after our final exams and sent downcountry to run amok in the real world, I wasted three months recovering. Still, all those years of military school have prepared me to be fast, faster than NileCorp-issued suits that try to propose my next movements for me. The red fades. The suit's screen clears when I detach my harness.

My quick exhale warms the inside of my helmet. A row of billboards synchronizes on the street level, changing from Eveline ads to a news segment. I barely catch President Sterling taking the podium, the crawling ticker at the bottom announcing RELATIONS SOUR FURTHER WITH MEDALUO—INCIDENT IN THE NORTH SEA before the tear gas has clouded my vision, closing over the top of my head.

My suit switches on infrared capabilities.

I was eavesdropping earlier in the barracks when Teryn received the emergency briefing for this mission. She hadn't stepped far enough into the hallway before answering the video call on her handheld. The trucker protest was forming along Seventh, three blocks away. The riot bots would intentionally push them toward us and then detonate, conveniently offering cover from the surveillance cameras pointed at the entrances of our target building. It would save NileCorp from having footage of its forces barging into civilian businesses: more fodder to sell to the tabloids, more ammunition for hit pieces on the governance of Atahua and the country's reliance on private military contractors.

"Everyone else, get to your assigned entrances. He's not getting away this time."

Gravel crunches underfoot when I pivot. I circle the exterior of the skyscraper, the tall lobby unmoving on the other side of the thick glass. Infrared shows nothing in my way at the back entrance. By official registration, some hedge fund owns the building, abandoned by well-to-do businesses who continue to pay rent but no longer perform operations on-site. One security guard clocks in during the day, then is paid to mind their business after-hours once the nightclubs and tattoo parlors and dog-fighting rings set up shop. That's classic downcountry.

"I'm in place," I say. My voice is hoarse. I haven't spoken aloud since we left the base. Teryn turns any complaint into a motivation speech, and if I'm not in the mood for her usual spiel, I've learned to keep my mouth shut.

"Enter the stairwell," Teryn instructs immediately. "Get closer to the nightclub."

I push through the back entrance, surprised to find it isn't locked. In the dark, my suit warns there's movement to my right, but it's only a tendril of tear gas slipping through with me before I shut the glass door and hurry into the main lobby. The space is open-concept: dilapidated pillars that hold up a white ceiling, the front desk a strip of metal lifted by steel beams sprouting from the tiled floor. I make a cursory scan. Empty. I hurry for the elevator hall.

"Ma'am." Smith's voice pipes through my earpiece, getting Teryn's attention. Our unit is split down the middle among the six contractors. There's Teryn, Mint, and me. New graduates. Fresh blood on the base, intent on doing a good job because our team leader, Wright, intimidates us. The other three don't care about impressing him. They're Nile Military Academy graduates who are a decade older, bored of the job and struggling to be granted a promotion that puts them in charge.

"Ma'am," Smith prompts again. "The locks are broken on the second-level balconies."

"What?" Teryn exclaims.

I push open the door to the stairwell. It's quiet—and glaringly bright, doused in an intense violet from LED striplights running up all four corners. The infrared of my suit switches off automatically against the onslaught, but I still can't see. I tap the back of my suit to open the helmet. The stairwell door shuts behind me.

"I'm moving up," I report, drawing my firearm. "Nothing here—"

"Hey," Mint interrupts into the comm line. "Our surveillance is scrambling."

My steps pad up to the second floor quietly, the rest of my sentence forgotten. The nightclub is accessible from its main entrance along a skywalk, or from a side entrance leading into the building stairwell. Teryn and Mint have entered: Teryn as a field scout and Mint to keep watch using the cameras around her. Smith and Buchanan have eyes on the skywalk. Penrose stays on the platform jutting off the thirty-fifth floor, where we rappelled from, acting as a backup sniper. I'm the only one stationed here.

"From what?" Teryn demands.

"It's signal interruption," Mint replies. I come to a stop outside the nightclub, the faintest whisper of music thumping past the soundproof walls. At this I pause, my grip tightening on my firearm. The only entity that could block *our* signal is . . . "Someone from federal must be on the scene."

"*Why?*"

No one answers Teryn. The Atahuan government offloaded this task to NileCorp, contracted us instead of a federal bureau to capture Nik Grant. But we've already attempted two capture missions and failed both times now, so maybe they're losing patience.

"Federal only scrambles surveillance if they're up to something," Smith says. A snide edge colors his voice, obvious even through the comms. "I wonder what."

Wright has been out of commission with an injury for weeks. Under normal circumstances, if Atahua's most wanted anarchist entered Button City in that time, the task to mobilize and lead the charge that would apprehend him should have gone to another unit at the base, or to the contractor in our unit with the next highest seniority—Smith. Instead, they gave it to Teryn. Eighteen-year-old Teryn Moore, the niece of James Moore, the CEO of NileCorp.

"We won't know until we know," Teryn decides. Either she didn't pick up Smith's dig, or she chooses to ignore it. "Eirale, do you have a visual?"

"Negative," I answer.

"Capture unit, proceed as planned. Our target is in the building."

Teryn and I went to Nile Military Academy together, though the first time I spoke to her was after graduation, when I introduced myself in the Button City barracks. She was good enough to make valedictorian, yet I haven't been able to match that repute to the soldier I've worked alongside. She's capable, I suppose. She's quick and she's smart and she takes a few seconds every morning in front of the tiny mirror in the barracks to straighten the collar of her uniform and ensure that NileCorp's logo is polished clean on her chest.

She also hesitates on the field and leads us astray in moments when we need cohesion. If we fail to close in on Nik Grant a third time, the rest of us are going to have our jobs on the line. Teryn, meanwhile, will be fine. No one fires their own niece.

"Any visual inside?" Smith asks.

"Negative," Teryn answers. "Keep every balcony secured. Once we give chase, he will have no qualms about making a leap onto the street."

I tap my foot, its echo traveling across the stone floor of the stairwell. The sound is quickly swallowed. We don't have enough soldiers on the perimeter. Penrose should have been situated on the skywalk too. Or we should have combined with another unit and doubled our efforts, given our previous failures.

Nik Grant first gained public infamy after he bombed a military base outside the capital. Three casualties, one a commander . . . but more importantly, the damage took out a whole surveillance grid. The government flailed directionless for a week trying to determine the culprit and left the District of Melnova to operate blind until their servers were fixed. The nation speculated viciously about the possibility it was Medaluo's work. A terrorist emerging among the ethnic Medans who called Atahua home. Someone recruited on their ancestral ties to turn the cold war hot. Then an identical bombing targeted a NileCorp base, taking out a team of contractors, and in hours NileCorp had identified the perpetrator and generated a headshot for the news. It confirmed he was Atahuan, born and raised. Unlikely an agent of a foreign enemy power, but rather a domestic anarchist. NileCorp didn't release his name initially. Their representatives refused, in fact, which led to speculation that he was a former contractor with a grudge. That was quickly put to rest when they relented with a sprinkle of biographical information: he was only seventeen years old.

Considering these recent attacks, Atahua's Federal Bureau of Defense has entrusted our security forces to execute justice, NileCorp released in a statement. *Due to the perpetrator's status as a minor, we feel it is best to keep his information out of public scrutiny. Please report any sightings on the NileCorp website.*

In the next footage the live camera crews got of him, he was spray-painting the rubble of his bomb site, finishing the last letter on his message: MY NAME IS NIK GRANT, LOL before disappearing. A clear middle finger to NileCorp for wanting to conceal his identity.

With each of his subsequent attacks in the last few months, he has only grown larger than life. The news splatters headshots of Nik Grant to encourage Atahuans to report any information they have about his whereabouts, and the image continues to be no less baffling. He could have been one of my fellow cadets at the academy, slightly blond in the right light and frowning with the insolence of a class troublemaker. Atahuan media spins up one new theory after another about why he wants to destroy his own country—maybe a tragic past as an orphan, or secret parentage from an extremist group—all to avoid addressing the likely truth: he despises NileCorp, and he's doing everything in his power to ruin the company. He's become notorious for his slogans, which are spray-painted over his bomb sites to support conspiracy theories and have been spreading like wildfire: NILECORP KILLS ITS CRITICS; INDISPOSITION IS REAL; LOG OFF BEFORE YOU LOSE YOUR MIND.

"The secretary of defense is here," Mint suddenly declares. "I see him. At the back, near the bar."

"Hm," Teryn says. She hesitates. "I suppose we leave him to his business. It probably has nothing to do with our task."

At least Teryn is very good at tame, controlled responses. Anyone else would have asked what sort of business Chip Graham could possibly have in a dingy downcountry nightclub. NileCorp contractors know our defense secretary's face about as well as we know President Sterling's. In times of war, while President Sterling addresses the public, we get Chip Graham. On paper he may be in charge of the Atahuan military, but the military has so many holes in its infrastructure that the country wouldn't feel a difference if it were dissolved tomorrow. There's no need to funnel money into the military when NileCorp exists to plug up the holes. NileCorp salutes to

Chip's directives instead and passes the assignments down a cohesive line of corporate soldiers.

"Possible target sighting near the tables," Teryn reports. Her tone changes, sharpening for combat.

"Ready on your signal," Smith prompts.

A few minutes pass. My palms prickle with sweat beneath my gloves. I change my grip on my firearm.

"Never mind," Teryn says eventually. "It's a lookalike. I've gone through the northwest quadrant. Mint?"

"Nothing in the south so far," Mint answers. "Everyone's moving around too much for me to confirm if I've surveilled all patrons."

That's the problem with trying to capture a fugitive in a nightclub.

"I'm seeing some movement in the third-floor offices," Buchanan contributes. "Any chance of it being the target?"

"Can't be." Smith's answer is slightly muffled—he's turned away from his mic, speaking to Buchanan directly. "Ward's on the stairwell. She'll have seen him move."

A new layer of sweat breaks down my back. It's certainly impossible that he got past me. There's only one route.

"He could have climbed the exterior," Buchanan returns.

"If he's climbing the exterior to get away from us," Teryn says, "he would have made a break for it rather than approach the third floor."

"Maybe he was already situated there," Mint says. "It's not the first time we haven't—"

A scream interrupts the rest of her sentence, piercing into the shared comm link. I flinch, my hand flying up to my ear in haste. It must be someone directly beside Mint if her mic has picked it up. I barely have a moment to brace before the door in front of me flies open and a mass of patrons pour into the stairwell. They funnel through the thin hallway outside the nightclub's side entrance, moving in such a stream that the two adjacent doors don't have any opportunity to close behind anyone. It disintegrates the nightclub's soundproofing. The music is suddenly loud enough to taste, the base piping up and down the stairwell.

"What's going on?" Smith demands. "What's all that screaming?"

I barely make way for the crush, pressing to the wall to avoid the patrons scrambling through the threshold of the exit and hurrying down the stairs. I catalog each of their faces, needing to ensure Nik Grant isn't slipping out in this chaos, but the ultraviolet light plays tricks on my sight. Everything has an odd sheen to it. No matter where my gaze settles, I have the urge to look away immediately, a magnetic repulsion between the world and my perception of it.

"Excuse me!"

I grab a girl out of the crowd at random, stopping her in her tracks. Though she attempts to continue forward, her arm stretching out for a friend who proceeds without her, she can't break free. My grip is immoveable.

"What happened?" I demand.

They don't turn off the thunderous music inside. I have to shout to be heard. Electric strobe lights dart into the stairwell too, slashing through the bodies like a skipping rope I'm not jumping with in time.

"Let go of me," she screams. The three piercings through her left eyebrow catch the strobe. Its glare almost blots out my vision. "Someone fired a gun in there."

I do let go of her then. My own firearm is still clutched in my other hand, hiding at my side. The girl is quick to run off down the steps. The rest of my unit continues shouting instructions through the earpiece, but I haven't been listening. My attention returns to the patrons. I run an eye along teenagers with scarves tied over their faces to hide from facial recognition cameras. Older men in suits ushered by personal guards.

A server in waitstaff uniform coming through the door and making an immediate right, walking up the stairs. I can't make out any other detail under the strobe lights. It doesn't matter. No one else is ascending.

I bolt forward, pushing through the crush of people.

"I've got him," I say. "I've got him. He's in the stairwell."

The moment my feet hit the stairs, taking three at a time, Nik Grant bolts. He hurtles skyward, trading subtlety for speed. Teryn demands that I wait for her. Smith is yelling for me to hurry with a location so he can adjust his harness accordingly and block Nik's exit from the correct floor.

A bang echoes from above. One of the stairwell doors has been flung open, striking the wall. I crane my neck and risk looking up directly through the middle of railing, catching the telltale flicker of shadow before its door closes again.

"Fifth floor," I report. "Get to the fifth floor!"

I close the distance rapidly. There's a moment of resistance when I try to tug—he's tied something to the handle—but I yank again and snap the plastic cord that he looped with a knot.

I emerge into a ghostly hallway. The floors that aren't utilized by down-country opportunists appear largely the same, exactly how their owners left them. They're the remains of abandoned offices, crowded with boxes along the walls and mold climbing up the side of the tall windows. I'm careful while I walk toward the open-plan desks, stepping over a broken chair arm and the faulty bolt lying beside it.

A creak sounds behind me.

I whirl around, lifting my firearm. "Freeze."

Nik Grant goes still. There's little light at the mouth of the hallway, so I can't parse his expression. He lingers in the shadows, only half his face visible under blue and flickering pink bleeding in from the billboards on the street level.

"Put your hands up," I say evenly.

His hands stay where they are. His head tilts. "You again."

I was the one who almost got him on our last capture attempt. I had him blocked in, within a few feet and my cuffs prepared, but then somehow he set off a glaring flash bomb. By the time I opened my eyes, he was gone.

"There's nowhere to run," I say. "Put your hands up, or I have instructions to shoot."

"You know, it's never made sense to me why Wards work for NileCorp," Nik says. His tone is easy, as though we're making small talk on the bus. "It may be law that you enroll in military school, but no law says you have to continue on as a corporate soldier to clear your debt. What's your opinion?"

I keep my arm steady. I don't speak my question, but . . .

"Yes, I know you're a Ward," he says, answering it anyway. "Eirale Ward. I looked you up."

"I'm giving you three seconds." It's not a far cry to see a Medan face in Atahua and assume they're a Ward. When the cold war between Atahua and Medaluo started, most Medans living in Atahua decided to flee rather than be treated as the enemy. For centuries there had been a significant presence of Medan immigrants in Atahua, and within a few years—as people raised the funds to escape to Cega or another island in the Western Territories—the number dropped to paltry amounts. Those who remain now either have too many ties to give up, or they're orphans born into this war with nowhere else to go. Wards of the state, branded as property of Atahua down to the very name.

Nik Grant takes a step forward.

I shoot.

He avoids the first bullet, already moving out of its path before I pull the trigger. Despite everything I know, despite the hours we've spent on base watching surveillance footage of Nik Grant to prepare for apprehending him, I'm still taken back by how fast he is when he rams into me.

I avoid falling on a wholly instinctive lurch, regaining my balance right as he swings a fist. Instead of blocking him and risking my momentum, I veer away, then try to recover my stance and straighten my shooting arm, but Nik predicts where I turn. He grabs my elbow, twists, and suddenly I'm pressed chest-first to the wall, my firearm pointing skyward behind my back. My suit whines in the protest of danger.

"Tell me, soldier," Nik Grant says into my ear. "Why were you posted in Kunlun last year?"

When the billboards go black outside, the darkness in the hallway turns whole and blanketing. There's no boom, but the abrupt, accompanying silence indicates another detonation has gone off. An electromagnetic bomb somewhere in the building, cutting out the voices that had been piping through my comm link. My team can't hear me. I'm on my own.

"What are you talking about?" I demand.

"It's a very simple question," Nik says. "Just tell me why you were posted there. Tell me what you did."

I raise my foot behind me and kick, striking his knee. Though I hoped that would be enough for me to tug free, Nik doesn't let go. He pushes my arm up, hard in the wrong direction with my shoulder. In that flash of screaming pain, I drop the weapon.

"I"—Nik kicks the gun with a huff, sending it skittering along the floorboards—"read your files. I'll know if you're lying."

I slam my head backward. Nik grunts, his grip releasing, and I immediately swivel, searching for where my firearm has gone.

I get the feeling he's allowing me to shift to the offensive now that he's disarmed me. The hallway flares with abrupt green, lit by the advertisement that returns to life on the billboards outside. My earpiece offers a bit of static, too, then:

"*Eirale*? Eirale, come in—"

"I already said fifth floor," I hiss into it. "Fifth floor, hurry *up*—"

Nik Grant is going to run for the windows.

I gauge it in the turn of his left shoe, in the flicker of his eyes under the awful green light and his attention latching on to the glass. The moment he starts forward, I lunge to stop him, colliding with him to send us both toppling to the floor.

"They will discard you, soldier."

I slam my forearm over his clavicle. He stops struggling. Both his arms stay splayed on either side, locked where I can see them.

"Don't move," I seethe.

"They will use you, then discard you. If you're lucky, maybe they'll post you upcountry first. You won't even feel it when you're squeezed out."

"Good," I snap. "Maybe then I won't have to watch your stupid tapes over and over again."

Nik blinks. "Ouch."

My earpiece keeps spitting overlapping voices at me. I finally use my free hand to grip the mic in my suit collar, shouting, "I *said*, fifth floor!" but seconds pass and Teryn continues asking for a location. I'm still blocked out.

I shift only the smallest amount. Nik says, "Trouble getting through?"

His shoulder twitches beneath my arm. It's only then that I notice he's wearing an earpiece himself.

"Change of plans," he says. He's not talking to me. "I have something interesting here."

"Excuse me?"

I catch the sleight of hand too late. A dark patch of something appears in Nik's palm. By the time I'm attempting to move, to put distance between us, he's already slapped it onto my neck.

. . . .

I'm not unconscious for long.

Two minutes. Maybe three. I scramble upright, lurching into a sitting position.

I haven't moved. I'm still on the fifth floor, the billboards continue to emit green into the hallway, and the window is wide open, the moth-bitten curtain fluttering with the wind.

Shit.

I wince, pulling the patch off my neck. The micro-needles across its surface emerge with a thin smear of blood. I'll need to get the wound checked to make sure Nik Grant didn't give me some disease.

"Can anyone hear me?"

The sudden cacophony of responses would confirm yes, I'm transmitting through the comm again. I stumble to my feet. There's no chance that Nik will still be within sight, but I hurry to the window anyway. Indeed, he's long disappeared, but my eyes widen to register eight, nine, *ten* black cars parked all around the building.

"Eirale, where did you go—"

"He was here," I rush to say. "I went after him on the fifth floor. I'm coming back down."

I shoulder through the door into the stairwell. It's quiet. The ultraviolet LED has been replaced with an ugly, normal white light, calmer on my eyes while I round the landing, counting the fourth floor, then the third. Mint is trying to speak into her earpiece—*They want us out. They had a threat called*—and with someone else at the same time. She's arguing with federal. Government people.

I make it back to the second floor, then along the thin hallway. Inside the nightclub, the lights have come on as well, white-blue to replace the strobes. Not all the patrons ran out. There are still clusters milling around the walls, nervously wringing their hands. I push my way past them, searching for Mint or Teryn.

Then I see the blood.

"Don't come closer!"

I'm suddenly at the receiving end of ten rifles, red lasers pointing a collection of dots onto my suit. The nightclub is smaller than the blueprints made it seem—or maybe the chipping black paint on the walls pulls everything closer together. I've approached the back of its dance floor, beside the bar. And everywhere I look, there are federal agents. Holding weapons, directing camera drones, setting up caution tape.

"What's going on?" I mutter, intending it for my earpiece, for my team to answer. I raise my hands to either side of me, keeping them in sight for the agents. "Why are they pointing their guns at *me*?"

"Eirale, over here." I hear Mint in my ear, but there's a double echo, her actual voice coming from nearby. My eyes flicker to the side, and I catch a glimpse of her green braids over the shoulder of a federal agent. She shifts until I can see her face properly, her folded arms wrapped tightly around her torso. Her head tilts, gesturing to her left, and I follow the trail of blood on the floor up to a booth.

My breath snags in my throat. A man slumps over the table, his face pressed to the metal at an awkward angle. Judging by the red spreading around him, oozing onto the tiles at his feet, I have to imagine there's a bullet embedded dead center in his forehead.

"Is that Chip Graham?" I murmur. I don't want to move my mouth too much. I don't want the federal agents to read what I'm saying, but my hands must lower in shock because they rush to scream at me, yelling to stay still or else they'll shoot, they'll fire immediately.

"I've been trying to tell them we were after Nik Grant tonight and that *he* did this," Mint hisses. "But the footage already leaked onto the feed."

"What footage?" I demand. The federal agents are starting to approach me. One is taking out cuffs. I can't understand what could have possibly prompted this reaction, why their rifles remain pointed at me, until Teryn's voice breaks over the comms, ice cold:

"You, Eirale. There's video of you shooting the defense secretary."

2

LIA

I can tell our backyard hasn't been cleaned in a while because last month's broken tree branch is still lying by the picket fence.

The early-morning wind howls against the window, rattling the latches. Downcountry sunrises don't bring much light anymore, not like the way they've redesigned them upcountry. I hate how gloomy everything is at this hour, how empty the world feels. Shadows shift in the room like the mist outside—heavy and viscous, hemmed with weight. Dad says I shouldn't sit in the alcove because it's too exposed, and the window could be easily smashed. Our house is in Haven State, east of Button State and two hours away from Button City, where the daytime sky is always tinted vaguely brown. When the winds quiet, I can hear our electrified perimeter: a faint, steady hum that Tamera swears isn't noticeable.

We've never had an incident at the house. The general public—despite their constant accusations that my father is a Medan spy—isn't stupid, and they know he's not here downcountry. Dad, like every other senator in Atahua, keeps his physical body in the District of Melnova, inside a locked hideaway office within the well-protected Capitol Building. On his reset days, he'll be walking around the Capitol, summoning coffee to be delivered by service bots.

No one is getting past the fence, in any case. No looters, no hitchhiking vagrants looking for a warm place to hide out. I suppose there's the rare chance someone comes by to throw something for protest's sake, which is the only scenario I can imagine there being danger. SENATOR'S DAUGHTER CONKED BY A BRICK. Rather pathetic for a headline. I shift away from the window.

The television on the wall switches segments, starting the latest breaking news coming out of Button City. When I tilt back to listen, my hair protests the motion, caught around my shoulders like a black shawl. Apparently some government official was murdered last night. They don't say what the official was doing in the city downcountry to begin with, where he was at risk of getting murdered. Nor do they mention that these sorts of assassinations seem to be happening more and more often, despite the innumerable security initiatives NileCorp launches at every quarterly presentation to "*protect Atahua.*" Before anyone can mull too long on the details, the newscasters turn the segment over to a James Moore interview: an old one that I've practically memorized because I've watched it so many times, and I wave my hand to mute the television.

"Lia, are you up here?"

"Yeah," I call back. "Alcove."

Tamera's footsteps draw closer to my room. I busied myself enough yesterday when I first logged out of upcountry, going from the treadmill to the rowing machine to the pull-up bar installed on my door. Now I'm just impatient to finish my mandatory twenty-four hours downcountry. Monthly users in the Pods stay upcountry the longest, but we still need to reset downcountry—in the real world—to prevent our bodies from deteriorating. Most of my grade at the academy do it together: on the first of each month, they're all spat out from their Pods in the dorms of Nile Military Academy, free to move around as long as they don't leave campus. While they use the time to socialize, to go for a run around the school grounds and shake out their body, I wake up here.

As much as I grouch and grumble, critically afraid of missing good gossip in the time I'm away, I know that Dad only insists on having my Pod at home in Haven State to keep me safe. Aside from skyrocketing crime in the few remaining major cities, our mere existence in the real world is dangerous now. It's why they invented upcountry, after all. Half a century ago, it would have been unfathomable to imagine how we have to live now. When Tamera reminisces about her childhood, she had blue skies in the real world and a minor flu season that took her out for a couple of days at most.

Then the seas started to flood the coasts, the very air turned cancerous, and the pandemics mutated at a rate that killed us faster than we could inoculate against them. The factories refused to stop pumping toxins into the clouds, and the megacorporations wouldn't unplug their machines eating up freshwater. What else were people to do?

When NileCorp invented StrangeLoom, it promised a server to each nation. They would virtually replicate their streets down to the shape of the cobblestones, and the property that anyone owned "downcountry" would become theirs "upcountry" too. I've had a ridiculous number of assignments on the famous presentation where James Moore introduced those terms to the world, how he paused after speaking both words as though he knew he was making history. Upcountry solved a problem without having to rectify the damage they were doing. The planet tried to wage a war after decades of torment, and NileCorp took its civilian combatants away. Now most of the world's population has migrated to experience life online, and though this existence is all I have ever known, people sure do seem happier for it.

I flex my hands, watching the curve of my knuckles, the lines of my bones shifting and straining. My handheld device is already buzzing with updates on the feed, posts from my classmates returning to virtual. Rayna promised to collect all the reset-day gossip for me, so at least that'll make an interesting lunch debrief.

Tamera pokes her head through my door.

"Do you want any breakfast, honey?"

"I'm okay." The security system beeps from a panel by the television. It's announcing an external temperature change, which could mean a dust storm is blowing in. I already have no desire to go outside, ever, but our house system's diligent notifications only add to my repulsion. I'd probably shrivel like a raisin if I stepped outside. A radioactive raisin.

"Are you sure?" Tamera presses.

"I'm sure."

Tamera puts her hands on her hips. "Real food is good for you."

I don't have any memories of my adoptive mom because I was too young when she passed away. Tamera is the closest maternal figure I've known—though, technically, she's my adoptive great-aunt. While Dad is busy in Melnova, Tamera's the one who takes care of me. She lives here, at the Haven State house, staying close on the off chance my Pod needs maintenance while I'm inside. During the day she'll log into upcountry as a daily subscriber, help Dad out at the Melnova apartment, and when it's time to take some rest, she'll come back down, getting sleep in the real.

I huff, throwing my legs over the alcove.

"But, Tamera," I whine, "I'm so not hungry. Perilously unhungry. In fact, I might throw up if I get a single bite inside of me."

It's not entirely theatrics. I'm usually somewhat nauseous when I come downcountry, even though the reset is supposed to be refreshing. Once I get back into the Pod, the nutrient line will keep me fed. I like the nutrient line. Most other cadets, like Rayna, go downcountry way more than mandated to work out and feed their real bodies. They say that no amount of training upcountry can replace physical exercise in the real world. Meanwhile, I'm convinced I could stay logged in forever if the mandatory reset didn't exist. The Pods are built to hold us indefinitely as long as someone is topping up the nutrient line, and my body never shows signs of decline when I'm forced to log off. Clearly I'm doing fine without popping down as frequently.

"All right, well"—Tamera checks her watch, waiting for the band to flash—"you still have about twenty minutes before your Pod unlocks. I'll make you some coffee or something. Your father always takes tea upcountry, but if you ask me, I don't think they've quite perfected the caffeine reaction...."

Tamera's mostly talking to herself as she disappears back into the hall, then down the stairs to the third-floor kitchen. On my reset days, she doesn't go upcountry until I do. So she waits with me, bustling around a wilted house with little to do. Secretly I think she's impatient to return to the Melnova apartment where she has a set list of tasks: buy ingredients to cook with, dust the furniture, put plants out on the porch. When I video-call Dad, I always see Tamera in the background, cooking despite her insistence that it's all just pixels. Her dyed blond hair and happily plump shape make her appear younger, but Tamera lived a whole life before upcountry was invented thirty years ago. She speaks of virtual as a false reality, a copycat plane trying to replace the true experience. It's why she only uses a Claw headset and doesn't want a Pod of her own, so that she can be in and out as she pleases.

The windowpane rattles again. On the television screen, James Moore mouths through the NileCorp origin story, and I finally clamber off the alcove, contributing the audio for him in perfect synchrony: *"The future is online. The future is digital."* The StrangeLoom icon flashes in the corner, an infinity-shaped arrow swallowing itself up like an ouroboros, and I wave the television off entirely.

Eighteen more minutes. I pad down the hallway. In the bathroom, the small touchpad for the light is always farther away than I think, and I grope my hand back and forth on the wall. My mirror image barely resembles a person hovering at the hazy gray entryway, more a silhouette than a body, more a phantom than anything solid. I don't like being downcountry. I don't like the empty white walls, the cold tile floors, and the clinical sterile smell that pervades every corner of the house except for the alcove, never going away no matter how much I try to create ventilation in my room.

The round bulb flares on. With the light, I'm suddenly crystal clear in the mirror, and my vision lurches. Everything appears flat. I have to take a deep breath. I force myself to count: *ten, nine, eight—*

It's called Wakeman Syndrome. For as long as upcountry has been around, so has the disorder that afflicts the 0.5 percent of people who question their reality as a result. It's named after President Elliot Wakeman, the guy in charge when NileCorp introduced StrangeLoom and started allowing people upcountry. Wakeman was halfway into his second term when he went off the rails and tried to launch a nuclear weapon at Cega. Despite being downcountry at the time, he was convinced that nothing was real and he needed to wake up from a simulation. Atahua's western neighbor barely escaped annihilation because the vice president talked him down and had him committed for psychiatric help.

A rather fitting disorder given his name, and the term stuck.

Breathe, breathe.

I've only told Dad about my symptoms, but he thinks I'm overreacting. He says it's not Wakeman Syndrome, that I'm just too overworked at school. He offered to refer me to his therapist so I can talk through my feelings—*normal* feelings, he insists, for someone of my age and ambition. He thinks I need to pick up some hobbies, try to enjoy life outside my grades. In elementary I studied excessively to ensure I'd qualify for Nile Military Academy, and now at Nile I study excessively to make valedictorian. Of course I've grown paranoid that I'm nothing but an incomprehensible warp of pixels and code. All I've known is putting good work in and extracting good results. When I'm not upcountry as an avatar, when I'm supposed to be relaxing as a real girl, time feels blurry, and the things that I've done mere minutes ago feel as though they've faded hours into the past. I get the sense that time ceases to exist, that if I think too hard about it, I'll accidentally break out from its hold and become lost in a floating void.

"Lia?" Tamera's voice floats in from the stair landing. "Which mug is yours? The blue or the green?"

"Blue," I call back. "Thanks!"

On Dad's official government About Me! page, they call me Lia Sullivan, even though by their own law that's not allowed. There have been one too many Medan child spies pretending to be orphans, which means that while Atahuans can take us in, love us, make us a part of their family, we can't ever shake off the Ward surname, and we're still mandated to attend military school once we're of age. Wards are also responsible for their own school fees, so we all go in debt to the schools, and our adoptive parents can't take on the burden. It's a protective mechanism for Atahua, allegedly, but everyone knows what it achieves. Atahua needs spies for their cold war too, and this guarantees them their most precious resource: Medan faces who can blend in when they're sent to the enemy nation.

So when Dad messaged me the appointment slot for therapy last week, I declined. I can't risk the academy suspecting I have Wakeman Syndrome. They won't want a cadet struggling with a disorder in NileCorp's private security forces, and the only reason I work so hard at the academy is to secure the most desired posting after graduation. I'm going to stay close to Dad, in Melnova. I'm not going to be used as ammunition in their war.

I reach behind my head, touching the slight hollow at the top of my neck, where my hairline starts. There's no scar. The procedure is so small and routine that the skin heals over perfectly to encase the chip inside. I got it when I enrolled on the StrangeLoom system at five years old—everyone does to allow full immersion through neural signals. Sometimes I wish they'd left a scar, just so I'd have some minor difference between my body and my avatar. Just as proof that I have real skin that can be cut.

My hand twitches, unexpectedly itching as though I've been bitten by a frenzy of fire ants. I scrunch hard, making a fist when my arm returns to my side.

"I swear, Lia, I don't know how there are so many mugs in this kitchen."

Tamera again. While she continues chatting idly from downstairs, I reach for the shelves beside the bathroom sink, trailing my fingers along the items. One of the fine-tooth combs sticks above the rest, its handle thin and tail-like, sharpened at the end.

Before I can think twice, I have the comb in one hand, pressing into the palm of my other. Its sharp end sinks into my skin, burrows parallel to a vein, carving an indent. Then I push harder, harder. My hand stings fiercely, but it's not enough. As long as it is bearable, it might be nothing but a virtual sensory response, manufactured to make me believe in a generated reality.

Break, I urge, imagining my skin splitting apart. *Show me something undeniable.*

"Lia!"

Tamera, suddenly, is at my side, grabbing my wrist. Though I don't resist, I keep the sharp end down, and when she pulls my hand away, the comb drags across my palm forcefully.

I really do wince this time. The comb clatters to the floor, striking against the tiles with a horribly discordant sound.

For a few seconds, the scratch is only bright red, a raised welt. Then blood beads to the surface, seeping through the damaged membrane. Little dots surround the cut in varying sizes before the red drips downward, landing one drop on the floor tiles.

It's not much, but it's something. It means I'm real. I'm *real*. StrangeLoom doesn't encode blood.

"What has gotten into you?" Tamera hisses.

"Nothing," I answer at once. "Nothing. I had an itch."

"An *itch*!" Tamera grabs a towel, then wraps it around my hand tightly to stanch the cut. "You didn't need to press so hard."

I wrinkle my nose, lifting the towel off to peek at the scratch. The bleeding has already stopped. I feel much better. A tension that had been building and building in my chest these twenty-four hours has been allowed a release, a hole punctured through my chest to begin pressurization.

"I'm okay, I swear," I say.

Tamera isn't so easily deflected. She frowns, still looking at my hand. I don't know when exactly it happened, but I've gotten a whole head taller than her, so she needs to hold my arm far above her eye level to keep it elevated.

"Come to the kitchen. I'll give you a bandage."

"It's already stopped bleeding. See?" I show her my palm. "A bandage will just get gross if I leave it on for a month inside."

"Lia."

I stick out my lower lip. "Tameraaaaaa..."

"All right, all right," she relents, dropping my hand. "Come on, then. Twenty-four hours are up."

We walk back to my bedroom. The moment Tamera steps in, she goes to open the side window's curtains, which doesn't change the lighting situation. She seems to realize it too, pausing before drawing them half-shut again.

"Are you going straight to school?" Tamera asks, turning around.

I pretend to check the watch on her wrist. "I thought I'd enter on a Button City landing station to do some luxury shopping first."

Tamera gives me a wry look. "A simple *yes, I'm going to school* would have sufficed."

"Sorry. I can't deny the urge to be a smart-ass."

I never miss school anyway, not even when I'm ill. There's zero chance I'll miss a minute during this critical week, when final exam postings are expected soon. Each grade I get could change the outcome of the race for valedictorian. As much as I'd love to think I've got the title secured, there's one competitor who's always been huffing down my neck.

Tamera pushes open the Pod cover. My Pod is installed in the corner of my room so that its wires can be plugged into the port in the wall, which makes the setup look rather sarcophagus-like. We have ports in every room, feeding into the cables that grant upcountry access, provided that Dad continues paying the subscription fees associated with our log-ins.

"I checked your nutrient line already, and your level is fine for two back-to-back months," Tamera tells me. "If you need the entire ten weeks for your posting, though, I'm sure it'll alert me to replace it too."

It's supposed to be my responsibility to make sure the Pod has suitable levels before I log in, but Tamera likes to take care of everything in the household. It's nice. At the academy, they have emergency nurses on standby in case someone's Pod falls low on nutrient levels, but cadets can also easily log themselves out, walk over to the nutrient room, and shove a replacement into the Pod. The only time it becomes trickier is during our final exam posting, because if we're being hacked into another country, we can't leave until the posting is finished. In this specific case, NileCorp allows us to skip one mandatory reset day, knowing that it's worth the risk if we want to stay in a foreign server. If our Pods are well maintained, two months in virtual won't do us any harm.

Tamera tuts, peering into the Pod now. I left the Claw lying on the pillow, not on the hook on the side where it's supposed to go. I smile sheepishly while I climb in, but I haven't damaged any of the electrode rods.

The Pod has all sorts of other bits and bobs that make it suitable for long-term stay. Nodes stick out from the sides, attaching to my legs, to my arms, to my torso. NileCorp has had decades to perfect its stasis technology, zapping the body at the right intervals while our minds are upcountry to make sure nothing atrophies in the real world. I slide the nutrient needle into my arm.

"Comfortable?" Tamera asks.

I adjust one of the Claw prongs, slotting it onto my head. The back needs to be aligned with the chip in my head. "Ow. Why is this so tight—"

She reaches in, unraveling a bit of my hair that got stuck on the Claw.

"I'm good. You can shut the Pod." I pause. "Thank you."

Tamera nods, then reaches in to touch my face briefly. "Have a good time at school. And good luck if I don't see you before your posting."

She closes the cover. The Pod goes pitch-black. In darkness I sigh with relief, waiting for the screen above me to buffer before the launch message appears. It recognizes my face after a few seconds, the text at the top displaying, WELCOME BACK, LIA. No need to enter my log-in credentials again—it'll only prompt me for my password the next time I've renewed my user ID. A map of Atahua and its territories shimmers to life, offering at my disposal every upcountry landing station where I could go. True to its purpose, the map of upcountry is identical to a map of downcountry, each street and building facade replicated by NileCorp's satellites. I zoom in on Button State, then flick the map slightly above Button City, sixty miles north in a town surrounded by bright red trees with a river to the east and a castle floating on the edge of the water. I've performed this process hundreds of times. At this point, it's as familiar to me as breathing.

I tap my destination. Press confirm. The mist inside the Pod begins to blow: a cooling, numbing sensation sinking to the bone. The Claw gives me a small electric zap to tell me it's about to kick in.

A STRANGE LOOP...

My shoulders relax. My breathing eases. The map dissolves for the engine's greeting words, the same three-lined phrase since StrangeLoom first hit the market.

ON A STRANGELOOM...

Letter by letter, each of the words appears, then fades. By the time the final part comes, I'm under in an instant.

THE FUTURE HAS LOADED.

• • • •

The academy has a landing station outside campus for arrivals into upcountry, but it's deserted when my avatar pops in. Early-morning landing stations for public schools in the city would be abuzz with activity while daily users make their entry, but all cadets at Nile Military Academy must board as monthly users. Yesterday everyone logged off half an hour earlier than me while I was finishing up some homework, which means they came in earlier too. I'm alone when I walk the short path up to the gate.

NILE MILITARY ACADEMY, the sign out front declares. EVER READY.

I grab the sign as I pass, squeezing cold metal. The cut on my palm obviously didn't copy over to virtual, but I feel the sting on my avatar, nonetheless. When I let go of the sign and continue walking, I receive a small pop-up in the corner of my vision.

Please refrain from any action that may damage academy property.

"Sorry!" I call out, swiping the pop-up away. No one's actually listening. The alerts are automated, warnings triggered by the rules NileCorp sets inside its property. If I accidentally damage the sign, it'll stay like that. StrangeLoom promises to scan the real world to create upcountry, but it's not continuously updating afterward. They'd have to bring in engineers to restore its image, or just get a new sign in virtual. Both of which take effort and money.

I blink once, opening my display to see the time. I really should hurry. It's a big campus, and there are certain areas that I have to navigate carefully, perpetually slippery because of the wet mud. I open my messages and find Rayna. She probably wouldn't have gone back to sleep after logging in with only forty-five minutes until first period, but in typical Rayna fashion, she'll still roll into her class right before the bell on purpose. I send **HELLOOOOO RISE AND SHINE!!!** to her inbox.

The wind blows at my eyes as I trudge onto the gravel path toward the school. Our shared calendar tells me Rayna's first period is math while I go to PE.

"Cadet Lia," the gate guard, Mr. Nell, bellows when he spots me. "You're going to miss your entire first class at this leisurely rate!"

I pick up my pace. "Sorry, sorry," I grumble. "Do I have time to change—"

"No, cadet! Report to the gymnasium, cadet!"

Most cadets on campus call him Mr. Yell behind his back. "Yessir. Have a great morning, sir."

My avatar reloaded with yesterday's combat uniform: the clothes I was wearing before logging out. I'm glad I'd changed first and hadn't just pulled myself downcountry in my pajamas. There's nothing I can do about my loose hair, but at least it's shorter in virtual. More manageable than the length it's grown to downcountry.

In Atahua, we get very little adjustment on how we look upcountry. Our first scan happens at the NileCorp registration center, when we turn five years old and qualify for StrangeLoom credentials. They'll put us under the cameras, issue a user ID, then make the quick incision to implant the chip that interacts with the Claw. We renew our StrangeLoom credentials every year—those without Pods go back into the NileCorp centers, and those with Pods only have to press a button. The scans are completed in seconds, and our avatars are updated to appear exactly as we do downcountry when we log in again.

We're not without options, technically. We could buy hair extensions or get haircuts up here. There's even a thriving plastic surgery industry that has learned how to make avatar adjustments using legal code alterations.

The plastic surgery industry, meanwhile, is entirely dead in upcountry Medaluo. Over there, users have a cosmetic adjustment page in their very display, letting them change the shape of their avatars' chins and the brightness of their teeth within reason. The feed debates all the time whether avatar customization should be allowed, arguing about how harmful it is to our perception of beauty when people can change how they look at a whim.

I don't mind that Atahua mandates cosmetic adjustments to be blanked out. One less thing to worry about so I can focus on studying instead.

My classmates appear in the distance, streaming out from the gymnasium in two rows. I'm late. They've started their first jog around the campus perimeter. Another pop-up shimmers into the corner of my display.

You are three minutes late to first period!

I break into a jog to catch up. The last thing I need is my participation grades slipping, especially when physical education is a bogus class upcountry. It's more about building habits and relaxing the mind. We must learn to push through discomfort. Spar with one another on the mats to quicken our mental reflexes and then do it again in the real during reset days.

I've argued with Dad about what I might be missing out on if I don't practice what I learn. I haven't stepped foot on the physical campus—it's too far to travel to when my Pod is in Haven State. I can work out endlessly at home, but for all I know, I could end up as one of those cadets who graduate and suddenly can't figure out how to throw a real punch when I'm a contractor posted downcountry.

It's happened before. The Pods are built to preserve our real bodies for optimal function, but that doesn't mean everyone puts the nodes on correctly; nor does it mean that we can build actual muscle while upcountry. I've obsessed over former cadet testimonials who sue NileCorp for firing them when they're weaker than expected and lain awake at night wondering if that could happen to me even if I do make it into their private military. Those cases never win. If people aren't as competent downcountry as they are upcountry when they were offered a job, that's their own fault.

My hair streams behind me as I gain speed, the strands lifting with the wind. On my reset days, I can count to a hundred doing push-ups. The treadmill at home was intentionally placed in Tamera's room so we can hang out if I'm running for hours and she's knitting something. I've performed perfectly fine every month, with no indication that I won't be able to transfer my skills.

A thrill sparks down my spine as I close in on the back of the cluster. I veer slightly right, joining the group of cadets.

"Better pick it up, Nat."

Natalie Ward visibly jolts from the scare. A beat later, her expression smooths out when she sees it's me. "Oh, just overtake me and let me suffer in peace. See you at lunch, bitch."

I laugh, pushing forward. The eastern side of campus overlooks the river, where the sweet birch trees hang off the ledge and deposit handfuls of yellow-green leaves into the water. I weave and glide, steadily enough to avoid tiring myself out but keeping at a pace that cuts me ahead of a few classmates, then another. People have different stamina paces, even upcountry. However fit we are in virtual usually depends on the limits our own minds set for us. Other cadets have often accused me of having a big head, so maybe I'm competent upcountry by sheer faith and willpower.

The campus grounds curve up on a gentle hill, then back down in a muddy slide. I keep my footing delicate, arms held up for balance. I know the sharp rocks here by heart. None of our instructors are supervising us short of the status updates that the system must be running to the academy. Still, no one is going to struggle or go off-course to dally. We're not the only military academy outside Button City, nor are we the oldest or biggest, but we're the most prestigious. It takes the top scores on the entrance exam to qualify for entry. There's a certain standard that Nile Military Academy sets, one that every cadet is increasingly aware of each time the common room's screens are streaming the latest breaking news. NileCorp owns us, and where NileCorp goes, renown rains down. The very nature of life as we know it is owed to NileCorp.

I skid at the base of the hill. It doesn't put any misstep in my stride—I recover in an instant and continue, approaching the end of the perimeter.

When I'm the only one who runs up to Coach Chelsea, the warm swoop of achievement cradles my stomach. I've pulled to the front significantly.

"I thought you were a cadet from Tier B," she calls to me. Her hands are propped on her hips. "I didn't expect to see any Tier As for another ten minutes."

"If you want me to go double and join Tier B's run too, just say so," I reply, coming to a stop. I heave a deep breath in. My lungs strain, then steady. NileCorp's long regulatory manuals will spell out which exact actions upcountry will create which reactions in our avatars, but it's easiest to assume the StrangeLoom engineers did the hard work and the usual logic we're used to downcountry follows. They're meticulous. They've gone as far as to ensure our breath will stink after a night of virtual sleeping, which means monthly users also need to brush our teeth every morning.

"Half of Tier B is back already," Coach says, "but you could probably catch up to the other half if you go now."

"Okay." I pretend to lurch back toward the hill, taking the route of the other class. We didn't overlap in the middle because Tier B runs through the proper path of the forest rather than the edge overlooking the river, where Tier A goes.

Coach Chelsea rolls her eyes good-naturedly and checks her watch. She's one of many people who will still buy antiquated items upcountry. She could just as easily blink to open her display and look at the time, but I suppose it must be nice to lift her arm and perform the action she got used to in the years before virtual.

She waves for me to proceed into the gymnasium, where Tier A and B will merge to resume class. I go through the outer doors, wiping down my shoes at the entryway. I have another pair in my locker, but I don't know if this is enough mud to warrant a change.

The gymnasium's inner doors slam open. The sound is loud enough to jolt me, but I relax as soon as I see who it is. Kieren Murray, dressed in class uniform rather than combat gear for physical education. He's definitely not in this period—I'm pretty sure he has Atahuan Literature now. Not that I've memorized his schedule or anything.

"Ward," he says, and despite his smile, it instantly sounds like a taunt. "I've been looking for you."

"And to what do I owe the pleasure?" I return his smile, sickly sweet, while I go to open my locker. I make the decision to change my shoes then purely to skirt around Kieren and busy myself. He hates it when people don't give him their full attention. "We're twenty minutes into first period."

"I thought maybe you would have smelled final exam postings dropping and levitated your way to the nearest board."

My smile drops. "What?"

It can't have happened any sooner than seconds ago if I haven't heard about it yet. Typical of Kieren to make it sound like I haven't been paying attention. He and his twin sister, Hailey, don't keep their Pods on campus either, so for all I know he also logged back in right before first period.

He looms closer. "Did you do it?"

"Do what?" I demand. I've never dropped a bit so fast. We can go back and forth in classic fashion another day—are *final exam postings* out?

"Don't pretend you don't know."

"I *literally* don't know what you're talking about."

Oh, Kieren Murray, my dear nemesis. I've been the largest pain in his ass since the summer before ninth grade, after we were accepted into Nile Military Academy based on northeastern state entrance exams. We befriended each other at a New Cadet Orientation party, then swore enmity just as quickly the next day when we were seated side by side for a second ranking exam to establish class tiers. Somehow, he and I ended up *sharing* number one because we had both not only received perfect scores but maxed out the bonus points the exact same way. Though they did their due diligence and investigated us for potential cheating, the system didn't note either of our heads looking up even once. No chance of cheating. In retrospect, it's shocking that they let me share that rank with him instead of shoving me to number two given that Kieren's own father is the academy headmaster.

Four years have passed, and nothing has changed. I rile him up so badly before tests that there are always rumors going around school about how we must be secretly hooking up because no two people can truly care that much about scoring higher than the other. Rayna is frequently talking me down from sending a blast to the feed debunking the claims. Not that it matters, but Kieren and I have only kissed once. And we were thirteen years old, so it doesn't count. I don't know whether I'm more offended by the insinuation that I would partake in hookup culture or that I need another reason to give Kieren Murray an aneurysm beyond being better than him.

"The posting, Ward." Kieren throws his arms up in the air. "This is unheard of."

Dad might think that overworking is what fuels my anxiety and derealization, but being the best is what makes me feel most alive. Kieren, consequently, may be my primary competitor, but he's also my greatest source of joy.

I keep that to myself, of course.

Carefully, I poke one finger at his chest, trying to push him back. "Can you ease up a little? If anyone steps out right now, those rumors are going to be at full fire."

"You—" His hands grab at the space between us as though he wants to strangle me but can't quite bring himself to do it. "Fine. I'm going to go sort this out since I apparently have to do everything around here."

With an abrupt motion, Kieren pivots and storms away.

"Is it something I said?" I call after him. "Baby, come back. I can change!"

He gives me the finger without looking. If I can't get further retort out of Kieren, this is probably serious. I'm already grimacing before he disappears through the doors properly. *Final postings.* It's early. I didn't expect them this morning of all mornings, the moment we've returned from a reset day. We still have one more unit to cover in class.

I change my shoes quickly, then slam my locker closed. Inside the gymnasium, Tier B's cadets who have returned already are clumped around the far wall. Drills will be starting as soon as the rest of their class and mine arrive, so it's unusual for everyone to be congregated by the announcement board. They're installed all across campus, each one accompanied by a holographic animation of the NileCorp logo overhead, looping in the StrangeLoom icon's infinity shape. Sometimes the boards are displaying upcoming events, and other times they're crowded with headlines of breaking news that the academy wants cadets to be aware of. Today, the board looks sparse.

"Is it postings?" I ask, rising onto my toes at the edge of the crowd.

Gena Wilson turns around. Her eyes widen. "Lia, you're here!" She shuffles aside immediately to let me through. "Go look."

I push into the crowd, trying to shift closer without prodding other cadets. I hardly need to worry. When my classmates spot me, they hurry out of my way, making a path for me to proceed forward.

This is getting really weird.

I get to the front. I scan the words at the top of the board at once. Final exam postings, indeed. My heart slams to my throat.

Postings and announcements are always made by class ranking, so I expect to see myself in the first row. But my name is nowhere to be found. It's not in the second row either. Nor the third. Now my pulse is starting to hammer. I move down the list slowly, carefully reading the two columns: the posting on the left and the cadet to the right. I see Rayna, posted to Medaluo. I see Hailey Murray, Kieren's sister, also posted to Medaluo. That's more unusual. Each individual cadet is designated to a location upcountry, followed by a short description of what their mission goal is. Most stay within Atahua. A fraction are sent to other nations. Cadets of Medan or Pyaish descent will almost always be sent to Medaluo. It's a given that that's where I'll be posted.

At last I find my name at the very bottom of the board—which is a warning before I even register the rest of the words. It's on a row on its own, separated from other postings.

I stare, aghast. I rub my eyes, then stare some more.

But no matter what I do, none of the words change.

SPECIAL JOINT POSTING	**CADETS**
Medaluo	Lia Ward & Kieren Murray
See Headmaster for details	

"Shit," I mutter.

3

EIRALE

They take me in.

It doesn't matter how much I protest that I'm innocent, or that my team members claimed I wasn't at the site of the assassination. I articulated clearly to the federal agents what we were doing at the nightclub. NileCorp received word of Nik Grant's presence tonight, and we showed up. If something horrible has happened, he is responsible. That's simple observation and deduction.

Somehow, I've still ended up in the back of their transport van, my wrists bound together with magnetic cuffs. The windows are barred. A barrier seals the front away and conceals the driver. Two agents sit in the van with me, speaking quietly between themselves. I can't hear them, though I suppose I'm not trying anyway. I halfheartedly tune in and out of the radio playing from the speakers: the civil war in Cega continues, Irisea has announced that they're cleaning the southern oceans. President Sterling will be making an emergency announcement tomorrow. To assign a new secretary of defense, I'm sure.

"All right, let's move it."

I'm being urged out of my seat before the van has come to a full stop. One of the agents takes my elbow, and the other hauls the door open.

Gauging by his grip alone, the agent escorting me isn't very strong. MILDENHALL, his lanyard says. He's pale, spindly, and the bald spot at the back of his head is shaped like a certain anatomical part. I bet I could outrun him.

Then Mildenhall pushes me to the sidewalk, my eyes scan the federal facility in front of us, and I change my mind. The line of uniformed military extends around the entire perimeter. I'm not running anywhere. They will shoot me before I can make a full turn on my heel.

"Inside. Come on."

The other agent's lanyard says PERRON. She walks ahead toward the building, the small heels of her shoes clicking audibly on each step. A few curious civilians peer over from their encampment down the road, lit a hazy orange from the fire burning in an overturned bin. They know better than to intrude in government business and certainly know to stay a healthy distance from a federal facility. By the time we've come to the door, there are no more onlookers straining to see.

Agent Mildenhall nudges me through the vestibule. On the first level, I scan the empty desks we march past, the screens dark and the holographic clocks turned off. Button City emits a murmur no matter the hour of the night, and beyond the window comes a series of faint car horns. I didn't know federal even had a facility downtown, but I'm not surprised.

In the interrogation room, they seat me without ceremony. A lamp flares on.

"Let's cut to the chase," Agent Perron says. "You can make this easier for yourself. A full confession will appeal to a jury far more nicely than us prying the truth out of you."

"I don't know how many times I can say this." I stay very still in my seat. "That's not me in the footage."

We'd stopped trusting sourceless video evidence about twenty years ago. Unless it came straight from the recording, it's too easy to doctor faces and people into evidence. Surely these two know that whatever video they have won't stand up to scrutiny.

Perron leans back in her chair, then lowers a pair of glasses at the top of her head. They jump to life, lighting up before her eyes. Maybe she's watching the footage again.

"Live deepfake doesn't work that fast," Mildenhall says. He remains standing.

"It's definitely moving that fast in some labs."

Maybe I'm supposed to keep quiet until NileCorp can get their lawyers here. I want to believe my employers will consider me too valuable an asset to neglect, but I have no one to plead my case within the company. Wright won't be easy to reach while he's recovering from injury. Teryn said nothing when I was being led away, which probably means she's not contacting her uncle personally to ask for help. She's always harping on about NileCorp greatness and our role as soldiers in maintaining it. Mint might have been willing to argue with federal and insist that I was framed, but Teryn turns her nose up at anyone damaging corporate reputation. There's no help coming there.

"Eirale Ward, if you took this as an assignment for Medaluo, now is the time to come clean."

My head snaps up. "I'm not a spy."

"Yeah, that's what you people all say before you're proven to be a spy."

"You were alerted to the crime as it happened," I say. "Then you were sent the video directly." The kerfuffle at the nightclub confirmed it, but calculating from the timing alone, the federal agents arrived at the scene before the doctored video even made it online. "You don't think that's weird? You don't find anything bizarre with the fact that someone has now posted the video to the feed?"

These are federal agents. Their education must have covered the incredible likelihood of tampered evidence. Most of the world spends their time in a computer-generated reality. No one takes video footage for the truth anymore. In court, prosecutions require eyewitnesses and undeniable human testimony. If they use video to prove anything, then there ought to be multiple angles from multiple sources.

Mildenhall puts his hands into his pockets. They sink in deep. He either has enormous pockets or freakishly small fists. "You seem to have the perfect answers, don't you? Medan folk love little cryptic idioms."

"I don't know what that means."

I haven't seen the circulating footage yet. But I'd assume the lighting was poor. The crowds were persistently shifting. If the video was sent to agents labeled RE: NILECORP CONTRACTOR EIRALE WARD SHOT CHIP GRAHAM, I can imagine that it looks convincing at first glance.

Mildenhall leans toward Perron. He whispers something into her ear, making an effort to cover both sides of his mouth so I can't read his lips. The lamp is too bright anyway.

"I didn't kill him," I say once more. My voice stays calm. "I have no ties to Medaluo and no reason to kill Secretary Graham."

"I'm getting here," Perron says, squinting into her glasses, "that you attended Nile Military Academy and finished a final posting in . . . Kunlun?"

My posture stiffens. "Yes."

"Any reason your corporate record is redacted from us, Eirale?"

Because NileCorp promised to keep it private. All graduates of Nile Military Academy have a mandatory final exam posting performed in virtual reality. That was my chance to prove myself in an otherwise middling academic career. I scored well enough to qualify for NileCorp's school, but I went under the radar once I actually attended the academy—no awards, no special projects, no friends. It was unlikely I was going to be assigned to NileCorp's forces, which was the aspiration for most graduates. If I was lucky, maybe a security job at a smaller company would take me, or I could leave the field entirely and live paycheck to paycheck downcountry while paying back the debt of military school. No one does that, of course: I'd need two lifetimes to erase my debt if I worked outside of corporate forces as a Medan, and since the schools lend the money, they also set the time limits before they can hand us off to the parent company for forfeiture. My life would be over the moment I missed a payment.

I hadn't had a choice in this path. By law, wards of the state are yanked out of the foster system at age twelve and into whichever military school will take us. It creates the perfect cycle. The state doesn't have to keep supporting its orphans, and while we pay back our education, Atahua gains soldiers.

"I've done confidential work," I answer. "Ask your Federal Bureau of Defense. They're the ones who took the information I retrieved."

"And for that," Mildenhall says, "you killed Secretary Graham?"

"What? *No.*"

Last year, the Atahuan media publicized claims that Medaluo was inventing technology at the cost of human rights up in Kunlun, and the feeds went wild. Kunlun is the only city in the world that exists upcountry without a downcountry equivalent. It's the birthplace of virtual reality as we know it, a rendering created by the first servers testing this technology before StrangeLoom introduced the ability to mimic our real world. As a matter of historical preservation, Kunlun was allowed to stay as a part of Medaluo's servers. Only citizens can enter, though—and citizenship to Kunlun can only be purchased for an astronomical price. Once a user is granted access, entry is possible exclusively through an additional, highly protected second password that a Pod or the Claw prompts upon selecting the open space north of Medaluo.

Like every other cadet in Atahua with a Medan face, I was put on assignment to Medaluo for my final exam. I don't remember what my task was. I don't remember why I finished in Kunlun, or how I even got there. I woke downcountry in the dorms, barely coherent and alive only because the school nurses received a warning that I was seizing in my Pod and pulled me out. After I stabilized in the hospital, NileCorp's CEO showed up himself to debrief me. James Moore told me where I'd been, then asked me how much I could recall, whether there were any additional details outside of my recordings. I had nothing: the seizure had put giant holes in my memory. Moore thanked me anyway. Said my findings were a matter of national security, and that I did a great job protecting Atahua. Once I was healed, I would be assigned a good posting on one of his teams.

I haven't heard from him since. I haven't regained any of my memories either, and NileCorp isn't exactly jumping at the chance to sit me down and tap me back into the confidential material I dug up for them.

Agent Perron gets up. I itch my wrists against the cuffs, turning my hands back and forth in my lap. After she leaves the room and the door slams shut behind her, Agent Mildenhall sniffs to fill the silence, mumbling something under his breath about late hours and a lack of cooperation. They'll file the report that way, I expect. Eirale Ward refused to answer our questions. Eirale Ward made our jobs harder, because we couldn't push her directly into the casket of guilt we'd opened, ready and waiting.

I don't say anything more. I've learned, through my childhood, that no amount of cooperation is enough for someone unwilling to extend goodwill. My innumerable foster parents. The dorm mothers at the care centers. Before the academy, I survived by staying silent when left alone and staying calm when picked on. *I didn't break the plate. I didn't pull out the garden herbs.* I can't remember the names of my foster parents anymore—it wasn't the seizure that wiped those memories, only the passage of time. I can't picture their faces outside of a pale blur in my head. But I remember how I needed to handle their quick rise to anger, their inherent suspicion toward me because of who I was.

"People from NileCorp are on their way," Agent Mildenhall announces, breaking the silence after several minutes.

"With lawyers, I hope," I mutter.

"Your employers don't have a legal right to offer lawyers yet. It depends on how the bureau processes you."

Goose bumps prickle my arms underneath my sleeves. I am still dressed as a NileCorp soldier even if I've shed the combat suit. Head to toe in black, my trouser legs tucked into my boots. They took the handgun and the earpiece. The slots at my shoulders and the pockets around my torso are empty.

This entire time, I've been waiting for something to happen. Some evidence of my culpability being a setup, brought in by an assistant sidling into the room or an anonymous tip on a phone call. The walls vibrate with the humdrum background noise of wires, their machines that run analysis on Button City, their scanners watching the perimeter for a hint of trouble.

A week after I was pulled out of my posting, Atahua held a press conference to condemn Medaluo's actions in Kunlun. The feed had been wondering why NileCorp's soldiers appeared on their streets, so they needed to say something, no matter how vague. In response, Medaluo issued a hand-wave for what *"may have been interpreted as a violation, but, please, be assured that we will work with the international human rights committee to ensure our future cooperation and, once again, we implore the Federated States of Atahua to respect our sovereignty."* I was never mentioned in relation to the scandal. Though I've watched all the news coverage I can find about the incident in Kunlun, I haven't probed for additional details, nor explicitly asked what I had uncovered that warranted a sea of soldiers appearing as backup. I became a corporate soldier myself shortly thereafter. I'm paid well. Every day I wake up at the base, train, and take meals. It's more than a Medan orphan in Atahua can ask for while tensions with Medaluo are at their worst.

NileCorp finished using me, and I'm supposed to be reaping the benefits now. They'll continue this arrangement with the newest graduating class of Nile Military Academy. They'll throw their cadets into the fray and make full use of the legal loopholes that let students fight Atahua's cold war without consequence, then offer rewards to keep us quiet and happy.

So if this situation doesn't resolve itself, I don't have high hopes that NileCorp is going to risk much to help me. The company would rather I not go to jail, but that's because I need to finish paying back my school debt with service. All the same, a few thousand dollars of unpaid debt probably isn't worth my legal fees to get through a scandal. My face is still Medan at the end of the day. Bad for optics. Bad for national morale. I'm an easy sacrifice to throw to the pyre.

The chair digs grooves through my clothes when I shift, changing which leg I have thrown over the other.

"Once again," I try a final time, "we were in the middle of a capture mission for Nik Grant when the defense secretary was murdered. Perhaps the country's top anarchist had something to do with it?"

Agent Mildenhall isn't paying attention to me anymore. He's looking down. Rapidly tapping a message on the handheld in his lap. Here and there, insurgents have been popping out of the woodwork to protest Atahua's current administration, but they're usually quickly arrested once NileCorp sends its private forces. There is nothing NileCorp cannot find. Nothing NileCorp cannot see.

Nik Grant's ability to evade capture is highly unusual. With that sort of skill set, I have no doubt he could set me up. The only question is: *Why?*

"Multiple cameras caught Nik Grant exiting the building before the shot was fired," Agent Mildenhall deadpans after a few seconds. "His list of crimes remains long, but this one seems to be yours."

"Suddenly I'm hearing it's important to consider the presence of multiple cameras," I return. "I was still in pursuit of Nik Grant after the shot was fired. Footage of his exit was fake."

Agent Mildenhall lowers his handheld. His head tilts.

"Which terrorist organization is it?" he asks abruptly. "Freedom Runners? Coalition?"

I haven't heard of any of these organizations he's listing. "Excuse me?"

"Which one of them recruited you?"

"*None*," I say.

"You're an independent actor, then?"

"That's not what I'm saying at all."

The room quiets. Agent Mildenhall huffs and looks away. I only stare ahead, waiting.

When the door opens again, it's not Perron returning. The three men waiting at the entryway are military.

"Let's go, please."

I stand. The quick obedience isn't feigned, though Mildenhall frowns like he's taken aback by my willingness to comply with the order. Clearly I'm not getting anywhere trying to convince him. Since no one has ever cleared their name before with fruitless arguing, I may as well be pleasant to deal with.

"Meet Agent Perron in the prepared cell," Mildenhall says to the soldiers. "Then report to your squad leader that we're finished up here. Thank you for staying overtime to deal with Medan perps."

I don't say anything. My gaze, seared by the bright lamp, stays level while they lead me out of the interrogation room into the hallway. We go up two flights of stairs, the facility eerily silent around us. Two of the soldiers walk in front of me, one behind. The rest of their men seem to have cleared out. We stop before the locked door at the end of the stairs, and my boots scuff against the linoleum.

The first soldier scans his badge against the panel beside the metal door. Its light remains red. The soldier, frowning, scans again.

"Did you store the badge with your handheld again?" the soldier beside him says. "You know that shorts out the magnetic stripe."

"I didn't," the first soldier replies shortly.

I tip my head down, swaying it side to side. There's a strain in my neck.

"Hey," I say. "Do you hear that?"

The soldier turns around, his badge pressed to the panel. His nose is crinkled, his top lip curled with a faint hint of disgust.

"What?"

I keep listening. "It sounds like a helicopter. Weird for one to be arriving at this hour."

The moment the words leave my mouth, the lights go out. My heart plummets down to my stomach. The soldiers take a beat to react. One of them yells out loud. The other two pull their handguns from their holsters. There's the high-pitched shatter of glass, and then the windows to our left disintegrate with a bright flare from the night outside. I flinch, pressing as closely as I can to the banister. If there's some sort of attack on the facility, I won't be looped in with Atahua's federal agents—

The silhouette of a person dives through the window, immediately unhooking a harness line from their belt. I search the stairwell for something, anything, to hide behind. Nothing. Before I've had the chance to consider whether it would be better to run, the silhouette from the window comes right for me.

"Wait, wait—"

They reach to grab my wrist. I go for my quickest defense, straightening my arms even while they're stuck together with my cuffs. One of the soldiers fires a shot in the dark. It misses. This masked figure, meanwhile, has predicted my exact move and grabs my elbow instead. Before I register their counteractive measure, they have their other arm looped through my waist, and I'm being picked up, thrown over their shoulder.

This has turned from merely dire to a catastrophic situation.

I have one gulp of air to scream before I'm yanked out of the third-story window, making a rapid plunge for the concrete ground. The wind whistles against my ears. My sense of balance turns upside down, fighting to understand which direction gravity has flipped.

We come to a halt just before hitting the pavement.

"Come on, soldier."

I recognize that voice. I don't believe it. I'm too flabbergasted to react, but then my rescuer releases the rope he caught, depositing us onto the sidewalk beside the federal building. The line of military is gone. My feet stop the moment they meet solid ground, so he grabs my arm again, hauling me forward.

A helicopter has descended near the pier. There's an alarm shrieking from the federal building. Red and white lights flash from the exterior, but the agents haven't made it out the door yet.

"When we reach the ladder, you're going to climb."

"I'm not climbing." I have to shout over the helicopter's frenzied whirring. My short hair whips into my eyes. "I'm not fleeing the scene with you."

Nik Grant yanks off his ski mask. "You'd rather be prosecuted for treason? Because trust me, they *will* prosecute you."

I fight to squeeze air into my lungs. The night shouldn't feel so cuttingly cold when we've long left the husks of winter. Each swallow tightens my throat.

The federal agents emerge from the building.

"Forget it," Nik Grant snaps. "This isn't a choice. Let's go."

Atahua's most dangerous anarchist, who is only a teenage boy barely three inches taller than I am, yanks me with him until we've approached the hovering helicopter. Nik flings my bound hands onto a rung of the ladder.

"Either hold on or fall off. *Lift!*" The latter part of that command is called up to the people inside the aircraft. Gunshots ring into the night, fired from the steps of the federal building. I throw a glance over my shoulder, both hoping for some intervention and praying there is none. My hair tears into a frenzy, writhing like loose wires and obscuring my eyes while the wind picks up with takeoff. I scramble to hook a leg through a lower rung so that my arms aren't straining for grip. The shots keep ringing out, coming close enough to strike the ladder and bounce off with a metallic bang before the helicopter hefts properly into the dark clouds.

"I'm sure I don't need to warn you not to try anything at this point."

Nik nudges my ankle with his own leg, securing my footing. His voice hovers close to my ear. I resist the impulse to fling myself off only to see what might happen if I did. He'd probably follow me and drag me right back even if we've both splatted on the ground.

The ladder starts to retract back into itself on a winding mechanism, pulling us higher, higher, until there's an arm inside reaching for my elbow and yanking me in.

"I have to say . . ." The girl doesn't release me once I'm on my feet. Her hands stay at my shoulders in the dark interior, making a thorough examination of my face. "I really didn't think this was going to work."

"Lack of trust, Miz. Didn't I say it would be fine?"

Nik clambers in, slamming the helicopter door closed. It seals away the roar of sound outside. With the engine flying steadily, I could almost believe we're standing in a train car on the ground instead.

A beat passes. I'm taking in the space, the bags stashed in the corner, the clean seats that make the helicopter appear entirely new.

"Why did you break me out?" I ask carefully. My voice is hoarse.

Nik Grant doesn't say anything. The girl—Miz—thins her lips and busies herself with a handheld screen. She possesses a discomfort that Nik doesn't. He stares at me outright, perfectly comfortable to let the uneasy moment draw long.

"I asked a question," I prompt. "The least you owe me is an answer."

"I thought the answer was obvious." Nik raises an eyebrow, as though he really is skeptical that I would need to ask. "We broke you out because we put you in there. We framed you."

I stare at him. *I* knew I didn't kill Chip Graham. *I* knew there was a link between our operation for Nik Grant and this assassination. But *why*—

"I need your cooperation for our mission, and this was the only way to get you," Nik goes on. "Come to Medaluo with us, and I'll give you back the real footage that clears your name."

It takes me a moment to process his words. A moment to comprehend that this wasn't only a setup to make me look guilty. It was a setup so that I would be motivated to keep myself out of prison.

Nik waits patiently. I suppose he wants my easy agreement. My gratitude for breaking me out of Atahua's interrogation rooms.

I lunge at him with my hands outstretched.

4

LIA

Headmaster Murray's office is located at the center of campus, in the A Block building beside the great sycamore, and I'm disgustingly nervous the moment the doors close after me.

I make my way down A Block slowly, worrying about every possibility that could unfold with this posting. If there's one thing I know how to do well, it's worry. There are moments where I'm paranoid that I could start overthinking and then get stuck in a loop forever, cycling through the various outcomes of an upcoming scenario so many times that I keep creating new realities inside my head. When NileCorp named their engine StrangeLoom, it was supposed to reference the idea of *a "strange loop,"* where the creation reaches back to influence the original, erasing any sense of a beginning or end. Whether the chicken or the egg came first is the most classic strange loop. Whether or not my world is kept on a tight leash because I catastrophize through my every move and end up exactly where I started had I not thought at all, is another.

Unsurprisingly, Wakeman Syndrome often goes hand in hand with an anxiety disorder. I shouldn't self-diagnose. Sometimes it feels dangerous to even *think* about what might be wrong with me in case NileCorp overhears it. If anything is logged on my record, NileCorp won't want to take me after I graduate.

A Block is empty when I proceed through the winding corridors. Other cadets are in class. While I'm dragging my feet, I open my display and scan down my contacts list. I've already been excused from next period, so there's no harm in taking my time. Dad has activated Do Not Disturb mode on his profile, but I call anyway.

The line doesn't have the chance to ring. Immediately, a pop-up appears to tell me I'm being transferred to his assistant.

"Lia," Freya greets. "How's it hanging?"

Freya has been Dad's assistant in the Capitol Building since she graduated ten years ago—I still remember when she first started, because she was the one who kept me company while Dad was running around for meetings.

"It's good," I say. "Is Dad there?"

"One second." There's shuffling on her end of the line. Ambient noise makes upcountry phone calls feel more realistic, even though we're being connected avatar to avatar and the system has the capacity to isolate only the speaker's voice from the mic. Freya's desk is right outside Dad's office: she'll be peering through the window to see if Dad's free or on the phone. "Yeah, I'll transfer you in. Your dad's been sending calls to me lately because he's getting a lot of international spam."

I frown. "Spam? With *his* security?"

"I know. Probably an information leak. I'm going to resume trawling through the dark web to see if I can find anything as soon as I pass you over."

Freya's funny. Though I don't think she's kidding.

"Thank you. Good luck on the dark web."

"I appreciate it. See you, Lia."

A click echoes through the line. Two seconds later, I hear Dad clearing his throat when he picks up.

"Lia? This isn't our usual call time."

Our usual call time is in the late evening, when I'm in my dorm room and Dad is back at the apartment. During the day, there's always some breaking emergency that'll drag him away two minutes into a chat. Dad hates messaging, so we rarely do that. It's largely a security measure, given the bot accounts that have popped up in the past pretending to be him. He has it worse as a public figure, with so many voice clips and written statements available online. The rest of us aren't as worried, but on Dad's advice, I've established an identity check with Rayna before we open a new conversation with each other. He thinks the two of us never stop texting. Which is true. It makes us good targets for scammers.

"I'm calling with special news," I say. Phone lines are possible to fake too, technically, but NileCorp is really working hard on countering that within upcountry. They've got to give people *some* sense of safety. "Final postings are out."

A long beat passes. That sort of silence is unusual for Dad, who could probably talk the ear off any of his constituents and their grandmothers.

"It's early," he finally says. "Where were you sent?"

"Medaluo, of course." I peer behind my shoulder. Still no activity in A Block—not even a creak of the building settling. It's too modern for that. The system wouldn't code it in. "I'm about to see Headmaster Murray. Apparently mine is a special posting."

"That sounds promising." His tone is strained. Dad always gets weird when it comes to Medaluo, when I remind him it's only natural that Atahua will try to use me as a weapon in their arsenal. He wants to believe that I could be like him, that I could make my own path if only I tried hard enough to resist the rest of the nation's perception of me.

But in war times, there's a world of difference between being fully Medan and half-Medan. Nothing bars Dad from being a senator, but a mountain of debt stands in my way from anything other than NileCorp security. It costs more to attend military school as a ward than an Atahuan. Go figure.

"I'll let you know what I get posted on," I say.

"Lia..." Dad trails off, and I hear his reluctance. He doesn't like the idea of a final exam posting out in the world beyond the academy's safeguards.

He would have banned me from military academy entirely if it weren't required by law to send all wards through. "Come for dinner tonight. We should chat about what you've got coming up."

There's one reason I've worked so hard in school, one final goal I've been counting on to reap the rewards. At Nile Military Academy, the valedictorian of each grade is allowed to submit their preference for where they're stationed within NileCorp's newbie ranks, and it's always honored. I've had a brutal four years, sure, whatever. But if I make valedictorian, I can join Capitol security in the District of Melnova. I could work my way up into being a part of Dad's detail, and he would never have to worry about me again, nor I him. Teryn Moore graduated as last year's valedictorian, and she's at the Button City base now. I follow her on the feed to get her every update, though she doesn't post that much. I'm sure being the NileCorp CEO's niece meant she'd get any posting she wanted anyway, but I already knew that she was going to be the top performer even when she was at the academy. When the grade above stayed overtime in PE, I would linger to watch her on the climbing ropes, nod along to myself to take mental notes on what she was doing well. I bet she aced her final exam posting.

I need to be ten times as good as Teryn Moore if I'm going to invoke the same competency.

"I can't leave the academy tonight," I say. It's a five-hour train from Button to Melnova. "There's no time to travel."

"Log out and log back in. You'll be on campus again before bedtime roll call."

I wince. Unfortunately, I hate going downcountry enough that I refuse to use the method, even if it's for a few seconds. Most people vastly prefer the pseudo-teleportation, but I need to travel properly, cross virtual space as though it's real. It messes with my head otherwise.

"Maybe," I say. "I'll let you know. I have a lot of work to do."

"All right." There's murmuring on his end: Freya has stepped into his office to summon him. "I have to go now. Talk later. Love you."

"Love you too."

Dad hangs up.

As a public figure, there are some things about his background that he's never told me himself—the internet does that work for him. Even while I'm merely hovering over his saved profile, suggested searches appear without prompt in case I'd like to browse further. Senator Henry Sullivan. Who is the Federated States senator of Haven? Henry Sullivan wife death.

I grimace, navigating out of my contacts list. It's as if he knows what the automated suggestions are showing me because I get a text from him at that moment: a simple waving animation that has his face rendered onto it. He got a whole pack of them made to use when he has to chat with his constituents. He reserves the silly ones for me.

I send back a **hehe**.

Before me, Dad and his wife had a birth daughter. The baby got sick when she was really young—some form of cancer, though they never publicized which one. Dad took time off from appearances. From the old posts I'd snooped through on the feed, it had seemed like she was getting better.

She passed away two weeks after her fourth birthday. Twelve months later, the feed announced that Henry and Mallory Sullivan had adopted a daughter—me. *It's important to the both of us that we're not abandoning* Atahuan *children because of our war with Medaluo,* he'd told reporters, making a targeted remark at a recent slate of anti-Medan crimes in Atahua. In that interview, Mallory had been pressed into his side, seemingly there to lend him her support. Every time I watch the footage again, hoping to pick up some new detail about these bygone days, all I can think is that she's the one who looked like she'd needed the comfort, her expression subdued.

Mallory Sullivan—my mom, I suppose in technicality—was born Mallory Meng. Unlike Dad, who largely looks Atahuan despite his half-Medan background, Mallory had two Medan parents who immigrated to Atahua before the cold war started.

Mallory died in a car accident a year after I was adopted. I don't have any memories of her, not even the faintest indicator of what she smelled like or how she hugged. She and Dad needed to spend time downcountry to raise me until I was old enough to be granted StrangeLoom credentials and use upcountry—and it took her life.

I blink fast, trying to control the sudden urge to tear up. My display opens a swath of tabs, not understanding my eye movements, and I mutter a curse, closing everything at once to get it out of sight. My vision clears. Only the empty corridor of A Block waits ahead.

Dad loves me, but sometimes I wonder if he *likes* me, because chances are that he never wanted to be saddled with me without his wife, and now I am his by a sense of duty. A ward of the state, clinging desperately to the identity he gives me outside of it. He's strict about where I can go and what I can do, and as much as I protest it, I know it's only because he wants to protect me the way he couldn't protect his wife and his first daughter. I used to watch him clean the photos of Mallory sitting on the mantel like clockwork each morning. I would linger in the doorway on the anniversary of her death every year when he was lighting a candle for her, not wanting to interrupt. He'd turn around, and he'd beckon me to come have a look.

"Do you miss her?" The conversation is one of my earliest memories, one small fist clutching Dad's leg because I didn't want him to walk too far. I must have been six, barely used to my life yet.

"Of course I do. I miss her so much, and it will always hurt a little for as long as I'm without her." He gave me a candle. "But she would be so happy that you're here with me. We'll take care of each other, you and me. Won't we?"

My dad has lost so much, and I am all he has. I will be good, be the best, be everything anyone could ask for in a daughter, because otherwise what was the point of him sacrificing so much to raise me?

Dad has not required this of me. He doesn't need to. If I am all he has, he is all I have. His approval is everything to me.

A door slams open above, audible from the ground floor. It gives my pulse another jolt, reminding me where I am and where I am supposed to be getting to. I take a deep breath in. A deep breath out.

I resume moving forward.

Our headmaster doesn't have an assistant to facilitate his meetings. He wants to be readily available for the student body, which means that when I come right up to his door and knock gently, he doesn't actually hear me past the radio he's playing in his office.

"... *Atahua is often cast in a negative light during global negotiations for having started what is now termed a* cold war *with Medaluo. Our intent to protect our self-interests is perceived as hostile. It's easy, folks—we just want to keep Atahuan products at home....*"

I knock again, harder, figuring Headmaster Murray didn't hear me. This time, he switches the radio off and calls, "Come in."

I step into his office.

"Hello, sir."

It's practically a squeak, but Headmaster Murray doesn't remark on it when he looks up from his computer screen. Kieren's dad freaks me out. He's a mountain of a man, his shoulders square and his neck always very red. He's nothing like Kieren, who appears lanky from the outside, hiding the build he's got when he takes his shirt off to spar in PE. Undoubtedly a tactic on his part to distract me. Which only *occasionally* works. And anyway, who isn't flustered by the prospect of having to touch a naked torso?

I don't really have a reason for quaking like a duck anytime I'm in Headmaster Murray's presence, but if I had to choose one, it's because he was once the head of security at NileCorp. He only left to take the headmaster role at Nile Military Academy when his two oldest children started here, and with every second I spend in his office, I'm convinced that I could say something wrong, do something wrong, and he could call up his old contacts at NileCorp to directly report that I'm useless.

"Lia, I've been expecting you." Headmaster Murray gestures to the seat. "Please."

There are three chairs facing his desk. I shuffle to the one on the very left, sitting delicately. Kieren's already been through. I can tell because the chair on the right is skewed at an angle, the rug underneath pushed from the brusque movement of someone getting up.

"I have to admit," I start, "I wasn't aware that a joint posting was a possibility."

Cadets team up frequently, sure. If a group of us are posted to Medaluo, then chances are high that many will be located in the same city at the same time. We can share hotel rooms. We can combine efforts to hit a place together with different goals. Some cadets are told to acquire information. Others are ordered to survey new developments in certain industries or regions. Collaboration can be a useful tool.

But I've never heard of two cadets with the same directive.

"Things have been changing lately, Lia." Headmaster Murray clicks his mouse, closing something on the screen in front of him. Computers are an unnecessary object to render in virtual, but a common one, like the watch Coach Chelsea wears. We can access everything on the internet by blinking open our display, but working for hours on end using our avatar's eye movements gets tiring.

"The academy gauges our needs with the changing geopolitical landscape," he continues. "That's why we're sending everyone in a week early. Less chance of Medaluo blocking us when they know it's exam season."

"I understand," I say. It makes me nervous to even appear like I'm arguing, so I buffer around my words: "But . . . and not to question the decision or anything—it just feels, to me, that perhaps a special joint posting maybe shouldn't . . . be me and Kieren?"

Headmaster Murray turns away from his computer. He laces his hands together, leaning back in his chair. There are pictures of his three children on his desk: Kieren and Hailey side by side, then twelve-year-old Weston. Next to the photo frames is a golden penholder. I recognize the specific brand of fountain pens because Kieren uses them in class. Most of our classmates pull open a virtual keyboard and take notes for their personal files. Kieren prefers pen and paper. Who knows what he does with the notes once he retires to his dorm since he can digitize them in a blink anyway. Maybe he eats them.

"Is there any trouble?" he asks.

"No! Of course not."

Headmaster Murray gives me a look. "I thought you two were friends. The board thought such a collaborative task would require cadets who were already very well acquainted."

How do I even begin to explain the relationship that I have with Kieren? We're... not *not* friends, I suppose. We've known each other for years, since the first night of New Cadet Orientation. We'd gone about our daytime activities separately, ignorant of the colossal threat walking the campus, only coalescing when we ended up at the same party that the upperclassmen hosted. It was exactly as I'd expected for a military academy rager: cadets screaming, drinking, and throwing themselves off the roof of the club house to see if StrangeLoom would have them bounce off the bushes—truly testing the limits of how upcountry won't allow serious injuries. I'd found myself in a quieter room, trailing behind Natalie Ward, who I'd befriended earlier in the day. Everyone who joined the circle on the carpet was offered a cold silver can with no identifying information printed on the surface. The only person who'd declined like I did was Kieren Murray.

I immediately sat next to him. I figured we had something in common. Before the year formally started, the academy always overlooked drinking on campus. It would be a different matter once classes were underway, but it was too hard to crack down now when all cadets partook. Except for us, I suppose.

"Not to your liking?" I asked.

"I prefer hard drugs," he returned.

I reached into my pocket and offered up the scrunched-up tissue paper I had. Kieren looked down slowly, then at me.

"I was joking."

"So was I," I returned. "The only gold dust in here is my snot."

It surprised Kieren that I had met him at his level. I could tell when his manner shifted and his scowl relaxed. His eyes smoothed out, widened to warmer brown. Hailey poked her head into the room a few minutes later, clearly to check whether he was still moping, and Kieren was quick to introduce her, then hurry her off.

That first exchange earned his quick friendship. We hung out together the entire party. We liked the same obscure historical events, shared the same opinions on Atahuan politics. I was already envisioning bringing my every thought to him over the next four years so we could debate back and forth until we were blue in the face.

I turned out to be mostly right, with some deviation. The second time I met him at his level, he didn't like that so much, and Kieren Murray changed his tune on our burgeoning camaraderie after they declined to break our first-rank tie. It's a shame, because I really do still enjoy debating him.

"We're in the same circles," I settle on, finally answering Headmaster Murray. "But we're also very—uh . . . *competitive*. You remember when Kieren pushed me over during the relay race."

That was tenth grade. Headmaster Murray frowns, likely trying to recall the memory. "I thought you said that was an accident."

"It was." To be fair, it was because I'd tried to trip him first. "He was still pretty happy about my distress."

Headmaster Murray sighs. We're getting sidetracked. "Believe me, I'm aware the final exam posting is usually a cadet's moment to shine. The board gave this plenty of consideration before making their decision. Your performances will be individually graded. We'll require permission to access your avatar recordings—anything personal or possibly sensitive will be filtered out by the system."

I don't like the idea of the academy fine-tooth-combing through my recorded footage just to figure out if I had a better performance than

Kieren. I tend to panic in the moment and work things out as they happen. I'd much prefer to be judged by my final product.

"But—"

"This is big, Lia," Headmaster Murray cuts in, anticipating my rebuff. "The directive came in from federal. To tell you the truth, the board is shocked they want two of the academy's cadets performing it. It's the sort of mission they should be giving someone ten years into their career."

Slowly, I sit up straighter. I'm enough of a people pleaser to nod along to the clear praise, but I'm also not stupid. Insurgents keep blowing up members of the military while they're off-duty to make a point about how much they hate the current administration. Just earlier, the feed was spreading crime scene footage of a hit—I didn't watch it, and by the time I was browsing, it had already been deleted. It'll get uploaded onto the back channels soon, and then the extremist forums will pick it up to blame the Medans in the country, to insist Atahua needs to launch a nuke on Medaluo while it still can, wipe out the enemy and seize a victory in this conflict sucking our nation dry.

Atahua's government departments need the helping hands despite their monstrous budget, and NileCorp's cadets will always land a few exam postings that are critical to federal's war effort. It's a get-out-of-jail-free card for Atahua, the perfect excuse if we're caught committing international espionage. We're a private company, and we're only students. We're children, really, and children can't be held accountable. So I highly doubt the board was that shocked by this directive, no matter what it is.

"All right," I say slowly. "I'm ready."

The headmaster slides over a black folder. "We think Medaluo created an AI weapon."

My spine deflates. Medaluo allegedly creates a new AI weapon every two weeks. Each time there are rumors that they've reached the peak of technology and will win the cold war by seizing the StrangeLoom system, and then each time the research still isn't strong enough.

"And might they actually have something," I ask, "or is Atahua being paranoid?"

Again, I add silently.

The cold war had already started by the time StrangeLoom was invented. Maybe as the two most powerful nations in the world, Medaluo and Atahua could have built something doubly effective if they had collaborated, but every new election here brought more bills cutting ties. More politicians who hated how Medaluo was overtaking Atahua. More Atahuans who were intent on confronting the matter.

"Atahua is right to be paranoid," Headmaster Murray chides.

I keep my mouth shut. I should have known better than to voice anything less than patriotic. My ethnic identity already puts me on thin ice. The headmaster taps the briefing in front of me, and I reach for the black folder.

Medaluo's government was actually the first to experiment with fully immersive virtual reality, but it only had enough power to generate Kunlun. They wasted too many resources trying to draw up a new world, encoding streets and roads and plants that adhered to the laws of physics. They didn't think to scan our real world and let artificial intelligence do the heavy lifting. *We're just mimicking reality,* James Moore would declare at the NileCorp conference to introduce his new creation, StrangeLoom. *There's no need to go inventing a new one.*

And James Moore didn't even start as an engineer—he was a graphic designer in the lowest bowels of NileCorp, hired right out of college after he won a mascot art competition. They didn't end up using his mascot. They didn't really care to. NileCorp was Atahua's largest company, a mass retailer for people to buy everything under the sun, and in the years it had been around, it had streamlined operations to the point of controlling each logistical node. It made sense for them to continue expanding into the arms of more powerful consumers. Weapons and military equipment. Schools and soldiers. The government of Atahua was its most insatiable customer.

So back then, if there was any place to propose ideas about a virtual reality landscape, NileCorp was the company for it. In his interviews, James Moore attributes his inspiration to waking up horribly sick one morning and realizing he couldn't risk attending his little brother's birthday party—but how nice would it have been if that risk weren't present? He brought his ideas higher, then higher, and as the news kept talking about Kunlun and how soon Medaluo would advance on its work, Moore was given a division to direct: StrangeLoom.

He's never admitted that his team must have stolen Medan government technology, but no matter where you read his origin story, there's someone in the comments talking about how it's impossible they invented StrangeLoom that fast without help. After Moore proved that the engine functioned on a global scale, Atahua pumped billions into the StrangeLoom division to become its primary investor. Federal and NileCorp intertwined more than ever before: Atahua set the rules of our new world without parallel. Irisea signed on quickly, eager to demonstrate itself a rising ally. Among rivals, Cega changed its tune first—expected, given its position at Atahua's western border, but it led to a domino effect across the other Western Territories. Eventually, even Medaluo was forced to cede its stubbornness and admit defeat by using StrangeLoom, opening its server and becoming the last major country to sign on. It's hard to stay out when life starts moving elsewhere. When people are leaving the physical plane in an upward direction.

But Medaluo has never forgotten that Atahua swept its burgeoning technology out from underneath them, and they've been desperate ever since to gain some foothold. They've been fighting for control over NileCorp's virtual world, where they have no choice but to live.

Which likely has something to do with the briefing I'm holding in my hand.

"*Operation Coldwire*," I read aloud. The rest of the opening page is entirely redacted.

"You'll find field photos starting on page five and research logs on page twenty. You don't need to understand the exact science behind it. You just need to understand that Operation Coldwire is Medaluo's attempt to create a weapon functionally able to hack into StrangeLoom by language command. Think of a chatbot loyal to Medaluo and able to stick its fingers into administrative code whenever it wants."

My head snaps up. "Oh, *shit*."

"Language, cadet."

I grimace. "Sorry. So it's been made already?"

"The weapon has already been made," Headmaster Murray answers. "But it's also been deleted."

I frown. "I'm not sure I understand."

"Here." There's an incoming transmission, and I flick my eyes, accepting Headmaster Murray's file download. A news article.

"Their lead engineer is someone named Chung Yin. You know him."

For a moment, I assume Headmaster Murray is making a barb. Ethnic Medans are used to the insinuations that we'll turn spy eventually, especially at a place like Nile Military Academy. Many of us end up assigned in Medaluo for NileCorp's intelligence collection because we're Atahuan assets who blend nicely undercover . . . up until the moment Medaluo discovers our presence and offers us enough money to turn. Some politicians say it's in our blood. Some want us all rounded up and kicked out of the country before we can destroy it.

Then I look at the picture attached to the article and realize I *do* know him.

"You were young when he was in Atahua, so maybe you don't recall anymore," Headmaster Murray goes on.

"No, I remember him," I say faintly. Before boarding at the academy, I lived with Dad at the apartment in Melnova. He was one of Dad's friends, coming by every few weeks to get a drink and chat on the balcony while I was doing my elementary school homework. Dad had me call him Uncle

Chung. When I was eleven, I realized I hadn't seen Uncle Chung in a while, and when I asked Dad why, Dad said it was because he had taken a job elsewhere and moved.

"Chung Yin was born an Atahuan citizen," Headmaster Murray says, "but he chose to revoke it when Medaluo offered him a job."

My head snaps up. I feel like I've been shocked by a strike of lightning, frozen to the floor. We hear the accusations. We hardly hear of it actually happening.

"I didn't know," I say. "My dad never told me."

"I imagine Henry didn't know the extent of it. We only very recently received word about what Mr. Chung has been doing with Medaluo all these years, and it turns out it's secretly building a hacking bot."

Every month, the International Assembly raises protests against NileCorp—and Atahua, peripherally—about the limited control that countries have over their own servers. NileCorp might give Medaluo the ability to make their avatars prettier, but they can't change anything about their streets, their maps. StrangeLoom's settings are immutable. It builds everything upcountry off its downcountry satellites, and NileCorp doesn't release anything for a country's own engineers to play with. It establishes the power balance upcountry firmly. NileCorp is Atahua's watchdog, and so Atahua is the global king.

Hacking StrangeLoom would mean Medaluo quietly meddling with every bit of society without us knowing what exactly they're hitting. People's messages. Bank accounts. Inventory objects. Our very sense of reality. Medaluo would be inserting puppet strings into Atahua's throne.

There's another incoming file from Headmaster Murray. I open it, finding myself looking at a satellite scan of some compound.

"You're aware of the function of national data centers, yes?" he asks.

I would hope so. "As in, the giant server rooms where the government stores their data?"

"Correct."

"I'm familiar with the concept."

He nods. "What you're currently looking at can also be found on page fourteen of your brief. Medaluo has been building Coldwire directly inside their data centers. It ensures the highest level of protection if there aren't any second access points—no external offices to break into, no remote locations to hack. On his official resume, Chung Yin has been made supervisor of the Ministry of National Defense's servers. He's actually the lead engineer who steers Operation Coldwire using those data centers as office spaces."

I flip back to the previous file transmission, scanning the news article again. In the picture, Chung is significantly older than I remember. The years haven't been kind to him downcountry. Scientists and engineers are some of the few people who end up in the real often as an occupational hazard. Tests still have to be run. Servers have to be updated.

His hair is graying in streaks on both sides. He's dressed in a button-down that seems a size too big for him, but the large white lab coat mostly hides the baggy fabric. A pair of glasses hang on a chain around his neck—old glasses, the sort for myopia, not the ones that people wear downcountry to replace their handhelds.

"And now it would appear Mr. Chung Yin has gone missing."

My head jerks up, minimizing everything in my display. "What?"

"The servers show he isn't logged upcountry anymore," Headmaster Murray goes on, despite my reaction. "The Pod in his home is empty, and the cameras lost sight of him after he left work that day."

I'm blinking rapidly. There's certainly foul play here. People don't *go missing* anymore. Facial recognition will identify them in an instant, even if only a snippet of their forehead flashes at a security camera.

"Under usual circumstances, we might assume he's checked into a spa retreat somewhere to enjoy some time off. However, Operation Coldwire then disappeared from Medaluo's data centers. Hard to argue that isn't suspicious."

But a file the size of an AI program can't be deleted that easily. There are always methods of reversing the wipe.

"Is that the assignment, then?" I ask. "Recover the file?"

Headmaster Murray gives me a dull look. "Of course not. That would take an enormous amount of data sifting. Lia, we want you to find Chung. Read the brief. There are two possible objectives: either confirm he is dead and no longer a threat to our way of life, or locate him so we can move in and turn his loyalty. The most likely explanation for a voluntary disappearance is that he has upset Medaluo. Ripe ground to bring him back to Atahua."

I finally flip through the folder properly, past the redacted introductory page. A sinking feeling has started in my chest. This is what I am being evaluated on. The most important exam of my life, and it's to use my personal connection to some friend of my dad I haven't seen in almost a decade. An engineer who probably doesn't even remember me and likely has no interest in coming back to a country he gave up.

"Chung disappeared from Upsie, so you'll start there. He did have offices across the major cities, which means you may need to travel for a comprehensive search." The second page of my brief says MEDALUO: A GEOGRAPHIC SURVEY. "We have resources we're receiving live updates from. You'll be given more information by a contact on the ground. Be ready to act and move at a moment's notice."

"But he disappeared from downcountry Upsie," I say. Final exam postings are always virtual. They can only inject us into the enemy country when NileCorp has control over the system, after all. It would be heinously more difficult to smuggle students into real-world Medaluo.

"Correct. You're still a cadet. We're not putting you on the real field. If he's retreated downcountry, he will have left signs upcountry too: file uploads, monetary withdrawals, communications with businesses. Why did he disappear? Who did he upset? Did he delete Coldwire himself, or is someone else out to get him? Can we offer him protection?"

Headmaster Murray's eyes glaze for a moment as he reads an incoming message. After a few seconds, he nods, then blinks to clear the message.

"NileCorp's engineers are coming tomorrow morning to send you into Medaluo's server," he continues. "You'll get an early start on the rest of the class. Any more questions?"

My hands tighten on the folder. I'm making creases on the paper. Before I can overthink it, I blurt: "Why Kieren?"

"I'm sorry?"

Headmaster Murray doesn't appear offended right off the bat, which is promising. Less of a chance he's immediately marking me down as an insubordinate cadet who can't be trusted with a task. Or as someone scheming to get his son off a prestigious posting.

"I only mean to ask," I say carefully, "why does it take the two of us? I can handle this myself. I know I can."

"I'm afraid that's up to the board's discretion," Headmaster Murray answers.

"Did they consider anyone else for the role?"

It's crystal clear why they want me. Their reasoning for Kieren isn't as overt.

"I'm afraid that isn't information I can divulge." Headmaster Murray stands. No smile, but no sneer either. He's impossible to read, and I stay perpetually nervous. "If that is all?"

I hurry to rise. My chair squeaks back, its legs pushing into the rug just like Kieren's on the right did, and I resist a sigh. From test scores to the way we stand.

"Yes, sir."

Headmaster Murray gestures to the door. "Kieren is already packing, so you should too."

• • • •

I skip dinner and opt to lie on the carpet of my dorm room instead.

It's comfy. I've never been one to need luxuries, but I'm glad that this is a facet of upcountry. The carpets are thicker, and the walls are cleaner. StrangeLoom will replicate everything large-scale with no exceptions, no matter how much the politicians deem abandoned lots to be eyesores and call for adjustment. But the system allows for plenty of reasonable changes if NileCorp is at the end of the supply line. Clothing retailers can sell as many virtual pieces as they want. Restaurants can make as much food as there is demand. Everything upcountry is eerily real up to its most basic state, when one will find that NileCorp has stepped in with their pixels to replace original sources. Virtual farms are mere stillborn mimicries that are never harvested; virtual fabrics all come from the one mega StrangeLoom.

At the pixel level, upcountry uses only NileCorp materials. Of course it would be softer, nicer, smoother.

I puff out a breath, my hair fluttering off my face.

Kieren and I usually share a regular table in the cafeteria—though we occupy two opposite ends of the very long surface—and it's clearly killing our friends that neither of us, it seems, is there tonight. They're dying to find out more about the joint posting, gauging by the group chats I've muted. They have questions. Theories and rumors that I'm not allowed to clarify. I've got CONFIDENTIAL stamped over every page of the briefing folder, which I've since opened in my personal files after Headmaster Murray sent the digital version.

While I stare at the ceiling, I read the briefing again in my display, my eye movements flipping each page quickly. The geographic overview of Medaluo begins with a photograph of Upsie's skyline. Short for *"Land of the Upper Sea,"* Upsie isn't Medaluo's capital, but it's the first city that comes to mind when anyone thinks of Medaluo. Upcountry, those skyscrapers are the country's financial and economic center. Downcountry, Upsie's location by the country's eastern coast means that it's being subject to the rising tides year after year. Trash slogs through the flooding streams, and the torrent destroys any ground-floor apartment on lower elevation.

The real city is worse for wear, approaching utter abandonment in certain sectors.

I wouldn't admit it out loud, not in this climate, but a part of me has always looked forward to the final posting just so I can see upcountry Medaluo at least once. I don't want to be stationed there for the rest of my life paying back my debts, and I definitely don't want to be there downcountry, which is where corporate soldiers are most needed. I'd still like to experience its virtual replica, though. Walk Upsie's streets. Eat Threto's food. Now the time has come . . . only I'll have a tagalong.

"This is ridiculous," I say to my empty dorm room. I still can't believe they're sending us *together*.

A knock comes on my door. *Kieren*, I think instinctively, and I flip onto my stomach, propping myself up with my elbows and brushing my bangs back into place.

"Come in," I call.

My door flies open and hits the back wall with a loud slam.

"My life is over."

I scoff out a laugh, dropping off my elbows and returning to the floor to peer at Rayna. She's changed into pajamas already, so she came from her own dorm, not the cafeteria. Her hair remains loose down her back rather than twisted up in that piece of foam she insists will create heatless curls, though, inevitably, by third period each day, her ponytail is once more as straight as a metal ruler.

"Why?" I ask. My cheek brushes against the carpet threads. "Did you go viral on the feed with a stupid post again?"

"No," she grumbles, closing the door and marching into my room. "It's—what happened in here? Why is it so messy?"

I've started packing, but my suitcase is only half-filled, and I'm at a loss for what else to bring. I don't have many clothes in virtual. Rayna, on the other hand, has a bit of a shopping addiction, by which I mean she has a tendency to black out and buy everything in a new-release catalog.

"I need to bring clothes if I'm going away for ten weeks," I say. "I'm sure you saw the posting."

"I did see your posting." She plops down on my bed. "But I'm actually more concerned about *my* posting."

I finally pick myself up off the floor, sitting upright. Though Rayna is wailing like it's the end of the world, this is a very normal display of emotions for Rayna Ward. We've been best friends since ninth grade—or more specifically, since our second day of classes at Nile Military Academy, when Rayna asked to borrow a hair tie and was so grateful when I had one that she burst into tears. Rayna's adoptive mom is a high-level lawyer who decided she wanted to raise a child, though she was unpartnered and above the usual rearing age. Like me, from the moment Rayna was taken in, she hasn't known any other home, even if the law prevents us from being formally claimed.

Unlike me, Rayna is close to her mom in the weird, mushy Atahuan way. She's grown up comfortable with expressing herself.

"Don't tell me...," I say. "It's because of Hailey, isn't it?"

Rayna puts her face on my pillow and screams into it. I let her do her thing. Sometimes Gena will message from next door to keep it down if Rayna and I are jabbering too loudly, but she's probably in the cafeteria for dinner.

"I was supposed to have asked her out already," Rayna bemoans. "I'm out of time. We have two days left!"

"It could be worse," I say. "If you were me, you'd actually only have half a day left."

"You know she wished me luck when I left the cafeteria? That's officially the twentieth and twenty-first words she's ever exchanged with me."

I give Rayna a wry look. Her face is still buried in the pillow. We've been in the same social circles with Hailey Murray for as long as I've been neck and neck with Kieren Murray in our academic career. Rayna has had plenty of opportunities to talk to Hailey—plenty of parties and idle chatter during lunches. She just makes excuses for herself every time. "You're ridiculous."

"I *know*! I'm the most useless lesbian in history."

She releases another muffled scream. I'm trying very hard not to laugh.

"Look on the bright side," I say. "Hailey's posted to Medaluo too. What is she assigned to—military base counts in the cities?"

"Yeah," Rayna says, muffled. "And I'm surveying the electric grid. We're never going to cross paths."

My mind has been circling and circling about why federal would ask for a joint posting. Self-assurance and self-doubt consume me with equal weight. They need me for my connection; they need me for my face. Kieren is more trusted; Kieren can't be relied on to handle it himself.

"What about this?" I say to Rayna. "A white girl in Medaluo probably wants to team up with a Medan cadet—*ahem*—such as yourself. She'll look more natural in the cities, like she's visiting a friend rather than engaging in intelligence collection. Ask Hailey if she wants to combine efforts."

Suddenly, Rayna hurtles out of my pillow pile.

"That . . . is not a bad idea at all," she says slowly.

I splay my arms. "People call me the queer whisperer."

"No one calls you that."

I grab a bundle of socks next to me and launch it at her. It lands dead center on Rayna's forehead, and with a shriek, she pretends to have been hit by a bullet, pantomiming impact before collapsing against my wall, lolled at the neck.

We're quiet for a moment. Then Rayna's eyes fly open again.

"Anyway." She tosses the socks back at me lightly. "Weird what they're doing with you, huh?"

Oh, *now* we're talking about me.

"I can't figure it out." I put the socks back into my suitcase. They're mismatched, a gray one and a pink one wrapped together. "Half of me thinks they're afraid I'm going to turn rogue, so Kieren is keeping watch. The other half wonders if this posting is so important that sending two of us is a contingency against one person getting abducted and tortured midway through so that at least the other can still finish the task."

Rayna grimaces, appearing queasy at the thought. She's the type of student who wants to perform within the bell curve. Getting posted on something important is her idea of a nightmare. "I don't think anyone is getting tortured upcountry. You could just log out."

I point a finger at her. "Exactly. Posting failed. The torturers win."

"Good gracious," Rayna mutters. "I'm glad I just have the electric grid."

"If we go to war, the electric grid is the first thing Atahua is going to hit," I counter. "Everything you learn about its distribution upcountry contributes to how we kill it downcountry."

"*Yay*. Can't wait to die in war before I get to open my orphan file."

"Don't *say* that."

Rayna's been obsessed with her orphan file for years. All wards of the state are issued one to catalog their basic information: date of birth if known, country of origin if known, date of handover to the government, birth parents. Mine was always unlocked—there's nothing substantial in the file. Both of my parent sections are blank, information unknown. But Rayna's is locked until her eighteenth birthday, which probably means there are identifying details about her birth parents that she's not allowed to see until she's mature enough to know hunting them down would be a bad idea. If her parents are alive, there's got to be some reason why she was raised as a ward instead.

"You're right, you're right," Rayna says sagely. "I put in a request to have the file opened publicly on my birthday anyway. Hopefully I turn eighteen and *then* we declare war."

"*Rayna*."

A pop-up appears in the corner of my vision. I have a message.

KIEREN: Hey.

"All right, I have to finish packing," I declare. "Are you coming to see me off tomorrow?"

Rayna hops up from my bed, taking the cue. "I don't think I'm allowed. Cadet privacy and all that."

Annoying. But I don't want to make a fuss with the headmaster any more than I already might have, and I suppose he's going to be overseeing our posting personally. We're an early start, *and* it's his own son being sent off.

"Fine," I say. I open my arms for a hug. "Then I'll see you in Medaluo. We can meet up once you get there. Message me when you're in the server."

"Can do." Rayna squeezes hard. She's short, but her arms have the strength of steel. It's all that weightlifting she does when she's training downcountry. "If you're spending so much time with Kieren, do you think you can ask if—"

"Absolutely not," I interrupt. "Do your flirting yourself."

Rayna snickers, letting go. "Love you! See you in enemy territory."

I blow an air kiss. She closes my door. A hollow sort of quiet sets in, the dormitories empty of activity. My display opens before me with a blink, my eyes already swiveling while I wander toward my window. The sill is ice cold on my hands when I place them down. I send my response.

> LIA: hi 😁

Kieren views my reply immediately, but two minutes pass before a new message appears.

> KIEREN: Instant response . . . It's as if you like me or something.
> LIA: i see that we're in a joking mood now
> KIEREN: 😁
> KIEREN: I want to apologize for earlier. I shouldn't have accused you of plotting this.

LIA: . . .
LIA: ok i'm waiting for the apology
KIEREN: [Sent a voice message.]

It's three seconds of silence. Half a second of a very loud sigh. Then: "Sorry."

LIA: you're so annoying
LIA: anyway did your dad say anything useful when he briefed you? as much as I love (🫶😊🥰🫠🫳) spending time with you, this is so weird

I have to manually scroll the list of emoticons that are triggered as suggestions by the word "love" to see what's available before making my selection. Every few months new obscure ones are added into the system, and it takes me a while to capture my exact level of drivel before sending it. Kieren waits equally long before his reply comes back.

KIEREN: Nope. I know as much as you do.
LIA: sigh

KIEREN MURRAY HAS SILENCED NOTIFICATIONS.

I blink. What?

LIA: bruh.

YOUR MESSAGE HAS BEEN DELIVERED QUIETLY.

LIA: you're the one who messaged me first

YOUR MESSAGE HAS BEEN DELIVERED QUIETLY.

LIA: is this some sort of sick power play?
SEEN AT 10:27PM.

Unbelievable.

Beyond the chat box I have overlaid at half transparency, the night stretches an eerie image. The trees sway in the dark. The moon mimics its current shape downcountry, waning into a crescent. This part of campus is deserted—since final exam postings were made, we're all fretting about our upcoming performance, about the last weeks we have as a cadet before being sent off to graduation and into the wide unknown world. Cold wind seeps through the lines of my window. I can't suppress the shiver that sweeps down my spine.

I flick away the chat box and close my blinds. I'll pack the rest of my suitcase tomorrow.

5

EIRALE

I come to with a start.

My last few seconds of consciousness trickle back. Nik Grant admitting that he framed me. Nik Grant flippantly explaining that he's made Atahua believe I committed treason so that I would accompany him on this mission with my innocence as incentive.

My attempt to choke him out.

I wince, shifting in my seat. The helicopter is still flying, though there's a bout of turbulence shaking the walls. My limbs have gone numb. They've strapped me down. It's my fault: I wasn't paying attention to the girl circling around and stabbing a sedative into my shoulder before I could get my fingers on Nik's throat. Without a suit, I'm left vulnerable to all their annoying needles and tranquilizers slapped wherever they'll go.

"You all right?" she asks now. She doesn't meet my eyes, her legs pulled up where she sits across the aircraft aisle.

"I'll kill you," I say blandly. "What does Miz stand for? *Misery?*"

"I wish," Miz says. "It's Mizuna, actually."

I scan her features. Short dark hair, cropped at her chin. Thin, small nose with a piercing looped through her septum. Brown eyes beneath her clear glasses, no hint of makeup.

"You're not Medan."

"No. A Ward like you, but otherwise Pyaish."

The helicopter shudders again, teetering harshly to its side. We must be flying over the ocean with these winds, and low, too. It's hard to parse when the machines run so quietly, the whirring blades barely audible other than a slight tremble along the ceiling. By the dryness of my mouth, the sedative has been worming its way through my system for hours, keeping me held under. My arms are still bound. A line of red glows on my wrists, tender to the touch.

Miz gestures to my bindings. "We can get those cut off you if you promise you won't attack Nik again."

"I promise."

She hesitates. Her gaze finally lifts, though it's exceedingly cautious. It almost seems like she's afraid of being within my line of sight in case I drip poison through mere eye contact.

"Are you lying?"

"Yes, I'm lying. What do you think this is?" I try to stomp my foot, but the straps are holding down my thighs too. My leg lifts a minuscule amount before it plods on the metal floors with a lackluster sound.

Miz tuts and shakes her head. She looks away again, tilting back against the wall.

"You need to tell your insurgent team leader to reconsider your plan," I say firmly. "I am not the best NileCorp has to offer. I'm not even the best that the Button City base has to offer. Teryn Moore was there—why would you take me instead?"

It's not good form to throw someone else under the bus, but it's a natural question.

"Why would we take Teryn Moore?" Miz asks. "NileCorp would be on our ass in five minutes flat."

Right. Because Teryn's important.

"You can't do this," I say, switching gears. "You can't force me to participate. It's—"

"Illegal?"

The interruption comes from the front. Nik has emerged silently from the cockpit, leaning at the threshold. Even when another shudder shakes the helicopter, he stays perfectly unmoving, one shoulder nudged solidly against the wall. He's put a pair of glasses on too, the screen flashing faint lines across his eyes while the display changes. Despite the one device already in use, he's also cradling his handheld close to his chest.

"You're awake far too early," he comments. "Go back to sleep."

"You shouldn't take me to Medaluo," I counter. "Atahua has spies everywhere. As soon as national surveillance picks up my face, you'll have NileCorp's private soldiers on your trail. It'll ruin your mission."

It's a strong argument, objectively. But Nik, slowly, wanders into the passenger area, unconvinced. He's reading something on his glasses. Atop the four bags dumped unceremoniously in the aircraft corner, there's also a briefcase and an open laptop. Its screen changes, the light reflecting off the metal of the wall. Nik must be connected to the laptop with the glasses. Quickly, he slides his handheld into one of the bags, tugging the zip securely.

"It's very easy to avoid surveillance. Don't worry."

Miz clears her throat from her seat. She narrows her eyes at Nik. Some silent communication must pass between them, because Nik steps toward me. I stiffen. He draws another step closer, almost like he's testing my reaction, and I react expectedly. By the time he's standing directly before my seat, my limbs have practically locked into place.

"We've been looking for someone for a while now," he says. "Someone... who went away, then came back again."

I stare, waiting for him to elaborate. Nik's frown deepens.

"Does the surname Sullivan mean anything to you?"

"I haven't a clue," I say honestly. "Sorry."

At the other side of the aircraft, Miz mutters something under her breath, then nods in response to a message that must be flashing through her glasses.

"Nik," she calls. "We're landing."

The opaque material around the walls starts to move, folding back from left to right to reveal a window panel built into the side of the helicopter. I bite down the protest hovering on my tongue. The world outside beams through the glass, and my breath catches in my throat.

Medaluo, from coast to coast, has a twelve-hour time difference with Button City. The image below is enswathed by the sunset, a haze of orange draped over the glass-topped skyscrapers. The helicopter hovers lower. My eyes trace the curved perimeter, taking in the shape of the coast. This must be Upsie. The city glitters with the declaration, with the clarity of its full namesake—*Land of the Upper Sea*. Shipping containers float near its piers; the leaden gray waves foam onto a concrete shoreline. A thin river cuts down the middle of the city, letting machines float along to make inland deliveries. Some of them transform into flight drones once they're close enough to the mega skyscrapers, soaring directly to the glass exteriors, where neon holograms unfurl in the burgeoning dark, running advertisements for upcountry subscriptions.

It's beautiful. It's colossal.

"Why aren't they shooting you down?" I ask quietly. "You're flying too close. We must be pinging every one of their sensors."

The window panel begins to close again. I react with a momentary pang of loss, a child with its new toy taken away, when the exterior slides fully into place and stops the temporary viewing.

"This is a Medan aircraft." Nik takes his glasses off, folding the device until it is small and putting it into his pocket. A strand of brown hair falls loose along his forehead, and he brushes it back. "It's cleared to be flying within this zone."

That was my first real look at Medaluo. The first look that I can remember, at least. There's a chance I was born here and brought over to Atahua before I was abandoned, but my orphan file is blank, and I have no real memories prior to the foster homes. When I cast my mind back to the earliest point of my childhood, I can only summon faint impressions of someone leading me around. A street in the rain. A siren in the distance—not a police car, maybe an ambulance. Nothing beyond that.

"How can this be a Medan aircraft?" With the window closed, I get ahold of myself again, tamping down my reaction. "We lifted off from Button City."

"And in Button City, we were an Atahuan aircraft." Nik's hands suddenly glint with something silver. He's pulled a pocketknife. "Keep up."

I shrink back. My pulse hammers with panic, jumping to the most likely conclusion. I can only do what anyone else would in that moment, at risk of being slashed by a deranged anarchist.

I reveal that I've undone the seat straps while he was distracted and lunge at him again.

"Hey!" Miz exclaims. "Hey, come *on*!"

Nik doesn't have any time to brace before I've bowled him over onto the aircraft floor, using my knees to pin his hips. His arms flail back in a split second of surprise, and I make a desperate reach for the pocketknife.

I underestimate his reaction speed. Nik's elbow twitches lightning fast, tossing the weapon away. The flash of metal spirits into the corner of the passenger area. When I go for it, releasing one knee and weakening my hold, Nik flips us both over, trapping me by my leg. His mouth hardens into a line.

I recalibrate my options. He has me pinned now. I'm on my back. I don't want to squirm and show weakness.

With great reluctance, I splay my hands to indicate surrender. The sequence occurred so quickly that Miz has only just finished unbuckling her seat belt to hurry over.

"There is no need for any of this," she hisses.

"She attacked me," Nik says. His voice is pitched low, like he's barely restraining himself. I suspect he'd much rather knock me out entirely than show leniency and lock me in place.

"You're kidnapping me," I say. "What else should I be doing?"

Nik lessens the pressure on my leg an infinitesimal amount. Perhaps he doesn't intend to, but I feel it.

"You're not being kidnapped," he grumbles. "Far from it."

"I'm being held at gunpoint to work for you."

"Is that what you want?" In a flash, Nik pulls a handgun from a holster hidden in his trousers. The metal is piercing cold when it touches my chin. He presses hard, lets the imprint of the muzzle dig its mark. "Will this help?"

I don't move. Nik Grant is one person. One boy, really, wreaking havoc against a world power and its forces . . . but it's becoming apparent to me why we've struggled to capture him. His eyes, bright and gray before, have turned entirely flat. If I provoke him once more, he may just shoot, my usefulness be damned.

"No need." Wright claims I have a tendency to slip into a monotone. That I should cut it out when superiors are speaking to me. *Lacks deference,* he insists. "You've got me," I say through my teeth. "I'm not going anywhere until you give me that footage."

This plan they have put together is clearly effective. All these attempts I'm making to get free are acts of childish insubordination. If I've been framed, I won't go crawling back to my country without proof that I'm innocent. Clearly no one from federal was taking my word for anything.

Nik tilts his head. The gun stays where it is.

"I convinced my team that you were the one we needed," he says. "But to be honest, if you're too much of a NileCorp bootlicker, I might be wrong. Maybe I got the wrong person."

"Maybe you did." My jaw is starting to cramp in my effort to remain still. "Between NileCorp and certain death, I made my choice a long time ago. Throw me into the water now if that's a problem."

Atahua may not love me, but I am Atahuan all the same. If I had somewhere better to go, I would have gone, but I don't. The paltry existence I've been granted in Atahua is a life that I have worked for, bled for, no matter how corrupt NileCorp is. Being a corporate soldier sucks, but it's something. It's not as bad as government military. It's not as bad as being another body slumped on the streets downcountry staring at a handheld all day and scrolling the feed, because most Medan orphans shoved into military school sure aren't afforded anything more than that if they can't serve their purpose in this cold war. The better jobs don't want us. The service jobs want robots.

Working for NileCorp is *something*. What else do I *have*?

Nik draws the gun away abruptly. My chin throbs with relief, the threat of steel removed. He pulls his knee off my leg too, allowing me to stand.

"Thanks," I mutter.

Bootlicker. I wonder how Nik Grant was raised, where he was born. NileCorp didn't offer any of that information for the capture mission. Even if its data scraping capabilities probably know what Nik Grant ate for breakfast on his seventh birthday, we operated on a need-to-know basis.

Still, some backgrounds don't need a declassified write-up. I see his pearly white teeth. I watched each careful fold he made on his sleeves while he gazed out the viewing window. If I am NileCorp's bootlicker, what cushy childhood did Nik Grant climb out of to afford him the resources as NileCorp's anarchist?

The aircraft shudders, then stills. A faint "*woohoo!*" sounds from the cockpit, signaling the presence of a third member of their team.

We've landed.

"Perfect timing." With another sleight of hand, the gun disappears somewhere within Nik's clothes. Even Miz looks a little shaken, her eyes flicking to confirm the weapon's disappearance. She starts toward me in an effort to help, but I'm back on my feet before she can make contact. I dust off my elbows.

Nik shoves open the aircraft door. Night waits outside, cool and violet.

"After you, soldier."

6

LIA

Before Nile Military Academy, I was a huge stickler about my grades too.

The private elementary school that Dad put me in didn't rank their students, so at least it was less obvious how intense I was about it, short of the perfect 100s on my tests. I haven't landed anything below a 95 in my life. If I scored a 98 on an off day, I cried in the bathroom and then mopped up my tears by the time Tamera was coming to pick me up and take me home. Back then, home was the upcountry Melnova apartment.

Dad usually wasn't off yet when I returned from school, so I'd sit in the living room and get started on my homework. I had always known that Atahuan law mandated my attendance at a military academy once I finished eighth grade and graduated elementary. The official list of the top fifty military schools in Atahua never changed. Nile Military Academy was consistently number one, so that was where I would go.

I was diligent about my plan. They started giving us assessments in the fifth grade, and I opened a new tab in the notes of my display solely for studying and keeping a schedule. If Tamera saw me zoning out at the coffee table, it wasn't because I was watching a video on the feed. I was always trying to work out a problem before my eyes zigzagged around to type.

Tamera only logged out after dinner. She would go back to the Haven State house downcountry, where she insisted she liked the space for sleeping. Until it got late though, she kept me company in upcountry Melnova. She'd bring me snacks to eat, then chop fruit for me to nibble on. From what I garnered, it was mostly Tamera who raised Dad too, so she always fussed like his mother, complaining that he needed to let her know when he was coming back from work so she could get started on dinner.

I remember the last time we saw Uncle Chung in that apartment. Dad did send word that he was en route. When the front door opened, he was in conversation, something related to work. I hadn't been listening, not really. It wasn't a big apartment, so they appeared in my peripheral vision as soon as they entered, but I had my display overlaid on 90 percent opacity. Algebra was a topic I struggled slightly with, and I was getting so close to solving for x on the hardest problem in the set.

"Hi, Lia," Chung greeted.

"Hi," I said back.

Dad walked into the kitchen. Chung took off his shoes.

"Lia," Chung prompted again, and I knew what was coming. I abandoned my math problem and blinked away the display. "Cast is to bone as grand gesture is to . . . ?"

A beat passed.

"Trust," I answered.

Chung pointed a finger at me. "You're getting too good at these. I'm going to have to think of some new ones."

I snickered. "You mean your machines aren't coming up with them for you?"

"The machines aren't that smart yet. They'll get there."

Dad emerged from the kitchen then, a glass of whiskey in each hand, one perfect ice cube lodged like a buoy in the liquid. He passed one to Chung, freeing his hand to ruffle my hair when he walked by.

"How's the homework coming along?"

"Good." I opened my display again. "I think I'm better at solving analogies than solving for x."

"That's only because I hang around so much." Chung's voice echoed back over his shoulder as he followed my dad to his office. "Make your dad befriend a mathematician and you'll be sorted."

I knew what Uncle Chung did for work in the labs beside the Capitol Building. His area of study was language modeling. I only came up to his elbow, so I often wandered over to him when they were chatting and stood there until he noticed me and brought me into the conversation. His research would help our computers grow smarter. It was what would let engines like StrangeLoom react faster to commands. Funding was strong—investors fueled by the spirit of the cold war. The race to rule the world was, at the end of it, about technology. Atahua wanted to be the most powerful country in the world. Medaluo wanted to be the most powerful country in the world. When our world was virtual, whoever regulated that space won everything.

But Uncle Chung wasn't trusted. He was bypassed for projects. He wasn't given sensitive Atahuan data to work with.

All this I overheard, I understood, even at that age. After I hadn't seen Uncle Chung around the house for almost a month, I asked Dad where he was, where he'd gone. It was the same answer, time after time, until I eventually forgot to keep asking: *I don't know.*

"You know they won't count this in your participation grades, right?"

I continue stretching on the gym mat. I had heard Kieren's footsteps the moment he came through the door, though he tried to stay quiet. He wanted to give me a fright, I'm sure. I don't turn to face him.

"I actually want them to take some away," I say. "I've too many. It's unfair on you."

"They definitely will when they see the broken lock."

I swivel around then, my legs still splayed. The gym was locked when I arrived, early enough that the sun wasn't up yet. But I really needed to get in. "The lock is not broken."

"It's scratched, Ward."

"It is not!"

Daylight presses into the tall windows only now, hints of red breaking over the horizon. It's hard to stay tired upcountry. A lack of sleep is more a nuisance because nothing is open and no one is around, rather than a burden on our health. I've learned that if I push through the first few minutes of grog at 4:00 a.m., I'm wide awake before long. I should have known Kieren would be up at this time too.

"I suppose no one will be looking closely," he relents. Kieren comes to a stop at the edge of my mat. He folds his arms.

We're both dressed in civilian clothing, prepared for our injection into Medaluo's server. Where I've gone for baggy and big, copying what I've seen on the feed for Medans my age, Kieren is still Atahuan to the bone, linen trousers and a collared shirt. He must have been up even earlier than me. He's had the time to brush his hair until every strand is in order.

I spring to my feet.

"Five-second warning."

"Absolutely not," Kieren says immediately. "My shirt doesn't stretch."

"Sounds like loser talk."

He's already taking off his shoes even while remaining resistant. "Lia, I swear, if you rip my shirt—"

I charge. He swerves the first blow I throw, but that was a distraction: my left hand comes up to tap his side, hard, marking a point. We've sparred enough over the years that he knows my tricks—the best way to win against him is to take him by surprise.

Even if it's not entirely a surprise. Kieren recovers in rapid time, going on the offensive when he ducks.

"That's such a cheat move," he hisses, spinning backward. I barely skid away. "You wouldn't have two knives in a real situation."

"I would have thrown my one knife from my right hand to my left"—

I grab his wrist, opting to embrace the hit rather than dodge it—"with a cool flip."

I roll onto the mat, forcing Kieren down with me. He's quick to take advantage of the momentum. Right as I'm regaining balance, the base of his hand makes contact with my shoulder, dragging it to mark a point. I earn another on the inside of his knee when he hurtles up.

Kieren steadies himself at the head of the mat. He splays his hands for surrender.

"Okay," he says. "I'm probably bleeding out at this point."

I narrow my eyes. I don't believe it, but even half a second of hesitancy is enough. Kieren lunges and grips my shoulder hard; when both my hands go up to brace against the contact, his other fist drags across my stomach, marking an incapacitating hit.

I huff, shoving him away.

"You always do that."

Kieren looks smug. "Win?"

"No," I grumble. I mimic his motions. Never one abrupt hit, but contact that stretches left to right. "You drag out each of your marks."

"Because I would slash you. That's what I'm practicing." He brushes out the wrinkles in his shirt. "It's reliably a better method to disarm without killing. Stabbing can hit a crucial organ or break an artery."

This is the first time I've actually asked why he does that, though I've watched Kieren rely on the same maneuvers for years. I suppose if there's any moment to inquire, it's now. We're going into our first field assignment, the first instance where the acts we practice on a sparring mat might somewhat matter. It's still upcountry. Emergency services will be called automatically if anyone brings out a knife. But that doesn't mean there won't be other sorts of roughhousing if we're caught lingering around places we're not allowed in.

"Hm," I say. I shove my shoes back on. "You don't want to kill someone trying to kill you?"

"If someone is trying to *kill* me, I'll stab." Kieren's gaze goes blank. He's checking the time. Morning grows brighter past the windows, voices floating along the path outside while the dorms begin to wake. "But I assume most people are only grappling with me. Security doing its job. Foreign agents fighting for a piece of the asset. Opponents backed into a corner." He blinks, his eyes focusing again. "That warrants a survivable slash, I'd think."

It doesn't surprise me to hear Kieren's reasoning, but it still takes me a beat to process it. It's a line of logic that feels distant in my mind. Getting to the end of military academy is enough of a challenge. I haven't been training my instincts for the field and the fights to come. I train to be outstanding in the present. Quick hits. Solid marks.

"Almost time?" I ask.

Kieren nods. "My father's waiting for us in his office. NileCorp is here."

"Off we go, then." I roll up the mat, pushing it aside. "How did you find me here anyway? Missed me so much you searched the campus?"

"I couldn't live with myself if I didn't maximize the time we spent together today," Kieren intones. "But no—this was the first place I looked. You're kind of predictable."

"Yeah, yeah," I mutter. He is, too, so that's not a problem with me.

In the locker room outside the gym, I fetch the suitcase I'd left by the door, and Kieren picks up his backpack. We walk along the path to A Block in silence, my suitcase's wheels making a racket on the uneven stones. A few faces press up against the dorm windows to watch us when we pass, curious enough to gawk. It's only an early posting for the two cadets directly competing for valedictorian. There's no third contender on our heels: everyone else in our class was left in the dust in tenth grade. Without a doubt, the one receiving the medallion at graduation will either be me or Kieren.

"After you," Kieren says, opening the door into A Block for me.

"Thank you, you're so kind."

He sends me a request for a tip. I decline the pop-up in my display, then send him back an emoticon with my face rendered over it holding a middle finger.

The door closes behind him. With that resounding thud, our spectators are shut out, only the long administrative corridors ahead bearing witness when I turn to Kieren and say:

"So you know that I was acquainted with our person of interest, right?"

His brow scrunches, then smooths in a flash. I watch him carefully.

"Were you?" he returns, casual. "I might have heard something about that."

Which means he's been filled in.

"Before you ask," I warn, "I know no more than you. There's nothing useful I can offer for information."

Kieren keeps his gaze ahead. "Good thing we're being sent in to obtain new findings, then."

He's uncharacteristically calm for a matter I thought he'd want to pry into. If we were walking into a joint posting where Kieren was the one who knew the missing man, I'd be asking him every question under the sun. Even if Kieren couldn't answer any of them, I'd at least be following protocol to exhaust my options.

"Right," I say. I make no move to hide my frown. Kieren gestures ahead to our destination, letting me proceed first.

Headmaster Murray's office is busy when we step in. NileCorp has sent a whole team by the looks of it, three milling around the room on their handhelds and two with goggles over their eyes. I'm tech-literate enough that I can log in and out of StrangeLoom, type my credentials where I need, and on occasion, troubleshoot any loading problems. I'm not tech-literate enough to understand how they inject us into Medaluo's server without Medaluo noticing.

I suppose when NileCorp owns the entire infrastructure, there's a lot it can get away with.

"Hey, nerds."

Kieren's twin sister is splayed on their father's chair, her feet kicked up on the desk. I don't hang out with Hailey often—it's too intimidating for Rayna, and I'm hanging out with Rayna first and foremost. Still, Hailey is waving at me as enthusiastically as she greets Kieren when she sits up.

Headmaster Murray stands at the other side of the office, staring off into space in a way that indicates he's typing into his display.

"Hey," Kieren says. "Did we miss anything?"

"They can't exactly start without you," Hailey replies. "It's been very anticlimactic so far."

Her head lolls back on the seat. Hailey Murray reminds me somewhat of a rag doll, and it's entirely incongruous with the rest of her sharp energy. She tells great jokes, and she has a knack for breaking the tension in any situation. She's perceptive enough that she's always the first to spot ninth graders hovering around our lunch table at the start of the year, and she'll hurry to wave them over to sit. But the world will be underwater before I see her hold good posture for any longer than a few seconds.

"What did you expect?" Kieren asks. "A circle of fire opening up from the floor?"

"That's probably a daily occurrence in this office," Hailey replies.

Headmaster Murray offers no retort. He's still typing. In that awkward silence, Kieren and Hailey exchange a glance, then both roll their eyes in complete mimicry.

Envy froths up my throat, forces me to look away. I used to wish so badly that I had a sister, someone to keep me company in a shared bedroom so we could gossip in the dark and whisper secrets through the night. Instead, I was left awake with only the sound of my own thoughts, with my incessant, obsessive fixations about what I'd done wrong that day, ruminating on and on and on until I eventually fell asleep out of sheer mental exhaustion. I wanted a sister for the company, but maybe I just wanted the alternate world where the sister I could have had hadn't died. In that world, I wasn't a replacement child, just a second one. And maybe there, I wouldn't have this crushing, sickly weight in my chest all the time.

I open my display. My cache must have cleared overnight, so when I click into my conversation tab with Rayna, our old messages are archived and not in direct view. Identity check time.

> LIA: beaver

Rayna's already awake—shockingly. I get an instant series of responses.

> RAYNA: ew
> RAYNA: good morning, cadet!
> RAYNA: pufferfish
> LIA: i've actually heard that's quite good

Our identity check is opening with an animal we would be willing to eat. We still haven't run out of examples. It works well because we've been getting increasingly outlandish with our answers, and so either one of us would feel it instantly if the scale shifted. Scammers these days are too sophisticated—they're scraping data sold from the feed and filching from the thousands upon thousands of catalogs that NileCorp stores of our activity upcountry. NileCorp knows everything about us, and as a by-product, if they get a rogue employee who wants a side hustle selling information to someone's AI company, there's virtually no way to distinguish between your actual best friend and a bot who has analyzed her every verbal choice.

I suppose nothing is foolproof, but this comes close.

> LIA: in headmaster murray's office right now with all the murrays
> LIA: scary
> RAYNA: horrifyingly beautiful

LIA: that's not what i meant
LIA: and ew??
RAYNA: ugh not the headmaster obviously. gross

"Let's go through the run-of-show one more time, shall we?" Headmaster Murray suggests, blinking out of his display. I do the same quickly, minimizing my chat with Rayna and hoping no one noticed my inattention. "Once you're installed in the Medan server, we won't be able to pull you out and plant you back in without triggering their security, so you'll have to travel upcountry Medaluo using your own means. A virtual card has been attached to your credentials—everything you spend on it will be reimbursed at the end of the posting."

"Is it likely we'll travel far?" Kieren asks.

"Hard to say," Headmaster Murray replies. There's very little warmth in the answer, no extra attention to indicate this is his son he's about to send on an extended mission. He's speaking directly to me instead. "Once you're in the server, a NileCorp outpost will be in touch. They'll be your best point of contact when it comes to the posting."

The brief said that communication back to Atahua will still be open while we're in the Medan server. I should hope that means I can continue to make calls to Dad without being pinged.

I suddenly have an incoming call in my display. Dad's avatar pops up, as though my thoughts summoned him.

"My dad is calling me," I say, wincing to cut into the run-of-show. "Is it okay if I . . . ?"

Headmaster Murray looks to one of the engineers. "Any estimate on when we're ready?"

"Enough time to take a call. Don't worry about it," the engineer replies. He must see fine under the unwieldy goggles, because he offers me a thumbs-up. Medaluo knows to expect cadets entering their server at the same time every year when final exam season rolls around, so they do their best to toughen up security. Even within NileCorp, it takes a second to find the back doors.

"All right." Headmaster Murray nods. "Go for it, Lia. I think we've covered everything."

"Thank you. I'll be quick." I accept the call. "Hi, Dad."

"Lia, I'm glad I caught you. You're about to start your posting?"

"Yeah." I shift on my feet. "Sorry I couldn't come home last night."

Dad sighs over the line. There's a slight echo. He's probably walking between meetings in the Capitol Building, under its tall ceilings and through its cavernous corridors. "Hopefully you'll be done with the posting quickly, and then you'll have a bit of time to relax in Melnova before graduation."

It's nice what faith he has in my abilities.

"In and out, definitely," I say.

"What have you been assigned to?"

My eyes flick up. Headmaster Murray is observing me, his gaze no longer flitting around to type. There's no threat in his expression, but I see a warning present all the same. We're not supposed to divulge details, even to our parents. Confidential means confidential. "Only a survey. I can't say too much."

"Mm-hm." I imagine Dad nodding on the other end. He's not often an emotive person, but I know the difference between an apathetic *mm-hm* and a curious *mm-hm*. This is the latter.

"I think we're about to be sent through now," I say. "Thanks for checking in."

"Very well." He pauses. "If you need me, I'm always here, okay?"

The sentiment takes me aback. It's not that I doubted it—Dad has never pushed me off or ignored me on purpose. But there's something anticipatory about a remark like that, a presumptuous need to prove himself lest I forget.

"Okay," I reply. I don't know what else to say. "Love you."

"Love you too. Good luck."

"Bye, Dad."

Click. Though the line drops, I keep the box open a beat longer, watching my call log register the exchange. There's a new whirring in the room. It sounds like miniature fans inside the engineers' goggles.

"I was wondering," Hailey starts, getting her father's attention, "whether this means I can skip class today."

Headmaster Murray frowns. "I'm not sure why."

"Emotional support for Kieren. I need to be at the ready."

"Hailey. That is not a legitimate reason to skip class."

Kieren scoffs quietly. Only I'm standing close enough to hear the sound. Unsatisfied by the lack of permission, Hailey's switching tactics to argue that Headmaster Murray is lucky she even asked him first.

For twins, it's fair enough that Hailey and Kieren don't act anything alike, but it's almost bizarre how much they don't look anything alike either. Kieren's short hair is dark like coarse coffee grounds, his eyes a hazy brown. Hailey's eyes are soul-searing blue, her whole face freckled and her wavy hair lightening into dirty blond. They possess no resemblance in their features, but they do share an abstract resemblance to catalog models that have been photoshopped to death. Too symmetrical. Too pristine.

"How much longer?" Kieren asks the first engineer.

"It depends on where your user file is in the system," the engineer answers. "As soon as I isolate it, we'll get rumbling."

Kieren props his hands on his hips. He sways his arm. His elbow knocks into mine.

"Where are we going to meet?"

I glance at him blankly.

"In Upsie," Kieren clarifies. "Hackings will randomize our entry onto any landing pad within city parameters. If our avatars get separated, we should decide now where we convene."

"Right," I say. "I was going to bring that up too."

Kieren knocks his elbow into me again to convey he doesn't believe me. I whack him back equally hard.

"How about the premier's statue?" I suggest.

"That's a tourist hotspot. It's way too busy."

Once we're both in, we'll have the same server privileges and can directly message again. "So? Just text what you're standing next to."

"Sensory nightmare, Ward."

Okay, fine. "How about the Star Hole?"

The Star Hole is a ditch by the border of Upsie, where the urban city starts to transform into sparser villages. There are very few places in Medaluo that still qualify for rural, but certain hotspots will remain relatively untended. After a teeny-weeny asteroid hit the border there, it got massive media attention for resembling a star until the Medan government roped it off. Upcountry has diligently re-created it, the ditch large enough to be picked up by the satellites.

Kieren points at his face. "I think we should stick within the city center where tourists would viably be."

"Plenty of Atahuans visit the Star Hole."

"An Atahuan tourist went viral on the feed for spray-painting a crude message on the Star Hole and got thrown in jail for two weeks. I don't want to get hauled away before we can even start our assignment."

Annoyed, I blink open a map in my display. I did hear the news about the tourist because Teryn Moore reshared it on the feed, and I read up about it quickly so that I could contribute a comment. I don't need Kieren telling me about it.

I zoom onto a random street in central Upsie.

"Lovers' Café on Sky Blue Street," I read out, identifying the first establishment rated over three stars. A beat later, the warm prickle on my neck spreads to my face. "Uh, but—"

"That sounds fine with me." Kieren's expression remains level.

"Fine," I confirm.

"Fine."

"Fine—"

"All right!" the engineer declares happily. "Cadet Lia, close your eyes."

That's unexpected.

"Good luck!" Hailey sings from the desk.

"Wait," I say. "Why do I have to close—"

My entire world shorts out. The pixels strain; the colors bleed. I spin, trying to grasp some sense of directionality and instead give myself severe vertigo in a void of nothingness. Extreme absence stretches as far as it'll go, pervading three hundred and sixty degrees around my physical form.

I need to breathe. I need to remember I have no physical form here. I am an avatar, and if something were to go wrong, someone only needs to yank the Claw off my head downcountry for me to exist again.

The affirmations don't do much to ease my panic. It doesn't change the way my world has warped. Nor does it curb the feeling of being cast adrift.

I squeeze my eyes shut. That makes it worse. Suddenly I am entirely in free fall, and when my arms flail and my legs kick out, there's nothing to catch me.

Please, I beg the system. *Please don't lose me.*

My feet suddenly meet solid ground. The abrupt presence underneath me is jarring enough that a shock runs through my body and up my spine, electric upon contact.

My eyes fly open.

Beautiful abyss.

I'm staring out into the night sea, the waves sparkling with neon light. Upsie's waterfront embankment. I'm here. I'm in the server. The colors glisten off the endless black, and I whirl around with a start, searching for the city.

I smack directly into someone else newly entering on the landing pad. The woman gives me a strange look.

"What are you doing?" she asks in Medan.

It takes me a moment to register the language switch. A moment to fully parse the words, to let years and years of classes and practice come together in an instant, to remember *Today's unit is on conversational openers! The very first thing we're covering is the infamous "What are you doing?" which, yes, is colloquial and may be a question of concern to ask if you are all right—*

"Nothing, nothing," I reply, rolling my shoulders. The clothes off my back came with me. My suitcase . . . did not. I must have let go of it before I was moved out of Atahua's server. "I'm fine."

The woman quirks her brow.

"Better be careful," she says, prodding me off the platform. "Don't linger too long. You don't want to cause a collision. You're sure you don't need help?"

"I—" I look over my shoulder, startled. Several more people have materialized on the landing pad during our short exchange, dressed in an eclectic assortment of nightclub casual and streetwear. They hurry off the steps as soon as they appear. In a somewhat orderly line, they proceed toward the city center, where the lights are bright enough to keep the entire strip of the embankment lit vividly.

The waves crash against the concrete embankment. I blink open my display, checking the time. 8:52 p.m.

"I'm okay," I answer, finally getting the words out of my throat.

My practice scores in Medan class were shaky during my first few weeks at the academy. I knew full well how to pronounce certain words, but I faked incompetence. I thought it made me more Atahuan.

Once I saw what my predicted test scores were going to be, I snapped out of it pretty quickly.

The woman doesn't look too convinced by my answer, but she nods and walks off. People in Upsie are busy. Loading times are lightning fast, and storefronts are always open. I stagger properly onto the embankment, toward the city that beckons.

She most definitely thought I was on drugs. Medans are accustomed to the experience of logging in and out since they have a far higher daily user distribution than Atahua, and though I'm particularly used to staying virtual for a month at a time with the academy, lots of ordinary Atahuans have a monthly subscription too. In Medaluo, most users don't prepay as we do: they log on when they need to—either during the daytime with their employers compensating the fee or after work for nightlife—and are charged accordingly.

I blink, maintaining caution while activating system features. When my display overlays my vision, it shows me a profile that looks identical to the one I see in Atahua, except for the short serial number of a fake visa accompanying my photo. Data trackers upcountry will register my presence as an Atahuan tourist. Other avatars looking at my face will assume I'm an ordinary Medan going about her daily business.

The small INBOX icon in the corner of my display is unblinking initially, all my messages read. Then, before my very eyes, I see the notifications stack up from a modest 1 to 5 to a concerning 12 within a few seconds. I'm certain it must be an error, until I click in and realize they're only ads. The first is some AI tour bus that leaves from Upsie every day to embark on a cross-country adventure. The next is a casino. Then, a restaurant's Buy One, Get One Free notice.

This is ridiculous. I firmly mute notifications for all messages other than ones from people listed in my contacts. Then I navigate to my directory and find Kieren's profile.

LIA: u up?
LIA: jk lol, did they get you in yet

I swipe my display closed. He'll reply in due time. The waterfront is cold, most definitely encoded to be several degrees chillier than the rest of the city, and I resist a shiver, running my hands up and down my arms. I can't believe I'm here.

Upsie is lit up in every color fathomable to the eye. I walk off the embankment area, crossing the road to the green pedestrian light. The self-driving vehicles waiting at the red stoplight are all taxis, painted blue to indicate their function. No one spares a second glance my way, which is relieving after that woman's comment. A tiny dog yaps on the other side of the road. When I pass by, the owner smiles at me, tugging the leash. Most real dogs downcountry are dying out, either from starvation or abandonment. People can't tell the difference anyway. If their real life is lived upcountry, then that virtual dog is as real as any flesh and blood kept downcountry.

I reach the main road. Holograms beam down from doorways, harsh and erratic depending on what they're announcing. I'm looking one way, then another, and it doesn't matter how weirdly I move because I don't stick out. I *don't*. My face blends in, my features resemble everyone else, and I could bellow out loud in the middle of the road with the incident forgotten in seconds. I'm just a Medan in Medaluo.

"Whoa," I whisper out loud, looking at my hands. They shimmer back the green of the twenty-four-hour pharmacy, then the pink of the underground train entrance. I don't drink, but if I did, I imagine this is the sensation people are always after, enough warmth unfurling from my stomach that my perception of the world is off-kilter.

Maybe this is all. Maybe this is why I've been afflicted with Wakeman Syndrome, stubbornly at odds with the nature of my reality. My eyes track the avatars strolling the streets, the couples ducking under the swooping hologram of a dragon, the friends arm in arm on their way to a bar. I stop dead center in the street, spotting a fast-food chain that Atahua has too, and then that feeling in my stomach suddenly pushes up to my chest, transforming into hot discomfort.

In Atahua, my options are acing military school for a career I can choose, or something middling that shoves me into a miserable existence. In Atahua, I have grown up spending every day trying to be the best, and instead . . . I could have just *existed*.

"Comedy show, miss?"

I jolt. A man with a light-up hat offers me a flyer, and I take it. The moment I scan the first line, I practically have to shove my eyes back into their sockets at the price of the entry ticket.

"Thank you so much," I say, already walking away. "I'll consider it."

I fold the flyer up. Maybe I could have existed upcountry happily in Medaluo, attending comedy shows in a crowd without standing out, but most likely I would have been downcountry, inching closer to a premature death with the next climate disaster or virus that attacks my immune system. No one wants to admit it, but upcountry grew popular early on because the unhoused populations were getting unmanageable. City hubs were impossible to navigate past the slumped bodies and makeshift tents and the smells—and if the government refused to do anything about it, people chose the selfish option, the easy option, the pretty option. They built another world and fled.

My fantasy dissolves, bit by bit as I continue down the main road. Dad and Mallory adopted me in Atahua, not Medaluo. I am dreaming of a life I would have never been afforded. I should consider myself so lucky that I've gained a comfortable home in trade for some bouts of delusion and anxious ailments.

My display screen lights up with a notification.

KIEREN: [hacker voice] I'm in.

I snort.

LIA: eta to the cafe in 20 minutes, walking over
KIEREN: I landed a little farther north. Finding subway now, give me 30.

I send a thumbs-up and keep my display open, letting the map direct me. Lovers' Café is a ground-level establishment located inside a skyscraper that's otherwise used for corporate business. I'm already on Hazel West Road, so it'll take one more turn before going west for Sky Blue Street.

I pivot on the corner, humming under my breath. It's then that a small warning triangle notification appears at the bottom of my display, which I've never seen before. It must be something only allowed by Medaluo's server settings. There are plenty of notifications that Atahua bans for privacy.

I open the notification, frowning.

One unfamiliar user has been following for 0.6 miles.

7

EIRALE

A self-driving taxi waits outside the helicopter, its rickety doors thrown wide open.

I take a step forward. My knee threatens to buckle, and I pause, suppressing the tremble. The newly fallen night is cool. Smoky. A shroud of gray hovers over the city on the horizon, a filter swept over the buildings to prevent its lines and lights from taking shape. I almost rub my own eyes, as though that might clear the picture.

"Go on," Nik prompts from behind me.

The grass brushes a slimy, wet touch on my ankles while I walk. Nik calls a warning about my head when I reach the nine-seater, but I ignore him, hauling myself in without watching for how much space is left between the top of my head and the taxi. I feel it scrape my hair roughly. A light dusting of blue paint flecks follows me into the back, sticking to the pads of my fingertips. I wipe it all off, then swipe my fingers through my hair, twisting it up.

"Can I have a pen?"

Miz follows me into the taxi first. She's frowning, hauling two bags in with her. "What?"

"A pen," I repeat. "The device that's filled with ink and is used to write."

"I know what a pen is," she mutters, reaching into her pocket. "I've been stabbed by a pen before. I'm warning you in advance: I can see it coming from a mile away."

Despite her words, she's still handing me a thin pen from her pocket. It's one of those plastic disposables that come with lottery scratch cards at the grocery store, the other end a slab of blunt metal to scrape the card.

Wordlessly, I take the pen and stick it in my hair to keep it up. Miz remains suspicious, but she slides across the seat, calling for someone named Blare.

The third member of their team trudges across the grass with two more bags and halts with one leg propped inside the taxi for balance. I blink. I had known there must have been someone else navigating the helicopter. I hadn't expected a *child*, still baby-faced with the sort of softness that ninth graders at the academy possess before morning drills harden them into stony cadets.

"What's this about?" I say aloud.

The kid looks at me in a panic.

"I'm agender!" they blurt out.

"I—" My disturbance gives way to confusion. "What?"

Nik comes up behind them. "Blare is having some revelations about gender lately. Please don't bother them about it. Blare, get in, come on."

My mouth opens and closes. Blare hauls the bags through with effort, then scrambles into the car, settling next to Miz.

"I'm adding child labor to your list of crimes," I say to Nik.

He slams the sliding door closed. "That's discriminatory against equal-opportunity labor."

"Are you joking? Please tell me you're joking."

"Yes, I'm joking. And it's not child labor if it's voluntary."

That's blatantly untrue. "How old are you?" I ask, pivoting the question to Blare. "Thirteen?"

Blare shrinks into their shoulders. "Maybe!"

I swivel to Miz. "You had a thirteen-year-old flying the helicopter?"

"It was on autopilot the entire time. No one uses manual flying for a cross-continental journey," Miz returns, fussing with the glasses in her lap. She's taken them out of her pocket to clean them. "And besides, I'm the one usually overseeing the transportation. But I figured it was better to put Blare on flying duty than risk them getting in *your* way."

I resist a huff. I suppose I did try to start a fight in the helicopter. Who knows—maybe I would have behaved myself if I had known there was a *child* present. Blare should be going to school and spending time on the feed exploring the limitless bounds of gender expression. Not running around with anarchists.

"Leave them be," Nik prompts again. "You're the only one being brought on for involuntary labor."

I grit my teeth. Nik casts a quick, verifying glance over me, as though he'd expected me to debate his flippant remark, but I say nothing more. My own school years were hazy. I didn't have friends at the academy. There were cadets like Teryn who I knew in my periphery, but I sat alone at lunch and didn't ask to borrow anyone's notes in class. It wasn't uncommon at military academy—plenty of us were realists, well aware that we were only going through these years to be sent out and sacrificed in a line of fire. I kept myself company. Sat in my dorm searching stupid things on the feed like *what does it mean to be girl? can u be nonbinary and keep using she/her? problematic to use she/they just to signal to people that ur gender identity is a little funky but you don't particularly need to be they/them'd?*

The taxi's engine whirls to a start. No one joins me at the back, where the three seats blend into one. Past the empty driver's and front passenger seats, there are four in the middle—two by two on each side with an aisle between. Nik settles on the left side. Miz has put on her glasses opposite him: she's connecting to the taxi to give it directions. On the right side, Blare's attention stays firmly on their hands, like I'm going to tell them off if we make eye contact once more.

Nik and Miz come across as exactly the type of people to be society insurgents: the likely rebels who *would* be going against NileCorp, against our accepted way of life. Blare is not. Blare could turn into me five years down the line.

Not that me right now is an admirable place to be.

I fold my arms tightly, tilting my body to face the window. We landed somewhere to the north, by Upsie's outer edges. The helicopter remains parked in the hills while the taxi pulls away. Either someone is coming soon to fetch the aircraft, or it was stolen to begin with and its use has run out.

The pervasive smoke follows on our tail while the taxi shudders onto a gravel road, picking up speed. No particular source contributes to the air quality tonight. In the outskirts, the factories always clog the skies until they're treacly. There are few streetlamps ahead, but the self-driving taxi doesn't need anything save its own lidar, zooming forward.

"Okay." With an effortful heft, Nik climbs into the back and drops onto the long seat beside me. I stiffen, subtly shifting away by an inch. "Atahua has launched a manhunt for you at the federal level, so it serves your best interest to keep your head down with us. You get caught, you get hauled in without evidence. Don't go blaming me if that happens." He pulls something out of his pocket and tosses it at me. It looks like a pimple patch. "Put that on your forehead. It'll scramble surveillance from identifying you."

I do it without protest. The worst that can happen is a breakout on my forehead.

"Tell me what you want from me," I say dully. "Let's get this done as fast as possible."

"Thank you for the enthusiasm, soldier. I knew you'd come around."

This is baffling.

"There's a Medan government program broken up across three files in three locations," Nik begins. His manner is nonchalant. Almost bored. "An enormous amount of data, and top secret at that. Intelligence networks in both Medaluo and Atahua were told the files were deleted. We want to steal these files before the truth comes out that they were merely hidden."

I run a quick mental calculation on the school year and the current month. It fits. Nile Military Academy will be preparing to send the newest graduating class on their final exam postings. I would bet anything that they're going to get involved. The Atahuan government loves to outsource everything to NileCorp, and NileCorp loves to use its cadets in training.

"And what's the program?" I ask.

The taxi goes silent. Miz makes a pointed gesture to squint into her glasses, pretending not to be listening. Blare is still staring into their lap, only with an added manner of discomfort, shrinking in their seat.

"Doesn't matter," Nik says. Though he'd been observing me before, his eyes have darted to the window. They reflect the moving shapes, the blue neon in the distance. We pass dark mills and billboards, abandoned cars and falling houses.

"Clearly does."

"Fine," he retorts. "It's classified from you right now."

Outside of bombing NileCorp property, Nik's second-most hindering behavior is his insistence on spreading a common slogan across his sites: *Indisposition is real.* Indisposition has been debunked. It's something that used to only have traction in anonymous forums, the idea that NileCorp possesses malware capable of infecting a user in StrangeLoom and destroying their mind.

Ever since Nik Grant, though, the idea has been taking root among the masses. Some people are growing afraid of logging in, claiming they could be Indisposed by saying the wrong thing. It's ridiculous. He's clearly working off conspiracy theories, so who knows what other flawed information he uses when putting together his missions.

I sigh, folding my arms.

"How am I supposed to help you without knowing what you're looking for?" Never mind whether this program even exists to begin with.

"You come along for the ride. We'll let you know when we need you to weigh in."

"You," I seethe, "ruined my life to get me to *weigh in*?"

Nik reaches a hand into his pocket. For a moment I'm convinced he'll attack me again. I need to prepare to be on the defense. Find the nearest blunt object that can help me fight.

He only pulls out his handheld. I have no clue when that migrated from his bag to his pocket. I'd definitely watched him zip it into the front pocket earlier.

"Here are the blueprints for each location holding the file. Upsie. Threto. And Kunlun."

The tension in my body shifts entirely, finding a new target.

"Kunlun?"

"Don't worry too much about Upsie and Threto. Those files are hidden in their national data centers." He's pretending he doesn't hear my shock. "It will take some work, but breaking in is doable."

Despite myself, I take the handheld and enlarge the PDF on the screen. Nik watches me like a hawk, tracking each movement of my finger. I treat it like I'm looking at a new mission, needing to understand the brief before NileCorp gives us the environment in mixed reality to train. I find those practice runs on the base more difficult than the real thing: I perform better if I've memorized the details before going in, even if that doesn't tell me what to expect when they re-create our target locations down to the hex code of the graffiti. They ask us to run through all the most likely scenarios in those mixed-reality rooms, but half the time, the most likely scenario is just the first one. Not every mission is as difficult as capturing Nik Grant. Usually we're only guarding high-priority officials entering Button City or transporting critical goods. No need for practice runs two to fifteen. I once asked Teryn if she was also always getting tested on her reaction speed to another unit of NileCorp soldiers converging in on her, and she looked at me as though I'd lost my mind. The engineers on the base design each experience to be unique to the soldier, working off instructions from the previous run about what our weakest flaws are, and for whatever reason, they really want me prepared to be ambushed by a rogue unit. I can't begin to parse why. We've never encountered anything close to that on a real mission.

"I don't know why you're showing me this," I remark plainly. "You already had this in motion before framing me. I suspect you know how to get into these facilities."

Upsie's data center is an enormous building that spans several wings across a field. Only one entrance, which means getting past a personnel screening turnstile, locks on the server rooms, and passwords on server access. Threto isn't as bad: it's a smaller building with more exits. It may actually be harder to move through the city itself without raising suspicion from government surveillance—Threto is the *Land of Three Towns*, the major hub of the country where all roads lead in and out, highly watched and tightly governed.

I make an attempt to give the handheld back. Nik doesn't take it yet, despite the careful eye he keeps over my grip on the device. He reaches his arm and swipes on the third PDF he loaded for me.

I look down.

"Oh, sure," I say. "Hilarious."

"I'm showing you this because these are the only blueprints we have for Kunlun."

It's a picture of me. My ID photo as a NileCorp contractor. They took it in the hospital, only a week after I'd woken so they could get my registration started. I appear dazed and bedraggled, with visible swelling along my jaw, barely aware what year it was, never mind what I had encountered in virtual. My body wasn't supposed to come under any harm while I was upcountry performing my final posting, but the nutrient line had tugged out when I seized, and the nodes in the Pod had failed to accommodate the frantic amount of activity happening. They say I was lucky I survived. They say I was lucky that a bout of memories was all I lost.

I push the handheld back properly. "You said you read my files."

"Yes."

"The censored files in the NileCorp database."

"Correct," Nik answers.

"Then you already know," I say. "I don't remember anything about Kunlun."

It's not only my memories of hacking into Kunlun that remain a wide, gaping hole. It's everything that came before it too, the moment I was injected into Medaluo's server. I can't remember how I stole into Kunlun. I could speculate: though Kunlun has no physical downcountry equivalent, the servers that store its streets, its buildings, its data are in Offron—Land of Outer Frontier—at the northern edge of Medaluo, where Kunlun was first built. If there's anywhere that makes sense to hack into Kunlun, it's Offron.

But that's where all of my speculation disintegrates. Upcountry Offron and Kunlun are two separate cities. No one at NileCorp will explain to me what exactly I did to cross that distance. It's better that I don't know, in fact, so that I can avoid situations like this exactly: being held under duress by anarchists to get them into highly secure locations.

"No matter." Nik puts the handheld away. "We start work in Upsie anyway."

I don't understand. Nik and his team have gone through all this effort to bring me along for their mission. They've killed a man, dragged my name in the mud, sent Atahuan federal after me.

And then he's flippant about whether or not I can actually help them.

It doesn't make sense.

"Do you know something I don't?"

It's Nik's turn to jolt. For the briefest moment, panic flutters over his expression, and it's a welcome change from the noncommittal, blasé coldness he's been wearing otherwise. "What?"

"Do you know something," I repeat, "that I don't? On the plane you said you were looking for someone who got lost and asked me about the name 'Sullivan.' Suddenly you've left that out of this explanation."

"I didn't say *lost*," he mutters. "I was just double-checking something. You don't know it, so I left it out."

"I have ten weeks of missing memories," I counter. "If I don't know it, I could just have forgotten. Tell me what you were checking."

"It's simply not relevant here if you have no familiarity with it."

"What do you mean—"

The taxi hits a severe bump, shaking the entire vehicle. My gaze whips to Miz. She took over self-driving capabilities just to do that on purpose.

"We're approaching the city," she announces. In the time since I've looked away from the window, the car has pulled onto a main road. It drives parallel to a highway overhead, where the underside is clustered with electric wiring that glows a hazardous white sheen. Other vehicles chug down the five-lane road, their exteriors rusted from the elements, the passengers inside made ghostly by the light.

"All right, no more time for chatter," Nik declares. He climbs out of the back seat, lumbering forward to the bags in the aisle. Miz warns him to watch his head on the next turn, and the taxi jostles off the road into a tunnel, leaping across a ditch in the road with enough momentum to threaten to flip. For a moment, it's utterly dark in the tunnel. Then we emerge out the other side, and instead of a highway overhead, it's skyscrapers and their iridescent advertisements, swirling through the night and making a dive at anything it senses beneath it. It's buzzing drones making deliveries at rooftop-level, zipping along the buildings and finding a good window to hover in front of before releasing its package. It's people—movement in the apartments, movement in the night markets, a low rumble that can be heard even through the sealed windows of the vehicle, a murmuring of conversation overlapping at every tier of Upsie.

A wave of something undecipherable turns up my throat. Some mixture between disgust and nostalgia, the desire to take in Medaluo and the sick churn that immediately sets in when I realize this awe is what Atahua would point to if I were accused of being a spy. Sooner or later, some Medan who frequently scrolls Atahuan news on the feed will recognize me in physical space, and then that'll be that. The pictures will go online; the outrage will spread. Atahua will mark me as a traitor until I get the video back. Atahua at large may continue to mark me as a traitor afterward, but that won't matter. As long as I get my job back. As long as there's a roof over my head and a bed at the base.

"Where are we going first?" I ask.

"Hotel." At Miz's direction, the taxi pulls into a side street. Here, short light poles grow out of the cobblestone every few paces, illuminating the alley a plain white-yellow. "I need the night to invade the data center network and get some information. We'll want employee details."

Nik yanks down one of the seats abruptly. He looks at me for an infinitesimal moment, and I can only conclude that he wanted a reaction out of me. Make me jump, give me a fright. My face stays blank. He's turning before anyone else can observe the exchange, already opening the taxi door and stepping out prior to a full stop. "Let's move. The less time we spend on the street with cameras, the better."

The taxi brakes beside a thin, low-rise building. Our destination, I assume. Miz and Blare exit after Nik, the two muttering between themselves while they separate the bags. Miz is still largely avoiding my gaze, but Blare's eyes lift for a moment. They smile cautiously, offering me the gesture before clambering off. Only then do I follow suit, my shoes touching down on the sidewalk's lumpy tread.

It's quiet. A fragrant smell wafts from the inner end of the street—I follow its source, squinting past the lights to find an old lady with a food cart parked around the bend. Despite the hour, despite everything that I assumed about downcountry in a dying city, expecting emptied and desolate streets, there are enough people walking about that two buyers hover by the cart, waiting for their onion pancake orders to be made. They stare forward blankly, scrolling the feed displayed on their glasses, their hands shoved in their pockets.

As soon as I've climbed out, Miz sends the taxi off. Faint music trickles from a skyscraper next to the low-rise building. Gauging by the lights, only the first five levels of the forty are functional.

"We're staying next to this thing?" I pose it as a question, but my tone is entirely judgment. "It could collapse in the middle of the night."

Miz waves me forward. "It won't."

Partially functional buildings are common in Button City too. Those who own or rent property downcountry are owed its upcountry value: every nation that signed on for a StrangeLoom server agreed to those terms. But that means no one can give up their downcountry property if they want to operate upcountry. There will always be some skeleton downcountry. One guard watching the investment bank's offices so that the company runs upcountry. Two cooks in the restaurants downcountry making the dry sandwiches only attainable by bot delivery so that customers upcountry can order cocktails and steaks.

There's a couple walking out from the automatic doors when I step through. One of them looks right at me. She continues staring for a beat too long. Maybe she's wondering whether she knows me, where she knows me from. Far more Medans access Atahua's feeds than either government would ever admit. It's easy to tell when there are Medan users debating in the comments of touchy posts because they'll use a very particular nose-picking emoticon that Atahuans don't have on our keyboards.

The couple walks on. I enter the lobby. They don't call out, and when I do turn my head back to track where they've gone, they're already around the corner, off to enjoy their night.

"In case you're wondering," Nik calls from the elevator, "Miz is posted in your room, so don't try to run."

Miz comes through the automatic doors then, grimacing. The directory beside the elevator shows the first three floors to be offices. Fourth and fifth are hotel rooms. No formal lobby anywhere to be seen, and six, seven, and eight are blanked out, rendered undecipherable by scratch marks. Maybe another company's office space, collapsing downcountry after automation took over their industry.

"We start in the morning."

The elevator doors open. An elderly woman steps out, pushing a cleaning cart. The scent of heavy bleach wafts alongside her slow amble, her supplies rattling. She pushes into the door for the back stairwell, a loud slam declaring her exit.

In the ensuing silence, no one moves until I do, waiting for me to step into the elevator first. I oblige. There's a camera blinking in the corner, but when I follow the wire trailing out its base, it goes nowhere.

Miz enters and stands to my side. Blare is similarly close when they find a spot in front of me. I'm almost surprised this team of kidnappers hasn't bothered handcuffing me, hasn't made the move to keep me sedated until we get where we need to be. It's a lot of faith that I'll remain reasonable. NileCorp's private forces aren't known for that. NileCorp has a 99.91 percent survival rate for its soldiers because we aren't trained to care about who gets caught in the line of fire. Shoot first and pay for it later amid a mess of corporate jargon. We're not going to get into trouble because NileCorp as an entity is too big, too nebulous to bring down for one soldier's trigger-happy fingers.

"By morning," Nik continues when the doors close after him, "I mean the break of dawn. We're going to get to these files before companies like your NileCorp pick up the scent."

"If you want me to get us into Kunlun," I say, "you'll have a better chance of success if you tell me what you're looking for there. What sort of data is it? What kind of file? Every part of Kunlun is stored in Offron's servers anyway—can't you break into Offron's data center and search there instead?"

We reach the fourth floor. The elevator doors slide back.

"No. We can't." Nik steps out, strolling down the corridor. Blare hurries to follow him, the two disappearing into a door on the left.

I turn to Miz, slowly, menacingly, and she barely blinks. It reminds me a lot of myself when I'm in those mixed-reality rooms trying not to look out the corner of my eye, because I know they're about to throw the rogue NileCorp unit at me again, and it takes all of my discipline not to fight them off. Better to keep them at bay as much as possible and focus on the actual mission. In this case, I'm Miz's annoying rogue unit.

I follow closely when she exits the elevator. She scans her palm on the door opposite to the one Nik and Blare went into, and the lock pops open.

"You have your palm data stored with reception?" I ask.

"It's a 3D-printed skin layer," she mutters.

"Fake bio-credentials?"

"Yes."

Miz tosses her bags on the floor, then plants herself on the chair, a handheld device on her knee and her glasses snug. Now that she's pointed it out, I see the thin line across her fingers where the layer she's wearing over her palm ends.

I walk around the bed on the left, inspecting the moth-bitten sheets. Miz doesn't want to chat, which is fine by me, but it strikes me as bizarre that I'm feeling an air of blame. As if I've done something to warrant this treatment.

"What's your problem?"

I've asked the question casually, equal to an inquiry into what temperature it is or what we're having for dinner.

Miz lowers her glasses. Her brow furrows. "Excuse me?"

"Surely I'm the one who should be mad," I say, "given that you kidnapped me. What's with the cold shoulder?"

Now Miz scoffs. She reaches into her bag and takes out a second handheld, balancing it on her other knee.

"Don't take it personally," she replies. "You just seem a little soulless, and I don't see the point of acting otherwise."

I sit on the bed. "All right."

Miz frowns to herself. If she expected to offend me, she'll be disappointed. I have no urge to counter that.

She taps her glasses. They turn opaque from my side, ensuring I can't see any hint of what's displayed before her eyes.

"Get some sleep," Miz says plainly. "Let me know if I'm making too much noise."

8

LIA

Warning: Unfamiliar user has picked up speed.

I don't overthink my strategy: I bolt, sprinting down the busy street. The other pedestrians barely pay me any mind. My feet thud on the pavement to the rhythm of my pulse, flinging me in and out of the crowds as I attempt to find some sort of cover.

How did this happen? I've been here for a grand total of ten minutes, and I'm being *followed*. Maybe I shouldn't be running away. Maybe this is only going to get me caught faster.

Crap. *Crap.* At the very least, I have to meet up with Kieren first so we both get docked by this stalker. If I go down, I'm taking him with me.

I make a sharp left, sighting a pair of automatic double doors leading into a particularly round building. I'm hurrying up the steps three at a time before diving through, and then I've entered a shopping complex filled with screaming children and the rhythmic clatter of arcade machines lining the center platform.

Think. Think, Lia.

"How do I open this?" I grumble under my breath. I force myself to slow, not wanting to draw the attention of mall security. At random, my display opens a map, triggered by my eye movements.

A small blinking dot enters the shopping complex too. I almost come to a complete halt. I'm not only being followed—I'm being *tracked*.

I swerve, avoiding a group of teenage boys. In their chatter, they don't notice the small dance I do to prevent smooshing into the wall before I pick up speed again around them. The shopping complex descends several levels underground. I take the escalator, glancing over my shoulder. There are too many people, too much activity. It's impossible to pick out my pursuer.

Suggestion: Make emergency call?

"No, absolutely not," I mutter, dismissing the alert. What is my stalker going to do, kill me? We can't die in virtual. The system didn't encode bleeding, so we can't even get seriously hurt short of slight bruises—and those don't last long. They bloom as an attempt to keep upcountry feeling as real as possible. Injuries that are any more severe automatically alert authorities in the system to perform a cursory check. Violent crime doesn't exist upcountry, and it's not because of society's improved character; it's because all opportunities have disappeared.

It tends to send most of those perpetrators downcountry, where rates will only grow higher.

I hit the lower level, stepping off the escalator into the middle of a food court. The signs declare TASTY TAKE-OUT! and BEST CHICKEN EVER, their ordering screens flashing bright to lure customers and their bots behind the counter working at high speed.

Tempting as it is to sniff around the Medan food and try everything Dad is cautious about letting me have in Atahua, I keep walking, swiping a tray. The repository machine beeps at me, recognizing my user when I reach my hand out, and my display tells me ten cents—*We've already converted the payment to Atahuan currency for all your tourist needs!*—have been docked from my wallet, available for refund upon return of the tray. It's not worth returning it for ten cents, so I keep moving, weaving past the tables and their order codes floating from the screens in the middle, steering clear of the numerous tiny bots driving around the food court to deliver plates.

The restrooms are empty when I push through the swinging door. I check the three stalls one by one. Clear. I breathe in, breathe out, then lift the tray, waiting for the dot on the map to get closer and closer. The Nile Military Academy handbook would advise against this. The handbook for final exam postings also never said that apparently someone would be able to immediately hack my location. What are they tracking? My avatar? My user panel in the system? Is this someone from the academy keeping an eye on me, and Medaluo's privacy settings have given them away?

The restroom door opens a crack. And as I swing the tray, I've entirely missed where I thought there would be someone to strike, because a *cat* has nudged its face against the entrance and trotted in.

"Sh—" I barely stop myself from dropping the tray on the cat's head. It's fluffy. Black. My heart rate slowly starts to beat evenly again. "Hello."

The cat blinks. The door closes behind its long tail. Suddenly, a wave of cold sweat breaks down my spine and squeezes a grip over my stomach because I'm still looking at the map in my display, and the user tracking me has entered the space too. I'm staring at a cat. So why is the map showing me that this is a user?

I just about faint when the cat starts talking.

"Oh. I didn't think it would be you."

Then it disappears. Literally. Its body shimmers and blinks out of virtual, leaving only empty space behind. My display doesn't note an unfamiliar user on my trail anymore. The map closes itself.

A new notification blinks into view.

> **KIEREN:** Where are you?
> **LIA:** bruh you won't BELIEVE what just happened to me

• • • •

I push through the doors into Lovers' Café twenty minutes later, huffing from my exertion. Kieren's already there, as proven by the multiple messages I have from him pointing out my tardiness.

"Welcome!" the hostess greets. "Can I offer you a menu?"

It's shockingly pink inside. Not the fluffy, pastel shades, but a metallic sort of fuchsia, painted wall to wall and beaming from the colored bulbs underneath the booth tables. I spot Kieren in the corner, his fingers tapping on the table. He's the only one sitting alone.

"No, thank you," I say, pointing over to Kieren. "He should already have ordered what I want."

It's absolutely bustling while I attempt to make my way over to the corner. Much as the name implies, the Lovers' Café only has two-person tables, and they're all full. Kieren must have had immense luck snatching a seat, especially with the amount of customers who are standing around, waiting for a moment to home in on an empty table.

I try to navigate past a couple standing right in the walkway. One girl is hanging off the other's neck, brushing her nose against her partner's. Neither notices when I push through, finally reaching Kieren.

"Yes," he says the moment I meet his eyes. "I ordered you one too."

"Hopefully not the same thing you got," I say, peering into his cup before I sit. Kieren likes his coffee black, no sugar, no cream. It's unimaginable to me.

"I wasn't born yesterday, Ward."

Right on cue, a server pushes out from the kitchen, carrying a tray. He's wearing a headset decorated with a bow, likely to communicate with the bot servers if any of them go astray.

"Table sixteen, you've finally got company!" he bellows, grabbing a large cup off his tray and setting it on the table. "The coffee you preordered for your girlfriend."

Kieren jolts. His eyes widen, like he's being accused of a crime. "She is not my girlfriend."

"Oh, I'm so sorry," the server hurries to say. He grabs two napkins off his tray, putting them down too. "For your wife."

Then he's off before Kieren can make another correction.

I reach for the cup, careful to slide it in front of me without disturbing the enormous mound of whipped cream.

"Am I going to find a ring in here when I drink?" I ask. "I'd rather not choke on a huge diamond."

Kieren's fuming. "That's not funny."

"Notice how I said huge. I'll have to reject anything less than two carats."

"Can we get back on topic? What's this about a talking cat?"

I set the cup down after a sip. There's likely cream on my top lip, so I take a napkin and pat it away before speaking.

"It's exactly as I said over chat. It followed me, then opened its mouth and said human words. I can't imagine that's *legal*."

"It's not." Kieren swirls his cup, catching the dregs trying to clump at the bottom. "Or at the very least it doesn't comply with StrangeLoom's terms of use."

"So what was that all about?"

There's a common saying we have at the academy: *If someone seems to have outsmarted NileCorp, it's probably NileCorp.* Insurgency groups that swoop in to steal a prototype; union protests around a new handheld release that grow large enough to draw national scrutiny. Even if the outcome isn't immediately clear, ten steps later the result will end up benefiting NileCorp somehow.

"Why don't we ask?"

An invitation enters my display, looping me into an outgoing call. Kieren has Headmaster Murray saved as **"dad . . ."** which seems unnecessarily punctuated. It rings a few times before his father answers, not with a greeting but:

"This is rather fast to have findings already."

"We're getting settled," Kieren says. "Are we being contacted already?"

"Sorry?"

Kieren peers around the café. It's unlikely anyone is paying attention to us. Even more unlikely that Medaluo could monitor our line, given the hundreds of thousands of calls being made at the same time. Still, we need to be careful. They'll have automatic sensors imposed, triggered by certain words to listen in for foreign agents.

"Our contact," Kieren says again. "You said we'd be acting from a contact on the ground. I wanted to check when they would find us."

A tut comes across the line. "Have you found lodging? Established a workstation?"

"We're only trying to cover our bases," I interject. Kieren's clearly annoying his dad, and it doesn't help that he didn't explain why exactly we're calling. "I suspected we were followed. We wanted to check it wasn't our contact."

"No," Headmaster Murray says. A beat draws long over the line. Maybe it's some setting in Medaluo, but I can't hear any noise fillers. When Headmaster Murray doesn't speak, it's as though the line isn't even active. "Once your avatars log a hotel on your tourist visas, the call from your contact on the ground will come in. It's not a good look that I have to explain this."

My posture stiffens. Kieren's mouth hardens into a line.

"Why do you think we were followed?" Kieren asks. "Any suggestions are welcome."

"I'm going to have to circle back on that."

"What? Just tell me what you think. Is it possible that there's a threat from Medaluo here?"

"I'll circle back. Keep the social chatter to a minimum, Kieren."

And Headmaster Murray hangs up.

"You know..." Kieren pushes his empty coffee cup to the middle of the table. "He didn't used to be such a *dick*."

Headmaster Murray clearly doesn't think there's a problem. I suppose it does sound silly when spoken out loud. If Medaluo knew we were in their server, we wouldn't be sitting in a café making a call home. We would be in a dark room with government agents, blindfolded while Medaluo tries to keep us from logging out long enough to question us.

I take another sip of my overly sweet coffee. Medaluo doesn't govern its country as Atahua does. It doesn't have several branches of government, checks and balances among its departments. Medaluo has one federal agency maintaining its affairs and the largest national military in the world. There are no corporations with their fingers in the national reserve, no powerful families outside of the ones that work for the government. If someone upsets the Medan government, there is nothing to stop their agents from dragging them in downcountry and making sure no one finds them again.

"I have to imagine this was a coincidence," I finally say. "Let's not press on it anymore. I don't want us *actually* getting the government's attention."

I'm not particularly fond of the Atahuan government either, but at least it's significantly harder to vanish in Atahua. At least there, we can go kicking and screaming, with hundreds of accounts on the feed chattering about the wrongdoing. Medaluo is most frightening for its silence.

"Maybe we should," Kieren mutters. "Maybe that's how we actually get something done."

I frown, waving my hand in front of his face. His eyes have glazed over. Any casual passerby would assume he's staring at something on his display, but I'm well acquainted with his furrow of concentration. This is Kieren lost in his thoughts.

"Hey," I say. "Relax, would you? We're on a missing person's case, not the elimination of the cold war."

That seems to bring Kieren back to earth. His shoulders slump. At the front of Lovers' Café, the door thuds open for a double date spilling over from the restaurant across the street. A small cleaning bot swivels under our table, slurping up the few droplets of coffee that splattered out the side of my cup without my notice.

"Thank you," I whisper down to it.

The bot lights up with a flash of pink.

I sit comfortably for a moment, finishing my coffee. Despite the loud ambient hum, I can hear the hostess laughing by the door, so entertained by whatever the customer at the front of the line has said that she's bowed over. The café warms from the activity, and the glass windows creak open an inch on automatic regulation.

"Do you ever get the sense that my dad has a wire feeding him answers?"

The question comes entirely out of left field. My eyes widen, my attention snapping back to Kieren. He's being serious.

"I don't think I've spoken to your dad enough to make that judgment call," I say carefully. "What do you mean—that he's under NileCorp's thumb for everything he does?"

It's rare that someone can disappear without a fuss in Atahua, but it's also rare that anyone is making a fuss at all. *Every* Atahuan is under NileCorp's thumb to some degree simply by using upcountry, where our activity and messages are cataloged in their servers down to the minutiae. When federal and NileCorp are so tightly collaborative, most of us are convinced the police will knock on our door merely at an inflammatory thought toward the company.

There's still plenty of crime. Petty thefts, robberies, homicides. NileCorp might know about it while someone is putting together the plan, but that doesn't mean they'll waste precious resources to stop it. They don't care if the old man living in the box downcountry got his throat cut in the night. They don't care to stop someone's electronics from getting stolen. More money feeds back into the supply chain when NileCorp branded replacements are bought anyway. I'm sure they'd like to prevent the hits that go higher—it's not to say nothing escapes NileCorp notice when there have been plenty of military that anarchists are targeting recently. But most perpetrators are caught before long. Only a few end up as big-name problems, and even then NileCorp will no doubt catch up eventually.

"He goes beyond being under their thumb sometimes. He's practically their walking mouthpiece," Kieren grumbles. "He used to be different when I needed help. He might have been strict when people were watching, but if it was just us behind closed doors..." His shoulders crawl up to his ears. "Look at me, protesting that my dad isn't *nice* to me anymore."

I shift in my seat. "I'm sure it's hard for him. He doesn't want to be accused of playing favorites."

A clunk sounds beneath the table. The cleaning bot has nudged up against Kieren's leg. He prompts it away, back onto its correct path, and it whines in confusion. It probably got thrown by the lack of wrinkles in any of Kieren's clothes and thought there was more smooth surface to roll onto.

"Unbelievable that I thought he might actually help." The bot finally pivots, turning for the next table. "Before Hailey and I started at the academy, he told us he took the job to keep an eye on us. Our education was the only reason he left NileCorp's corporate ranks." Kieren pulls his leg up onto the chair. "But it doesn't really seem like he cares much about us one way or the other, does it?"

I don't know what to say, so I stay silent. My dad is a public figure too—I know how it feels to be tiptoeing around what responsibility he owes the rest of the world. It seems cosmically fitting that Kieren has the same conflict. As different as Kieren and I are on the surface, our minds have always been mirrors. It's the reason we've been able to go head-to-head without tiring all these years later.

Another notification appears at the edge of my display. Kieren has sent me a pinned location.

"I was looking around for lodging while I waited. There's a hotel one block over."

Ah, I see. It's time to change the subject.

"Okay," I allow. "Lead the way."

We leave the table, bringing our cups to the collection trolley. The hostess waves goodbye, and I return the gesture, dispensing a tip at the door through my display. We step onto the street, me trailing slightly behind

Kieren. His backpack came with him, but I'm terribly lacking. I hope Hailey returned my suitcase to the girls' dorms. I'm going to be mad if Headmaster Murray sent it off to get recycled.

"It's just around here," Kieren announces. "This one."

I'm browsing the online marketplace while I follow Kieren up to a low-rise building, its lobby bustling with some upscale event. Attendees dressed in suits and gowns pour through the glass door with us, waiting for the large elevator to arrive. I select a toothbrush, then a set of cotton pajamas, and complete the purchase.

"Wedding?" Kieren asks the group waiting at our side.

They turn from their chatter, perking up with intrigue. I hadn't been looking closely at any pedestrian faces while I'd wandered in from the embankment; nor had I paid anyone particular attention in the dim café, save for Kieren, whose face I know rather well. Here, though, under the golden lights of the building atrium, I suddenly feel the need to sidle out of view, put a hat over my head and pull it low.

"Corporate event," one woman answers, smiling. "You coming?"

I've seen Medaluo's cosmetic adjustment filters on the feed. I've seen the pictures, the videos. It's still astonishing to encounter it in person, the symmetrical chins and the white teeth and the perfectly curved noses. Without thinking about what I'm doing, I'm checking if I've been given access to the filter adjustment sliders, but mine are still blanked. Tourist pass. Ugh.

"No," I contribute before Kieren can decide this is an opportunity. "We're unaffiliated."

"It's open anyhow. Seventh floor!"

The elevator doors slide open. We step in with the corporate partygoers, jamming into the tight space. Kieren casts me a look to ask why I interrupted, and I return his expression. I'm right behind a tall man—height isn't adjustable, but the dip of his shoulders likely is, the exact slope of his neck. At the fourth floor, the elevator doors open, and I'm distracted enough that Kieren has to grab my elbow, extracting me with him.

"We missed out on free drinks, Ward," Kieren says after the doors thud closed.

"I can't believe it," I say, clearly fixated on another topic. "What must it be like to not have pores anymore?"

Kieren puts his hands in his pockets. My glare suddenly turns on him.

"I guess you wouldn't know."

"Hey," he protests. "I have pores."

"Yeah, yeah," I grumble. "Where's check-in?"

Kieren blinks for his display. "Self check-in. The website says it'll activate when we reach the fourth floor. . . . Okay, here we go. I'm browsing, I'm browsing . . ."

He trails off. A few seconds later, he's still frozen.

I tap my foot. "Are you holding your breath? Do you need CPR?"

"Bet you'd like that, wouldn't you?" he fires back, resuming his normal respiration. "I'm only seeing one room available."

"Just get it," I say. "We can share the space."

"Are you sure? There's another hotel ten minutes away. That might be larger. This one only has two floors."

I resist the urge to sigh, to slam my forehead repeatedly into the wall, not because of what Kieren is saying but because this day has been so long, and as far as my body is aware, it's still morning. I would love to check in and take a shower and not feel like the grubbiest person in the entirety of upcountry Upsie. Maybe sit for a minute, moisturize my various pores, and finally begin the next course of action to take us into our posting properly.

"I already ordered stuff to this hotel."

Kieren's eyes focus. "Why would you . . . ? Oh, you dropped your suitcase. How did you drop—"

"*Get the room!*" I hiss.

"Fine!" His brow twitches. He's made the selection. "Room 408. It's right ahead."

Another notification appears at the side of my display to confirm that

Kieren has shared a key card with me. Someone's leaving their room down the corridor, so we get our act together, smiling primly while the man walks through and heads for the elevator. He barely looks our way, eyes glazed for his display. The moment he disappears into the elevator, I stride along the thin carpeting, searching until I spot 408 in golden cursive adorning a plain black door.

The handle turns smoothly under my palm, a cool puff of air-conditioning caressing my cheek as soon as I shoulder through. On an automated setting, the soft lights come on and the red curtains draw apart, revealing the lower-level views of the city at night. The dark picture glows with busyness, even at this hour. Drones zip up and down the street, perfectly visible at hotel window height, blinking yellow, blue, pink to signal their task. The television fixed on the wall starts to speak to welcome its guests, and I wave my hand to shut it up. My eyes pivot, finding the interactive wardrobe, the color-changing lamp . . . and the one bed.

"Wait—"

Kieren steps in too, letting the door close with a thud. "Don't say I didn't warn you."

9

EIRALE

After my final exam posting, I woke confused in Button City. The last full memory I had was at the academy upcountry before going into the exam. Short of screaming from the intense pain, I wasn't really conscious when I was pulled out of my Pod. I wasn't responsive at all during the airlift out of the Button State campus and into the city.

I gave the nurses a fright when I tried to move. The hospital hadn't expected that I'd be alert so soon. I slipped back under within seconds of that initial burst of energy, but the machines attached to my body shrieked like the end of the world had approached. Horrible spikes and dips, I'm told.

After that, my recovery was slow. Each day I opened my eyes for a few minutes, trying to parse what had happened, dissect clues from the doctors talking in my vicinity. I heard peculiar terms thrown around, *brain function minimal but improving, muscle activation*. What was most alarming wasn't that I could hardly move. It was that I couldn't *remember*. If I had been that close to the verge of death, I would have expected to know what the cause was.

I didn't recognize my visitor at first. The hospital ward lowered its lights and the noise in the hallway went quiet, which told me they had cleared the space. The door opened, and he approached my bedside surrounded by security. He was dressed simply: a plain white T-shirt and dark trousers with a black belt. My neck shifted an inch; my eyes managed to swivel when he settled on the chair. Security waited outside the door too. They were uniformed in sturdy suits, the NileCorp logo stitched above their chest. At that point I knew who this was, not because of his face but because I had studied up on the number of soldiers he hired into his personal security force. It was a good position. Something I aspired toward.

"Hello, Eirale," James Moore said. "I'm sorry you're unwell."

I couldn't speak. As far as I could gauge, there wasn't damage to my throat, but it was like the part of my brain trying to deliver the command for verbalizing my words was fried. I tried to say that it was okay and that I didn't really feel unwell, but if I couldn't do that, it was true after all. It *wasn't* okay. I *was* unwell.

"Please accept my deepest gratitude for the work you've done for us," James Moore went on. "I'm sorry that this happened to you. In the early days of StrangeLoom, it was at the top of my list of requirements that people should never be hurt using it. It's unfortunate how much the world has changed since then—how much has slipped out of my control."

I watched him as he grasped my hand. I couldn't manage anything other than a beady stare, though he smiled warmly. I thought, in that moment, that if I had a father, he would be somewhere around Moore's age. He might be hurrying to see me while I recovered and greeting me in this exact manner. But I was an orphan, so what I got instead was a visit from my all-powerful would-be employer. What I got was something purposeful, a visit to make his wishes known to me. Moore's fingers were clammy. It didn't fit with the rest of his appearance. The careful smile and the clean blond hair brushed back from his mild-mannered face.

"The whole point was to connect us without harm," he said firmly. "No more carcinogens soaking into our skin, no more pollutants in our lungs just because we wanted to enjoy the sun on our face. If I hadn't managed the project, someone else would have, don't you think?"

He wasn't expecting an answer to his question. Moore's grip tightened, almost to the point of pain, and I had no ability to react.

"StrangeLoom is a societal good. It would be for the best if we keep this quiet, Eirale. Every incident that my engine has caused is burned into my mind. But so is every great stride. Do you know how long after StrangeLoom went live that every member state in the International Assembly had signed on? Only five years. It took ten before virtual reality's economy surpassed the real. After fifteen, federal declared downcountry Atahua to be defunct, financially speaking. I intend to continue on an upward trajectory. I'm glad that we didn't lose you among the ranks of incidents. It means you can help us ensure it never happens again."

I managed the smallest movement of my head, the semblance of a nod. It must have been enough for Moore, because the tension dissipated in his expression. He stood with relish.

"I'll be in touch again when you have recovered." Security in the room shifted, preparing to accommodate his exit. "Take the time to heal. You have the Button City base waiting for you once you're ready."

• • • •

I pretend to be asleep until Miz finally puts away her handhelds. Wait until I hear her rustling into her bed, then settling.

When her breathing evens out, emitting soft, gentle snores, I give up the pretense and open my eyes, opting to stare out the balcony window.

I've never been more awake. I keep straying back to the memory of James Moore in my hospital room, the day I realized that somehow the results of my final posting had landed me a comfortable position at a prestigious base. After I recovered, I'd been granted a salary far more generous that I'd expected or ever thought to ask for. It was the best-case scenario I could have encountered upon graduation.

Yet I still can't fathom what I might have done to warrant it. And maybe a part of me doesn't want to know.

I shift slightly against my pillow, narrowing my eyes. Miz left the curtains undrawn, so I have a perfect view of the neighboring building. *There*. The light blinks again. Maybe a malfunctioning silent alarm.

When I move to sit up, wanting a better look, my body responds easily. Enough time has passed since my hospital bed that it seems like a faraway dream, an event happening to someone else, played through my eyes. It feels absurd to consider that I'd been immobile while James Moore was in the room, that I hadn't gotten the chance to speak. I do admire him, despite NileCorp's wrongs in the world.

Moore wasn't in touch again. His NileCorp representatives were, so I suppose that still counts. I was smoothly transitioned into Button City. Officially registered as a corporate soldier.

Another blink, coming from the neighboring high-rise. I'm moving silently at once, swinging my feet into my waiting shoes. This makes the fifth flash, and I've been counting the seconds that pass between. They're increasing on ten-second intervals. It's not an alarm, and it's not random.

NileCorp.

Miz's snoring echoes through the room. Slowly I creep across the floor and open the door inch by inch to prevent the hinges from squeaking. Miz doesn't stir. The hallway is almost pitch-black, interrupted only by pinprick lights embedded in the carpeted floor. It was emergency escape path lighting once upon a time, repurposed after the world went virtual so the building owners could save money on bills downcountry. Room 407, where Nik and Blare disappeared into, is dark behind its door too.

I slip out of the room, beelining for the elevator. Under normal circumstances, I'd assume the stairwell to be a quieter route, but I already heard how loud the exit door was when the cleaning cart lady pushed through. There's no sign of life inside any of the other doors on the fourth floor. My shoes are noiseless on the carpet.

The elevator doors glide open. I slink inside.

It doesn't move for a long moment. Agonizingly, I eye the digital display until the box finally begins to descend, the red *4* switching to *3*. A blinking light within view of my window either means someone is trying to get *my* attention, or Nik's team is being cased, and this is a signal between unit members who are closing in. Regardless of which situation it is, I'd like to see what's going on.

When the elevator arrives on the ground floor, the doors are so slow that I push out before they've fully opened, my eyes stinging from the sudden onslaught of fluorescent lighting. I wait just a beat.

Before the stairwell entrance thuds open, and Nik Grant marches out.

I break into a run. My shoulder thuds hard against the entryway in my haste, but I ignore it, making a sharp right. We had come in from the main road, so I go the other way, taking the obscure, small streets.

"Where are you going?" he bellows after me. "I can track you!"

I keep running. The system on his glasses can map exactly where I'm going, but I don't need to get away. I only need to stay ahead.

Upsie unfolds grid by grid, most of its alleys and entryways hidden until I've approached directly. Where there aren't operational buildings, its streets stay dark. I take a left to throw off Nik's tracking, hurrying down a ramp and plunging into a parking garage. There's a fire flickering here, burning from a metal box. Sleeping figures stir at my entrance, but I pivot fast for a stairwell, not waiting around to be noticed.

I don't go far. At the nearest landing, I leap for the ledge of the window, easing the glass up. The frame is brittle—my foot almost eats right through the rotted wood before I've clambered out the window and dropped back onto the sidewalk, gritting my teeth. The impact shoots sharp pain up my feet and knees. I trace a line along the night. Count up the windows of the high-rise that looms over the otherwise dark pathway.

I almost miss it. Just as I'm about to charge at its base, the light comes again.

To my east, a drone rockets into the sky, beeping erratically to begin a search. I sprint forward, slamming through the glass doors and calling a greeting to the night guard behind the front desk, entering the back before he can respond.

There's a man sleeping in the stairwell. The night guard isn't doing a very good job. I leap over the man before his loud snort can turn into a proper rousing. It's not as though he'll have much luck on the floors or getting into any of the apartments, because if there are occupants inside their Pods, their security system will summon the police instantly on intruders.

Begs the question then about who exactly is shining that signal.

"Eight—nine—ten—" I count under my breath, turning and turning on the staircase, tracking each floor I ascend. I'm aiming for fifteen. My step only slows somewhere on the twelfth floor because I've picked up the hint of a breeze.

I stop abruptly when I round the landing. The windowpane here has been broken.

An arm closes around my neck.

"Don't shout. He'll be here in less than a minute. When he does arrive, you will play this off. He can't suspect you saw me here."

I recognize that voice. *"Teryn?"*

"Listen to me," she says firmly. I'm not struggling from the grip she has on my shoulder, but she still keeps a tight clamp anyway. "NileCorp knows you're innocent. They found artifacts that the footage was a deepfake as soon as they analyzed it. It's enough proof that Nik Grant set you up."

I don't take the time to reel. I digest the new developments in a snap: Teryn has followed me into Medaluo; my employer has always known that I didn't commit treason. Which suddenly means I'm not actually here for the reasons I thought.

"Then I can come home?" I hiss.

"No." There's a slam downstairs. "NileCorp was waiting to see why you were set up before contacting federal to clear the air, but then a better opportunity fell into their lap. Stay here. Keep going wherever Nik Grant wants you to go."

The hole in the window makes a suctioning noise with the cold wind. The elements are picking up outside, bringing the first sign of a night storm.

"That's not going to work," I say. "He set me up because he wants me to get him into *Kunlun*, Teryn. I can't get him into Kunlun."

She pauses. Her arm doesn't slacken.

"Offron, then," she decides. "Take him as far as you can in his mission. Our forces will close in on him there."

I can hear footsteps. The initial slam must have been Nik coming into the building.

"Can't I hand him in *now*? He's right within reach. He'll show in seconds."

"Company says no. It sounds to me that he's after something we want."

"We can't get it after he's secured? He said he's searching for a program."

"To my understanding," Teryn says slowly, "that program is not something we can access. Nik Grant needs to acquire it first. Can you manage that?"

A slow panic bubbles up my throat. Coats my tongue.

"Okay. Yes. I can manage it," I whisper. "What about—what about the charges against me?" My words jumble together, my speech tripping in a fit to cover everything before Teryn disappears. The company wants me to be the wheel steering Nik into dark waters, but I was trained to be an invisible cog in the backup motor. This isn't my usual line of work. "The entirety of Atahua thinks I'm a traitor. Can you make it known internally, at least?"

"Your name will be cleared when this is over. We can't risk tipping off Nik Grant that you're in touch with us."

"The longer this goes on, NileCorp may not even believe it—"

"Enough with the negotiation," Teryn snaps, and I stiffen. "You were given the fortuity of spearheading this task. There is no '*your name*' to clear. There is NileCorp who has thrown its lot in with you, and when you succeed, we all succeed. Is that received?"

I swear my allegiance to my team, my unit, my company. We're all asked to recite the oaths when we're inducted onto a base. Our names printed onto the corporate logs of NileCorp security and signed off under James Moore's approval.

"Received," I say.

"Good. I'll be nearby."

Teryn releases me, and then she's gone, slipping through the door for the residential twelfth floor. The handle clicks. I'm already running for the window, slamming my elbow through the glass and hoping the noise is enough to cover for her.

A sharp gust of wind howls into the stairwell. The rain has started at a steady mist. Gray and murky, creeping onto the ledge and immediately coating my hands when I grip the windowpane to push myself on.

Nik finally reaches me, closing his grip around my upper arm. I don't turn to look at him.

"That's enough," he declares. "You and I both know you're not going to throw yourself off."

"Maybe not." There's always a smell that accompanies downcountry night rain. Reedy, lush, dirt-sodden. It's what moss would smell like if left to grow in the crevices of old property, forgotten on each turnover of ownership until its presence becomes unbearable. "But I could attack you. You don't have backup. You probably only had time to grab one weapon, and if the gun wasn't within reach, then it's something more makeshift." I lurch forward an inch. His hands are slacker than they should have been. His fingers tighten to steel instantly upon prompt, but it's too late. I already proved that he wasn't being careful enough. "Maybe this was my plan. I saw the red light blinking on your door and knew you were watching me through the camera. I couldn't risk you waking the rest of your team and ganging up on me. I had to lead you farther away. Somewhere I could throw us *both* off a very tall ledge."

Nik has stilled behind me. The wind picks up. I'd always thought that one day, like every other soldier since the formation of nation-states, I'd give my life to my country for some paltry act of service that wouldn't make a footnote in the historical accounts. After swearing into NileCorp, I realized

I'd even overestimated my impact then. At no point was there any mention of Atahua in the oaths, the rules, the speeches. My loyalty was to my company. My company was who I'd end up giving my life for.

"Are you certain that you could overpower me and make the lunge?" Nik asks. "Should we test it out?"

I likely could. But I won't.

I take too long to respond, and a biting metal sting on my wrist replaces the tight grip Nik had on my arm. He secures the other end of the magnetic cuff to himself.

"Don't play tough," he declares, yanking me off the ledge. "You're only creating more trouble for yourself."

"I had to see how dedicated you were," I return. "Wasn't sure how much I meant to you, and all that."

Nik kicks aside a shard of glass that had landed near his foot. The rain splatters through the broken window. A droplet hits him square on the nose, but he doesn't pay it any mind.

"You're our expert. If this was a loyalty test, I don't know how it gets any more loyal than selecting you personally."

But how did I appear on their radar? How did they come across anything relevant in my files that they decided could help them, unless they were already digging for specifics in the NileCorp database? And then, factoring in the coincidence that I was on the very team sent to capture Nik Grant when he first entered Button City, affording them the opportunity to set me up . . .

I make a vague noise.

Nik's eyes narrow. Lightning shudders from the clouds. Quicksilver in every direction. "What does that mean?"

"Nothing." There's no sign of movement from the rest of the building anymore. Wherever Teryn has gone, she's hidden well. If she's brought a team at all, I pick up no indication we're being watched. "You've got me. Take me back."

10

LIA

I close the door, thanking the robot that brought me my purchases from the marketplace. I'd chosen a random delivery app, whichever one had the fastest driving speeds across Upsie's city center. In Medaluo, they all feed back into one conglomerate anyway—Golden Eagle, owned by a government official's brother-in-law—so any choice is an illusion. Dad has been trying to shut down Golden Eagle's subsidiaries in Atahua, fearful of Medaluo stealing Atahua's data.

Which is a task solely to accommodate Atahuan patriotism given how much data about Atahuans our own NileCorp holds.

I rumple up the plastic bag, tossing it into the trash can. Kieren is lying in a starfish shape on the bed, making himself at home. He pays me no mind while I unwrap the toothpaste I ordered, squeezing a dollop onto my toothbrush before putting it in my mouth. I brush thoughtfully for a moment, still eyeing Kieren.

"Are you going to unpack?"

He frowns, lifting his head slightly. "What?"

My mouth is gargled full of toothpaste, turning my question into *Arff aah to unpah?* Given Kieren's unique ability to take my limelight in class and raise his hand to say my answer first, I would have thought he'd be able to understand me.

I go into the bathroom to spit out my froth. The full immersion of virtual reality doesn't actually come from the photorealistic pixels or the physics engine: it comes from our bodily functions. That's how James Moore opened his presentation the first time they went public with StrangeLoom at a NileCorp event. Though they had been memed to death by people commenting *bro wants us to hallucinate peeing,* it sure did the trick once it went live. If we have to perform our usual menial tasks upcountry, there's no separation from the real. I put my toothbrush at the edge of the sink.

"I *said*," I try again, "are you going to unpack?"

"No point," Kieren replies. "We might be on the move again tomorrow."

"It would take you, like, ten minutes to unpack your clothes." I emerge from the bathroom, putting my hands on my hips. "Maybe five minutes to put everything back in if you rush."

"I have a routine. I can't just take stuff in and out. It's been ordered like soil horizons, each bedrock of clothing speaking to a specific—"

"Okay, okay, forget I said anything," I interrupt, scooping up the pajamas I left on the table.

I return to the bathroom and close the door. While I change, the mirror reflects back the sides of my arms inexplicably dusted with grime from the mall, and I grimace. Of course Kieren would let me walk around looking like this. There aren't any towels—it's a budget hotel, no amenities on offer—but I grab toilet paper and scrub.

It's just when I'm reaching for the last splotch that my entire display fills with a call, and I tumble off-balance, hitting my hip against the side of the bathtub before going down.

"You all right?" Kieren calls in.

"Yes!" I snap. It's not his fault that I was taken by surprise, but I'm still mad at him adjacently. "You're on this too?"

"I'm seeing it. Should I answer?"

"*Wait.*"

I stumble to my feet. When I exit the bathroom, Kieren remains diagonal on the bed, though he's flipped onto his stomach now. He's braced on his elbows, casual while he flips through a comic book. There's a stack that he plucked from the front pocket of his bag and placed on the bedside table, scattered alongside various Atahuan-language newspapers that he must have picked up on his walk between the landing station and the Lovers' Café. I scan the large print, which screams, NIK GRANT'S DARING ESCAPADE, NIK GRANT AND ATAHUA'S DOWNFALL, NIK GRANT AND—before hurrying to sit at the foot of the bed.

"Ready."

The call connects. With the both of us on a shared line, our systems communicate and void the double display, projecting into the room instead.

There's no image cast onto the wall. Only a quavering audio waveform, bouncing up and down when a voice says, "Hello, cadets. You can hear me well?"

"We hear you," I answer.

"I've never seen this call origin before," Kieren adds. He's swiping through the metadata on the display still open in his eyes.

"It's a back channel to make sure we don't get any wiretapping." The waveform shrinks small while the line rustles. The caller is rummaging through paper on their end. "All right. Cadets Lia Ward and Kieren Murray, welcome to your briefing on the ground."

I got mentioned first, I mouth to Kieren.

Kiss my ass, Kieren mouths back.

"I'm Kam—that's spelled with a K—officer number 4092, stationed in Medaluo under NileCorp employment and assigned liaison for academy exams," our caller goes on. "All material relevant to your posting will reach you through me. If you are contacted by anyone else claiming to possess information, assume it to be fraudulent and get in touch with me immediately, understand?"

"Yes," Kieren and I answer in unison.

"Great. So easy. I'm looking at your administrative task list, and your first step tomorrow will be to register Mr. Murray with Voluntary Declaration of Foreign Visitors at the nearest precinct. Miss Ward, you are welcome to join him if you want to declare yourself an Atahuan tourist, but chances are low you'll be asked for identification."

We nod along. Even if Kam can't see us, I suppose the sentiment is understood. I can't envision the person that accompanies this voice—it's been altered to be rid of any identifying features, no indication of man or woman, old or young.

"Shortly following registration, you may proceed to the last-known whereabouts of Mr. Chung. We—as in the company—will have your entry route prepared accordingly. Find what you can inside. You're looking for likely causes of his disappearance, his next steps." A pause. "Gauging by how thin your briefing folder is, I gather your academy believes this should be a quick examination."

Personally, I thought our folder was rather thick. We have ten weeks to complete our final posting. NileCorp wouldn't design it to be as easy as infiltrating Chung's last-known whereabouts and simply reporting on his possible motivations.

"Sorry," I interject. "I thought our briefing said the goal was to find Chung."

"That is correct."

"You think that'll be doable only having his last-known whereabouts?"

"It depends on whether he's on the move or not," Kam answers. "We can recalibrate accordingly after. This line is open to your call at any time if you want to report in."

Without any further pomp, Kam hangs up. The screen disappears from the wall, the audio waveform collapsing.

"That was anticlimactic," Kieren says. "I'd assumed there would be more information."

"They did say it was a NileCorp outpost contact, not a source," I return. Register with the precinct. Proceed to the Upper Sea National Data Center, where Chung was seen exiting. "Does tomorrow's plan sound right to you?"

"Yeah," Kieren replies. "It sounds right. You?"

I nod. With that exchange, I'm made certain about our next steps. Our mutual approval does more for me than the call from NileCorp, than any briefing they wrote out for us. I worry often that I don't form enough of my own opinions, that I'm only adopting what I've heard from others. When I contribute to any discussion, I enter a mode of performance, speaking for the sake of it, disagreeing only to impress. We may be on a posting now where our recordings are actually judged at the end, but even when I'm attending classes at the academy, there's always an invisible committee nodding to my words, and I'm never quite saying what I think: I'm saying what would be best to believe.

Half the time I can't fully trust my opinions until I obtain positive reception, but I do trust Kieren. His confidence doesn't waver, and it's nice to be on the right side of it.

The pause between us lulls long. I run a quick search in my display.

"The precinct opens tomorrow at nine o'clock," I announce. "I suppose I'm going to sleep."

Kieren tilts his head. I wait a beat.

"Are you," I try, "going to offer to take the floor?"

"Absolutely not."

That synergetic moment was nice while it lasted. My back teeth grit together. "Can you at least straighten up then, so I can have half the bed properly?"

With the comic book still clutched in his hand, Kieren slowly shifts his long legs, adjusting onto one side of the bed. Then he resumes reading.

"You're unbearable."

"Thank you."

"You should brush your teeth."

"Okay, Mom."

I grab the edge of the blanket and toss it over his head.

"Hey!"

With a click of my fingers, I turn the lights off, getting comfortable on the mattress. "Good night." I'm a flurry of activity on purpose, jostling him left and right when I shove a pillow between us. The bed is large enough that I doubt we'd touch in the night anyway, but it's more for the sentiment than actual necessity. "Don't disturb me when you get up for the bathroom."

11

EIRALE

I don't sleep.

Morning comes, and Miz stirs, stretching her arms over her head. She rolls upright groggily. Her first move is to glance at me. My unblinking eyes must give her a fright, because she makes a noise, flinching.

"Okay, sure," she mutters when she recovers. "Too good to get under the blankets?"

I'm not often tired. A consequence of my time upcountry during the academy. I didn't sleep much then either, convinced it wouldn't have a detrimental impact, and the habit has stuck.

"I overheat easily."

After Nik deposited me back in the room, I spent the night thinking instead. NileCorp wants me to stay with Nik. Nik wants to get to Kunlun. If I'm going to push him into NileCorp's hands, then I do exactly what Nik Grant wants. I'll draw him a path into Kunlun.

Miz clambers up, ambling to the curtains. I'd pulled them closed after I returned, not wanting to draw anyone's eye to the location of my little excursion. With the new morning, Miz pushes the fabric to either side of the balcony. The dilapidated room brightens. Its stains in the corner form discernible shapes. The peeling wallpaper behind the television reveals a ring of mold that almost resembles the insignia of Atahua.

Though light glows through the glass, it has a lifeless quality to it, polluted by the perpetual layer of smog haunting Medaluo at its stratosphere. The skies are expectantly gray, spotted with darker clouds that I see only when I stand and walk to the balcony glass, craning my neck for the strip visible past the tall buildings. Four floors down, on the ground level, the lady with the food cart has disappeared.

It's quiet in Upsie. Mornings usually are downcountry. The city has been cratered from its financial epicenter out to its factories. The former has transferred its personnel upcountry—they'll be logging in from the safety of their home right about now—and the latter has switched to automation. If there is early movement on the street below, a lone bicycle or a tattered car, it is someone off to keep watch over an empty building, ensuring it isn't vandalized while operations stay virtual. Someone going out to a manor and nannying the infants until they turn five years old and are mature enough to be scanned into the StrangeLoom system.

Or someone who can only work in the real, like those in the national data center, toiling away at the servers.

"Air quality isn't too bad today."

"Winds must be blowing pollution north," Miz replies dully. She tugs the curtain, like she's trying to smooth out the creases and tatters. "It'll be worse in Threto. The mountains lock the smoke in the basin."

As the day starts growing brighter, that's when the activity increases downcountry too. Tents on the streets rustle. Squatters who were taking refuge in abandoned buildings exit before they're caught by patrol officers.

"Threto," I say, "is also notoriously gridlocked by Medaluo's government surveillance." And consequently, impossible to enter or exit unnoticed because of its position in that mountain basin.

Miz shrugs. "We'll be fine. We'll hack through it."

To get into Threto, they're going to need to do more than scramble the cameras. It's not Upsie, the city where foreigners are expected. In Threto, they'll need the cameras to think we have existing identities registered in the city, or else their police drones will be after us in a split second.

"Why are you doing this?" I ask suddenly.

"Sorry?"

I knock a knuckle to the glass. "This. Terrorizing Atahua. Adventuring through Medaluo with—and forgive me for assuming here—an end goal of terrorizing Atahua some more."

"Why are *you* doing what you do?" she returns. "Loyal to NileCorp without any reason."

"The reason is survival under capitalism," I say. "Back to you."

Miz huffs, shoving her hands into her pockets. It pulls the loose material of her dark green trousers. Something tickles the back of my brain. It's the same itch as smelling a perfume that I haven't used in years. The déjà vu of visiting a site I've seen in my dreams. For ten weeks, I was in virtual Medaluo performing a mission I can't remember. Any plan I come up with here to get into Kunlun *must* take some inspiration from what I decided to do last time. I am still the same person. I wouldn't think differently just because I don't have the memory.

"Have we met already?" I ask before Miz can speak again.

She rears back. "We—" Her jaw makes a sound when she takes a moment, amending her answer. "No. Of course not."

A quick knock on our door interrupts my retort, which is for the best because I was going to accuse Miz of lying. Nik marches in. He looks like he hasn't slept either, still in the same collared black shirt, a clump of his curly hair flat at the side. The glasses don't hide his dark circles.

"Good morning," he says.

"Not really," I reply.

Blare comes in next, chomping on a persimmon. They look bright and rested. They've also hung two bags off each shoulder, which doesn't seem sustainable. "Are we going?"

"Let's walk through the agenda first."

Nik takes out his handheld, pointing it at the wall. He slides his finger across the surface, and a beam of light shoots from the top of the device, projecting its screen onto the white wall, the right edge slightly cut off by the television. He frowns. Pinches the screen on the handheld, and the projected light shrinks by a few inches too, fitting neatly on the wall without being cut off.

"Our target location is the Upper Sea National Data Center, which holds a file that comprises one-third of a program we're after," he begins without fanfare. The blueprint appears on the wall. "There's a main front entrance and a side door used for mail collection. Upsie's data center sits east of the city in an industrial area. Security will be alerted to any lurkers. We need to use the main entrance with legitimate credentials if we want to avoid notice."

He swipes his finger, changing the projection.

"Here are the eighteen employees working at the data center today. I'm welcoming thoughts on whether there's anyone in particular we should be targeting."

I read through the brief profiles displayed on the wall. Miz must have written this up, or at the very least sorted the information she found to put this together. Name, age, position, title.

"I still don't think it matters," Miz says. "Whoever we can clone from the parking lot."

"There's the matter of the human fail-safe," Nik supplies. It sounds like a reminder, like they've discussed this prior and hit a wall here too. "Any secure facility is going to put an additional barrier in front of someone simply bum-rushing an employee for a badge. In this case, it's the person running the reception desk."

"Unfortunate," Miz mutters.

Nik ignores her. "We need to think about which credentials make the best case that the receptionist doesn't ring an alarm."

Blare bites down noisily on the persimmon. I've narrowed my eyes, and Nik must take that for some sort of response.

"Soldier," he says, "we may not be in Kunlun yet, but your input is appreciated here nonetheless."

"Trying to test me?" I ask wryly.

"I'd quite like to know what you're thinking, so yes, I suppose it is a test."

I tuck my loose hair behind my ears. NileCorp is waiting in Offron. NileCorp wants the program Nik is after, all three parts of it.

"You're speaking about the receptionist being a human fail-safe," I say. I gesture at the wall. "I don't see them here."

"This list is only the employees with security clearance throughout the facility," Miz explains. "They're the ones who can get us into the server rooms. The receptionist can only enter the lobby."

"Pull up the receptionist's profile."

Nik frowns, visibly trying to catch up with my train of thought. Nonetheless, he taps open a new window on his handheld, and in seconds he's on a government page, navigating the full roster for the data center's public-facing employees.

"Here."

Xixi Leung, graduate of Upper Sea University with a degree in information studies. She's young—somewhere in her early twenties. I look from her smiling picture, to Miz, then back again.

"What time is it?" I ask.

Blare checks the watch on their wrist. Nik lets them have it, though the time is sitting in front of him on his glasses too.

"Six in the morning."

"Around two hours before employees are expected at the data center, I'd estimate," I say. "Any chance we can find Xixi's address?"

Miz's glasses light up too. "You know what they say about our favorite surveillance state: *If you hold it, you may as well upload it.* I'll browse through traffic cameras and search for a snapshot of her license at police checkpoints."

"Are we bum-rushing her?" Blare asks.

"Yes," I say simply. "And once we do, someone still needs to show up for work so they don't report a missing receptionist." I look at Miz meaningfully. Her eyes catch mine behind her glasses, then flit away upon instinct. A second later, she freezes, understanding my idea. She turns slowly to the image of Xixi on the wall.

"You're kidding," she says.

"You look more like her than I do."

"No one is going to think I *am* her."

"They don't need to," Nik cuts in. He's understood too, and by his tone, he's on board. "The employees will assume someone new got brought in. The cameras won't be immediately suspicious if you have some resemblance to her, and we'll get a face covering on you so facial recognition in the surveillance system won't identify you as an intruder. This only needs to buy us enough time to get in and out once we clone the first available credentials from the parking lot."

Miz drags her hands down her face. Out of the corner of my eye, I can sense Nik inspecting me, sentry to the slightest change in my expression.

I suppose he liked my contribution. I wonder if he set me up to suggest it, whether he offered up all the dots to connect. Again and again, I encounter the same simple question. *Why?*

A quick *beep beep beep* sounds from Nik's pocket. While I jolt, everyone else in the room scrambles, immediately prompted to action. Miz rushes to pull the curtains closed. Nik has already turned on his heel, waving Blare into the hallway.

"What is that?" I ask. "What's going on?"

"Let's go," Nik returns. "Our presence here has been registered."

12

LIA

In my dream, I'm happy about a bowl of soup placed in front of me. I wrap my hands around the ceramic, and its warmth envelops my fingers, settles deep into my palms. The aroma wafts up—hearty, smooth, a hint of spice. My mother made this for me. She loves me, and I am safe. She brought me into this world. She'll do whatever it takes to make sure I'm ready for it. The soup wavers when a shudder jolts through the table. I lift my head to ask my mom if she felt it too.

But when I call out, she won't face me. She won't even look at me.

I startle awake.

My pulse is beating a racket while I make sense of my surroundings, emerging from my daze. I'm in the hotel room, I've been placed in Upsie, it's early morning, and today we begin work on our exam posting.

I breathe out. The dream felt so real. I can still smell the busy kitchen and feel the heat emanating from something lovingly prepared. I'm not sure what any of that was about, whether I was remembering Mallory or my mind made it up for fun. It definitely wasn't my birth mom—she was long gone by the time I had the motor functions to pick up a bowl of soup.

My body shifts, trying to rise. More of my senses return gradually, but the phantom sensation of something warm remains pressed to my skin.

I move my hands, and they're fine, adjusting until I can get onto my elbows and peer down—

I freeze. I don't know why *my* first instinct is to avoid getting caught, even though Kieren is the one using me as a pillow, his head resting on my stomach and his back to me, legs curled so that they don't dangle off the bed. Suddenly I'm unsure if I'm breathing too hard, if the slight movements of my torso are enough to wake him.

"Kieren," I manage to whisper.

His shoulder twitches, but he doesn't stir. Kieren sleeps in a way only someone who feels safe can, without bracing for sudden disturbance, without guarding his vulnerable undersides. The image is almost comforting.

"Kieren," I say again, louder this time.

Still no response.

I smack the back of his head. Lightly.

"Ow!" he protests, rousing awake and sitting groggily. "What gives?"

"Comfy, were we?"

He glances down. In live time I track the moment he makes sense of where he was sleeping, where he must have been sleeping if he's just sat up in the middle of the bed.

"Wow, Lia," he says. "I know you liked me, but you didn't have to drag me on top of you in the middle of the night."

I hurl a pillow at him. "You are such a—"

• • • •

While Kieren is showering, I put on the hotel kettle, standing guard by the water and making two tiny braids in my overgrown bangs. I'm sifting through our briefing in my display again. It's become a nervous tic at this point—I've read everything cover to cover, twice.

I've taken notes on Kam's ground briefing. They didn't recommend any of the miscellaneous matters that other cadets might be tending to, like buying transport cards or withdrawing cash, so I figure our task doesn't warrant them.

In Upsie, our presence in and of itself won't be suspicious. When NileCorp has matters outside of the coastal city, though, they like to send Medans. Patrolling police officers aren't going to stop a face like mine. Non-Medans will be asked for their tourist pass. If they don't have one, they will be questioned, their entire itinerary closely examined in suspicion of being a foreign agent.

I'm not sure how many foreign agents they've actually caught that way. A large part of it is for the theatrics. So that people at home feel safe.

"Ward!" Kieren bellows from the bathroom.

"What?" I answer, equally loud. My display automatically closes, triggered by my shift in attention. I finish tying my small braid with a clear elastic band.

"There aren't any towels in here."

"I know." Without hesitation, I grab the tea towels on the counter and walk into the bathroom. There's a yelp, and then the rapid rustle of the shower curtain.

"Can you *knock*?"

"Here."

"Okay! Thank you!" Kieren says, strained. Half of him has stepped out of the shower, and the other half remains inside the water spray. In a scramble, he's bunched the clear curtain in front of him to stay decent, and I toss the tea towel at him.

"Need anything else?" I ask. "Happy to help."

"Lia, get *out*!"

Laughing, I swivel around, closing the door behind me. My display puts the briefing back in front of my eyes when I go to pour boiling water into two to-go cups, dropping a tea bag into each. We must be staying at a hotel designed for foreigners, because tea bags are a travesty in Medaluo. While the tea steeps, I mark the page I was on and close the briefing.

Kieren emerges from the bathroom, flinging the door open. He's dressed now—a tight T-shirt and black sweatpants. I raise an eyebrow in comment. An attempt at a tourist look, I gather, but his appearance is too sharp to be entirely convincing. Kieren Murray is the type of person to live in button-downs and khakis, maybe a pair of jeans if he's feeling spicy. When he runs a hand through his wet hair, it drips a neat row along his shoulder, like even the water is afraid of messing up his appearance.

I'm still wearing the same clothes from yesterday.

"Ready to go?"

"Yes, sir."

The tea is extremely hot when I pass him his cup, and Kieren takes it with a sniff, trying to determine what it is without opening the lid. It's busy in the hallway. Two doors stay propped ajar for their occupants to have a lively conversation. A cleaning lady pushes her large cart along. We're forced into single file to skirt around it. At the elevator, a woman is leaving her room at the same time and enters with us, giving a brief nod but otherwise staring ahead with her gaze unfocused, watching something on her display.

We stay silent the entire way down. The elevator reaches the ground floor. As soon as we emerge from the hotel's main door, the woman swerves in the opposite direction to us, her shoulder bag thudding against her hip. There's a key chain in the shape of Threto's skyline dangling from the bag strap.

"Did you hear about the zoo in Threto where they painted a dog to look like a panda because they didn't have the cash to import an actual one over?"

Kieren has already finished his tea. He tosses the cup into a trash can at the corner. We turn out the smaller street for a main road.

"That was a propaganda campaign, Ward," he says. Immediately, the bustle starts around us. Upsie in the morning is a different city. It trades the nightlife for the coffee runs, the neon for a stream of gray and beige. Avatars who came in for the bars and the karaoke have logged out and left space for the daily users entering to work. Now it's all pencil skirts and briefcases and pedestrian lights going off every ten seconds to facilitate a flow of people walking from landing stations into their corporate buildings. "You didn't see the correction note that got added?"

"What?" I open my display quickly. I run a search to find the post again, and sure enough, a clarifying note has been added to the Atahuan news account that uploaded this to the feed. *Post is intentionally portraying Medaluo in negative light by implying their zoogoers wouldn't know the difference between a dog and a panda. Threto National Zoo dressed up these dogs as pandas on purpose to open a "panda dog" joke exhibit for a viral moment.*

"Damn," I mutter. I'd trusted it without thinking—Teryn Moore was the one who shared it with an angry emoji and put it on my feed, so I'd reacted accordingly. "It got me."

"Don't feel too bad. Who's ever heard of opening a joke exhibit to get hits online?"

The places that need more frequenters to stay afloat, I suppose. We approach the crosswalk light, and Kieren indicates we can cross to the other side of the road while the perpendicular light is going. I can see the precinct already, a red and blue blinker flashing from the wide double doors as though there might be a chance of mistaking the bright sign out front too, declaring the station to be operating on the second to fifth floors. It's a very round building, shaped like a beehive built from steel.

Kieren and I break from the crowd after the next light and head into the building. He takes the steps up two at a time, but I make a more careful trek, watching where I'm placing my feet. There's an old man and an old woman by the entrance in the middle of an argument—their accents are thicker than I'm used to, the sort of Medan that was spoken back when the country still raised children in rural regions, when different areas could develop twangs and idiosyncratic sounds. It's all straight and narrow city-polished syllables now. Purely to be nosy, I turn on Global Ear in my settings—and suddenly their words switch to Atahuan, translated by the system before it hits my perception. They're arguing about a traffic ticket.

Kieren casts me an amused look to signal he's eavesdropping too, and I switch off Global Ear hurriedly, as though he might be able to tell I cheated by some glint in my eye. The academy teaches us language acquisition diligently despite the alternatives available. Global Ear is great for tourists, but not so much for undercover students. When we're relying on Global Ear, we can't actually tell if someone is speaking a different language than us, which makes things horribly awkward if we reply in Atahuan.

"I'll wait here," I say inside reception. I would have forgotten it was daytime the moment I entered through the doors. Heavy drapes smother the windows, blocking all natural illumination. The naked orange bulbs on the reception desks cast a sharp glow in the morning's stead.

Kieren nods. "I shouldn't be long. I can't imagine they're going to ask me anything hard."

He heads toward the receptionist. I fold my arms, resolute to stay put, but my eyes wander the ground floor's rounded walls, finding a directory that announces floor six as a lawyers' office and floor seven a nail salon.

The bulbs on the desks flicker. Kieren is waved into the elevator, exiting the lobby. I stay put for a full two minutes before my attention snags on one thick exposed wire that runs along the wall, then down a set of stairs. Each time the bulbs flicker, the wire glows pink like a summoning. Brighter and brighter.

I go to investigate. It seems an odd design choice until I curve around the desk and inspect the descending staircase, where the wire ends with a pointed arrow. *Ah.* It's only showing the way to the basement.

Kieren's interview will need a good fifteen minutes or so, assuming he doesn't mess up wildly and get the military called on us. I have time to spare.

I start down the steps, sniffing at the aroma wafting up. Just as my nose predicted, I reach the basement and come upon a small collection of shops, each one thronged with building employees waiting to make their pick. They're serving Medan breakfast foods that I've seen in the feed videos I watch. Fried dumplings, soy milk, dry noodles. The walls glow in varying yellow and blue, lit by the wires that thread through the shop signs, and I don't draw any attention when I slink into the busy space, tipping my head back to read the menus. Though my mouth waters, it doesn't feel right to take a seat among the employees of the building. It's too blasé, too forgetful of what I'm doing here. I am not in Medaluo for a cultural heritage trip.

"Sample?"

The server bot behind a counter extends its arm, offering a chunk of a meat bun with a toothpick through it. The other stalls have lines, but this one is empty. The server's facial emoticon looks sad, the square surface of its head scuffed and missing a piece on the left.

"Thank you," I say, taking one.

As soon as I try the sample, I know why the stall is so empty. The meat inside is at once sweet and too salty, which doesn't seem physically possible. Maybe it's not—perhaps the system coded this wrong, and the human owner of the stall hasn't caught the mistake yet. I barely stop myself from gagging, quickly swallowing the sample. I'm glad I've already shielded my expression away from the server. I don't want its sad emoticon to turn even sadder.

The basement level isn't large, so I reach the end of the shops quickly. The final stall hides a discreet corner that turns into a corridor, running a short length before it gives way to an emergency exit marked with a neon green sign. I would have expected to find a bathroom or a supply closet hidden here, but instead my eyes land upon a booth pressed to the wall and a seat inside glowing red. A.I. LOVE PSYCHIC! the exterior reads. YOUR HIGHLY ACCURATE READING.

I slink over to the booth and pull the half-drawn curtain aside, settling myself onto the red seat.

"Welcome."

The sudden greeting comes with all-surround sound. I jerk back, hitting my skull hard on the booth wall, and my display immediately offers a pop-up asking if I need help. I swipe away the notification with a wince. There's no danger here except my own lack of spatial awareness.

"I didn't even activate you yet," I grumble. The screen in front of the seat has woken up. Though there's a voice speaking to me, there's no visual depiction of the bot, only an audio waveform that trembles to signal its presence. It's just like the call we had with Kam, except this is an intentional choice to help us forget there's no one real present. In tenth-grade economics, my final project was about the millions of dollars that get dumped into market research every year to choose what sort of AI a select group of audience is most receptive to. Artificially generated faces creep most people out. Service bots that use anything other than the plain emoticons get significantly fewer customers. Driver bots should be nothing more than text on a screen to respond to emergency stop instructions. I guess the love psychic market decided to forgo the face entirely and focus on voice.

"I sensed your presence in my domain," the booth replies. It's soothing, vaguely female. That specific timbre must be extensively market-researched too. It must also switch languages depending on the user sitting inside, because I didn't have to click anything to activate it in Atahuan. "Would you like me to begin your psychic love reading?"

I pull my legs up and cross them. "How can a machine be psychic?"

"How can humans be psychic?"

It's got me there. "Fine. Go on."

A pop-up appears in my display asking for five Medan dollars. That's like fifty cents in Atahua, so I send it without thinking twice. The screen ponders for a moment. Its waveform vibrates, the booth purring.

"I'm getting a lot of resistance from your aura," the booth says slowly. "Focus your energy on what you want to understand. Think of two questions about love, and then ask me one."

I resist the urge to laugh. I'm the one who sat down in this seat voluntarily, so I'm not allowed to roll my eyes, but of course it needs a question. It's failed to read anything out of my mannerisms. I fidget too much for an algorithm to decide which twitch was intentional.

"Okay," I say, tilting my head back. "Will I ever be in a normal relationship?"

The question falls from my mouth before I know I'm going to ask it. I watch the screen's sound wave display turn flat entirely, processing in silence.

"Define normal."

"You know." I wave my hand around. "Pull a search for every depiction in media. It's pretty well-defined already."

"I understand. And you identify with the majority depicted in this media?"

"Probably not." I pause. "I suppose that's where my question comes from."

"I am running a quick scan on your feed," the booth reports. "Three percent of the human population is asexual or on the asexual spectrum. *Normal* fits there too."

My eyebrows shoot up. "I didn't realize you were allowed to look at my feed."

"You identify as demisexual in your social profile's bio. The answer is right in front of me."

"You're supposed to be a love *psychic*."

"Psychic in the age of technology means I am all-seeing to data. Your question is very easily answered. Your normal can be constructed on your terms."

Whoever built this booth should be sued for false advertising. It's not a psychic love AI, it's a data-conscious love AI. They probably reuse this code in therapy services somewhere.

"I don't think that explains everything," I say stubbornly, "and I feel wrong for it."

"You have friends who identify similarly, is that true?"

The booth's tone rises on the end of its sentence, as though it might be a question for me to answer. I know it means it as a statement. It's probably scanning through my friends list on my feed.

"Yeah." Every few weeks when I have a solution for Rayna's misery, she's rolling around the floor bemoaning that she can't just *get over Hailey, okay? It's hard for me to like someone, and when I do, it's all-consuming, so please, Lia, just help me talk to her, I'm so bad at this.* "A few."

"And do you think they're... wrong for it?"

"No," I say instantly. "Of course not."

"Then why think differently for yourself?"

"You tell me," I say. "What does your psychic reading say?"

It asked me to think of two questions, after all, one spoken, one kept. In the back of my mind, within proximity during any exchange, always hovering somewhat within reach, there is one question: *Why don't I ever feel* right?

I'm always loath to leave virtual because it takes away that reason for there to be a barrier between me and the world, me and being normal, me and how most people experience emotion and sensation. I hate that going downcountry takes away my excuse for that disconnect, that there's only my organic body down there, and if I think too hard on why, why, why I can't respond the way everyone else does, I fear my clutch on reality may disintegrate, my arms and legs will stop moving, and I'll find that I've never been real, that this is some mass hallucinated state and I don't exist.

"Your user panel tells me you're a tourist from Atahua. Do you think this has any bearing? To grow up in a place where you are cast as the enemy must have shaped how you view yourself."

"Of course it did," I say, and then I'm irritated, because even this stupid psychic box in Medaluo thinks being Medan is why I'm constantly floating one layer removed from everyone in this world. "So?"

"Deep breaths, please. If your pulse elevates any higher, I have to call emergency services."

I glare at the booth's waveform. "I'm fine. I'm calm."

"It seems to me that your future holds having conversations with yourself," the psychic booth says. "There's more to sexuality and love than defining your exact position and stance. In the end, it's about figuring out how much you're willing to accept. What you have decided you deserve.

What you make peace with in the space you fit into. I see love for you. It's up to you to let yourself have it rather than keep it outside."

I have to fight the urge to scoff. As nice as the sentiment is, it seems absurd for it to be as simple as me *deciding* I should feel less wrong in the space I fit into. If I could, wouldn't I have *done it by now*?

"Ward, there you are."

The curtain suddenly flings open. It gives me a great fright, though at least I don't hit my head again when I swivel fast.

"Oh, hey," I say breezily. "Did you finish your interview?"

Kieren holds up a card. I recognize its blue color for the tourist pass, so I'll take that as a yes.

"What are you doing in here?" he asks in return.

"Can't you tell?" I gesture to the screen. Conveniently, the booth has gone quiet on me. I suppose my five dollars have been used up. "I'm getting an AI psychic love reading."

Kieren's gaze sweeps over the booth slowly. I can see how badly he wants to make fun of me. He's just struggling to decide what to address first.

"You know most of these things have real people on the other end, right?"

I blink. "What?"

"Yeah." He cranes his head into the booth, scanning along the top. "They call it AI to disarm you into talking, but actual AI tested poorly with consumers. They liked the humans better. These companies hire people downcountry to sit in front of a laptop for a few bucks every hour and chat when a booth gets activated."

I should have known the booth sounded too astute. I clamber out of the seat, miffed that I've needed Kieren to correct me on Medaluo's way of life twice in the span of an hour.

"Whatever," I mutter. "You were taking a long time. I had to amuse myself."

Kieren tries to get in my way when I stand. I stomp on his foot. Accidentally.

"Ow," he hisses.

"Do you *mind*—"

I cut myself off, spotting a flash of movement behind him. Something has followed him into the corridor. A blur of black movement: I barely would have noticed if it weren't for the obnoxious glowing red of the booth, lighting up the space and reflecting back in the cat's eyes when it sees that I've spotted it. It darts away.

"Kieren," I gasp, yanking his wrist and breaking into a run. "It's the talking cat!"

13

EIRALE

We pile onto the subway.

I expect the train cars to be as empty as the station, but the seats are crammed tight, passengers with their arms curled around their stomachs, faces covered by masks, flashing glasses perched on their noses so they can browse with their hands free.

The doors close. An automated announcement declares the city center to be the next stop, and the subway surges into movement again. We've tracked dirt into the train car upon entering, though that's the fault of the dilapidated station. Other passengers don't make any remarks. At the far side, a half-empty bottle of soda rolls back and forth, splashing liquid onto the floor with each turn.

"You're not afraid that surveillance is going to follow you onto public transport?" I say to Nik. We evacuated the hotel and hurried across the street into the subway station with such haste that I still haven't registered what exactly we were running from.

"What?" Nik bellows.

The roar of the tracks drowns me out completely. One of the windows has been cracked open in the train car, which means I can barely hear myself. At the very least, the other passengers aren't going to hear me.

"I said," I shout, "you're risking public transport surveillance?"

Again, Nik goes, "What?"

My hand lashes out, gripping his collar hard and pulling him down. It's such an abrupt move that he complies, his ear brought to my mouth.

"There's a camera!" I shout. "Right above us!"

Nik turns to look.

"Don't worry about that," he says. He doesn't make the effort to shout, but now my hearing is enough to collect the shape of his words, my lip-reading filling in the blanks. "Public transport surveillance is older than what's on the streets. Easier to mess with."

I release his collar, frowning. I've rumpled the fabric there, but Nik only has to reach up and pat the creases casually before his shirt is straight again. He's kept his other palm flat over his jacket pocket the whole time, protecting his handheld inside. I have to assume we're not riding far to reach the address that Miz found for Xixi Leung.

The train car shudders when it passes along rough tracks. There's a row of three seats to my side, but only one man sitting there, the seats on either side of him taken up by his bags. He has his glasses on a transparent setting. I can see what he's doing on his screens, albeit mirror flipped. He cycles between different apps to access the feed. In fascination, I watch him scroll for five seconds on each interface before getting bored and opening a new one. There are multiple ways to access the feed: on one app it's text-based, and on another it's video-forward. They used to be owned by separate companies, but the moment any app grows prominent, NileCorp purchases them as subsidiaries, so it's hard to perceive them differently when our profile is shared across everything. As much as I scroll the feed too, I try not to put anything on it.

The man, with his transparency settings as bright as daylight, types in a post declaring that he hates it when perfectly normal Medan girls cut their hair to Atahuan styles—

"*Excuse* me—"

"This is our stop!" Miz shouts, grabbing my elbow. The train car slows, then comes to a halt. Before I can say anything, she pulls me off along with half the other passengers, all spilling out at this stop with their backpacks and knapsacks.

"Did you see that?" I ask.

"I try not to read backward if I can help it. It gives me headaches," she replies. She lets go of me quickly. "But yes, I saw that. Please mind your business. Getting into a scuffle that has you thrown into Medan jail counts as failure to hold up your end of the bargain."

A clap comes from ahead. Blare, trying to get Miz's attention after they've already jumped the turnstile to avoid scanning out. Nik's even farther ahead. He pauses by the staircase just long enough that we've seen where he's going before surging out first.

Another commuter checks my shoulder hard while walking by.

"Ugh," I mutter. The train car may have been full, but the exodus into the station still doesn't warrant walking so closely to me. The space is large. The black marble walls are scuffed with dirt, the painted orange ceilings flecking wherever there is water damage seeping from the pipes overhead. At one point they built these stations to accommodate the rush-hour crowds coming into the city in the morning and leaving in the evening, but downcountry has downsized since then.

"This way."

I follow Miz. I'd had my eye on the commuter who slammed into me, but they disappeared into thin air, turning the other way upon hopping the turnstile. Miz goes first when we approach, easily lifting over the arm. I duck instead, and while I'm out of view, I stick my hand into my pocket, confirming a suspicion.

That lumbering commuter was someone on Teryn's team. And gauging by the tiny metal sphere hanging out in my pocket, they've slipped me a tracker.

I emerge from the turnstile with my expression smoothed out, my arms swinging at my sides. Miz isn't paying attention anymore anyway, resolute on staring forward. Blare waits for us before we ascend the steps out of the station into central Upsie under the cover of the other commuters. They disperse in varying directions, but we walk straight slowly, catching up with Nik.

"I've mapped us," he says, already walking again the moment we approach. "Three blocks away."

I sniff. Something is burning in the distance—chemical and metallic, wafting from the poisoned sea on our right. Last night's rain is going to start again soon too. It had finished falling by the time I was hauled back to the hotel, but the clouds stayed plump, waiting for their next opportunity. I'd give it a half an hour more before it bursts.

"Backtrack."

I don't hear Nik's instruction in time. As he turns, I slam right into him, still eyeing the clouds, and instead of waiting for me to maneuver properly, he grabs the sides of my arms, turning me around.

"Hey, hey"—I twist away—"I can do that myself."

He must think it's a complaint against the contact. A flash of alarm crosses his face. Nik releases me, splaying his hands out to prove himself unoffending.

I was only thinking about keeping him away from my pocket.

"Why is there police?" Miz hisses. "Surely not for us."

"It looks like they're roping off the street," Nik murmurs in reply. He picks up his pace. I didn't get a chance to see, and it's too late to crane my neck back without inciting suspicion. "It's not for us. They would already be searching the area otherwise. It could be general reports of foreign presence. Maybe NileCorp sent a few lackeys."

I face forward. I go where Nik steers, obedient while he pauses to check our diverted route. We turn into an alleyway, continue past a restaurant's open back door. Oil and salt thicken the air's scent, heavy against the humid threat of rain. Two line cooks stand outside for their break, eyeing us suspiciously. One of them says something under their breath.

"I think we almost got robbed," Blare whispers after we've emerged from the alleyway.

"Not a chance," Nik replies. "Too many cameras."

"That doesn't stop people from manipulating footage," I mutter.

Nik frowns. The next alley spits us out onto a wide road.

"We're here."

Up ahead, four residential high-rises appear, our target being the one on the farthermost left, half-tucked behind a copse of browning trees. These are some of the tallest buildings I've seen yet in Upsie. A pair of rats scampers through the abandoned computer pieces at the mouth of the alley, unafraid of our presence while they weave in and out.

Security will be tight. The buildings are well kept, which means there are definitely upcountry users sleeping inside. In every major city, the wealth of the neighborhood is discernible by looking at what time of day its residents are walking around. There are some blocks where residents are downcountry all the time, scraping together day passes to go upcountry only for a nice dinner. Those parts are frequented at every hour. Other areas outside the heart of the city are never frequented, the houses entirely motionless, the driveways dragging dried leaves across the concrete with a gardener coming occasionally to rake them. That's where the proper upper class live, those who work upcountry and only come down for reset days. It's easier to immediately distinguish the difference in Medaluo, because the government is fast to snap up unhoused wanderers and break down their encampments. They'll send them somewhere rural. Atahua just leaves them to lie around when they enter the nicer areas, knowing it will drive sales for more security alarms when the residents panic.

Here, I'd bet there is movement once at the start of the day, another rush at the end of the day, and hollow in the middling hours. That's for the working population who live in between, stepping out for a well-paying downcountry job and coming home to live their after-hours upcountry—meet their friends, see their family. They can afford these apartments because even when most of the world moves to virtual, some jobs never go away. It's similar to being a corporate soldier, I suppose. The pay is good enough to incentivize the risk of coming down. We might get stabbed by a random robbery, but nothing equivalent upcountry is hiring the same.

"Confirm the address, please," Nik says.

"Confirming," Miz replies. "Seventh floor."

"Scalable."

"You need harnesses and ropes if you're going to scale a building," I counter.

"We've got them." Nik waves forward. "Miz and Blare, take a window approach. Quick, quick."

They follow his instructions without protest. I suppose those heavy bags on their backs and shoulders must be good for something, though I wouldn't have expected them to be lugging around harnesses.

"Just them two?" I ask.

"Yes. You're staying with me. Someone's got to open the window."

Nik's scanning the ground, eyeing the abandoned materials left around us. Half a bookshelf. A six-pack of energy drinks that have been emptied out but slotted back into its paper casing. A box that might have once stored a gift delivery. He makes a thoughtful noise, then scoops up the box.

"Does this look like trash?"

"Yes," I answer without hesitation. "It is, in the very literal sense, trash."

"I know, but does it *look* like trash?"

I stare at him. Nik Grant, infamous anarchist. Nik Grant, enemy number one to an all-seeing entity like NileCorp. Asking me if he's holding trash.

"If you hide the oily smear there"—I point at the corner—"I could be convinced that it's new."

"Great. Come on, soldier."

I can't quite smooth down the confused notch that hits my brow. It's still there by the time we're approaching Xixi's building, the glass exterior reflecting back the suspicion I'm wearing in the curl of my lip. Nik pulls open the front door, one arm balancing the box.

I pass through the entrance.

The doorman looks up immediately at our entrance, rising behind the front desk. The dissonance in downcountry design is a sight to behold: smooth marble surface, beautiful and costly and long-lasting, only the desk sits on wooden floorboards that creak and shift, one unhappy resident's temper tantrum away from putting a foot right through the thin paneling. Tall, impenetrable plexiglass to keep the doorman safe from intruders, a small display screen even built into the bottom so he can scroll the feed, though the raw wires sticking out of the fried bulb overhead are more likely to take him out.

"Hello," Nik greets him. "We're here for Xixi in 7C. It's her birthday."

The doorman taps the screen embedded in the plexiglass. "I don't have any expected visitors logged."

"Because it's a surprise." Nik raises the box he dug from the street trash. His Medan is so easy. He has an accent, the sort of tonal clutter that anyone with Atahuan as a primary tongue brings through, but he still speaks as though he should be listened to, as though the imperfections shouldn't matter. "We brought cake. You won't ruin the surprise, will you?"

The doorman frowns. "It's against building policy to let visitors up without informing residents. I'll call up."

"At the very least," Nik implores, "can you say it's a mystery delivery from her company? She's been having such a difficult time. I really think she would appreciate the surprise."

Though the doorman looks annoyed, he thinks on it for a moment and then nods. I clearly haven't given Nik enough credit for his improvisation. *This* is what NileCorp should have been adding to my mixed-reality training rooms.

"Miss Leung," the doorman says into his earpiece when Xixi answers. "You've got a delivery from your company. A mystery, they say. Can I send them up?"

I hear the slightest echo through the earbud, an expression of surprise. Xixi must reply in the affirmative, because the doorman nods and gestures we can proceed to the elevator.

Nik makes a whole show of protecting the "cake" when he turns the corner. One of the elevator doors is already open, waiting for us, the button for the seventh floor lit by the front desk's instruction. We likely wouldn't have been able to activate the button inside if the doorman hadn't allowed it.

"You're making it seem far heavier than cakes actually are," I mutter under my breath.

"It's an expensive cake," he mutters back. The elevator doors close. Despite appearances, the machinery makes a heinously loud clatter before it begins to move. I'm braced for the chance of it breaking down as it hauls up each floor at a snail's pace.

When the elevator opens on the seventh floor, I hear the jangle of keys first. My arm flies out to warn Nik, but he's heard it too. He jabs the button to close the doors. We don't want to run into anyone here. We don't want any of Xixi's neighbors to have made note of us, because then they can provide descriptions when inevitably there is news about Nik Grant in Medaluo, news about a fugitive plotting something against the nation of Atahua and the whole world tunes in with curiosity.

But there are two voices in conversation. Coming from the left, where apartment C would be.

"Wait," I whisper quickly, grabbing Nik's arm to take him off the button. "It's her."

"... all this business with Chung. I've only been here eight months. I bet you this is some veiled threat to get me to stay."

That has to be Xixi. Her voice is high-pitched with the faintest hint of a lisp. Her keys clack together in quick succession while she locks up. Nik and I hold as still as stone. He reaches carefully into his jacket.

"Keep your head down today. There's no use arguing with them about this."

The other voice is deeper. I hadn't thought to suggest checking whether she had a partner, but he clearly lives with her. That was an oversight.

I feel a nudge on my hand. Without looking, I open my palm, and Nik slides something into it. I swipe along the cold edge to identify the item. Tranquilizer. One dose, by the weight of it.

"Ready?" Nik whispers, barely audible under his breath.

"No," I answer.

Xixi and her companion arrive in front of the elevator, stopping short. Nik commands, "Go!" and I drop to the floor, rolling on my shoulder to stay low. I rise only when I've suddenly situated myself behind Xixi. She hasn't yet thought to move out of the way; I take a hold of her shoulders. In that moment of contact, she has the brief chance to jolt, to attempt pulling away, but I already have one end of the tranquilizer pressed to her neck, and my thumb shoves hard on the button. The needle shoots out. I count: one, two, three—

Xixi slumps into deadweight. I catch her before she falls, keeping her on my arm.

In my periphery, Nik has incapacitated the man already too. He hasn't bothered to catch him.

"Bring her in first," he tells me, stepping over the unconscious body.

I watch Nik lean down and pick up the keys that Xixi dropped. Callous and quick, as he was that night in the club. I don't care much for our politicians either. They know what they signed up for. They continue proxy wars in other countries for no reason save to fill their own pockets, and when angered anarchists rise as a result, they only have themselves to blame.

Still, I suppose I expected some sense of mercy from Nik Grant for his ordinary victims. He's not like me, looking out for myself. He's trying to change the world.

But I see only coldness. Here, now, then. He is long beyond anger.

"Come on," he calls back, opening Xixi's apartment.

I wonder what happened to make him this way.

"I'm coming."

I drag Xixi back to her door. Inside, Nik goes to let in Miz and Blare, who are both hovering outside the window with their harnesses flapping with the wind. We're lucky that Xixi didn't activate her home security system when she left: they're impossible to disarm without the multiple passcodes, but most downcountry users don't turn them on unless they're in their Pod. It's too annoying otherwise to go through the steps every day.

While I deposit Xixi on her couch with a grunt of effort, Miz and Blare clamber through. Xixi's unconscious form slumps onto her cushions. Miz pushes the window closed with a thud.

A beat passes. I collect my breath. I haven't had to lift anything heavy in a while.

"What . . . happened?" Blare asks, breaking the tension.

"Unexpected visitor," Nik answers. "It's fine. I'll go move him in. Let's hurry."

Nik steps back out into the hallway, which leaves Blare the open space to beeline for the wardrobe. They pull out a turtleneck. Then a long skirt. The place is sparser than I imagined. A Claw has been left on the vanity chair, still plugged in with the mini side screen active. When I wander into the bedroom, there's another one in the port there, as well as a mattress with no bed frame. No curtains either. The gray clouds hover heavy on the other side. A single raindrop lands on the glass.

I return to the living room to find Miz crouched in front of Xixi, examining her face. She wants to imitate her look as closely as possible, I assume, so I scan the items on the vanity by the television and pluck up an eyeliner pencil. I offer it.

Miz doesn't make any move to receive it.

"I'm not sure if I know how to use that."

"Okay," I reply plainly. "I can help."

That doesn't seem to put her at ease either. Miz wrinkles her nose. "That's fine."

"Miz, stop being resistant," Blare supplies. They're half-buried inside the wardrobe, sifting through the shoes.

"I'm not being resistant," Miz fires back. "Sorry if I don't want this random girl holding a stick that close to my eyeball."

"I'm not a random girl." I pull the lid off the pencil. "I'm your kidnapped corporate soldier who gains nothing from poking your eyeball out. Besides, I'm good at this."

Miz pauses. She looks at me properly, which almost feels like a victory I didn't know I was working toward.

"You've done it before?" she asks.

"Well, not on other people." I gesture to my own face. "But I can do it on myself, so how hard can it be?"

"That inspires confidence." Despite Miz's begrudging manner, she does turn toward me, which I take as permission to proceed. I crouch down and bring the pencil to the outer corner of her eye, drawing the shape that Xixi has. The pencil hasn't been sharpened in a while. The black wax is stubborn upon application as a result, but my hand stays steady. I complete the line across her eyelid and move to the other.

"You're doing great," I offer. The reassurance comes as naturally as a fish flopping along a crosswalk. I am far from the type to coo to put someone at ease. But Miz is doing everything in her power not to twitch and mess up my work, so it deserves some indication that I appreciate the effort.

"It feels like a lifetime ago," she says softly, "but my best friend used to do this for me before we went to parties."

"Where is she now?"

I ask it without thinking. It's only the natural follow-up, an idle question to keep a conversation going.

"They killed her," Miz says. "NileCorp."

Shit. I finish the other eye. I'm saved from saying anything more or—worst-case scenario—from needing to apologize when the front door opens. Nik has returned. He sets the man against the wall, and I stand up, laying the pencil back on the vanity table.

"How's it going in here?" Nik asks.

"Just about ready," Blare declares, emerging from the wardrobe. They hand Miz an outfit they've picked out, dumping it into her arms. Miz, without complaint, steps into another room to change.

Xixi stays passed out. Entirely silent.

"I don't see her badge anywhere," I say.

"Attached to the keys." Nik shakes the bundle in his hands. "It's a small key fob."

"I would have thought there would be an actual picture attached to her entry badge," Miz calls from the other room. "What with this emphasis on my costuming."

It'll be in their database instead, I assume. We'll have to be careful not to let the cameras get too close to Miz.

She emerges from the room, opening her arms to ask for our opinions. A plain white turtleneck, tucked into nondescript jeans.

"All right," Nik says. "Good to go."

I pluck a disposable mask from the box that Xixi has near the door and offer it to her. "You should probably take the septum piercing out. In case it shows through."

"That's homophobic," Miz deadpans. Still, she does it. The nose ring slips into her pocket. The mask goes on. When I look between her and the woman collapsed on the couch, the image is convincing enough.

"Now we're good to go," I decide.

14

LIA

The cat must know immediately that I'm giving chase, because it darts up the stairs in a flash. I don't even consider slowing. No way.

I let go of Kieren to take the stairs three at a time, and then I'm zipping through the ground floor and slamming back out onto the street. I catch the barest glimpse of the cat scampering along the crosswalk.

"Hey!" I scream. The other pedestrians on the street turn to look at me. Shit. I switch to Medan. "Hey! Cat! Stop!"

Good one, Lia. Really advanced vocabulary they taught you in class.

I dart onto the road, catching the last few seconds of the green light. It's unlikely a car would hit me even if I crossed against the light, given how quickly automation responds to environmental roadblocks. Still, I hurry back onto the pedestrian path, my eyes pinned on the cat. I keep it in sight for the length of one long commercial street. I've practically come within three feet of it when the cat turns the corner, and suddenly I have to halt at the intersection because I don't see it anymore.

I drag in a deep breath, making a frenetic search and spinning in two full circles. The storefronts have started to play their holographic advertising for the morning commuters. The drones overhead increase in frequency, zipping by in twos and threes every minute to make deliveries.

Their buzzing is low, easy to tune out. Just when I think I've caught sight of the cat again whipping around people's feet, it's only someone walking their virtual dog.

"*Ugh.*"

I slump down, bracing my hands on my knees. A few seconds later, Kieren approaches holding a bottle of water, offering it out to me like I'm the stray cat collapsed on the street.

"Ran out of stamina?" he asks.

"I didn't see *you* trying to catch up with it," I hiss, snatching the plastic water bottle. On occasion, our avatars can push beyond our usual capacity downcountry, but that takes a shot of emergency adrenaline spiking past our mental barriers and a certain sprinkle of delusion. I'm annoyed at this cat, but we clearly haven't reached the level where I can keep running after it without remembering to be tired. "It bolted as soon as it saw me coming. I'm telling you, we're being spied on."

Kieren frowns while I chug my water. My tongue is parched.

"Upsie definitely incorporates stray cats as a part of the environment," Kieren says. "Most cats *would* be encoded to run from you if you give chase."

"I made eye contact with it. It followed you down and—"

I stop, mid-motion while putting the cap back on the bottle of water. Kieren raises an eyebrow.

"What?"

"You," I say slowly, securing the cap. We've been standing on a street corner to debate, and it's starting to annoy the passersby. I nudge Kieren to stand a little closer to the nearest building—FOUNDSYS, the sign reads over the door. A game development company, gauging by the bell chime of coins ringing from the foyer. "It wasn't following me. It was following you."

"Why would—" He cuts himself off. I wait, seeing if he'll put voice to what has just occurred to him, if he's only taking a moment to gather his thoughts.

Kieren stays quiet.

"What is it?" I prompt.

Kieren inspects the new pop-up on the wall, a trailer for the latest movie tie-in franchise popular in Medaluo. I've seen the ads on the feed, but Atahua won't play it in cinemas.

"Let's start making our way to the data center," he suggests. His gaze turns to me meaningfully. "We can go somewhere with fewer people."

• • • •

We cross the bridge into the east side of the city, up the hills onto the highest point of the rippling valleys.

The self-driving taxi was blowing startlingly cold air that we couldn't figure out how to switch off, and Kieren and I are both shivering when we arrive. I set the drop-off point at a five-minute walk away from our actual destination. I didn't want to run into any employees, nor have the taxi's surveillance capabilities grow curious about why tourists were going to the city's national data center.

"You want my jacket?" Kieren offers.

I clamp down my chattering teeth. "Keep your jacket."

Here, the sea is within view, starting where the sand bleeds out into foam. Medaluo's eastern edge is a muddled grayscale, pulled as blue as StrangeLoom will let it go before the satellites scanning the grunge downcountry grow confused in complaint.

The taxi drives off, and I don't make any move to start walking. Kieren comes up to my side, brushing right against my arm to offer cover from his jacket without admitting that's what he's doing. We stare forward, out into the waters, both pretending to be less interested in the sight.

I have spent most of my formative years inside the academy's gates. I know those grounds like the back of my hand. The Pod could let me go anywhere within the bounds of Atahua while classes aren't in session, but I don't.

So I've never seen the sea until now.

"You don't go anywhere on the weekends, do you?" I ask, though I know the answer.

"No time," Kieren says shortly.

He has me to blame for that. I've sacrificed weekends I could be at home to lock myself in my dorm instead, memorizing my essay answers for Atahuan Literature midterms. I've made use of extended breaks to stay on campus and get a head start on the following week's quizzes. I know how often I see Kieren wandering the common areas too when the winter snow is falling outside, when other cadets go downcountry to train or use their Pods to relax at a ski lodge. I know why I stay, know that he's always right on my ass, snaking up to me with that point zero five decimal difference in our GPA, and I have to imagine the task of catching up to me also consumes every minute Kieren might spend elsewhere. We're each other's puppets held up by the tension of the strings between us, and if one of us steps away, the other would only be left confused and feeble.

"I've always wanted to visit Temple Island," I say.

There are two categories that StrangeLoom won't translate upcountry. Cemeteries, and religious places of worship. It's a contentious topic—endless back-and-forth about whether this respects religion as something bound to the true plane of reality or if neglecting religion for virtual intentionally persecutes groups who are now dying off, who have a worse quality of life downcountry. At some point in the last few decades, there came a man-made island in the middle of the northern oceans, created by multi-Sect Atahuans and given independence as a nation-state in a bid for some sense of equity. Temple Island is no larger than five thousand square miles, more an archipelago of temples than one true landmass. It is the only country that has been entirely left off the maps upcountry, because its entirety is a place of worship.

"I didn't realize you were religious."

It's a jab. Kieren knows my day-to-day habits better than I know them myself. My rejecting default atheism would definitely not have gone without notice.

"What can I say? I'm fascinated by multi-Sect culture."

Kieren rolls his shoulders to stretch them. "Are you sure it's not the challenge of scanning the island to code for virtual? I remember your presentation."

I keep my eyes straight on the water to hide my shock. I cast my memory back frantically: ninth grade, a starter presentation in world history . . . If *I'm* remembering right, Kieren hadn't even been there that day. He and Hailey had been pulled out of class for family bereavement.

"I watched the class recording on my own time," he says before I can ask. "I think that's when I first realized you were going to be trouble."

I snort. "Because my proposal to do a clandestine scan of an island was so well prepared? What impressed you the most—the utter lack of respect for its residents or the loopholes I presented to insist it wasn't illegal?"

"The earnestness." He shoves his hands into his pockets. "You wanted to see it. You wanted an upcountry equivalent so that you didn't need to wait until you'd graduated and been assigned downcountry, until you had racked up the vacation days needed to travel over in the real. So you came up with a proposal and argued it to every possible point. I've come to expect that of you."

I'm almost amused. Somehow, Kieren is giving me too much credit while insulting me for being an annoyance.

"It was ninth grade," I counter. "Most of us hadn't lost that twinkle in our eye yet. What about Gena's presentation?"

He doesn't say anything. I turn to Kieren slowly. I wait a beat.

"Kieren . . . ," I say. "You *only* watched mine, didn't you?"

No reply. That's confirmation.

I jab him in the ribs. He flinches, but I go in for another jab. "*That's when I knew*—you big liar. You knew the moment I got the same score as you in the entrance exam."

"Okay, okay," Kieren relents. "I can't *believe* they kept our scores the same! My dad is the *headmaster*—"

On my third jab attempt, Kieren catches my finger entirely, wrapping his palm around it. I try to tug my finger back. He refuses to let go. In a smooth maneuver, he turns us both away from the water, toward the road and resuming our route to the data center. Though I let my feet follow suit, I feel a pang, a sense of loss to be leaving the sight.

"Now that we don't have the taxi and half the city listening in anymore," he says. "I suppose you should know something."

"Kieren"—I give my finger another yank, to no avail—"do you mind?"

"I don't, actually, thank you for asking." He continues walking without a bother in the world. "If you didn't have the strength to extract your finger, maybe you shouldn't have stuck it at me."

"I see we're victim-blaming now."

"*Victim*-blaming? I'm *perpetrator*-blaming."

"I wonder if the academy board is going to agree with you when they review this footage for our performances."

With a relenting huff, Kieren lets go of my finger. Chances are that when the board looks at the footage recorded of our posting, the system will automatically snip out the irrelevant parts, like me bothering Kieren by sticking my fingers into his ribs. Still, the threat of being perceived as irresponsible is enough to shake Kieren back into order.

"As I was saying . . ." He checks our surroundings over his shoulder. The east of Upsie is made of chain-link fences and abandoned lots, factories blowing plumes into the air and mills processing raw material. The road echoes our footsteps with hollow reverb. We'd hear it if someone so much as turned the corner a hundred paces away.

"I get the sense we're not the only people assigned to this," Kieren declares.

I rub my hands up and down my arms to smooth out my goose bumps, but the taxi's cold freeze has largely worn off. The asphalt underfoot is sharp through the soles of my shoes.

"They implied as much, didn't they?" I ask. I'm not sure why Kieren is revealing this like it's illicit information. "The briefing opens with two objectives. Either"—I pull it in my display to read out the quote—"*confirm Chung is dead and his work no longer a threat, or locate him.* We're upcountry. Any follow-up on our findings has to be pursued downcountry."

I'm sure they've put me on this task because they think I have some personal tie to Uncle Chung, but he's not in virtual. If he's going to be recruited onto Atahua's side, we need to speak to him. And there's no way the academy would send cadets downcountry. We're not cleared for that yet.

"They implied NileCorp would have assets on standby depending on what we find, but that's not what I'm talking about." Kieren looks over his shoulder again. "I don't think we got the full picture about our task. Who clued them onto Chung's work to begin with when it's a top-secret Medan project? There could be Atahuan spies living undercover across the country, but to penetrate a government effort led by a former *Atahuan*? Medaluo probably watches him like a hawk. They probably have a thousand levels of security to prevent a leak from happening."

"Leaks do happen, nevertheless," I say. "No information is truly safe if more than one person knows about it."

"Fine," Kieren acknowledges. "A whisper traveling through intelligence networks is one thing. What about all the evidence they have now? Who gave NileCorp the footage to show where Chung was last seen? That belongs to the Upsie data center system. And in any regular mission, data centers are so well protected that it should take a whole task force to break into one. But NileCorp can just *get us in?*"

When he puts it like that, I have to admit it sounds too easy, especially given the state of global affairs. Still—we're cadets. We're being tested. We're not actually in the field yet.

"If we want to start picking holes," I say, "it doesn't make sense why they sent you, either. I'm the one who knows Chung. You're just a second high-performing cadet."

Kieren frowns. "Not the point here, Ward."

"Why not?"

"Because," he splutters, "it's just not the point! All I'm saying is that if NileCorp already has someone on the inside, why do they need us?"

I mull over the thought. Nothing comes to mind, no speculation, no hypotheses. In the time we've been talking, we're rapidly approaching the Upper Sea National Data Center, its gargantuan main building cresting the hill. Only the north side is visible from here, but the rest takes up two whole blocks, surrounded by a perimeter fence. Three other facilities sit within proximity of the fence: a containers terminal, a parking garage, and an abandoned lot. When we pass the lot, our steps are harmonized by a loud flapping sound, the tarp-covered windows of its battered admin building fighting against the wind.

"I want to suggest that this could be a test in the truest sense," I say. "That NileCorp already knows where Chung is, and the board is having us follow the path they took to find him." I glance over to Kieren. "But I don't think they'd waste their resources like that."

"No," Kieren agrees.

He pauses on the sidewalk, and I follow suit. We take in the scene. Despite its height, the blueprints say the data center is only one level, with the exception of certain server rooms burrowing lower underground. The vaulted ceilings catch the scarce morning rays streaming from the clouds. Most of what we can see through the glass walls appears to be lobbies and atriums.

"Then maybe," I suggest, "the actual task isn't finding Chung."

Kieren puts his hands in his pockets. I don't look at him, keeping my eyes fixed on the data center instead, but by proximity alone I can track each of his minute movements, the curious tilt of his head, the curl of his lip.

"What could it be, then?" he muses. "And why not tell us outright?"

I squint at the side of the facility. There aren't many vehicles in its parking lot, but enough to indicate a considerable number of employees already clocked in. Data center work is largely performed downcountry:

temperature control and energy regulation, server maintenance and new developments. When the information is accessible on either plane of reality, though, they can at least offload some cataloging work upcountry.

"I guess we'll know more depending on what we find," I say. I point to the vehicle parked outside the fence. "What is that? A delivery truck?"

Kieren squints too. I haven't seen a delivery truck in quite some time. Most packages are sent by bots and drones. They'll only require a person if they're larger or sensitive, like the documents Dad gets in Melnova to sign. Someone's got to be held responsible if a shipment goes missing, and you can't punish a bot.

"That," Kieren says, "is probably our way in."

15

EIRALE

Medaluo has wheeled out its newest line of security bots for Upsie's data center, which is going to be an issue.

"We don't really have an alternative, do we?" Miz asks. "This is the closest we can get."

Nik looms in the front seat of Xixi's car, his handheld device pressed to the window. The vehicle drove us here on her preloaded route, diverted only as we were approaching the Upper Sea National Data Center and noticed a whole row of metal guards installed around the perimeter. Now we're idling behind the admin building of an abandoned lot, staying out of sight.

"I didn't think they would have bots," Nik mutters. "Give me a few more minutes."

Nik's initial plan was to park at the data center while its employees were arriving for the morning and clone their credentials when they walked by. It's significantly harder now that the bots are blocking us from the parking lot, and Nik is trying to clone the key fobs while their cars are passing on the road instead. Unfortunately, none of the data center employees are driving to work holding their credentials dangling out the window. And they're going by way too fast.

Miz checks her watch. She needs to enter first, and soon, if "Xixi" is going to arrive in time, but it'll be for nothing if the rest of us fail to get credentials.

"We may need to get out of the car," Blare says, "and sneak a bit closer."

"Miz, you'll have to go in first." Nik lowers the handheld. "Proceed as we planned. We'll be in within the next twenty minutes, all right?"

"Yeah. Yeah, okay," Miz breathes. She looks nervous. She's been tugging at the tip of her nose, playing with a phantom ring she's removed.

"This will work," Blare offers quietly.

"Yeah," Miz says again. She stops fidgeting, pulling her mask up to cover her face. Blare offers Miz a small earpiece. She inserts it without further instruction. "Testing, one, two," she murmurs, and Blare nods, hearing the audio through an identical piece in their ear.

"You'll be fine," Nik says. His screen lights up again, attempting a new cloning sequence. In tandem, there's another car approaching, the sound of its tires following behind the electric signals of its owner's credentials. "Keep your head down."

Miz exhales. "Off I go." When she closes the door, its echo is compounded by the emptiness of the lot. Blare winces, quickly bracing the handle after the door closes as though they can suppress the sound. They cast their glance over to me. I splay my hands, not sure what exactly they want me to do to help.

Nik groans, his screen turning dark.

"Missed it again," he declares. "At this rate, everyone will have arrived for the day, and we won't have a way in."

Blare lets go of the door handle. "And you were so picky before on who you wanted to clone."

"Sorry if I wanted an all-access pass." While the road is quiet, Nik swipes to a new tab. "Forget the electrical engineers. I'll take anyone at this point. I'll take the unpaid intern."

Yellowing grass blows into the lot and swirls over the hood of the car. Nik sits back for a minute, his head lolled on the seat. As I predicted, it's started to drizzle outside, darkening the morning and dragging up sludge and grit. The air has the faintest tinge of orange, compounded by the dreary weather. With each car that rumbles past on the road, another line of dirt sprays near Xixi's car.

I push my forehead to the window, eyeing the mud bed forming around the vehicle. Nik's device can't seem to catch any of the employees arriving to work, but they're sure catching us in the splatter zone.

Downcountry urban areas are already relatively quiet. But outside the city center, the isolated edges bypass silence entirely and descend into barren paranoia. Here, there are few people with business to tend to. Anyone lurking has no good intentions. That includes us.

"Hey, Nik?" Blare says suddenly. "Channel one."

Nik straightens in an instant, reaching for the glasses he tossed onto the empty driver's seat. Whatever Blare sees on their handheld is communicated to Nik without missing a beat. Nik turns pale.

"What is it?" I ask.

"NileCorp."

I allow no visible reaction. My breathing stays the same pace; my hands are relaxed in my lap. Consciously, I walk myself through every step it takes to seem nothing more than mildly concerned, as though I'm only thinking about my own wellbeing as a fugitive.

Then Nik adds, "Medan security is murmuring about their presence in the city. They may know that we're going after the program. They'll want to intercept it."

My concern grows genuine. I can't make sense of this. Teryn said so too: *That program is not something we can easily access. Nik Grant needs to acquire it first.* In what world can Nik Grant retrieve a program that NileCorp can't? NileCorp hires first-class decryption experts. Yet somehow it's a better gamble to let me sit tight with Nik as a ticking time bomb than to make a capture and use a brute-force attack for the program.

"If they've only touched down, surely we won't run into them," Blare says. "I'll tell Miz. Miz? Are you hearing me?"

They turn away, facing the window to murmur into their earpiece. Nik, meanwhile, slowly withdraws his device from the window, his eyes pinned to the rainy day outside.

"Isn't NileCorp under the impression the program was deleted?" I ask.

"It was only a matter of time until they discovered otherwise," Nik replies.

Because of Nik? Is he already aware that they're watching him?

"And what does NileCorp know?" I push. "About the nature of the program?"

"They know enough." Nik puts his handheld into his jacket. "They can't have it." He pushes open his door and marches into the rain.

Immediately, I open my door too, throwing my legs out and standing. "Blare, stay here."

"But—"

I duck my head back in, just to make sure they understand me properly. "You're the getaway driver. Do not come." I put my palm out. "And give me the earpiece."

Their mouth drops open. "What! The car drives itself!"

"Are you going to listen to me, or are you going to waste the expertise I was kidnapped for?"

Blare gives me a grumpy look. Still, they pull out their earpiece and drop it into my hand.

"I have wet earwax."

I frown, looking at the small bit of metal. "Yippee. Stay inside." I shut the door firmly. By the time I've given the earpiece a cursory wipe and shoved it into my own ear, Nik's out of sight. I follow a hunch and stick close to the admin building, creeping forward parallel to the road. My shoes sink deep into the mud. It must be the sloshing that signals my approach, because when I finally spot Nik hidden in one of the bushes, he's already waving me over.

"What was that all about?" he asks when I duck down. "Did you tell Blare to stay in the car?"

"I'm doing what you won't," I mutter. Thirteen-year-olds don't need to be breaking into facilities. "Now you only need to clone two passes."

"Blare is actually our hacker," Nik says. "But they can do it remotely too."

I thought Miz was their hacker. Maybe they're both the hackers. I don't care enough about the clarification to ask further.

"You're not any closer here. You still won't be able to run a copy on the employees arriving."

"I know." Nik shifts, bringing his arm up. The screen on his watch has copied over the tab on his handheld. He unlatches his watch, then offers it to me. "I think if you approach the line of security, that should be close enough. I looked up the model of the bots already: They don't have visual cameras. Only infrared. We can walk past fine once we have credentials."

That means the bots guarding the facility will sound the alarm if people without credentials try to sneak through in the trunk of a car, but they're not going to know if people holding stolen credentials stroll by in the open. No visual recognition.

It takes me a moment to register what he's indicating by giving me the watch. Slowly, I begin to scrape back my hair, letting Nik hold the watch out for a few beats longer. My hair goes up in a ponytail—it's too short to get everything into a bundle, so I have tufts sticking out at the base.

"The blueprints," I say, taking the watch and strapping it onto my wrist, "they didn't mark out any server rooms. Are they underground?"

Nik nods. I expected so. It's a common feature when summers get too hot and the rooms use up excessive energy keeping cool.

"And you know the exact route to take once we're in?" I continue. "Because I need access to the servers too. While you rummage for your file, I can work on finding a way into Kunlun."

"Yes."

Nik doesn't say more.

"How *do* you know the exact route?" I ask.

"Irrelevant."

"Not irrelevant, because you think NileCorp might hit the facility soon too. Do you know more, or do they? Are they going to know you were there?"

"Assume we know best," Nik says tightly, impatiently. He's not hiding his alarm, his stiff shoulders, his gray eyes hurrying to shift into the distance. His disposition tells me he thinks he has said too much—but I don't know why.

The watch on my wrist beeps to signal it's ready for remote access. Nik takes the sound for his cue to start cloning again, the light on the other side of his glasses changing and covering up what might have glanced across his eyes. He gestures forward, onto the road.

I could press further. I could. But that would only prolong the mission without guaranteed answers, and besides, my aim is to get through this whole ordeal as fast as possible. I went to military school—if there's anything I know how to do, it's shut up and take instructions.

"I'll do two laps," I say. "That'd better be enough."

"Be careful."

I was about to stand, but my knees lock at his words. Nik turns briefly, seeing how I've stopped, and then his brow furrows to tell *me* off for being confused.

"Go on," he prompts. "Don't get caught."

That's more like it. I emerge onto the road. The moment I know I've become visible, I let my left foot drag, feigning disheveled. I've come from the promenade, and I've already been jogging for an hour. I shouldn't require any inspection because I'm not a threat.

I count five security bots, lined evenly outside the front of the data center. Their heads begin to shift when I draw nearer. I glance down at my watch to have something unsuspicious to do. Nik's remote access is moving around the cursor. My arm drops, slicing through the light rain.

I jog past at a leisurely speed, refusing to look at the bots. The one closest to the road shifts to track me as I go, but the others straighten their heads when I continue onward, running the east side of the facility. There are two more guards here, but they don't track my motion. The fence is high—it's unlikely anybody would succeed in jumping over without snapping their neck.

I catch movement in the parking lot as I'm passing by. Employees slowly getting out of their vehicles. Putting on coats, masks. Changing their shoes and leaving the spares in the trunk. Holding still enough to hopefully, hopefully get a scan of the credentials dangling off their keychains. In no time, I've reached the end of the facility, and the dead-end of the road too. Rather than run into Upsie's reeds, I pivot, starting my second lap.

"What's taking so long?" Miz's voice emits clearly into my ear. "If you come in any later, you're going to get noticed."

"Almost there," I mutter back.

"Wait, where's—"

"Blare's in the car. It'll be just me and Nik."

I pass the same bots at the side again, huffing and puffing. I don't dare glance down at what's happening on the surface of my watch, because if Nik is failing to connect, then this plan all falls apart. Back to the drawing board.

The bot guard closest to the main gate turns to look at me. I keep jogging, holding a constant pace until I'm out of view from the security line. Just as I'm looking for Nik again in the greenery, a hand shoots out from the bush and drags me down by the arm.

"Ow—"

"We've got it," Nik says in a rush. He holds my wrist out in front of him, syncing the watch with his handheld device. "All right. It's activated."

"It's copied?"

"Copied. Let's go."

Nik doesn't bother with a pretense for the guards. He marches up the road, forges straight ahead for the open gateway. It's not that I don't trust the technicalities of infrared, but that bot before had looked me square in the face, even if I was showing up differently on its radar. . . .

The guard doesn't turn at all. Its beady orange eyes stare ahead, staying level. I follow Nik quickly, striding through the gate and up the steps to the building before any of the employees still in the parking lot can collide with us on the way in.

"About time," Miz breathes when the door opens for us, letting us into the lobby. We're damp from the rain. There are dried leaves sticking to the back of my legs. Nik and I don't say anything when we walk to the turnstile. I'm through first, the watch on my wrist buzzing while the turnstile scans my credentials and lets me proceed. As Nik angles his handheld to scan, Miz pushes a folded square of fabric along her desk. I grab it as I pass, tucking the two lab coats onto my arm. Nik proceeds through the turnstile and offers Miz a quick nod.

"Take a left here," Nik murmurs when we've stepped into the facility atrium. I pass him his coat and shrug on my own, freeing my ponytail while I'm at it. A red carpet bleeds the length from the front entrance to the center of the atrium. It's the most amount of color in the building, yet still the threads appear matted and worn, smeared with old mud that has been tracked in over time. The lobby echoes with Miz faking a cough behind her mask, keeping her face down when she opens the door for the next employee coming in. With another gesture from Nik and a second left, we're already deep enough inside the facility that I can't hear her coughing.

"It's so empty."

Each room we pass appears desolate. Dust-covered computer screens. Dark workstations, lamps installed with various settings on the surface but the cords unplugged.

"The facility was built at a time when they needed more manpower regulating the data, but most of the work is automated now," Nik replies. "It's still a lot of employees for downcountry."

He pauses and glances at an exterior door that lies to the left, EXIT marked overhead. Nik proceeds onward. I let him guide the way, more interested in observing how he reacts to our surroundings. Two corridors later, after passing a large portrait of Medaluo's current prime minister, we come across a door with a complicated latch, a two-sequence scan on credentials and retina. Nik is clearly expecting the process, because he holds his handheld and then switches to a new page, holding it to the laser rather than his eye. The panel turns from red to green. The door opens to a set of stairs. Without taking the extra time to confirm where he's going, he steps in.

"You've been here before," I say when I follow Nik down. The hum of the servers sings a one-note chorus.

"Medaluo's data centers are broken up by departments," Nik replies in lieu of an answer. "The Ministry of National Defense only has two server rooms. Highly secure. Lots of redundant servers to prevent information from getting lost."

Highly secure, and yet he's made getting in seem so easy. A metal plaque flashes at the bottom of the stairs, greeting all entrants before they make the turn into the server aisles. *Supervisor,* it says, before the name is covered up with black tape. There's a phone number to call in case of error or emergency. I wonder who that goes to, given the state of its anonymous employee.

"You can take the main controller screen," Nik instructs. "Find what you need. I'll plug in with a handheld for my file."

Nik heads straight for one of the ports, connecting up to his handheld. I make a slower route to the central screen, the controller where on-site engineers can run maintenance from.

"Whose credentials did you copy?" I call over. I indicate the watch on my wrist. "Will it have access?"

"Technician. I don't think it's going to log in." Nik doesn't look up from his typing. "As soon as you get an idea of which box you want to get into, you need to message Blare for remote hacking. They're user 'dazzling underscore star.' Connect the watch to the interface."

I do as he says, then pull open a chat window.

me: Hi Blare, are you there

dazzling_star: this is kinda confusing bc it says i'm talking to nik and nik2 so i have to assume nik2 is Miss Earpiece Stealer

me: Yeah

me: Please standby for when I need you

dazzling_star: 😒

dazzling_star: funny how you need me despite your insistence on me staying in the car

me: Yes, and now you're able to hack remotely so if anything that proves my point

me: Checkmate

I start searching. Maneuvering through large blocks of stored information isn't feasible by any means, but without engineer credentials, I'm only browsing the file names across the boxes anyway. It's a fail-safe on the data center's part. Credentials that get us into the room won't get us into the servers. Credentials that get us into the servers often don't scan into the room, because those employees are probably working from upcountry.

me: Okay, do you see my view?

dazzling_star: yup i'm looking. what are you after?

me: I've pulled up a box with hundreds of pages of survey data. Can you see if anything in here mentions Kunlun? I bet there's an ad company out there that makes a note of Kunlun's citizens.

dazzling_star: okie dokie

dazzling_star: give me like ten minutes

me: Only ten minutes?

dazzling_star: you wouldn't believe the amount of back doors on the dark web

dazzling_star: (kid-safe dark web)

I huff. Still, Blare goes idle immediately to work, so I can't complain while I'm making use of their labor.

The problem with getting into Kunlun—the reason it is so impossible to hack—is that pesky second password. The system is already checking for citizenship, so only avatars with the designation can enter the space at all without setting off a dozen alarms. But even if someone were to steal a citizen's credentials, preparing to hack into the space wearing that citizen's avatar, that second password is going to halt them in their tracks. When entry to Kunlun is so exclusive, people don't tend to write their passwords down. It's nearly impossible to find any floating around the dark web.

I push away from the screen for a moment, rolling my neck and hearing it crack on both sides. At the end of the server, Nik hasn't moved at all from his initial stance, his feet braced and his posture hunched over his device.

My plan to get into Kunlun involves a bit more abstraction. There's one place in the entire world that won't require a second password into Kunlun: Offron's data center. The engineers need to be able to go up and perform maintenance, but an engineer living in Offron is unlikely to be able to afford Kunlun citizenship, so their activity will be carefully logged and recorded if they have a back door open like that. Kunlun's security will review every instance of people without citizenship coming in even through that back door to ensure safeguarding.

So we can't just use the back door haphazardly. We'll get kicked out in seconds with our own credentials. But we *can* use that door as Kunlun citizens.

I'll need a few candidates first.

The chat window lights up again.

> dazzling_star: i have two PDFs. they both look like Kunlun citizen lists. does this work?
> dazzling_star: [Sent two attachments.]

I open the files, browsing through the lists. They're plain text spreadsheets, pulled from some sort of city registry that takes note of energy usage by Upsie downcountry residents who spend monthlong stints in Kunlun. This is great. Plenty to work from. I'm just about to tell Blare that they did a great job when new messages come in.

> dazzling_star: **it's still encrypted dude. you might have located it with your bff trail but we need to isolate it among everything else on the server**
> dazzling_star: **oops wrong person**
> me: **???**

Nik's sudden slap against the server echoes through the room. My gaze whips over, then narrows. Blare must have resent their message to the correct recipient. Nik is muttering something to himself, clearly flustered.

"Is everything all right?" I ask. I type, *Thank you Blare I've got it* and disconnect, clearing my searches on the main controller.

"It's fine," Nik says. He's barely able to get the words out past his gritted teeth. "The file is right *here*, but"—he puts his hands in front of him, making it seem as though he wants to strangle the server box—"naturally, everything is encrypted."

"Blare seems like a quick hacker."

"Blare has a certain skill for stubbornly chasing down rabbit holes, but decryption takes more power. Servers are usually duplicated for redundancies too, which makes files easier to retrieve, but there's only *one* version of this, and the compute of handhelds alone will require *days*—"

He yanks his handheld out of the port. For a second, he appears to be giving up, calling it quits before we're caught so that there will be the opportunity to regroup and find another method.

I'm mistaken. Nik leans closer to run a palm along the rack in front of him, counting the blinking blue lights. When he pulls at one of the lower boxes, he's only examining the outer casing at first.

Then he's hauling the box all the way out, attempting to heft its weight into his arms.

"Whoa, whoa," I say, hurrying over. "Not with your handheld still in your grip. You're going to drop everything—"

I take his handheld from him. Nik jolts immediately, which makes him loosen his hold on the server and fumble it. It's more an instinctive response than deliberate nosiness when I glance at his unlocked screen, finding a chat log with two tabs open. *I hope I'll see you soon* is the last message someone sent, and that doesn't seem like it came from Blare. Before I can glimpse anything else, auto-lock kicks in and turns the screen dark.

"Be careful with that," he warns, regaining his hold on the server box. He shifts to adjust its weight and pulls the entire hardware into his arms.

I blink. "Are we stealing the server?"

"Yes," he grunts. "We need time to decrypt it before we can retrieve it. Grab Miz on the way out, would you?"

16

LIA

"I assume this is for you."

Kieren holds out the smaller jumpsuit of the two yellow delivery driver uniforms. The doors were left unlocked. Even the engine was still running, so we didn't have to figure out where the keys were or how they turned.

"I'm just going to wear this on top of everything," I say, gesturing for him to hand it over. "It clashes terribly with my hair."

He pauses, midway through pulling open his own jumpsuit. "Your hair is black."

"I know. That was my way of insulting the jumpsuit for being ugly."

I make a small hop, freeing the tight ankle hem caught around my shoes before I zip up snugly. NileCorp has gone the extra mile of attaching badges to the belt line with a picture of me smiling. I don't think I ever posed for that photo, so I assume they generated it on their own.

A small pop-up appears in my display.

> **This is an automated message: Hurray, you've made it to the truck! Remember deliveries go in through the side entrance.**
> **—Kam**

"Do you want to drive?" I ask.

Kieren's already getting into the driver's seat. "I feel like we're completing quests in a video game."

"I suppose that's not so far off from the point of an exam posting."

Kieren makes a grand show out of checking the mirrors and putting the truck into reverse. With only a small shift on the wheel, though, the vehicle easily pulls itself out from around the corner, then rumbles toward the gate and turns in. I press up against my window in search of the facility's side door, only the truck is turning again, taking itself to the walkway on the left. The route is loaded in already.

"See, this is what I mean," Kieren mutters. He doesn't want to trigger any listening ears on the dashboard's recording capabilities. "No way they're this prepared without someone who's already been in and out of this facility."

The truck comes to a halt at the data center's side entrance. I only make a pensive noise, stepping out and tugging my jumpsuit straight.

I go to open the back, pushing the doors wide and browsing the packages for something we could convincingly deliver. I shouldn't have bothered—there's another pop-up, a request for an augmented plug-in to make some changes to my vision. While Kieren calls, "Are we supposed to accept this?" I've already hit *accept*. Two of the cardboard boxes in front of me light up with a white glow.

"I'm taking the smaller box," I announce when he comes around. "Use yours to block your face."

"Rude," Kieren mutters. He picks up the package with more strength than necessary—it must be empty inside given how he almost flies back, his balance faltering for a few seconds before he steadies himself.

"I'm staying professional," I recite under my breath, quickly turning away so I don't laugh. "I'm so professional. . . ."

I hit the call button at the side door. There's no exterior handle, only a small panel with a camera eyeing us. I don't have the time to prepare a spiel before a woman in a white coat has come to open the door, waving us in.

"You know where to go," she says distractedly. She's not looking at me, which means I can keep my stare on her face, trying to make sense of the slight blurriness I'm getting. It's another filter feature. The woman is likely Tamera's age, somewhere in her fifties, but the system blots out the lines that decorate the sides of her eyes without entirely removing them. She must have dragged the slider all the way up.

"Please make it quick. We need the hallways cleared for management in an hour."

I nod. "Yes, absolutely."

The augmented plug-in illuminates a path at our feet. The woman proceeds ahead of us, finding nothing odd about the switch in their usual deliverymen. It helps that we don't falter where we're going, and when she makes a left turn into a lab, we continue forward, down to a door at the end of the hallway.

There are no interesting additions in the building, no bright lights or holographic art pieces. It looks exactly as it might downcountry, from the cracks in the walls where water damage dripped from the ceiling to the scuffed carpet. No cameras inside either. Can't risk having their surveillance hacked and spied on.

The glowing arrows end at a depot room, the door wide open and a bot sitting inside to scan items. Kieren and I exchange a glance. I suppose we do need to hand over these packages and let the employees wonder who ordered the empty boxes.

"Thank you," he tells the bot.

It doesn't respond.

"Now what?" I whisper outside the room. "Chung's office?"

"You go west. I'll go east?" Kieren returns.

I nod. We split, breaking into a quick stride. There's only so much allowance we have if an employee asks what we're doing, and a onetime excuse of getting lost before we absolutely must leave. Most of the rooms I pass aren't sensitive areas. Just plain labs, fitted with computer screens and desk chairs.

I lean up against a few of the larger, closed doors with hefty keypads attached to their handles. Those don't open when I try to push through. The server rooms, I assume. They come equipped with far more security.

I keep moving forward. Left turn, right turn. After a few minutes of walking, I hear the whine before I round the corner and come upon its source: a plainer, wooden door. The hum buzzes against my ears strangely, as though someone is playing a flute off-key outside the facility and the sound is wafting in through the wall.

I go to open the door. I hadn't expected resistance, given the lack of a lock, but it doesn't budge. No keyhole, no digital keypad. It's a regular handle.

"Hmmm." The door is coded locked. That's unusual.

I open my display, wanting to see what appears when I interact with the door. There are certain items in virtual reality that operate like this—movie posters waiting to move, hardcover books with digital versions—only revealing their extra functionality in our displays. They don't tend to accompany *doors*. Upcountry is supposed to feel real. In reality we use handles and locks.

But indeed, a virtual box pops up in my display. It leaves no room for confusion. The box is labeled with DOOR. A drop-down menu has it on Closed.

I tap the menu to open all the options.

OPEN

ERROR#z27LxQAwx4jDEw//access:2040070120580517XXXXX

My blood runs cold. *Closed* is selected. *Open* is blanked out, unavailable as an option. But the third *error* option is selectable—for me, at least . . . likely because the tail end of the gibberish is *my* user ID for StrangeLoom.

Or close enough to it. My unique last five numbers are blacked out. But the first eight digits are my birthday, the exact year, month, day—Dad chose it, because they didn't know what my real birthday was—and then the next eight digits are my ID expiration date in the same format, when I need to get new StrangeLoom credentials.

I'm frozen to the spot, uncertain what to do. While this *could* be someone else's ID with my very same birthday and ID expiration date, the very fact that it's selectable to me must mean it's mine. And even without the unique last five numbers on show, it wouldn't have been hard for someone else to narrow this down either. Only a handful of people in the StrangeLoom system will have an identical birthday and expiration.

I've hovered over the third option long enough that my display decides to select it automatically. The door handle clicks. I don't hear the off-key whine anymore.

Anyone can see this. How long has this been here?

Did Chung leave his office this way? For *me*?

I open the door slowly, unsure what I'll find. The room is dark inside. Quiet. Unmoving. No use lingering and getting caught by someone in the hallway at this point. I slip through properly, closing the door behind myself and leaving it unlocked.

I'm definitely in the right place. My eyes gravitate to the only illuminated part of the room: the adjustable cabinet lamp clipped to the bookshelf and a photograph tacked at its side, perfectly in that beam of gold. I inch closer, almost afraid that the photograph will disappear like a startled wild animal.

It's a printout of a digital article. Dad and Chung stand side by side, posing for the Atahuan media. The text of the article has faded into an indecipherable blur. But the headline is fully legible when I run my finger along it.

PROJECT WIT KICKS INTO ACTION

I've always known the story of how Dad and Chung became friends. Before I was born, right as the cold war was reaching its peak, the government announced a week dedicated to policy and technology, then sent its senators to its national labs so media outlets could cover what was most pressing for the civilians of Atahua. We weren't knowledgeable enough about our breakthroughs, our projects funded by tax money. We were proud of being a democracy, and so elected officials ought to put a face to elected projects, make sure the country was on the same page.

I've never looked into what exactly Dad endorsed. How did the media not drag Dad in when Chung left for Medaluo? Surely I would have seen the chatter, if not on my own feed at the time, then later, by algorithm, when I'm hovering over Dad's contact.

I open my display again, intentionally avoiding the updates from Kieren while he's checking the other side of the facility for the office I've already found. In the search engine, I type "PROJECT WIT" "HENRY SULLIVAN" "CHUNG YIN." When another message from Kieren comes in, I set my display to Do Not Disturb.

SENATOR SULLIVAN ANNOUNCES PROJECT WIT, GROUNDBREAKING AI TECHNOLOGY
From the press release, we see the Senator Henry Sullivan cite this as a diplomatic venture. . . .

KIEREN: *LIA*

I jolt in fright, registering the message. I hate it when people use the loud effect to get past my settings. I close the article quickly, confirming that Dad did endorse Chung.

LIA: i was just reading up on something can you CHILL

I put him on Do Not Disturb again, intent on making a proper search of Chung's office. Unfortunately, Kieren must know what I'm doing and sends everything following his initial message in loud mode.

KIEREN: *I CAN SEE YOUR LOCATION IN FIND MY FRIENDS*
KIEREN: *YOU'RE IN THE OFFICE?*
KIEREN: *I'M COMING*
KIEREN: *YOU'RE SUCH A WEENIE*

I swipe his messages away as fast as I can. In the rapid bursts, my display gets confused, not certain if I'm trying to pull open the article again or make another search or reply. When I flail my eyes in the other direction, trying to exit out of everything at once, my display freezes entirely.

"Come *on*," I groan. I swing my eyes across my display so furiously that I feel my head try to mimic the maneuver too. I really hope the academy doesn't watch this when they're playing back my recordings.

My display is dead frozen. Not even a flicker. I need to do a hard reset. I *hate* what NileCorp decided would be the hard reset mechanism for the displays sitting in our heads. . . .

I turn to face the inside of the door. Without time to grit my teeth, I pick up speed and run right at it, putting my full force behind the collision. My whole vision goes out for a second, pitch-black when I land with a solid thud on the floor. I wheeze an inhale.

When my vision snaps back, my display is clean and moving normally. I've only had to hard reset twice in my life, and unsurprisingly, it's always unpleasant. I blink, closing the display properly to avoid the risk of overwhelming it again. My forehead is pulsing. I'm going to have a bruise.

"Ow . . ."

And that's when the door opens, bringing Kieren in. He halts at the threshold.

"A little help?" I ask after several moments pass, lifting my hand.

Kieren bursts out laughing.

17

EIRALE

"You stole the *entire* box?"

Miz resisted saying anything while we were in Xixi's car fleeing the scene. She was silent while Blare inputted instructions to find the nearest mall, the car taking us into an underground parking lot beneath the mammoth structure. Unspeaking until the moment we pulled into the lot, the doors slamming after us to shut out any listening capabilities on Xixi's dashboard.

"Why would you *do that*?"

It's impressive given how her arms are gesticulating now. Her voice bounces off the low ceiling. I inch closer to a pillar on my left, keeping out of the way. There's one other car down here. It looks like it hasn't been moved in years.

"What else was I supposed to do?" Nik returns.

"I don't know"—Miz throws both her arms in the direction of the stolen hardware tossed in the back of the car—"make a *copy*?"

"I'm not going to make a copy and then leave the original in the data center. Once I've traced it, I've left the pathway for anyone else to pick up." Nik props his leg onto one of the loose stone blocks separating the white lines. "NileCorp is already sniffing around, so we move fast. We get to Threto and bring this server with us to decrypt and extract."

Miz takes a deep breath, her nose screeching with sound. She's since put her septum ring back in, freed of her Xixi costume.

"A missing drive means that Upsie's data center will know there was a break-in on their next inventory sweep, which could be as soon as later today," she snaps. "This wasn't the plan. What if we can't get into Threto because you activated a nationwide security warning?" She throws her bag down, its thud loud on the concrete ground. "You took a risk, dumbass, and you should have asked us first."

Nik turns away, scrubbing his face. He's accepting the telling-off. Blare catches my gaze from the other side of the car, then widens their eyes to convey a silent *Yikes*.

"Did you want me to leave the file there?" Nik asks. "Did you want me to leave the *program* there?"

They're speaking in code. It's obvious in the way they're emphasizing their words, and I have to imagine it's only because I'm listening.

"No," Miz hisses. "Of course not. But one file is nothing without the other parts. As long as everything is left in limbo, as long as Medaluo doesn't notice what's hiding in their data centers, there's always a chance of retrieval. If we're blocked out, then we're done for. If Medaluo puts up its defenses, it's over."

"You were always going to have a short operating time anyway," I say, inserting myself into the argument. Nik and Miz both whip around to look at me with a certain astonishment, as if they had forgotten I had exited the car too. "The *Be back soon!* sign you put up at the front desk isn't going to fool them for long. Once they send a bot to check on Xixi and find her passed out at her apartment, they'll go on high alert. The only question is whether you get half a day or two before they send notice to Threto."

Miz shoves her hands into her pockets, sulking. Nik considers my words for a moment, then nods.

"You heard our soldier," he says. "The goal now is getting to Threto. We're wasting time debating anything else."

Miz's entire spine is trembling, turning her height even shorter. She looks like she'll say more, like she has more resentment to fling around. Then her shoulders ease. She heaves a breath to cool down.

"I'm going to find a new vehicle for us," she decides. "We can leave in an hour."

• • • •

The twenty-first floor is a food court.

They leave me and Blare there. Nik must not fear that I'll run again, because I could definitely tackle a thirteen-year-old if I really wanted to.

Blare is typing away with one hand and occasionally spooning at a bowl of soybean milk with the other. My eyes flicker around, eyeing the sparsely occupied tables, the exits. There's a skybridge that leads into the other half of the food court, but that side is dark, its shops closed. One of the windows is also partially cracked—it's not bad enough for the owners to replace, but it's emitting a loud whistling noise.

Out in the open, I'm paranoid, keeping watch over every other person sharing the space with us. We've seated ourselves at one long table in the middle of the food court. An air filtration system howls above, maintaining constant ventilation. Teryn must be nearby. It's clear that we've finished in Upsie. Members of her team will already be drawing out a path to begin following us into Threto. If I were still in her unit, that's what I would have suggested.

"Hey."

Blare looks up. "Yeah?"

"How did you get involved in all this?"

Their plastic spoon halts midway to their mouth. It clanks back into the bowl.

"I . . . volunteered," Blare says. "I've always wanted to."

My nose wrinkles. "Do crime?"

"Um, *no.*" Blare's voice takes on a sneer. "Be a revolutionary. Maybe not everyone will agree with the way we're bringing change, but it's needed. Without us, NileCorp would be quietly killing people in their Pods, and everyone would be none the wiser."

I kick my feet onto one of the chairs. Despite my best effort to wipe my shoes down, muddy clumps stick to the sides, crawling into the crevices.

"Do you really believe that?" I ask. "That NileCorp is capable of Indisposing people?"

"I don't just believe it," Blare says. "I *know* so."

A loud clatter comes from the other end of the table. I flinch, spinning fast, but it's only a group of kids fighting over a toy. They've smacked a tray of dumplings onto the floor. I assume they're here unsupervised until a girl—the nanny—stands up to her full height, pleading for some order. She's young. No older than I am, though I doubt she graduated from any sort of academy. A shoulder bag is slung across her body, the screen on the front blinking through advertisements. Every fifth slide displays her own services: she's available to watch children from seven o'clock in the morning to ten o'clock at night for a flat-rate fee.

"If you give me the toy, I'm going to reward you with sweets when we get back. How's that?" the girl tries.

They ignore her. I count the clump of kids stretching their small arms: one, two, three, four, five—my goodness.

I swing my feet off the chair and stamp them down on the floor. The sound ricochets like a gunshot, and the children scream, freezing midmotion.

The nanny's gaze whips toward me, her eyes wide. Thankfully, she recovers before the children do, and she hurries to yank the toy away, putting it in her pocket.

"All right!" she bellows. "Home time!"

I turn around. Blare has gone back to looking at their handheld. Since they're not using the fork they were given with the meal's plastic utensil pack, I steal it, intent on scraping the mud off my shoes.

We sit in silence for a beat. My left boot is particularly gross, so I rest it against my other knee, nudging the flimsy plastic prongs at the sole. The nanny is having some trouble getting a long leash on to all the children. I keep watch out of the corner of my eye.

"You really don't remember anything about Kunlun?"

Now Blare's question comes out of nowhere. I swap the fork for the plastic knife when I come across a particularly stubborn lump.

"You've read my file, haven't you?"

"Yeah," Blare replies. "But NileCorp exaggerates all the time. Is it really a complete void, or do you have . . . I don't know . . . impressions?"

"It's a complete absence." Flakes of mud fall to the floor. It's barely noticeable among the other food scraps and litter left under the table.

"But it was *Kunlun*," Blare says. "How can you not remember?"

"What do you want me to say?" I counter. "Maybe NileCorp took my memories. You've heard of Indisposition. Now"—I drop the knife and wave my fingers around, imitating a storybook monster—"get ready for Ignorance. They go in with a malware. . . ."

"Don't be glib," Blare huffs. "It's rude."

It *is* unmannerly of me to tease a kid.

"In any case," I say, "I'm sorry to say the specialness of the place doesn't stop a seizure from eating up my memory. What's it to you? You'd think you were there or something."

Silence. I look up, and Blare has turned entirely pale, their handheld lowered. All my attention shifts away from my muddy shoes.

"*Were* you?"

Blare splutters, "No. No, I wasn't."

"Blare." I put both my feet flat on the floor. "Nik and Miz aren't here right now, so you can't get in trouble for saying anything to me. What do you know?"

"Nothing!"

I must be freaking them out. I press on.

"Look me in the eye," I command. "I have no memory of my final examination, from the moment my school transferred me in as an avatar to the moment I woke up downcountry. Anything could have happened in those ten weeks, so I really need you to answer a simple question: *Have we met before?*"

Their mouth opens and closes. Then, quietly, so much so that I have to strain to hear them, Blare says, "It could harm you to find out anything now."

What?

Their handheld starts to ring. Blare is saved from my scrutiny and dives for the opportunity to escape the interrogation. I am at a complete loss, so I don't push it further. At the other end of the food court, a maintenance technician is telling someone that the elevators aren't working, and customers will either have to wait or take the stairs.

The nanny has finally ushered her kids into a line. When she passes in front of us, my eyes almost glance away. Blare is nodding vigorously—I can parse Nik's voice coming through the line, even if his words aren't audible to me. I am still looking, but Blare is not, when the screen on the nanny's bag flickers and replaces the ad for a local casino with plain white text on a black background:

GET TO OFFRON WITHIN THREE DAYS.

It's gone in a heartbeat. The screen on the bag turns to a Buy One, Get One Free code for pickleball paddles. I might have thought I imagined it entirely if it had played any faster.

Blare sets their handheld down. "Nik says they're ready. He wants us to bring some food."

My ears are screeching with white noise when I nod. I don't glance around further in search of other screens. I'm not sure what else I'll see. Once I've read and comprehended direct instructions from my superior,

I can't act against it. Even if there's something here, information I'm hungry for right within grasp. Blare has just as much admitted that they were present during my final posting. Each time I watch Miz touch her nose, fold her arms, grumble a complaint, it's uncannily familiar. And Nik—Nik Grant, most of all, activates an instinct in me that I cannot understand. There's a pull in my gut to pay attention to his every move, that tells me I ought to be looking for something specific, and I don't know *what*.

"You go ahead to wait on an elevator," I say to Blare. "I can buy buns." I stand. "Also, give me some money."

18

LIA

Kieren hauls me to my feet, still grinning when I pat the dust off my backside.

"Something funny?" I seethe.

"You are, Ward." He looks around. "Find anything yet?"

"I didn't get a chance to search." No thanks to him and his incessant loud-mode messages. "I think we should rummage through possible hiding places and then call it a day. If he stored anything, it would more likely be downcountry."

The office is sparse. The article printout is an anomaly—there's no other decoration, save for a decorative cat penholder on the desk, and I could argue that's a necessity. Naturally, Kieren's eyes gravitate toward the photo with Dad.

"Is that—"

"Yes," I cut in. "I've already looked at the article it came from. Nothing useful for right now."

Kieren pauses. His mouth opens, poised to speak, before he suddenly presses his lips together. I must have frowned in response, because a flash of alarm crosses his gaze when our eyes meet.

"What?" I ask. "Do you disagree?"

"No," he says quickly. "I'll check the shelves."

He hurries into a crouch, running his hands along the lower brackets. I'm left blinking at his back. That was strange, but I can't exactly pick an argument with him about it. It would sound bizarre to ask Kieren why he seemed afraid to ask me more questions. About Chung. About my dad.

I shake my head quickly, redirecting my focus. Since he's on the shelves, I take the desk, turning on the screens. Chung's profile is down. That's probably something the data center did after he deleted their program and disappeared.

I kneel below the desk, peering at the items underneath. Two shoeboxes with different pairs of running shoes. I follow each of the wires to make sure they plug into the appropriate ports and confirm that there's nothing out of the ordinary.

Kieren clicks his tongue when I poke my head out from underneath the desk.

"Did you find something?" I ask.

He turns around, a small box in his hands. "What's this?"

A jewelry box, I'd guess. I'm frowning before I approach, both my hands splayed out eagerly for him to pass it over.

"It doesn't open," Kieren reports.

He sets the box in my hands. It *could* be a jewelry box, even if it's on the smaller side, but then again, I'm not sure what that would be doing in Chung's office. The surface is made of metal, only interrupted by two hinges along the razor-thin line that hints at where the box ends join.

I give it a tug. It doesn't budge. I shift my fingers, squeezing from the sides instead, and the entire box pulses.

I freeze. "Did you see that?"

"What?" Kieren asks. "You got it open?"

The box cracks open on my next attempt, its insides smooth and red and velvet, answering Kieren's question. It reveals a key. It's no longer than my index finger, but the teeth are round rather than jagged, different lengths from end to end.

"This is so strange," I mutter, picking up the key. "Why would—"

I almost clear the display intrusion out of sheer habit. It's one of those auto-banners that the academy likes to send, the warnings if I've knocked into campus property or the countdowns if I'm too far away from class and it's getting close to the bell. This banner, though, has movement. After my eyes scan it once, the pixels disintegrate.

Don't say anything.

My throat constricts.

"Ward?" Kieren prompts. "Did you just get frozen again?"

A new banner waves into place.

Understand you are being recorded at all times. The internal files of your display are secure, but the messages you send and the searches you make are not. The key is for the safe.

I flip the key around. When the banner disintegrates, I remind myself that I have to breathe, or else I've instantly given up whatever precious little advantage I've stumbled on to. Kieren and I are on the same posting, but it looks like we're accessing different information after all.

The office was coded to open for me. The banners are appearing directly in my display. What's happening here?

"It's a smart key," I say, showing Kieren the back. The shape is entirely a decoy. "Probably for a safe."

Kieren, immediately, narrows his eyes. "What are you seeing?"

Damn.

"What?" I try. "What are you talking about?"

"You saw a smart key and you assumed *safe*?" he asks, flabbergasted. "There's no safe at the data center. Everything is password-protected on the cloud."

He makes a reach for the key. Instinctively, I yank it back, close to my chest.

And that only increases his suspicion. "Lia. Hand it over."

"What is your problem? I recognize the brand, it pairs to a certain safe—"

He tries again. I dart out of the way once more.

"Lia, I swear—"

"*Wait*—"

Kieren finally snatches the key away from me, one hand wrapped around my wrist to keep me still and the other prying the metal from my fingers. I freeze, waiting for the accusation, waiting for the banners to enter his display too and his cries of fault.

But Kieren says nothing. He frowns, then turns the key over a few times, getting a good look. Nothing has appeared for him.

"I was *trying* to tell you," I huff. "It's this company, Beam-Man Security." I reach over to tap the key's round teeth, where the logo is engraved at the end. "Look it up. The safes open on smart keys and a fingerprint. It's probably in Chung's home."

A set of footsteps hurry by outside. Someone, in a rather flustered fashion, is calling for bottles of water—management is arriving. We need to get out of here before then.

"You think that's where our energy is best served next?" Kieren asks dubiously. "Chung's safe at his apartment?"

I shrug. "If you were working on a program that half the world wants and encountered secret reasons that lead it to be deleted, don't you think you'd keep the important stuff at home?"

"No," Kieren says. "I think I'd keep it in the real. Downcountry."

"He *worked* downcountry, but he had the funds to be upcountry. I'm sure he spent plenty of time at his upcountry Upsie apartment."

Kieren tips his head back. My eyes are swiveling impatiently to the door, but Kieren seems to be in no hurry.

"Lia," he groans, and I'm so unused to him using my real name that it sends a shiver down my neck. "Don't you think Medan police will have cleared out his apartment by now?"

"Wrong," I fire back immediately. "Maybe they stationed an officer to track who comes by, but they can't treat it like a crime scene. He's just missing. It's not illegal to go missing."

Kieren frowns. "It is illegal to delete government property."

"Which a normal precinct can't know about. Top secret, remember? Government higher-ups can only keep an eye on the situation. They won't report the extent of it."

Kieren still seems uncertain. "We should call Kam and check in. What if Medaluo's higher-ups are sending their own people to sniff around?"

"Then we should get to the apartment as soon as possible and see what's in the safe before them," I counter. "We're not out of moves yet. This is a critical path to pursue."

"It's like arguing with a wall." He gestures up and down his clothes, the ridiculous little outfits we've put on that NileCorp supplied. "How are we getting in without Kam doing prep work overnight?"

I make a rapid search through our briefing for Chung's apartment address. It's back in the city center, near Norca Road. At the same time, I get a small alert, a new message. This one wasn't triggered by any coded objects—I recognize Rayna's custom emoticon smiling toothily in the corner.

"Your sister," I say, speaking before my thoughts have entirely caught up to me. "Last year she hacked your dad's fingerprint scanner on his computer. She sent that prank blast out to the school."

Kieren rolls his eyes. "*Hacking* is a generous term for what she does. She browses the dark web for exploits and bothers the creators until they explain them to her."

"Message her."

"What?"

I'm already moving for the door. "Kieren. I think we're onto something. Message her!"

RAYNA: hiiiiiiii :D i'm in Upsie!
RAYNA: oh, and rattlesnake
LIA: toad, lightly fried
LIA: Norca Road please!!!
RAYNA: huh?
LIA: [Sent a location pin.]
LIA: wear something cute, Hailey's going to be there

• • • •

Both Hailey and Rayna are under an hour away by transit in different directions.

Kieren and I reach Norca Road first, parking the truck in an alley and leaving our jumpsuits in the back. A giant hologram of a green fish swims through the air where the street begins, the entire thoroughfare roped off for pedestrians only. Norca Road is Upsie's tourist hotspot—not to be confused with Norca, *Land of the Northern Castle,* the capital city of Medaluo. Vehicles aren't allowed on this road because both the ground-level sidewalks and the elevated glass platforms are already impossible to navigate without being pressed shoulder to shoulder with other people.

Half the faces here are foreign. Visitors in the server on vacation. No one gives Kieren a second glance.

"You know," Kieren remarks when we push into the crowd, "if NileCorp really wanted to step up its cadets, they should open restrictions on avatars. Let us change our faces to blend in where we need to go."

I give him a dirty look. "Huge ethical issues, Murray. *Huge.*"

"I'm just musing."

"You're too smart to muse on that. Be serious."

There's a simple enough reason Atahua doesn't open the lock on full avatar customization: it doesn't need to. Atahua has droves of citizens who are ethnically Medan—if they start running out of orphan children to use, they will recruit adults. They have no shortage of spies who blend in with the enemy nation, but Medaluo doesn't have the same. Medaluo is made up of Medans to the point that tourists stick out beyond the main cities, and any foreign agent of theirs sent into Atahua will possess a Medan face.

No matter how well they speak Atahuan, no matter how much they adopt the mannerisms of Atahuans, a Medan cannot be trusted in Atahuan society, will not receive security clearance in Atahua by law.

So NileCorp won't code that sort of customization, ever, because if they do and it goes wide, the one who benefits most is Medaluo.

"Rayna's twenty minutes away," I report, watching her location pin. "I think you should go ahead and find somewhere for us to convene. Somewhere our group will look natural, and not, you know, like we're plotting a home invasion. I can go buy a laptop."

Kieren pulls a face. He already has plenty of qualms about inviting Rayna and Hailey in to help us, but we've argued enough during the drive to Norca Road, and I clearly won.

"Buy a laptop?"

"You're not going to make your sister squint at her own display to launch an exploit, surely." I pivot before Kieren can protest. He's the one holding on to the smart key in his pocket, so it's more important that he get out of the crowds first in case someone attempts to swipe it.

"Keep me updated!" I shout back. "I'll join you shortly!"

I'm mostly only finding an excuse to go off somewhere and make a call.

In seconds I've lost Kieren in the crush of tourists, navigating forward with my map. Upsie has standardized its architecture—its climbing titans of steel, straight and tall—everywhere except here, along this tourist strip. A portion of the buildings I'm passing are short and far older, their rooftops paved with flat red bricks. Kieren scored higher than me on that presentation in Medan Language class. I stammered answering questions about the war with Pyam two hundred years ago, and Kieren had extra fun facts up his sleeve about the cultural preservation effort the Pyaish populations in Medaluo underwent to keep these buildings as a way to remember their ancestors.

I scan the stores ahead of me, inspecting the map in my display. The depth perception shifts, and I huff, realizing I should have been using the elevated platforms—the tech store is on the second floor, where the silver doors bulge out from the existing houses, where businesses rented out their extra spaces after the city installed the elevated platforms, intent on taking advantage of the foot traffic.

Rather than going around for the steps at the end, I grab the edge of the platform and haul myself up, squeezing through the thin space where the glass barrier doesn't touch the floor. The two closest tourists on the platform sniff at my behavior—an elderly Atahuan couple, which I can tell because they're wearing NiLeisure head to toe, and no one outside of Atahua takes NileCorp's fashion line seriously.

"Hi!"

I get the cheery greeting out before the store associate does, and she jumps to attention, intent on matching my pep. The air-conditioning in the store is on full blast. I can feel it in my nostrils.

"Welcome!" Her name tag says NADINE. An Atahuan name. For a moment I think she's not Medan, but then she comes closer. She is, only her features have been severely adjusted. Her chin is far sharper than any Atahuan or Medan alike, her nose thinner than a Popsicle stick—which can only be Medaluo's filters. It's not something frowned upon here, as it is in Atahua. It isn't seen as bizarre or deceitful. Everyone knows that's not how they look downcountry. It's like decorating a dress-up game avatar. Or switching up an alter ego.

"Can I help you look for anything today?" she asks. "The new model of handhelds just came in, guaranteed to be ten times more comfortable than your display. We can calculate a payment plan quicker than you can say *Wow!*"

I glance up. The store's name is Wow! Electronics.

"I just need a new laptop," I say. I peer around the aisles. It's entirely empty aside from Nadine. She's practically rising onto the tips of her toes in her enthusiasm to help. I've gotten away from Kieren's scrutiny only to meet another roadblock. "Actually, can I try out some soundproof booths first? Work from home is getting impossible with the social calls my mother is making in the kitchen."

"Sure thing!" Nadine chirps. "They're just around the back."

I follow her through the aisles. They don't put the handhelds under glass cases, nor lock down any of the computer monitors. Demand is already low in virtual, the devices made solely in case someone is sick of having everything right in front of their eyes. No one commits theft when they'd be identified instantly either.

Nadine brings me into a corridor at the back, where their soundproof booths are laid out in a row. I thank her and step into the first one, tapping around as though I'm testing out its firmness before I close the door after myself.

I activate the call immediately.

"Pick up," I mutter. "Pick up . . ."

"Lia!" It routes to Freya. "Aren't you on your posting?"

"I am," I reply enthusiastically. I don't want her to tell Dad that something is wrong. "Can you connect me to Dad? I just wanted to check in."

"Hmm . . . He's in meetings right now, but I can pass on a message."

My eyes flicker through the glass panel. Nadine isn't going back to work. She's leaning up against the entryway, watching me test the booth.

"Okay, I lied," I say. "It's actually a bit of an emergency. Please put me through."

Freya seems concerned now. "Is everything all right?"

DEFINITELY NOT, FREYA, I want to say. *THAT'S WHY I SAID IT'S AN EMERGENCY.*

"Please just check for me! Thanks!"

The line clicks. I get a beat of silence. It draws long. Longer. I hear only the tapping of my fingers against the wooden table, the plush leather booth seat settling under my fidgeting. Then:

"Lia?"

"Project Wit," I say without prelude. "Was there anything strange about it?"

A beat passes. "Excuse me?"

I open the briefing. I start to flip through the pages for anything I've missed, CONFIDENTIAL emblazoned on each page. "I can't say too much. But if you were to point out *anything* strange about Project Wit, what would it be?"

"Lia, I haven't a clue what you're talking about," Dad says. "Is this about your posting? You said you were on a survey."

Finding Chung's missing body is definitely a survey of his life and times, I suppose.

"Tangentially."

"Lia. Project Wit is no joking matter, however you've stumbled onto it. It was shut down for a reason."

I wait for him to elaborate. He doesn't.

"Before Chung left?"

"Yes." He sighs. "I'm sure that was a motivator for his actions."

"Why was it shut down?"

"Because some things actually don't need to be made," Dad says. "Especially not in a climate where racing to acquire it first means ruling the world. Leave it alone, Lia. Go back to your posting."

Unfortunate that I'm getting the feeling this is very related to my posting.

"Dad." I flip to the middle of the briefing, to Chung's picture. He has this look in his eyes that Dad gets too, right before he goes on television. Controlled, measured, absent—so that nothing shouted at him will provoke him. "This sounds concerning."

"We can talk more when you get home."

He's afraid of being monitored. A jolt squirms through my stomach, spreads outward and prickles my skin. By the time I've gotten home, this will be over, and I'll either have succeeded in this posting or failed to glean anything. I'll either have performed to the status of valedictorian and chosen my position, or I'll be nothing, just another cadet, another graduate, another unwanted resident of Atahua swept into the everyday drivel that makes up its workforce.

"Okay, I'll talk to you later," I say faintly. "Have a good day."

"You too. Love you."

He hangs up. Nadine must have been peering through the glass block, because as soon as I've stopped speaking, she knocks on the door.

How are we doing in there? she mouths through the glass.

I let her question hang, signaling that I'm checking on something. It buys me the time to reel, to digest what exactly that was all about. My dad has never been the most forthcoming person. That's expected, given his job. He waves off questions about the latest political scandal in Melnova; he hems and haws if I'm asking him his opinion on Medaluo. It's not that he doesn't trust me. He can't afford sound bites leaking on the off chance someone is tapping our call line or flying a miniature drone in the form of a bee through our balcony windows.

But between his reaction and Chung's office giving me secret banners in my display, I can't imagine this being regular, precautionary secrecy. My calls are monitored, yes. As are my messages to anyone back in Atahua... to be viewed by NileCorp, my future employers. So if Dad won't say anything, is there something here that *NileCorp* isn't allowed to know?

I push open the booth door.

"I need to think on it a bit longer," I say distractedly. My eyes swivel in rapid motion, making a search in my display. When the academy traces this later to grade my posting, this is more than relevant. This is what anyone would check up on knowing what I know and having seen what I saw in Chung's office.

project wit shut down atahua why

"Totally understandable," Nadine says. She gestures along the row. "Do you want to try out any of the other booths?"

"Um..."

The results of my search come back with various feed posts from twelve years ago. I don't see any official press releases or news coverage, so I highlight every opinion on the first page of results for a summary: **Project Wit was an AI program that aimed to truly understand language, which raised questions about its use in improving the upcountry experience.** *It would make a huge difference in productivity—rather than employing engineers building and improving StrangeLoom, this program implicitly grasps the nature of its reality, which allows it to easily do the job of ten engineers.* **NileCorp did not acquire Project Wit, as investors hoped. To the researchers' dismay, in fact, NileCorp felt threatened by the possibility that the AI would gain the capability to build a competitor to StrangeLoom.** *Once the research reached a certain point of success, Project Wit was building AI that could either enter StrangeLoom to shut it down entirely, or make a carbon copy that was a free and open reality, replicated using its own knowledge.* **Behind the scenes, trusted sources say the company bent the arm of Atahua's research departments and ended Project Wit.**

I clear my search, sweat building at my temple. An AI program built to understand language, able to interact with StrangeLoom and make adjustments.

Flip it on its head, spin it around a few times, call it a weapon instead of a bid to improve the upcountry user's experience, and it sounds a lot like Operation Coldwire, actually.

Nadine clears her throat. "Maybe this larger model here, with two seats?"

"No, that's okay," I croak, closing my display. "Just the laptop, please."

19

EIRALE

It's a nine-hour drive from Upsie to Threto.

We're slowing, turning off the highway and onto a main road, so we must be reaching the midpoint of our journey. I assumed we'd travel the full nine hours at once. It's a self-driving van. They don't exactly need to swap who's behind the wheel to take shifts when night falls.

Turns out though, the vehicle is electric, which means plugging in for more power halfway through. Stolen electric vehicles don't hold much charge. At least not enough to risk the full journey.

I stir from my light doze, shifting to face the window. Miz suggested stopping in either Satisci or Peacebrate, whichever ends up being easiest for refueling. On the map, it's a straight shot from Upsie to Threto. On the actual roads, the curving lines and squiggling hills add far more travel time. Our route so far has cut through the middle of several residential low-rises, which I gather is common in places where they needed to build an expressway but didn't want to demolish the buildings in its path. We've had to detour twice: the map hadn't realized parts of the expressways were shut down from a lack of usage and led us into dead-ends.

The horizon seeps grayer the farther west we go. The clouds grow darker too. Night arrives with the flip of a switch. I blink, and what I assumed to be a decrease in air quality snatches the sun away at once, the sky a canvas of blotted ink.

"You're awake?"

Nik's voice sounds suddenly in my ear. I hadn't heard him change seats to get behind me, and I jolt, spinning around.

"Sorry," he rushes to say, holding his hands up. "I come in peace."

My eyes flicker to the window. My pulse is thudding. "I think we're in Satisci, actually."

It takes Nik a beat to realize I made a joke. It takes him another to react, emitting a half laugh, begrudgingly gifted. Land of Satisfied Civilian and Land of Peaceful Celebration are close together, both smaller cities that continue hemorrhaging civilians with the years that pass. Downcountry, whether in Medaluo or Atahua, every midsized point on the map flows in one of two directions: into a big city where there is still a population, still jobs to be found, or the very opposite if someone has enough funds, into remote areas where they can be left alone to plug into a Pod and live in the virtual rendering of whichever city where they own property. Upcountry Satisci and Peacebrate remain well occupied, even as the real ones turn into arenas of ghosts.

"I looked at the two lists of Kunlun citizens that Blare got you in Upsie," Nik says. His expression has returned to its resting state—impassive. "What's the plan?"

I shift to cross my legs. On a bathroom break, I put away Teryn's tracker to keep it safe. It's in the sole of my shoes.

"We're already going to Threto next," I say. "You can't guess?"

"I can likely guess," Nik replies. "But I'd appreciate you talking me through it."

The unfortunate result of keeping the tracker in my shoe is that my left foot feels an infinitesimal amount heavier than my right. Though I know it must weigh less than a grain of rice, I still sense it, and I'm finding it difficult to ignore the difference. It lurks ever-present in my field of awareness.

It reminds me of what waits at the end of this. They'll want Nik dead eventually. It won't be called an execution—it'll be a hazard that they couldn't have foreseen, an inmate with a shiv. They'll want Miz, even Blare, imprisoned. They'll put Blare in prison garb far too big for them. NileCorp will not care that they're a kid.

I push the thought away quickly, then cross my legs again in the other order.

"It's nothing complex. You already have business in Threto's data center—and it's Medaluo's largest data facility. Exactly the place to hit for the most variety of information." I look over at Blare, who's lightly napping. "We run the names of the Kunlun citizens we retrieved in Upsie. See if any of their StrangeLoom credentials are retrievable. We'll need several options in case they log back in faster than we can change their primary passwords."

The StrangeLoom system will only allow one active log-in at a time: understandably, to prevent families who try to share one subscription. The moment we enter Kunlun, we'd be booting out the user whose avatar we stole, and we have to finish our business before they call for help to recover their account.

Nik nods. "And we'll retrieve their second passwords into Kunlun as well?"

"No." Kunlun is home to the richest people in the world. Their personal security, personal engineer teams, personal publicity will have a system set up to rotate new second passwords—weekly, daily, maybe even hourly. The second password is too precious to risk. "After we finish up in Threto, our next stop needs to be Offron."

My eyes flicker up. I don't know what I'm looking for—some signal, perhaps, that Nik knows I'm double-crossing him. Some gesture to point to him bugging me, wiring me, having recorded my entire exchange with Teryn.

We stare at each other for a beat too long. He has not reacted, so instead I'm the one who twitches suspiciously.

"What do they call Kunlun, after all?" I ask.

"The City in the Cloud," Nik answers, not missing a beat.

I nod. "You need to store the city in the cloud somewhere. Kunlun was invented in Offron—all the data is there."

We haven't seen any cars on our tail. If Teryn's team is following us, they're either maintaining drone watch or waiting for the tracker to stop. Or maybe they're not following at all. Maybe they've proceeded ahead and stationed themselves in Offron to prepare. Three days is not a long time.

"To break into Kunlun," I continue, "we primarily need to break into Offron's data center. If we plug a Claw into the maintenance ports that the engineers use, I expect that means we bypass the second password and log into upcountry the regular way. Use the credentials we've siphoned, and we enter as Kunlun citizens without raising their alarms."

The vehicle falls quiet. We've pulled off the main road, chugging toward the electric charging booth at a gas station. While the van parks itself into a slot, Miz reaches up at the front to turn on the interior lights. We all flinch. The bulbs are clinically bright, dousing us with such vigor that my eyes physically sting.

"I'm going to go activate charging," she announces. "Don't wake Blare if you can help it. We'll be on the move again shortly."

Miz steps out. Her door shuts. While she fiddles with the charging station cord, Nik mutters a complaint under his breath, leaning forward for the dashboard to dim the lights. A loud *click* reverberates from the van's exterior. The vehicle begins to hum to indicate a charge in progress.

"Do you even still have your chip?"

Nik turns slowly at my question, perched on the central console. He props his hands on his knees, keeping himself upright.

"You mean the chip that lets me go upcountry?" he asks. "Why wouldn't I?"

I didn't think that was a matter too unexpected to ask about. He's an anarchist, after all. One who won't shut up about Indisposition, insistent that any users who disappear from the servers but do not wake up must have had their minds deleted by NileCorp. The more logical possibility is that every once in a while, an error occurs in the Pods or the Claws, and people's brains go on the fritz. NileCorp pays an enormous settlement, the families mourn, and the rest of us continue with our lives in virtual.

"Given how many strong-worded leaflets of yours I've had to sift through fingerprinting," I say wryly, "I assumed you hated upcountry enough to want out."

Nik scoffs. "Yes. I have my chip. Thank you for worrying about whether I will be able to partake in the plan. Anyway . . ." He clears his throat. He evidently welcomes no further questions about the state of his subscription to StrangeLoom. "You think that will get us in? Entering on the maintenance ports?"

"It's the only method I can imagine that doesn't require those second passwords," I say. "We're not going to know until we try it. But even this gets you closer than anything you've brainstormed, right?"

He doesn't respond, which means I'm correct. The temptation to relish this competes with my disconcertment, growing with each passing second that I watch Nik for his reaction. In the other seat, Blare makes a loud snoring noise, harmonizing with the electric charging. They haven't stirred despite the light.

"It's not going to be easy," I warn. "Offron is Medaluo's most guarded data center."

"We'll get in," Nik says. He leaves no room for argument. It's not only a statement thrown at me. It sounds like a promise he's making himself.

"May I ask once again," I try, "what the program is?"

"Would it make a difference if you knew?" Nik returns.

It would. Because the longer they keep it from me, the more I'm convinced this has something to do with me. With what I uncovered the last time I was in Medaluo.

I lean forward on my elbows. "You have a lot to lose if I decide to go haywire and take the risk of returning to Atahua."

Nik shifts too. We're facing each other directly, our feet braced for the moment the bell goes off in the grappling ring.

"You wouldn't."

"Luckily for you," I counter, "I don't want to. I want your information. That's simple enough, isn't it?"

"I think you overestimate your negotiating power here."

"I think you don't understand how much I've already parsed." The vehicle shudders when Miz pulls out the charging cord. Her silhouette moves along the dark windows. My attention stays firmly on Nik. "The moment I saw you outside a video screen, I wondered if we had already met."

There's a reason I asked if he still had his chip, not whether he'd ever possessed one at all. If there was a time when I'd met him already, it had to have been upcountry last year. I scan him, and every detail is cohesive to what I'd innately expected. The faint scar on the left side of his dark brows. The paler strip of skin on his right wrist where he must have once worn a watch and since removed. The flash in Nik's gray eyes—terrified, for a brief second.

"I thought it was because I spent all that time studying you," I say. "My team in Button City split duties on the footage we had. We were only designated three each to take notes on and then pool together, but I found myself going to their boxes too just to learn a bit more information, gain a bit more insight."

What I don't say out loud is that I watched all his videos again, then again. Something kept bothering me, and I couldn't put my finger on it. I memorized how he moved, how he ran. I read through our brief front to back and spoke his name under my breath before I went to sleep, just to have captured a part of him first. The mixed-reality practice runs weren't depicting him correctly. When I almost got him on that second encounter, our eyes locked just as my hands faltered on the cuffs I was preparing. If he hadn't bested me the third time, knocked me out and escaped while I was unconscious, I might have started wondering if I was letting him slip away on purpose.

"I don't know how," I say, "but I think you were there with me in Kunlun. I think you know me."

"That's ridiculous," Nik counters. He's playing aloof, vacant. But I see him tapping his thumb to his index finger, then his middle finger. When he hits his pinkie finger, he reverses, repeats the process in a profane variation on counting prayer beads.

"Is it?" Ten weeks is a long time. "Let me prove it to you."

I hurtle forward.

This time I'm not trying to win. I have no intention to disarm. I'm not even trying to hurt him. My arm collides with Nik's chest; I push him onto the console, lock him down with the press of my knees. I take a swing, aiming right for his nose, and he blocks my hit by shoving upward on my elbow, breaking my trajectory before it can land. In the next breath I'm already shifting, attempting to stand again so that I can drive my elbow into his stomach, but Nik hisses, kicking me back.

He keeps his strike measured. I fly into the seats, my hair obscuring my eyes. Blare has woken with the commotion—they barely have the time to yell, "Hey!" before I skid along the floor in the small space, reaching for Nik's ankle.

I wrench at him, pulling him down. He has no time, no room in the van to maneuver elsewhere. And when his head thuds to the floor, when I raise my fist once again for a strike dead center on his face, he shoves his fingers into the side of my ribs, crumpling my form before I can make contact.

I prepare no next move when Nik goes on the offense. He takes the chance to incapacitate me, reverses how I've loomed over him so that his hands are clamped to my shoulders, his knee pinning my stomach in place.

And I say, "Point proven."

"What's wrong with you?" Nik snaps. He can't feign these instincts. Knowing how I move. Knowing exactly how I fight.

"You're bleeding!" Blare wails.

Nik doesn't let go of me. I don't break his gaze.

"The program," I say. I give him this out. We won't speak of why. I won't push him further on what he will not answer. But he has to give me something. Anything. "What is the program?"

Blare scrambles up, grabbing Nik's arm to haul him off me. He is unwilling, in that initial response. He lets go one hand at a time, afraid I'll charge again. Sensation returns to my left shoulder, then my right. When Nik straightens, he stays sitting on the floor of the van, close, wary. In tentative armistice, I mimic him, rising slowly so that I remain on the floor with my legs crossed.

Silence settles in the space between us, heavy as velvet, draped and pooled.

"The program," Nik finally says, "is a corruption exploit for the StrangeLoom engine."

Blare passes him a tissue, and Nik wipes the scratch on his temple where blood has beaded to the surface. That wasn't me. It's his own fault for colliding with the van.

"What does that mean?" I ask. "You'd be able to hack it?"

"Yes. To the very core level." He exhales, setting down the bloodied tissue. "I don't hate upcountry. I hate NileCorp's control over the invention. We could unlock NileCorp's settings on every nation's server. Delete the subscription model on users. Make upcountry a public right and freely accessible to anyone with a plug-in."

My eyebrows shoot up of their own accord. I understood his team were anarchists. I didn't think that meant they had such inexact ideas for the be-all, end-all of freedom.

"If you corrupt StrangeLoom," I say slowly, "what's stopping NileCorp from refusing to run their servers? They won't be making money anymore."

"Good," Nik replies sharply. "The next thing I want is NileCorp dead in the ground. They *shouldn't* have control over those servers. There shouldn't be one entity who stores every bit of information about every person who has ever gone upcountry."

"The servers would collapse without their maintenance."

"Maybe countries need to be taking over their own maintenance if they want a place to live. It'll force them to have their own system instead of relaying everything back to NileCorp."

I wait a beat, making sure I've heard him right. "You want *Medaluo's* government taking over their upcountry?"

Nik grimaces. "I didn't claim it was a perfect plan," he says.

"Medaluo has Kunlun, and they're doing fine," Blare offers.

"Medaluo does *not* have Kunlun," I say. "*Kunlun* has Kunlun, because Kunlun has more billionaires than square footage. Of course Medaluo's not going to shut them off from the world just because they can."

Even with a corruption exploit, I have trouble believing StrangeLoom couldn't just kick Nik right out. NileCorp has millions and millions of dollars of reward money every year set aside for hackers, prompting them to submit the smallest of loopholes rather than exploit them. Even the toughest underground black hats will help NileCorp for the payout.

No wonder the only entity that would even make a program like this is a national government. If monetary gain isn't the motivation, the only remaining reason is power.

"Don't you think," I say, "if the Medan government made something like this, it would benefit them most if you used it?"

"You see what the papers say about me already," Nik replies. "If I have to declare myself a traitor loyal to Medaluo to see NileCorp burn, so be it."

The passenger door flings open, bringing Miz's return.

"We're charged," she announces. She clambers back into her seat. Turns around. "Why are you both on the floor?"

Nik gets up, dusting himself off. He's clearly finished with our conversation, and I let him extract himself. He goes to the front, intent on telling Miz the series of checks they need to do to make sure the van hasn't been overloaded on the charge, and I ease myself back onto a seat.

"Off to Threto we go," Blare says quietly, doing their best to ease the tension. I nod to acknowledge their effort.

Still, when I fold my arms, I lean away, toward the window. The night shows no movement outside. Only empty houses and skeletal trees, faintly visible by city light in the distance.

If they knew me from my posting—Nik and Miz and Blare—why set me up for murder and treason? Why not ask me to come along, say that we were once acquainted, that my presence is needed?

Slowly, my gaze slides back to Blare. Their fingers fly over a handheld, the screen tilted so that I can't see what they're typing. At the front, Miz has put on her glasses. She's typing too. They're speaking to each other, right in front of me. When I helped Miz put on her eyeliner, she barely dared to move. That's not the behavior of someone who enjoyed my friendship in the past. That's the precautionary agitation of being around a complete stranger.

I breathe onto the window, misting the surface. None of this makes sense.

I couldn't begin to put together what memories have escaped me. What I did, who I knew, why I ended up in Kunlun. How I ended up in critical condition coming back down to my Pod. The fact that I was injured enough to damage my memories tells me everything, I suppose.

Whatever happened last time I was here, it didn't end well.

20

LIA

Kieren sends me a location for a building called the Pindrop.

It's near Chung's apartment, up at the northern tip of the tourist hotspot. I forward it to Rayna and tell Kieren as much, to which he replies with a frowning emoticon he's clearly doodled himself. Before I have the chance to respond, he's sent a complex landscape of a stick figure drawing, depicting the two of us getting arrested for revealing confidential secrets. I roll my eyes, swiping out of my display. He's so dramatic.

We've entered a quieter hour, a lull setting over Norca Street. The tourists have found their way to various stores for afternoon tea, exhausted and in need of rest. Gaps open among the wanderers that remain on the road. I zip and dart around their bulky backpacks, narrowly avoiding stepping into a ball of ice cream someone has dropped from their cone. The laptop bag I'd gotten from the store hangs over my shoulder, bouncing the device against the side of my leg.

The Pindrop is shaped as it's named, and I've already located it from several blocks away. It doesn't look like it should be capable of standing upright at all, never mind at its height. Its tallest point is the widest part of the building, a half sphere that glows red from the line of windows ringing the circumference. With every descending floor, the building grows narrower and narrower. The shorter establishments on either side hide the Pindrop's base, lending the optical illusion that perhaps it really does filter down to something needle thin. Once I'm directly in front of it, though, it's obvious that the building remains the same width from below the tenth floor. I breathe a sigh of relief once I'm inside the revolving doors. The whole thing probably isn't going to tip over. Probably.

The front desk at the Pindrop has both a person and a bot stationed. I almost don't know who to look at first when I approach.

"Where to?" the bot says first.

"Oh, um, top floor. The lounge."

The doorman rises from his chair, his posture stick-straight. The longer part of his waistcoat flaps with the air-conditioning roaring through the vents. "With me, please, miss."

He comes around the front desk, gesturing for me to follow. This is rather unnecessary, given all he does when he accompanies me to the elevator bay is press the big, red button that says ROOF LOUNGE, but I thank him anyway. He stays put. The elevator makes its way down.

"So," I say, only to fill the silence, "slow day?"

"No. Lounge usually doesn't fill up until after dark. You'll get a nice seat now." The elevator arrives. He inclines his head. "Have a pleasant visit."

I step inside. I have to imagine the bot is in charge of the residents who live on the lower levels, but the human is the face for rooftop visitors. Maybe he wanted a tip. The doors close. It's too late now.

The elevator starts to move, ascending the levels. Past floor eleven, I'm suddenly shot into daylight again, and I turn to face the city, blinking fast at the elevator's glass walls. The pulley chugs along the exterior of the Pindrop, offering a view of Upsie's entirety: the sharp rocks where the coast meets the water, the vast spread going into land, the edges of its western terrain where enormous industrial lights shoot different company sponsor banners into the atmosphere every night.

It looks bigger, somehow, when viewed on a map.

The doors open, having arrived at the roof. I almost don't notice. It brings me to a dark, winding corridor which wraps around the lounge in the center, gauging by its shape. My feet sink into the plush red carpet; there are paintings of dogs wearing hats hanging from the gold wallpaper. I'm about to capture a screenshot to send it to Kieren—thus make fun of him in a roundabout way for bringing us here—when I turn the bend and spot someone familiar gazing up at one of the portraits, clearly admiring it.

I gasp. Rayna turns. I lift my arms. Rayna squeals, "Wheeeeee!" and runs toward me until we've joined in a hug.

"Thank you for coming," I say when we draw apart. "I know it was quick, especially after you just got put into the server."

"Oh, I almost didn't come. I don't know if I'm mentally equipped to interact with Hailey yet." She smooths the wrinkles out of her silk shirt. "What happened to your forehead?"

"Don't ask." I spin Rayna around, walking her toward the door to the lounge that I've now spotted. "And you better keep it together. Don't *ever* say I don't do anything for you."

Kieren's waving at me the moment we cross the threshold, impatient. Hailey's already here, in the seat beside him, picking at a bowl of sunflower seeds. I ignore the slight tremble that has started in Rayna's shoulders and continue pushing her forward.

True to the doorman's word, the lounge is largely empty, staffed by bots at the bar and an open-concept kitchen window. There are only two other groups among the red velvet couches: an elderly couple with martinis in hand and three women in the middle wearing shiny dresses, celebrating. A server bot rolls out from the kitchen with sparklers on a cake. The women cheer, crowding together for a tiny drone they've launched before them for pictures.

"What is this place?" I demand the moment we reach the corner table, tucked to the right of the bar. "We're underage in Medaluo too."

"We're not here to drink," Kieren scoffs.

Hailey drapes herself on the couch. She still has half a sunflower seed shell in her mouth, and she aims it perfectly when she spits, letting it clink into the discard bowl. "Well," she sighs, "there goes my reason for being here."

I sit Rayna down by force, afraid that she'll get entirely distracted and remain standing if I don't.

"We're here," Kieren says with emphasis, "because this is the only building on Norca Road that has a view of Chung's apartment. See for yourself."

Oh. I hurry to the window, peering out. I spot the building in question immediately, easily recognizable after my extensive study of the photos in the briefing. I pull up the building's floor plans and count the levels, confirming Kieren's claim. This looks right into Chung's kitchen window.

"So what is this all about?" Hailey asks, sitting upright. "You have to give us the full scoop on your top-secret mission now."

She makes it sound like a game we're playing, leaning forward to debrief with her team members in the school courtyard. Hailey Murray has never been the type to take anything seriously: during formal classes, her uniform will be unbuttoned too low, and she'll insist on her civil right to keep the rings on each of her fingers when we're supposed to have changed for PE. It's not like any of her bad behavior at the academy matters after she graduates—NileCorp can't *not* take a Murray.

Kieren Murray, on the other hand, is an anomaly for working so hard.

"The overview is that we have a Beam-Man smart key to a safe we want to open. We need, one, a distraction to keep building security away so we can get into the apartment"—Kieren nods to a flustered Rayna—"and two, a method to bypass the fingerprint scanner that accompanies the smart key access." On the second part, he rolls his eyes at his sister, and Hailey grins as though he's paid her a compliment. She's scraped her blond hair back into a tight ponytail, which means, shockingly, there's much more resemblance between them than usual. Clean and proper.

"Sorry," Rayna says. It comes out a squeak. She clears her throat, acting as though she'd gotten dust stuck in there before speaking again at normal volume. "Did you just say I was keeping security away? I thought I was helping with retrieval."

"You are," I offer. "Helping us get in is a part of retrieval."

"I mean," Rayna says, "I'm pretty good at running cloning sequences on devices too."

Hailey quirks a brow. She rests her left elbow on the back of the couch, her entire posture slumping in that direction. "You want to take over for me instead?"

"Absolutely not," Rayna rushes to correct. "That wasn't what I was implying."

"I wouldn't mind," Hailey singsongs.

"Do you not want to be here or something?" Kieren asks his sister.

Hailey pouts. "When my dearest brother asks, how *could* I say no?"

A bell goes off at the kitchen window. While Kieren and Hailey start to argue, my attention pivots away, and I watch a serving bot roll over to collect the tray. It shrinks itself down to a lower height before rumbling to the elderly couple, depositing the soups. When they thank the bot, its neutral face changes to a large smiley.

I open my display, keeping my gaze on the bot so no one can tell I'm typing.

> LIA: Rayna . . .
> RAYNA: WHAT'D I DO
> LIA: stop touching your face like you're on the verge of a nervous breakdown
> RAYNA: i kind of am tho
> LIA: are u going to use this as an opportunity or not!!!!!!
> RAYNA: okay fineeeee!!!!!!!!!!!

"We need to get started," I cut in, interrupting whatever point Hailey was on. "Do you think you can manage it? Trigger the fingerprint scanner of a Beam-Man safe?"

"Yeah, of course," Hailey replies casually, crossing her legs. "My dad's computer was probably harder. I can adjust the exploit I already have."

"Great." I swing the laptop bag off my shoulder and throw it at Hailey. She catches it smoothly. I give Kieren a weighty look, a silent *I told you so* that I knew his sister would be useful. "You'll be okay to go remote here?"

Laptop bag bundled in her arms, Hailey slides across the couch to the farthest end, up against the glass, where she can get a good look into Chung's apartment. "Sure thing. You can wave at me from the window if I'm not pointing signals in the right direction."

"Rayna, do you want to stay here to trigger security remotely?"

Rayna makes the biggest, most startled eyes I've seen on a human being. I have half a mind to think she's fusing with an owl. A were-owl.

"Yes. Yes, totally," she manages.

Hailey pats the seat beside her on the couch, signaling for Rayna to join her.

I yank Kieren up by the arm, and we make our prompt exit. "Wait for our cue," I call to Rayna. "Thank you! Love you!"

• • • •

We're outside Chung's apartment building in six minutes. I eye the giant bees' nest that's hanging off one of the water pipes, unable to believe what I'm seeing.

"How did that get there?" I whisper.

"Engineer with a sense of humor," Kieren replies. I suppose it's either that, or StrangeLoom decided bee populations were lacking in Upsie. "Ready?"

I nod. I send Rayna a message, asking her to begin. She returns a smiley face, which I assume means she's working on it.

Kieren leans back against the wall. I bounce up and down on my toes. A minute passes.

"Read anything good lately?" I ask.

"What is this?"

I tilt my head. "What?"

"You're making small talk? Before we commit burglary?"

Still no indication that anything has been triggered to pull security away from Chung's apartment.

"We might not take anything," I muse.

"Burglary is just the act of breaking and entering." Kieren's not facing me, but I know he's got a smug twist to his mouth. "It doesn't need to involve theft. Common misconception."

"Do you get physically itchy if you don't correct me? Genuine question."

There must be a loudspeaker installed somewhere above us. A sudden, folksy tune starts to play, floating over from one of the balconies.

"You don't see me scratching, do you?" he asks.

I groan. We settle into a lull. I send Rayna another message prompting a time estimate for what exactly she's working on.

"I've been reading a lot of comic books lately," Kieren offers after another minute.

"Cool," I say. "Any standouts?"

Kieren shrugs. "I'm pretty much just catching up on one old series. It's about a boy who—"

Chung's building lets out an earsplitting shriek. Fire alarm. Rayna sends a reply telling me the back door stairwell has all its cameras down, and I'm on the move instantly. Kieren knows to follow suit without my prompting. We're up the steps in two strides, the heavy back door depositing us directly into the stairwell.

The fire alarm turns faint here, blocked by the insulation in the walls. Kieren surges ahead, taking advantage of his long legs on the stairs. Though I keep pace, I have to pretend not to be slightly out of breath by the time we're at the ninth floor. I'm sure Kieren's doing the same.

"Hailey, have you got the front door?" Kieren asks out loud. He must have opted to connect to a call rather than text.

We press into the hallway. I scan the corners first: the camera lights are dulled and down. Thankfully the doormen in this building aren't bots.

They're not checking system updates. They can only rely on the visuals.

Kieren approaches Chung's apartment and tugs open the door smoothly, holding it for me to slip in first.

Immediately, my neck prickles. The door closes after us with a click, and I take a deep, stale breath. A stack of magazines on the dining table. Various umbrellas hanging from the coatrack. Even a half-eaten bunch of grapes left in the fruit bowl.

"The safe is probably in the bedroom, right?" Kieren says.

I make a vague affirmative noise. While Kieren goes to the bedroom, I wander into the kitchen, positioning myself in front of the window briefly to offer a thumbs-up. Then I trail my fingers along the stove. I wipe the edge of the gas knobs.

"I've found the safe, Ward," Kieren calls, his voice echoing through the apartment. "Where'd you go?"

Outside, the fire alarm is still ringing, though I don't hear any resident leaving to evacuate. We're upcountry—the same protocols for safety exist, but there's little danger in what a fire can actually do. They're all just waiting for it to stop screeching.

I hurry to join Kieren. The bedroom is a similar situation to the living area. There's balled-up socks in the corner. A glass of water too close to the edge of the bedside table.

It all so *perfectly* resembles a scene mid-motion.

Almost like the place has been staged to look like someone walked out in the middle of a busy morning.

"Some help here?"

I jolt to attention, hurrying to join Kieren in hoisting the safe from the closet. It's a small, rectangular box, so flat in height that I can't imagine anything larger than a textbook lying inside. I give it a shake, and Kieren hisses *"Be careful!"* right as what sounds like metal clatters against the safe's interior.

"It sounded light," I remark. "Can't be anything that takes up the whole space."

"To tell you the truth, I didn't think people even owned safes anymore—especially not upcountry." Kieren peers at the scanner protruding from the front. "Hailey, did you say you needed the serial or the link number?"

A call request pops up in my display. When I accept, I hear Hailey's answer, looped into the group line.

"Serial number. Read it out for me nice and slowly."

Kieren does so, pausing after each digit to ensure Hailey has received it correctly. I push the water glass to the center of the bedside table. Hailey confirms that she has the number—she'll start running the exploit.

"Lots of safes in old movies," I remark when the line falls quiet. I mute myself so that Hailey can't hear me. "Chung showed me a bunch of those, actually. The film noirs with the detectives."

Kieren has turned around to peer through the bedroom window. We're too high up for there to be activity immediately outside. I have to assume he's only making a cautionary perusal. I can't see his expression when he replies, "Most likely items you'd keep in safes are cash, identification, and weapons. First two are digital now. Maybe it's a gun in here."

"Sure. Very likely."

He hasn't reacted to my comment about Chung showing me my favorite noir movies. It's not a lie: I did watch a lot of those on Chung's recommendations. Still, I wouldn't have mentioned it if I weren't waiting for Kieren to ask about the detail, to investigate whether there was more significance. It's unlike him.

"I think we've got it, babes," Hailey declares.

I unmute quickly.

"Key?" I prompt Kieren.

He hurries to dig it out, sliding the teeth into the small slot at the front. When he turns it, there's slight resistance for a heartbeat.

Then Kieren pulls hard, and the seal of the door shifts, opening.

"Success," he breathes, reaching in. He tugs out one item. The only item in the safe.

I don't even know what I'm looking at. It's a thin, square disk with a hole in the middle, encased in what looks to be plastic but seems heavy enough to be metal. Kieren turns it over, frowning. There's a sticker on the other side. In hurried handwriting, it reads PROPERTY OF THREE TOWNS NATIONAL DATA CENTER.

"A storage disk?" I ask. I can't help but be disappointed. I'd imagined a rare gem that would lead us to a smuggling ring. A pair of gloves that belonged to some spurned lover. Something *solid* that was more than just... more information to follow.

Kieren nods. "Floppy disk. Look. It's got a unique panel."

The floppy disks with unique panels are a pain. They were made in a call toward nostalgia, resembling the disks that were first popularized almost a hundred years ago. Only, to smarten up the design and increase security, each disk comes with a unique reader to access its information. It's essentially the layman's version of an encryption.

"Should we look for a disk reader?" I ask.

"I poked through the electronics already," he says. He taps the sticker on the disk. "If Chung only brought this home, then the reader is still in Threto, presumably."

Our briefing says Chung works across all the major locations, given entry to each of Medaluo's data centers. Fair enough if he ends up dispersing his sensitive information across them too to prevent access to thieves.

"HIYA."

Rayna's entrance into the joint call is a surprise, and Kieren and I both jump at the loud volume. He almost drops the disk, and I scoop my hands out, intending to catch it.

He regains his hold.

"APOLOGIES FOR THE VOLUME—I BROKE THIS SETTING IN MY DISPLAY THE OTHER DAY AND STILL NEED TO GET IT FIXED. PLEASE LEAVE NOW. ALARM IS STOPPING IN THIRTY SECONDS."

21

EIRALE

The WELCOME TO LAND OF THREE TOWNS sign is missing its top corner. I lean forward to get a better look, rolling down the window. We've been on the road for long enough that I'm itching to move. Different parts of my body keep going numb, asking for a change in my posture or some opportunity to stretch my limbs.

The dashboard beeps. Miz lurches upright.

"What is that?" Nik demands from the back. He's been at work on the floor of the vehicle, two laptops open with one on each thigh to decrypt the server.

"Vehicle wants to be taken off self-driving and switched to manual," Miz reports. "I don't know why—oh. Never mind. I see why."

We turn off the sharp exit from the expressway and immediately join a queue of cars. If the welcome sign was any indication, we've just crossed the boundary line into Threto. It must be the toll booths causing this traffic jam. The lights have gone out up ahead, so there's only the impression of the entry barriers, the one lane into Threto and the machines that process a fee for each entry and exit.

I get out of my seat, creeping forward for a better look. Blare, with a yawn, stands too, trying to join me by leaning between the front seats.

"Why are we stopped?" they ask. "Toll booths are automatic."

"Maybe the bot is having a bad day," I suggest.

The queue moves slowly. The booth becomes slightly more visible after another car is let through the barrier, shifting the line forward. Now I've spotted the traffic control workers in their orange vests and clipboards. One of them gestures for the next car to roll down their window. The worker says something, then points overhead at a bulky camera.

"They're doing thermal checks," I say suddenly. "Making sure no one has a fever before entering."

"Oh, shit." A subtle glow grows brighter from Miz's glasses. She's pulled open a video. "I don't know if we're going to make it through."

"What?" Nik and Blare demand together, their voices bouncing from different points of the van.

Miz taps the side of her glasses. With a click, it projects the video as a hologram hovering before her, letting the sound play on speaker.

"... *announcing a two-week closure in Threto's urban limits starting at ten p.m. tonight. This latest variant of avian influenza is moving fast, and we want to prevent the spread as well as we can. A reminder that the safest place to remain is upcountry, and if you haven't yet subscribed, this segment is sponsored by the Ministry of—*"

The video blinks off when Miz pushes her glasses up, onto the top of her head. The queue has moved again, and she eases off the brake, driving forward.

Avian influenza is highly contagious. The Button City base gave us our vaccines last month, but that doesn't mean I can't catch it still.

"This is ridiculous." Nik pushes aside his two laptops, marching to the front of the van too. It's crowded as soon as he joins, and Blare pulls a face, ducking so that they're not squished.

"It's 9:54 p.m.," Nik says, reading the time on the dashboard. "Legally, we should be permitted."

"Legally, they don't have to allow anything, especially if we can't provide a reason for entering the city," I say, pulling my arm free from his invasion of my personal space. "Where's the van registered to?"

"I'm changing it right now." Miz drops her glasses back down over her eyes. Her hands stay on the steering wheel. "We're coming from a warehouse in Upsie. It needs to be an emergency shipment. Any ideas?"

Five cars ahead of us now. The vehicles in the queue are being allowed through so far, but their license plates all indicate their origin place to be Threto. They live in this city, so they need to be let in.

"Give me a handheld," I demand.

Blare looks at Nik, thinking he'll respond. Nik doesn't offer his. Blare frowns, reaching for their own.

"Here," they say. "Nik is practically married to his handheld."

"I am not," Nik counters. "I'm protective of it."

It can't be the footage of me that he's wielding so preciously on the device. Something of that nature would live securely in the cloud.

"What's the issue?" I ask Nik, accepting Blare's handheld and opening the map. "Do you have one of those dating bots installed?"

I wouldn't have thought it physiologically possible, but Nik's face flames red.

"Don't be ridiculous."

"That really got a rise out of you." I zoom in on Threto, searching for major landmarks. "I didn't think you had the emotional capacity for an AI girlfriend."

"There is no AI girlfriend on my handheld," he intones.

I doubt he actually has a chatbot pretending to be his girlfriend on his handheld, but his reaction seems to say otherwise. The van shifts forward a little more.

"It must have gotten hard," I say. "Buzzing in your pocket while you're running from NileCorp, asking why you haven't said 'Good morning.'"

Nik rolls his eyes. I close the map and return the handheld to Blare.

"We're electricians," I announce, pivoting back on task. "There's an emergency at Threto's Tri-Split Dam. There won't be anyone working there right now to confirm if they call."

"How is that an emergency we need to be let in for?" Blare asks.

"Threto's gravity dam feeds into the world's largest power station. A small emergency in any section is a mega-disaster. Go with it—I can lead."

Miz pauses. She doesn't seem to buy it, her consideration drawing long. Then she nods firmly.

We reshuffle in the van. I take the front passenger seat. Nik and Blare settle in the row directly behind. I hear Nik telling Blare that they need to pull their turtleneck collar higher, try to cover up and appear older. The van inches forward, forward, and then we're only two cars away from the barrier, the skyscrapers taking shape ahead. Threto sprawls more than it climbs, formerly three ancient cities combined into one. Its location smack-bang in the middle of Medaluo makes it the access route for every traveler and mass shipment trying to cross the country. For as long as business operates, even downcountry Threto remains a hub, which means work trickling to its residents, but plenty of disease too. A city like Threto has to be trigger-happy with city closures. If it isn't careful, it will lose everyone living in the real to each new wave.

9:58 P.M., the dashboard reads. There's a long line of cars trailing behind us too.

The barrier lifts for the car ahead. It drives through, its rear lights blinking twice.

A tap comes on my front window, and I push the button to roll it down.

"In case you haven't heard, we're initiating a lockdown in Threto—"

"This is an emergency, sir."

Thirteen years at the academy attending language class every day, and I'm still shocked when I can speak Medan. I'm the perfect case study of an orphan severed from their culture of origin, the nerve ending cut and dead. In my head I believe myself entirely Atahuan, living in ignorant bliss until I glimpse myself in a mirror and am hit anew with the realization each time.

"We're with Jiang and Tang Electric," I continue. "There's a breakdown at the Tri-Split Dam in the lower-east component, and the city's going to experience severe shortages if it's not fixed immediately. Give them a call—ask for the supervisor."

The worker nods, noting something down in his clipboard for reference. I watch him take a few steps back, murmuring with another man in an orange vest.

"Jiang and Tang electric," Miz murmurs under her breath.

"It's catchy," I hiss back.

"It sounds like a dessert item."

The booth worker returns. "We're not getting an answer. You have badges?"

"Yes. One second." I twist my body, pretending to rummage behind my seat. Nik's sitting directly behind me, and I hit his ankles. He flinches at first, not following. Then I whack again and call, "It should be here somewhere—sorry, we're a very young company. Most of our credentials are online. I know I carry the lanyard, though."

Nik immediately reaches down too, retrieving his handheld. He's understood.

"It's got to be somewhere..."

I blindly grope around for another full minute, rustling plenty without finding anything. Eventually, Nik makes a fed-up noise and rolls down his window.

"Here," he says. "The digital versions."

The worker takes the handheld. He zooms in on the digital wallet database, scrutinizing the badges. I'm not sure how Nik got pictures onto them too, but I catch a flash of very realistic-looking credentials while the worker is scrolling on the screen.

"What are you?" he asks bluntly, giving the handheld back to Nik.

"Irisean," Nik answers smoothly. Then he says something that sounds like gibberish. I didn't take Irisean as an elective at the academy, so I don't know what Nik just said. I doubt the worker does either, but he nods.

"No cars on the road during viral containment, so go directly to your destination. If you must leave after, contact the nearest precinct for permission."

The worker waves for us to move ahead. The dashboard shows 10:03 P.M., and there's a sharp whistle blowing from one of the other workers, who raises both arms and signals for the cars behind us to turn around. They're closing. We're the last ones being let into the city.

"This is going to be a nightmare trying to leave," Miz mutters, easing the van forward. The barrier lifts. Our wheels crunch, gliding us right past.

"We should count ourselves lucky that we made it in," Nik says.

I breathe out, shifting to cross my legs. My foot dangles, the tracker inside sitting snugly. Teryn's not going to be able to monitor me here unless she rode ahead. Three days. If I'm to serve NileCorp well, I need to get us finished with Threto, and into Offron, in three days.

"We're unlucky that there's a new wave of influenza," Miz counters.

My eyes flicker to the rearview mirror, watching Nik loll his head into his hand, propped on the armrest.

"There's always a new wave somewhere," he says. "That's just downcountry. We should have planned for this. Now we've infiltrated at the worst possible time. The booth workers will have made a note for the surveillance network that our license plate is only permitted at the dam."

He must notice me watching him, because Nik's attention flickers up to the mirror too. He quirks an eyebrow. I uncross my legs and swivel around, facing him properly.

"Are you really Irisean?"

Nik scoffs. "No. I recited him a grocery list." He pulls out a box from his bag and tosses it at me. "Masks on."

• • • •

There is not a single blind spot in all of Threto.

"We've waited long enough," Miz says, twenty minutes into driving in circles on the inner expressways, avoiding each turn that takes us down to the city. "The cameras below don't cycle through active periods. Scans are repeatedly showing they're always on."

"We can't have the cameras identifying us until we're exiting the facility," Nik insists. "It's not enough time to get away. They'll circle us in mid-operation."

Threto is significantly more inland than touristy Upsie—which means a tighter fist over the city. Medaluo can manage affairs here without international news picking up their every move and publishing criticism on the feeds. Angry protests against the government are eliminated before they've started. Dissidents are taken away the moment they make a marketplace purchase for a clean banner to write on.

"What if we drive right up to the facility?" Blare asks. "Get there first and then plan an entrance route."

"We can't get off these highways," Nik answers evenly. "Police will be on our tail when we drive the wrong way."

The roads into Threto are built on an elevation, reserving the streets underneath for pedestrian use. The buildings to either side of us loom at thirty, forty stories high. Threto is sprawling, but Threto also receives the increasing burden of Medan rural drain. If people are moving here to keep themselves afloat, then the city must strengthen its pillars and patch up the holes on its undersides. Grow tall, grow bright, plaster advertisements on every available face of its skyscrapers until the electric bills are sponsored too.

"We could cover up the windshield?" Blare tries. "So that the cameras don't log our faces."

At this height, I can see directly into the apartment windows. Mothers scrubbing clothes in the bathrooms, fathers talking into headsets. The sidewalks have emptied out. Though there aren't cameras on the highway, there are digital eyes fixed on every building we drive past, pointed at the street level to make a note of visitors.

"Blare." Nik gives them such a withering look that I duck into my shoulders out of secondhand indignation. "If we cover the windshield, don't you think the cameras will find *that* suspicious and ping our license plate instantly?"

Blare folds their arms across their chest. "I'm just trying to help."

Nik sighs, reaching over to tap their elbow. "I appreciate it."

I eye the interaction through the rearview mirror. If Blare only met Nik after they were recruited into his ring of anarchy, they can't have known each other for much time. But there was a familial feeling in that gesture, long-standing and comfortable. Slowly, I take in the shape of Blare's eyes, the blue color, the light brown hair that ends unevenly at their chin.

"We still need to get off the expressway soon," Miz says firmly. "Hover any longer and the cameras are going to trigger an alert when we go down to tell the precinct we were circling."

"Fine. Let's do it." Nik leans forward, directing the wheel to one of the off-ramps. "As soon as we drive down, we need to ditch the vehicle. Threto city police will wonder why we're going in the wrong direction if our excuse was the Tri-Split Dam."

"You know," I cut in. "The problem isn't only evading identification. No matter how thoroughly we cover up, Threto surveillance will also ping their precincts as soon as multiple cameras fail to identify who we are." I shift to look over my shoulder, speaking directly to Nik. "They don't need to know we're Atahuans to come after us. They just need to be suspicious about why the cameras aren't logging registered Medans."

"There's nothing we can do about that," Nik says. "Our best bet is going by foot and hoping we avoid most of the city cameras."

A best bet is for gamblers. A best bet accompanies the spin of a wheel, the throw of a die. It's luck.

Corporate soldiers aren't trained to take bets. We are trained to make evaluations.

"Three Towns National Data Center is by the river, and we just drove in from the east highway boundary," I say. "That could be a five-hour walk."

"We'll go fast. Night is young."

"We have twenty minutes at best before the surveillance network has gathered enough data to determine they can't match us to registered civilians." I face forward again. The van has eased off the ramp. Miz applies pressure on the brakes, slowing for the pedestrian streets. "If they've noted our presence before we enter the facility, we won't have the time to search for your file. They'll have police waiting. We should be saving that twenty-minute mark to use after the break-in, for when we're leaving. Then it won't matter if they're coming to arrest us because we'll be fleeing the city anyway."

I shake a mask out of the box in my lap and snap it hard onto my ears. Its synthetic material seals down, clamping onto my nose and mouth.

Nik, meanwhile, hasn't put his on yet. When I look into the rearview mirror, his brow is furrowed. I get the feeling he wants to tell me off for being right. It makes the task a lot harder when we have a set amount of minutes we can be walking freely in Threto.

"Let me think it over for a second," Nik mutters. "I accept fault in this, okay? Threto closes down around this time every year when the weather gets warmer and people start leaving their apartments. I should have known better."

"No use self-flagellating now," I say sagely. "There's—"

On the left side of the pedestrian road, an entire row of buildings suddenly goes dark. My attention snaps to the window, searching up and down the rest of the block to see if their electricity was also cut. All dark.

"Did we do this?" Nik demands.

"No, just a coincidence," Miz replies. She hesitates, then turns the corner, rumbling onto the next road. "It's not uncommon when closures are announced. Power reroutes if everyone is ordering a bunch of stuff at once. We need to make a decision now. Eyes will be on this block when the lights come back on."

My face is still pressed to the window as I stare at the buildings. They're alien shapes in the night. Overgrown obelisks, planted in the sidewalk. Slender fingers, reaching through the clouds.

The idea forms.

"Hey," I say.

Nik leans forward. "Yes?"

"I've always wondered how you got away so fast after the statue bombing in Vermillion Bay."

Nik gets out of his seat. He hauls up one of his bags at the back of the van, strapping it tightly to himself. The Vermillion Bay, situated on the west coast, is Atahua's third-most populous urban area. The people there nickname it *The Million*. Yet, somehow, in his escape, Nik hadn't been sighted by a single witness.

"I don't think now is the time for an explainer."

"Nik Grant," I say, much more forcefully. "How did you get away so fast?"

He stops, a second bag hovering in his grip. His head stays ducked slightly, needing to minimize his height to avoid hitting the ceiling of the van. "By zipline," he answers. "There was a harness waiting one floor below. While the capture unit there thought I'd jumped for the ground, I'd swung to the next building and taken an exit route through the inside. They couldn't have responded in time." Nik straps the second bag onto himself, then pauses. "I'm sure you already knew that, though. With all your footage watching."

I did. It was a smart maneuver. It was something he planned with extensive consideration before launching that bomb at the marble statue of Atahua's first president.

"Didn't you want a plan to avoid wasting our minutes on the street?" I ask. "Do you still have that zipline?"

22

LIA

Rayna and Hailey are jet-lagged, which I don't exactly understand when they didn't even take a plane here. Still, they could barely keep their eyes open when we rejoined them in the lounge, after we declared the retrieval mission a success and thanked them for their contribution.

I offered them a nap in our hotel room, and now they're knocked out so deeply that I could call a demolition crew and neither would stir.

"Look what you did," Kieren says, his arms folded across his chest.

"What was I going to do?" I retort. "Wave them off and send them on their way?"

"Yes."

Despite his tough talk, Kieren keeps his voice lowered, not wanting to wake them. He's showered again, cleaning off the grime of burglary in the time it took Hailey and Rayna to conk out. His wet hair drips along the side of his neck. I don't know why he seems morally opposed to drying off properly before he steps out.

"Should we go somewhere quiet and call Kam?" he asks.

"Yeah." I point up. "I'm pretty sure the floors above us are event spaces. Should we try?"

Kieren signals for me to lead the way. We close the door behind us quietly, and I head for the stairwell rather than the elevator, figuring we'd probably have an easier time testing which of the floors are vacant. The fifth floor is another part of the hotel. On the sixth, I can already hear chatter through the heavy white door, and I keep walking. The seventh floor is quieter, so I pull the door and poke my head in, but there are waitstaff present, laying out white tables and setting out shrimp cocktails.

I close the door, heading for the eighth floor. When I open this door, it's entirely dark, the curtains drawn and the lights off.

"Great," I say. "Perfect."

Kieren is grimacing when he follows me through. "I feel as though we're about to get jump-scared by a ghost."

"Don't be ridiculous. That can only happen once."

In the early years of virtual, someone used an exploit to bring a "ghost" into upcountry for a prank, and it scared their victim so badly they logged out and knocked their head hard against their Pod. The prankster ended up doing time, and StrangeLoom fixed up the back door that allowed the exploit. Over the years, NileCorp has built barriers of every fashion so that nothing unusual can slip through.

Upcountry wouldn't be a very pleasant place if Chung's weapon cuts down what StrangeLoom has patched. Suddenly there could be ghosts on every street.

I pull aside one of the heavy velvet curtains, letting in the sunset. The sky is turning pink. Deep orange light cuts through the window beams, feathers onto our skin in uniform lines.

Kieren starts the call, looping me in with a request. I accept immediately, but I still feel as though I've missed the opening remarks when Kam picks up and says, "Security alerts are currently high across upcountry Medaluo with concerns that Nile Military Academy has begun their annual cadet postings. Report, please."

"Uh—"

I glance over to Kieren. Smoothly, he says, "We found a smart key in his office, which directed us to a safe in his home. Opened the safe. Retrieved a disk that came from Threto's data center."

He's summed up our day in as few words as possible. There's a beat of silence over the line. Then, instead of an affirmative acknowledgment:

"How'd you get into his home?"

I grimace. "We thought on our feet. Launched some attacks to distract security and unlock the doors."

"Did you wipe yourself from the system log afterward?"

Kieren and I exchange a glance.

"... Yes," he says, sounding not at all convincing.

"Please confirm," Kam says, sounding not at all convinced. "You performed it yourself and wiped your log?"

"We recruited help from other cadets," I say. It's not against any academy guidelines to do so. In fact, it's encouraged. It shows we know how to use the resources available to us. "Rayna Ward and Hailey Murray. They're tasked in Upsie too. Hailey used predownloaded exploits. She shouldn't be connected to them."

The line echoes with tapping.

"Kieren Murray, you have an impeccable math record and an application pending for the elite cyber division at NileCorp. Why would you let your sister step in with predownloaded exploits?"

I whirl around, flabbergasted. Even in the fading sunset, Kieren's gone visibly pale, his cheeks drained of blood. This is the first I've heard about this. The first I've heard about Kieren having any interest in a *cyber* division. Maybe he's great at math, but so am I. That alone doesn't put two and two together.

"I have a moral opposition to launching my own exploits," Kieren replies tightly. "And excuse me, but I don't think those files of mine are of any relevance to you."

"I have access to all your files. I am your ground contact."

"For the posting." This has clearly pressed one of Kieren's buttons.

A secret exposed, and he's scrambling by lashing out. "It's entirely irrelevant here and a complete breach of my privacy for you to judge what I should and shouldn't use."

"I think what Kieren means to say," I hurry to add, "is that we're sure Hailey did a fine job erasing her work behind her. Now that we have this disk from Threto, we need to get over there."

More tapping. It goes on for long enough that I grow uncomfortable, shifting on my feet. I feel as though I just watched Kieren get told off by a teacher.

"There will be rail tickets deposited into your display within the next hour for a train departing tomorrow morning," Kam says shortly. "Do not go buying anything on your own. Transport in Medaluo is registered to your ID and tracked by the government."

Then the call goes dead.

"Great job." I swipe the box out of my display. "Our contact is pissed."

"That's not my fault," Kieren grumbles. "She had no right to look at that. That's my personal information. I might not even get in."

I tilt my head. "She?"

Kieren shrugs, lifting his hands to imitate typing. "I thought I heard long nails. Presumptuous of me, I guess, sorry."

"Hmm." I lean against the window. The glass is warm, and I step onto the raised ledge on the floor to get closer. "So. Elite cyber division."

"What? It's a very high-paying position."

"It's atypical," I say. "Don't act surprised that I'm surprised. Or you wouldn't have been keeping it a secret."

Kieren scoffs. "We're not exactly the best of buddies, Lia. Prior to this posting, when would I have sat down next to you to tell you about my career dreams and aspirations?"

"There have actually been many times when you sat down next to me unprompted to talk."

"Yeah," Kieren mutters. "About the teachers. Or the lesson. Not . . ."

The vulnerable stuff. The stuff that I could use, and weaponize, and turn against him. He doesn't need to say it. I get the gist.

What makes Kieren's aspirations toward the cyber division so bizarre is its lack of respectability, and if Kieren is anything in a nutshell, he is respectable. The cyber division used to be known for sharing resources with the StrangeLoom division. As the years passed, it kept getting into scandals with international incidents, with Medaluo's accusations, and now they're mostly known for having Atahua's hackers. A good fraction of the cold war is fought by launching malware at each other over the ether. There's no honor, no integrity. Someone who trains out of Nile Military Academy doesn't aspire to go to that department. It isn't even a division where people get posted. It only accepts candidates on rolling applications.

"I truly don't understand," I say after a long pause. "I know you don't owe *me* an explanation, but you've spent so many years tearing yourself apart for academic excellence—"

Kieren tries to interrupt. "I haven't been tearing myself apart—"

"You have been, because *I* have been, and if you respect me at all, then you'll admit it," I snap. "Out of anyone, you can't lie to me. I know what it takes to keep up those grades, and I know how strongly you have to feel about what results come of it." I swallow hard. My throat is dry. "So what gives?"

He must know that, most likely, there's nothing we can do at this point to one-up each other. Whatever happens at the end of this posting, the outcome of valedictorian may as well be decided by a coin toss between our two names. He may as well treat me as a friend.

"What gives is that NileCorp is separated by head of security and head of cyber division," Kieren says tiredly. "My dad was former head of security. Despite his retirement, despite his current role, he has the right to pull files on all the private forces under NileCorp security. Once we're signed under that branch, we give up our claim to privacy. He'd be able to access my display if I'm upcountry. He could see what I'm doing at any point. My location, my data, my suit recordings downcountry. He'd see *everything* no matter which unit I'm assigned to...." Kieren looks away, his arms crossed tightly enough that his shirt fabric will be marred permanently. "Unless I'm elsewhere."

I hold my breath for so long that my lungs start to burn. I force myself to exhale, bit by bit.

"I didn't realize," I say when I've recovered, "that you hated him so much."

"I don't," Kieren counters at once. "I love him. He was my hero. I looked forward to Saturdays in elementary school because he could come home and take me and Hailey out to the park, and when we'd fight over who got to ride inside the tire swing for Dad to push, he'd say he was strong enough to push us both." The hint of a smile presses at his lips, his eyes lost in the memory. "I wanted to be just like him when I grew up."

That doesn't sound much like Headmaster Murray. I don't say it aloud, but Kieren must know I'm thinking it. His gaze flickers up.

"Yeah," he says in confirmation. "Not the man you know, right?"

"People change," I say weakly. "Stress, work . . ."

"I suppose so. But you asked for an explanation, so here's mine: I have to get away from his watch. I think NileCorp did something to change him, and I'm going to prove it."

23

EIRALE

The night wind cuts underneath my sleeves, slicing a trail with each cold howl. I lean over the roof edge. No barrier. Fifty-five stories feels very, very high from the top.

"All right, I think we've got it. I should be able to fly the drone from my glasses."

Miz tosses the drone up, and it stays floating, calibrating to its surroundings. The horizon doesn't so much twinkle as it buzzes, filled with innumerable sources of digital light. If it's not the underside of lower apartment windows wired with glowing repellent to keep out the mosquitoes, it is the roving red patterns dancing down the skyscrapers, tracing their glass surfaces. If it's not the flicker of the billboards installed on the street level, it is their reflections, sparkling off the wet puddles filling the potholes in the road. It must have rained over Threto earlier today. A faint trace of humidity still lingers.

"Careful," Nik warns. "If you fling it out of range, you're going to disconnect, and then we can't get it back."

"I'm not going to fling it out of range."

"Really, Miz? Because your hand is pulling back right now in a way that makes me think you're about to fling it out of range."

Chided, Miz lowers her hand, waving it to erase the trajectory she must be drawing in her glasses. The drone will take one end of the zipline and lock it onto the rooftop we want. Then the drone has to hover there until we arrive, pull the zipline back, and repeat the process.

It'll only require five buildings. Five connecting points before we reach our destination. For a route that spans a significant length east to west in Threto, it's really not bad. All I needed was a satellite map of Threto, and I'd calculated a smooth path that would bring us lower and lower to the ground, letting gravity pull at the zipline. The Three Towns National Data Center is located in the heart of the city, along the river that cuts a zigzag through Threto, unlike Upsie's facility in its east. Though there are a healthy amount of skyscrapers scattered between us and the river, there are also many shorter, steadier buildings. Those are the ones we're targeting after our tall start. Unused and largely empty, with all the cameras concentrated on the ground level in case of squatters.

"Do we want the harnesses?" Blare asks, picking through Nik's bag.

"Only the ropes," Nik answers. "Makes it quicker. I trust everyone can maintain a good grip."

Blare nods and pulls out a few sets of rope, made of the same material as the zipline. I stand aside, watching the scene. Nik goes to the edge of the rooftop and fixes one end of the zipline tight to the building. The line is unlike anything I've seen, clamping itself to the edge of the roof as soon as he activates a red lever to the side.

"It's magnetic."

A gust of wind carries Nik's voice away, but I know it is directed toward me. I've drifted behind him, watching him secure the line.

"Good tech," I remark.

"The best. No chance of a blunder."

The hologram playing on the neighboring building darts around the north wall to look at us. A dancing woman, rendered in blue and yellow, wearing the face of some model who must have signed her resemblance rights away for life. HAVE YOU PURCHASED LIMB INSURANCE? reads the caption running around her waist.

It wouldn't have been noticeable in the night otherwise, but the moving hologram lights up a piece of graffiti behind it, on the wall. I can't imagine how someone climbed up the building exterior to do it, but the spray paint was certainly applied with a steady hand. A near perfect circle, with four arrows pointing inward evenly around the circumference.

"Your work?" I say sarcastically, pointing to the graffiti.

Nik turns over his shoulder, his eyes narrowing.

"Believe it or not," he replies once he's spotted the source of my dig. "I don't belong to every anarchist group in the world. I don't belong to any, in fact."

"Forgive me. I saw spray paint and made my assumptions."

Nik doesn't rise to my bait. He's studying the symbol now, head tilted like he's trying to identify it. I kick a pebble by my shoe.

"In all seriousness," I say. "I'm sorry for attacking you."

Nik looks over to me again. "Are you yanking my chain?"

I point at his hand. "I think you're the one yanking a chain."

"What—okay." Finished with securing the zipline, Nik gets up, rising off one knee in a smooth motion. "You're real funny."

I wasn't trying to be funny. In fact, I don't think anyone has ever used the word "funny" to describe me.

"I'm just trying to apologize for, you know." I point at his temple, where there's the angry red scratch. "It's your own fault, but I'm sorry."

"That's a terrible apology."

"I'm sorry for attacking you to prove a point," I conclude. "I'm not sorry that I was clearly right. Or that you keep steering away from what is pretty evident at this point in time, and it's giving you a dark cloud of a mood."

Behind us, Miz picks up the other end of the zipline with the drone and starts to fly it off the edge of the roof, toward the first destination point

I selected for her on the map. In the entire time she's securing it, Nik only glowers at me, and I don't offer any leeway. I glower back.

I can't imagine myself befriending a team of anarchists either. But really I can't imagine myself befriending anyone, given my gaping history with forming meaningful connections, so what do I know? Maybe we were the world's most tight-knit unit of coworkers.

"All right!" Miz shouts. "I think we're ready to go."

"Great," Nik says. He brushes by me, grabbing the bags he set down. He's managed to shove the entire server box he stole in Upsie into one of his backpacks.

"I wanna go first," Blare declares.

"Grab a rope, then," Nik says. "Soldier, stay sharp."

I catch the rope he throws my way, clasping it close to my chest. Nik pauses, his eyes steady on me. I don't look away, mystified by whatever it is that my mind is scrambling to put together.

Either I get the truth out of him in three days, or NileCorp takes him away, and I live with never knowing.

• • • •

We cross the first four buildings with no trouble.

Somehow, I'm shocked by the brutal wind on every swing, swallowing gulps of cold air repeatedly and then having to force down my hiccups upon landing. Each building was selected to be lower than the previous to build speed, and *I* selected them, so I don't know why my stomach keeps dropping as though the plunge is unexpected. We want to be zipping as quickly as possible, lest some poor civilian glance out their apartment window and find themselves face-to-face with us in mid-air.

I roll out my shoulders, flex my palms. Just one more to go, and then the burning sensation ripping through my skin can rest. It's a shame that no one brought gloves. Who carries a zipline but not *gloves*?

"Connected," Miz calls. "We're good."

The final swing will get us next door to Threto's facility. We couldn't attach directly to the data center: the building was too low, standing at only six floors. Threto's space is far smaller than Upsie's too. No lawn, no perimeter fence, no vaulted ceilings where the sea breeze can float in on warmer days.

"Go first," Nik says to her. He's hauling Upsie's server box around in the bag on his shoulders, so he's moving especially carefully with each swing. "You can bring the line back with the drone as soon as we're through."

Miz makes a salute, then loops her rope around the zipline and jumps. She swings fast, but I notice the brief stutter in the middle, as though she's caught on something before her momentum resumes, landing at the other side and hopping off. This final stretch is our longest distance yet, so she's tiny when she waves back up at us to gesture that we can continue.

"Wait a moment," I say, but my conviction isn't strong enough. I haven't fully understood what looks wrong—I don't, until Blare has already looped their rope around the zipline, clutching tightly on to both sides, and pushed off.

They get halfway along the zipline at a good speed. Then they start to slow.

"Whoa, whoa, whoa," Nik says at once, hurrying forward. "What's going on?"

I know instantly what I did wrong. I ran calculations on our average weight, which is the only reason I decided to risk this final stretch rather than find another building in between. But Blare, being much younger, is also much lighter. The math didn't work on them for this one.

"Take over the drone," I command. "Bring it back."

Blare is starting to squirm. They can't hold on for this long. And if they let go . . .

"I swear, if you're scheming something—"

"I am not scheming something with a kid's *life*," I spit, and it's so vicious that Nik takes a step back. There's no time to argue. I trust he'll wrest control of the drone from Miz, and I go for the outer pocket of his bag instead, yanking out a harness. I'm inside the contraption in a heartbeat, offering no extra thought for securing each buckle. I hear Nik yell for me to hold it, to give him a second, but Blare doesn't have a second to spare, so I clip the harness onto the zipline, spinning the hook latch until it has closed.

Then, I dive.

The benefit of ziplining with rope, at least, was that we stayed upright across the journey. If my air-swallowing problem was bad before, I can barely squeeze anything into my lungs this time, the cold wind piercing needles into my face. Three seconds, five, seven . . . Blare must see me coming, and in an act of trust that I can't comprehend, they let go of the rope, their hands exhausted.

I catch them in the exact moment they begin to fall, one arm under their shoulder and the other gripping the bag they've got clipped across their torso. I don't breathe until the harness slams to a halt at the end of the zipline and collides with the blocker. We both go crashing into the water tank that Miz fixed the zipline to, and while Blare falls to the rooftop—their bag taking the brunt of the collision when they roll onto their shoulder, groaning—I make a frantic grab for the top of the harness, pulling the release mechanism and freeing myself before I swing back over the edge of the rooftop.

I drop to the rooftop on my knees. The sting is brutal, but it is a good feeling. It means I've made it onto solid ground.

"*Shit.*" Miz hurries to Blare, hauling them upright. "Are you okay?"

"I think my palms have second-degree rope burn, but otherwise I'm not a pancake on the pavement, I guess." They look up. Their eyes are wide. "You saved me."

"You were only at risk because I left out a calculation," I say, getting to my feet. My knees are bleeding under my clothes, and I'm startled for a moment because I can't even remember the last time I got hurt like this.

The academy, despite its exercises, rarely got us into scraps given that we spent most of our time up in virtual.

The zipline trembles. It pulls taut, and then Nik makes it across too, releasing his rope and neatly jumping off before he hits the water tank.

The night goes quiet. Only the hum of electric ads and electric stars. My breath is still coming fast. I heave a deep inhale, urging my pulse to slow.

"Everyone all right?" Nik asks evenly, shrugging his bag more securely upon his shoulders.

"Alive," Blare reports. They clean off their elbows, then turn to me. "How did you get to me so fast?"

It's because I sped myself up manually, I'm about to say. Then I realize that I hadn't actually delivered that instruction—I'd spoken half of the plan to Nik, and in my rush to get onto the zipline, I hadn't finished my thought. My gaze snaps fast across the zipline to where the initial end waits upon the previous building, and I spot the drone there, hovering with the line. It must have lowered again for Nik to get across, but the moment I'd attached my harness, I was going to tell Nik to use the drone to lift the line as high as it could go. My descent would be steeper, and I could get to Blare faster.

But I didn't need to tell him.

Nik meets my eyes. I tilt my head.

"What can I say?" he offers. "I pay attention."

His words are impassive, but he's slightly breathless, a low rasp catching in his throat. It isn't the strenuous activity getting to him. There's something else there, something that shows as an excited glint when he stares at me. As though he's daring me to ask for elaboration. If I didn't know better, I'd almost think he's trying to hold back a grin. He must be delirious.

Nik finally turns away, maneuvering the drone back with the zipline. He's quick to shove the equipment into the bag swinging from his waist, asking Miz to scan the perimeter, see if any alarms have been triggered by our presence here.

"Clear," Miz reports after a minute.

"Then we proceed," Nik says. He pauses. "Soldier?"

I don't know what to think. I take a step forward, and my knees tremble with a faint weakness, not entirely attributed to the scrape I took coming off the zipline. *Why?* If I'd barely understood what I was planning until I was doing it, how could Nik Grant possibly have known?

"We proceed," I echo.

24

LIA

I stare at Kieren, my mouth opening and closing.

"You think NileCorp *did* something to change your father?" I finally echo. "What—what do you mean?"

"I mean that ever since my dad left his job, he's been entirely different." Kieren scoffs, clearly hearing how ridiculous he sounds. "I can't explain it. It's as though he's been brainwashed. Or recruited into a cult. Or . . . I don't know—maybe if I had a better grasp on what happened, I'd actually be able to do something about it."

"You don't think it was his adjustment to a major life change?" I ask. "Pivoting gears from NileCorp to the academy is a pretty big deal."

"There's midlife crisis, and then there's losing your soul," Kieren says darkly. "And if you'd known my dad before he was the headmaster, you would know exactly what I mean. I've compared notes with Hailey and Weston. It's as if he walked home that day after quitting and the light disappeared from him. He grew mean. What NileCorp wanted would be the law. What the company asked for must be delivered." Kieren pauses. "He and Mom got divorced three years ago."

I jolt. I had no idea. They must have really kept it quiet if I hadn't heard the faintest rumor around school. Kieren's mom is a socialite. I've said hello when she's on campus, but I mostly see her on the feed because she livestreams all the time. Her shoes, her bags, her trips downcountry to get high-end manicures.

"I'm sorry."

"Don't be," Kieren returns. "It was inevitable. My mother's attendance at his academy fundraising events was already sparse. Nothing looked like it had changed once the separation went through." He puts his hands in his pockets. A moment passes, his gaze cast forward. "It doesn't make sense, does it? Why take a job to be closer to your kids and then act like you hate your kids?"

I don't have an answer for him. I almost want to grab him and hug him, but Kieren might find that degrading, so I stay put by the window, lolling my head against the glass.

How would NileCorp even have had a hand in that? Their technology is advanced, but I can't imagine it covers brainwashing. Hard to argue for cult recruitment too if it happened with the click of a finger.

"You'll get him back," I say quietly. The reassurance feels like the most natural response in this moment. It's not empty platitudes or condolences for what he's suffered. Kieren doesn't like that sort of drivel. When he wants something done, he'll do it. I trust that to be true, if nothing else.

His lip quirks. It's a soft gesture, made pinker by the setting sun. "Even if it means beating you for valedictorian?"

I shrug one shoulder. "Even then. I understand the play you're making here. Being valedictorian means NileCorp can't say no to joining cyber."

It suddenly colors everything I knew about Kieren Murray. I'd thought that his career would be sunshine and roses, that no matter what grades he got, he'd be cushy after graduation. He was a Murray. They *had* to post him somewhere prestigious.

And exactly that: the headmaster would want his own son in the division he once led. He would fight against any other designation. Cyber is the one place where they might decline his application. Kieren's been trying to ensure it doesn't happen.

"Thank you for understanding." He sniffs.

"Don't push it," I warn immediately.

It's too late. Kieren feigns tears, reaching up to dab his eyes. "I never thought this moment would come. Lia Ward, giving me permission to be the best."

"Hey, I'm saying you can *try*."

We can't sit in a genuine moment for long. I don't think we've had an entirely sincere conversation since we met at the pre-cadet party, before Kieren decided to take my test scores personally.

"Fine," he relents. "May the best cadet win. At this point, we have no choice but to collaborate until the end anyway."

It's a shame, really. It's always been about winning. Even in ninth grade, when neither of us had fully gotten our bearings down yet, it was already about making sure we were overtaking the other.

"You know," I say before I can stop myself. "It would have been nice if we'd collaborated from the beginning. Imagine if we'd combined test notes and exchanged ideas for projects. We would have been unstoppable."

Kieren stays quiet.

"I'm not blaming you for our rivalry," I go on, "but I am kind of blaming you. You decided to be rude to me first."

"Rehashing old wounds, are we?"

I point at myself. "They're very much still open and bleeding. Remember how nice the New Cadet Orientation party was?"

"Yes, well," Kieren says. "Unfortunately, after that first night we met, I developed such a raging crush on you that I had to wean myself off like an addict."

I blink. My thoughts short out entirely, then kick back at ten times the volume. He must be joking. There's no chance he's serious.

"What did you just say?"

"In hindsight," Kieren continues, refusing to repeat himself, "maybe there were better methods than being rude. But you were always so enthusiastic, and I liked your smile, so I was very intent on putting a stop to it. I'm naturally competitive, Lia. By the time I actually decided I wanted to be valedictorian, I'd already given myself a head start because scoring highest in the class infuriated you."

"*A raging crush . . .* ," I repeat, still stuck on that first chain of conversation. "We were thirteen. It only took one night for it to be that serious?"

Kieren's brow furrows. He almost appears offended.

"You kissed me dead on the mouth," he exclaims. "What is a thirteen-year-old boy supposed to think?"

"For, like, two seconds." I'm still flabbergasted. "And it was Spin the Bottle!"

"I was a sheltered child."

Kieren, despite the confession that I'm hearing for the first time, appears entirely casual, his posture relaxed, one shoulder leaning against the wall.

"I— This is— What—" I cut myself off. Meanwhile, I have to switch gears or else this is going to splinter my brain in two. "Okay. Sure." My eyes flicker downcast. "You poor soul."

"All right," Kieren says dully. "None of that, please."

"I've left you pining," I sniffle. "All these years."

Kieren rolls his eyes. "You are unbearable, actually."

"You're in a safe space. You can admit your undying love now."

"You are so—"

A screech of sirens echoes from the street, and immediately I peer through the window in search of the source. It catches Kieren's attention just as fast, his face right up against the glass when he strides to the window.

The sirens get nearer, then nearer.

Then the one police car stops in front of the building.

My pulse stutters.

"Hey," I say slowly. "What are the chances that Hailey didn't do a complete wipe of the system log like Kam was afraid of?"

Kieren stares down for a moment. He blinks, his eyes glazing for his display, and seconds later he says, "High. I'm on their radio. Chung's building reported suspicions of system tampering when their alarm sounded, and they sent their log to be investigated. *Shit.*"

Without any time to waste, Kieren makes for the door. I take one more peek to see that the officers have entered the building and wince, hurrying after Kieren into the stairwell.

"Are they tracking Hailey's credentials?" I ask. My breath huffs while we make our rapid spiral down the floors. "Is she in danger?"

"No names mentioned. I think you were smart to give her a physical laptop. They're likely tracking a live location for the device itself."

But as soon as they enter the hotel and locate the laptop, they're going to start looking at the security footage. Reviewing the patrons who came in and out. The ones who match street footage near Chung's building.

Kieren barges his way back to the fourth floor. I'm close enough behind him that I follow through on the same swing of the door. The lights in the hallway have dimmed, accommodating the burgeoning evening.

"Right now the police may only be following a cursory report from Chung's building," I say, "but it'll hit the radar of Medaluo's federal agents before long. We can't let them look into us until we're done with the posting."

"Shit," Kieren says again. *"Shit."* He pushes open the door into our hotel room. "Wake up! It's time to go!"

Rayna bolts upright instantly, her hair in three different directions. Despite her quick movements, her expression is entirely still asleep, failing to follow the situation. Hailey doesn't stir at all. She's probably too used to Kieren yelling at her to wake up.

"Get Hailey and Rayna up and moving," I tell him. "They have to come with us. They can return to Upsie after the heat has passed, but if they stay here and are taken in, it's going to loop right back to us and impact our posting."

I cross the room in a few strides, picking up the laptop bag that Hailey left by the coffee table. I take out the laptop. Then I bend it backward and snap it in two for good measure. They'll still be able to confirm that it's the device they're tracking once they find it, but no harm in adding an extra roadblock. I shove the pieces into the laptop bag, then stash the bag in the closet.

By the time I turn around, Rayna's on her feet already and pulling her backpack on, but Hailey remains groggily slouched on the bed.

"I literally can't even see straight right now," Hailey complains.

"When can you?" Kieren mutters. He's fetched both their bags. While I grab the toothbrush in the bathroom and the pajamas I left on the floor, Kieren simply hauls his sister up over his shoulder, and she flops like a marionette, letting him carry her. Rayna opens her bag to gesture that I can add my stuff in. I breathe, *"Thank youuuuuu,"* and then wave her along after Kieren, into the hallway, to the stairwell.

"What's happening?" Rayna hisses. "I was having such a nice dream."

"Turns out Hailey might not have erased her handiwork all the way through." I cast a glance over my shoulder. The elevator doors are opening. With a rapid intake of breath, I shut the stairwell door after us, hoping the officer hadn't caught sight of us leaving.

"And we're fleeing?"

"Temporarily!" I insist. "Your survey wants every major city, right? You can always come back to Upsie later."

Rayna yawns. She and I hurry down the stairwell in tandem behind Kieren, our feet synchronized. "Lia, if you wanted to hang out for longer, you could have just said so."

I roll my eyes, giving her an extra push out the door and into the lobby. It's quiet. Kieren sets Hailey down with a warning that she better walk. I'm impressed he made carrying her look so easy. He's hardly broken a sweat.

"I'll walk," Hailey says under her breath, "but where are we *going*?"

Great question. The first step is getting onto the street. Rayna loops her arm around mine, letting us appear to be on a casual stroll, maybe a group of friends heading to dinner in the city. A streetlamp blinks to life above us. It glows turquoise, matched to the night aquarium opening its doors to the right.

"Ward," Kieren says lowly, turning over his shoulder.

Rayna and I both look up. He grimaces.

"I meant—Lia. The rail tickets aren't in yet."

"Even if they came in now, they're for tomorrow morning," I say. "We need a new escape route."

"Are we going to call Kam?"

"No use. If she gave us morning tickets, that's likely the earliest thing she could get her hands on with legitimate methods." I open my display, poised over the browser. I'm not even sure what to search. We have to leave in a way that can't be traced if we're identified by the police back there. Railways and airlines are connected to our user IDs, as Kam said. We can't do taxis either—those are recorded. Precincts can run a facial recognition request through the systems, and the taxi company will tell them the exact route we took. The subway only goes as far as rural Upsie, too.

That doesn't offer us many remaining options.

"We could always stay in Upsie and hide out somewhere, can't we?" Hailey asks. She gestures for Kieren to return her bag now that she's mostly coherent, and Kieren shoves it back at her.

"It's dangerous," he says. "Surveillance within a city is all fed back to the same place. It makes it easy for Medaluo to find us just by asking the cameras to be on alert."

As opposed to lurking in Threto, before they know we've gone to Threto. They're not going to run a facial scan on the entirety of upcountry Medaluo. It would take forever.

"At least for the night, then," Hailey says. "Hole up and then take the morning train."

"Where would we hole up?" Kieren asks. He doesn't sound accusatory. It's a genuine question that has no answer. There is nowhere that goes unwatched.

"Maybe we go unconventional." Hailey points at the aquarium we're passing. "Fish cleaning back rooms."

"This is why I don't go to you for advice."

While I've been hovering over my display for so long, the system tries to offer me suggestions, noting that I'm at an impasse. It suggests searching sunset times for the week. Messaging Rayna Ward, not realizing Rayna is right beside me. Checking my spam folder, because I've been receiving an unprecedented amount of messages there.

I sigh, swiping it all away one by one. I've been keeping watch on my spam folder—before my eyes, the number grows from 498 to 514. A lack of privacy restrictions in Medaluo also means the adware works overtime.

Though I intend to close out from spam, my display has noticed me lingering, and it floats previews up at me. I pause. As tempted as I am by the restaurant bargains for spicy soup, that's not what suddenly has my attention.

THE GRANDEST BUS EXPERIENCE!!! Leaving from Upsie's port at 20:00.

COME ONE. COME ALL. The AI tour guide you've been seeking.

WE'VE GOT TO STOP MEETING LIKE THIS . . . at the edge of Medaluo! Follow us across the cities.

"Hey," I say, interrupting the insults Kieren and Hailey are throwing at each other. "I've got an idea."

• • • •

The bus is waiting at the northern end of Upsie's embankment, LIGHTNING SMART TOURS plastered across its side. There's no one else boarding. It'll drive on a loop regardless of how many tourists it picks up, and it'll perform its entire tour as well, even if it's to empty seats. No one uses AI-guided services anymore despite their initial boom during upcountry's invention. At first it seemed like tour guides and schoolteachers and sport coaches could be automated, just as accounting jobs and insurance brokers were. Then it turned out AI tour guides freaked people out too much.

Fortunately, though, AI buses are private companies. Our IDs aren't logged when we board, so no one is going to know we're here. Most of the companies running these tours are also at the brink of bankruptcy from a lack of customers. I doubt any of them are staffing their headquarters well enough to answer the calls from Medan authorities.

The four of us look among one another upon the embankment, all daring someone else to step onto the bus first. Its door is wide open. It would be welcoming if it weren't for the dead silence and darkness inside.

I take a deep breath, making the first move to step inside. As soon as I grab the handrail and enter the bus, the lights flicker on. A bot jerks to attention in the driver's seat. Its chest beams blue; its faceless silver head swivels fast in my direction.

"HELLO!" it bellows in Atahuan.

My hand flies to my heart. "Oh my—"

"Welcome, welcome, so sorry for the fright," the bot says, lowering its loud volume. Maybe it's been so long since it spoke that it needed to run an adjustment. "Please, take a seat. Is it the four of you?"

I'm patting my collarbone rapidly, trying to ease my pulse back into its resting state. "Um. Yes. Yes, four people."

"Great!" Clearly the volume adjustment isn't the issue—it's the enthusiasm meter. "We're setting off on the adventure of a lifetime in ten minutes. Remember you are safe here!"

I grimace, starting into the aisle. It's a wonder these things haven't all been discontinued, but I suppose I can't complain when it's benefiting us now.

Kieren climbs onto the bus next, though he pauses by the bot, staring at it a while. I don't walk far, sliding into the left side of the second row. After a thorough inspection, Kieren comes to my row and gestures for me to shuffle over to the window seat, and he plops down beside me. When Hailey and Rayna board, they both choose rows farther back.

"My name is Twelve," the bot says from the driver's seat. It reminds me of a particularly short puppet. It's got arms, and legs, and it could probably walk around if it wanted, but something about the way it sits in that seat makes it seem like someone's got their arm up through its body. "We will depart in approximately four minutes. Did you know Upsie stands for Land of the Upper Sea? The names across Medaluo are long and hard to parse for tongues used to Atahuan, so literal translations were made."

Twelve isn't expecting a response. Its light pulses again at its chest, and it reaches up to adjust its mirrors. Somehow, though it has no eyes on its smooth face, I sense that it is checking the rear window view.

"Ward," Kieren whispers, getting my attention. He leans in, pressed right to my ear so that the bot won't hear him. A shiver dances down my neck. "This thing gives me the creeps."

"What are we going to do about that?" I whisper back. "Do you want to shut it down and drive instead?"

"No," Kieren grumbles.

"It's just a bot. It'll get us where we need to go."

Kieren falls silent, which I take as his agreement to proceed. A few minutes later, Twelve bellows, "It's time to go!" and the bus begins to drive without any impediments. A tinny tune plays from the speakers while the large vehicle makes a turn off the embankment, clunking onto the road. "With an evening departure, our first stop is—"

"Let's skip the first few stops," Kieren calls forward. "We want to go to Threto. And no need for any guide description at the moment."

There's a long pause. Out of the corner of my eye, I catch Rayna going back to sleep, lolling her head against the seat.

"Hm!" Twelve chirps. "Why is that?"

Kieren clears his throat. "Just because."

"Our route is constructed to allow passengers to board at every stop," the bot insists.

"But we have a particular interest in certain areas for sightseeing," Kieren counters. "You may not get more passengers at other stops. Surely maintaining our customer satisfaction is very important."

The blue circle on Twelve's body lights up again. It spins twice in a counterclockwise revolution.

"Okay!"

I can't believe that worked. Twelve goes quiet. The tour bus accelerates, taking the ramp onto the highway. The buildings on either side of the bus flash by in prismatic streams. Virtual's pixels never look quite right when we're speeding through the space, and I think it's because everything else is rendered with such photorealism that StrangeLoom's engineers can't capture what the world looks like when it blurs. Upsie's structures around the highway develop a faint bend, tired at their middle and relaxing their spines.

"Feeling less creeped out?" I ask quietly.

Kieren leans back and folds his arms across his chest. He's eyeing the front, inspecting Twelve.

"I suppose," he murmurs.

That's a no, then.

I sigh, getting comfortable in my seat.

"It's nine hours until Threto," I say. "Better get some sleep."

25

EIRALE

Downcountry Threto under lockdown is noisier than I would have thought.

I pause at the landing, lagging behind. The elevators have cameras, so we're walking down the stairs. My head is spinning from the rotations. Each time I pause, Nik is quick to call a prompt, noticing when I pull behind by even half a stair landing.

Nighttime twinkles through the small window here. Very few apartments in the neighboring building have drawn their blinds.

"Soldier, move it."

I pick up my pace again. The city shutting may have forced us into an unconventional travel method, but it has also lightened the burden of entering the facility. They'll be down to their emergency guards only. The exchange on the rooftop was quick as we decided how we were approaching the data center. Even if we go in with the aggression of bank robbers, we should be out before security sends backup.

We cross the final stair landing with our footsteps quiet, keeping alert as we ignore the door into the building lobby and make another turn for the exit into the alleyway outside. Nik nudges open the door. He pauses, then closes it again to sniff hard. I think he must be smelling something, but when Miz offers him a tissue, I realize he's only got a runny nose. He blows into it. Opens the door wider, looks left, right, then proceeds out into the night.

"Camera at two o'clock," Blare warns behind me.

"Noted."

We curve around the building in single file. The Three Towns National Data Center is a humble, thin facility—no more impressive than a regular office block for some company that does mediocre consulting. The silver Medan characters at the front declare this a research center, but otherwise its exterior remains nondescript. We slink around tidily.

There's an access panel blinking red beside the glass doors. Nik ignores it entirely and opts to retrieve a crowbar from his bag, jamming it between the doors and forcing them open with a smooth *whoosh!*

While Miz and Blare are quick to hurry through the open entryway, surprise delays my reaction. No alarm shrieks. Nik gestures for me to move it, waving his arm.

I step inside. In the dark I can't see much of the reception: I mistake the large potted plants for standing guards at first, but by the time I've turned in alarm, my vision has adapted to the shadows. A water cooler glares its beady red eyes at us. The cameras above the front desk stare down diligently, and Miz taps her face, then Blare's, checking that they're masked in a way that covers as many facial markers as possible.

"This way," Nik tells me, steering left beside the reception desk.

"Something isn't right," I declare.

"Nooooo," Miz counters. She hops over the turnstiles. "Don't say that."

"Not saying so won't make it suddenly go away—"

"The room we need is right here," Nik interrupts, gesturing ahead in the corridor. We're still on the ground floor. There is one door on either side of the corridor, humming with a sound that only server farms can generate.

I peer around, searching for extra security functionality. I find nothing. "This doesn't seem very well protected."

"Threto splits up its departments with a strange organizational system:

Ministry of National Defense is both first floor and sixth." Nik pulls out a hammer-like tool. "They're relying on stationed guards and an unhackable lock. Lockdown means most guards aren't clocked in."

"How are you hacking an unhackable lock?" I ask.

Nik responds by striking the door with the hammer. All subtlety went out the window the moment he crowbarred the front entrance open, I suppose. The hammer smashes into the smooth metal structure, digging through the wires looped inside the layers, dragging them out in awkward lengths. Whatever that hammer is made of, it's sure doing the trick, because the hole grows quickly, larger and larger until it's big enough for Nik to squeeze into the server room.

"Blare, come in with me. Miz, the front." He pauses a moment, setting the hammer down on the floor and meeting my eyes. "Check the rest of the building for anything impending—alarms, employees. Warn us if anything will interrupt the data retrieval process."

I nod. "Don't forget to look for my materials," I say to Blare. "Run searches on all the Kunlun citizens listed in those two documents from Upsie and retrieve any StrangeLoom credentials you can find." A data center will be holding plenty of private text exchanges and personal notes. There must be a significant number of credentials floating around.

"You got it, boss," Blare replies. They dive through the hole in the door before Nik can. Nik pauses, mouthing, *Boss?* before following.

"Be careful," I say to Miz.

She tilts her head. I know the warning comes strangely, especially when the break-in itself had proceeded so smoothly, but Miz salutes. She hurries for the front again, off to guard the entrance.

And I proceed forward.

Sound is instantly different when I enter the stairwell. It's muffled, warped. My nose wrinkles, catching a whiff of something sour. I tug my mask down, trying to figure out what it is that I'm smelling.

I climb up the stairs, making a turn. Second floor. I push through the door to exit the stairwell, and it's entirely quiet. Slowly I poke my head into the rooms that have been left open here, inspecting the labs with their doors unlocked. At the end of the second floor, I follow an electric humming to a closed door, but it doesn't budge when I try the handle.

The hairs at the back of my neck prickle when I return to the stairwell, climbing to the third floor. I perform the same inspection—find the same empty workspaces and locked server rooms. There are pictures hanging on the walls here: the employees smiling at the cameras. I trail past them, lingering long enough on each to memorize their faces.

I check the fourth floor. The fifth. At this point, I should hope that Nik and Blare are finishing up. I push open the door to the sixth and final floor, meaning to make one cursory scan before calling it a job well done and returning to the group on the ground floor. But the moment I step into the hallway, I freeze.

A night guard did clock in for work. He's right here.

I rush to his side, kneeling roughly on the carpet threads. There's warmth still, emanating from his skin when I search for a pulse. It gives me false hope, thinking he'll only be knocked out. Any moment now, I'll find the sign.

I find nothing. His head is resting at a terrible angle. He's dead.

"Shit," I breathe.

I scan the dark. I almost expect someone to jump out from their hiding place, but the hallway stays quiet. A hum, though, is persistent here. I get up, following the sound. It's loud, then louder, and in front of it, I turn to find the door entirely melted through, a puddle of something sticky trailing into the carpeting.

I was smelling industrial-strength acid. It's still dripping along the sides, eating away at the doorframe.

I spin on my heel, breaking into a dead sprint to get back into the stairwell. We didn't trigger an after-hours alarm because one had already sounded and been shut off. Who was here? A different NileCorp team? Medaluo's internal agents? Another unrelated group?

I waste no time. I don't take the steps down so much as I fling myself from end to end, using the handrail for momentum. I hurtle back onto the ground floor so suddenly that I almost bowl directly into Blare, who's struggling with another heavy server box in their arms.

"We have to go," I announce. "Someone else was just here. Dead guard on the sixth floor. The countdown on security arriving started much earlier than we expected."

Nik pokes his head out from the server room, his eyes wide. A second passes as he digests my words. Then: "Any estimate?"

"I wouldn't be surprised if silent cars are heading our way right this moment. Guard was still warm." My attention turns back to Blare, clearly struggling with the box. "Do you need any help with that?"

"Nope!" they insist. "Miz is getting a bag. I'll fling it over my shoulder."

"You've got the log-ins too?"

"Multiple." Blare tilts their head to the side, to their pocket, indicating it's stored on their device. "We can review everything when we have a moment."

I nod. Miz hurries over, her expression frazzled and a large burlap sack in her hands.

"There's a car out front."

"All right." Nik packs everything up, shoving his tools into his bag. "To the back. If local police suspect it's NileCorp's presence, they might have sent military to get past the quarantine."

"NileCorp?" Miz echoes. "Why would they suspect we're NileCorp?"

"Because someone was here right before us," I say. I don't think it was NileCorp—or at least it wasn't Teryn because she's not going to interrupt her work capturing Nik. It could be a separate team. Another unit after Chung's work. If Teryn's task is confidential, other NileCorp forces may not know what they're interfering with.

"Through the window," Nik commands. "Split up if they engage in pursuit and the situation calls for it. Just keep your comms active. Don't go taking them out for a little ear break—I'm looking at you, Blare."

Blare grimaces. They're already fiddling with their earpiece, muttering something inaudible as Nik looks around, secures his bags, then pushes into the stairwell, heading for the window. He uses the same hammer that broke open the server room door. This time, it takes one hit before the glass smashes into smithereens, littering the stairwell with crystal fragments.

"Miz."

Miz goes first, taking Nik's backpack with the server box. On the ledge, she drops the backpack outside carefully, then reaches in again for Blare's burlap sack with the second server box. As soon as those are both deposited without incident, Miz slithers through the window easily, landing in the alley outside. Distantly, I catch the shudder of helicopter blades. No sirens. They don't want civilians complaining about officers breaking quarantine and spreading disease.

Blare is quick through the window too, though they grunt when they hit the cement.

"You, now," Nik says.

I don't pay him any mind. My ears are perked to the front of the building, waiting for the telltale footfall of someone, anyone approaching the entrance.

"One second."

Nik frowns. "This is absolutely not the time."

I'm not getting the tread of police approaching. Strangely enough, I'm getting a phantom ticking, echoing right above us from the second floor.

"Oh shit."

Before Nik has a chance to argue, I yank his wrist, hurtling us down the stairs into the basement level. I shove him hard on the final step, sparing a breath to get us low just as fire bursts through the ceiling, engulfing the ground floor.

26

LIA

I learned how to study through my dreams.

When I was younger, I had problems being overloaded with everything I needed to learn. There was so much to remember, so much to understand before I could move on from one topic. The fear grew paralyzing the closer I approached elementary graduation. That final year, eighth grade, I had been working my way through all the previous evaluations that Nile Military Academy uploaded online, the tests they used to rank new cadets into class tiers. My scores weren't good enough. I couldn't be hovering in the range between Tier A and Tier B, my designation depending on the bell curve of my classmates. I couldn't leave it up to chance.

Uncle Chung was over for dinner one night. I'd been thinking hard about my physics assignment. I was quieter than usual through most of dinner, and when Dad went into the kitchen to help bring out the muffins that Tamera made, Uncle Chung leaned in and said, "Lia, get ready."

I perked up. Our favorite game.

"Flash is to camera as disaster is to . . ."

"Friends," I answered in a snap. I paused. "I think a lot fits in there, though."

"Perfect answer," Uncle Chung praised. "There are a few that work.

Depends on who someone thinks about when it comes to illuminating their true colors. Many of my colleagues say *partner*."

"Well"—I lifted my chin—"I'm ten."

Uncle Chung seemed to find that funny. He was still chuckling when Dad returned with the tray of muffins. "And very smart."

I shrugged, bashful. "It just comes to me. It's like the word flashes in my head, and I understand what it says before I've fully read it."

"Interesting," Chung remarked. "Kind of like how we read in dreams."

I nodded, reaching for a muffin. I had those dreams too. Reading without reading. Understanding conclusions that emerged in my mind unbidden.

The next morning, I had an idea I wanted to test out. I wasn't going to stare at my flashcards anymore. I pulled open a video editor, uploaded all my flashcards as clips spliced to half a second, and saved the footage. Then I sat in front of it, watching. I'd hoped I would understand the material as though it were a dream.

It worked. It became the method I relied on the most for brute memorization. Nile Military Academy's tier ranking exam was a breeze when I didn't really have to think about the order of foreign occupation in Atahua prior to independence—the dozens of nations merely flashed in my head.

Strange how no one else has discovered this method. I'd have a lot more competition than only Kieren.

． ． ． ．

I jerk awake in a daze, still caught in the tethers of my dream about studying for a physics test. I'm entirely confused about where I am, why I was thinking about my assignments, why I'm absently reciting a formula.

The floor is moving underneath my feet. Nothing is registering properly, and dimly I conclude I must be having a slight episode. Most times I don't feel Wakeman's Syndrome unless I'm downcountry. But, every few months, it'll creep upcountry right after I wake up. Virtual sleep will hit my mind at the wrong angle, and it'll pinch its finger on whatever pipe in my head is funneling conscious thought. Panic starts to swirl. I am not tied to my physical surroundings. I am here, then I am not. I am floating, insentient.

"Lia?"

Some of my awareness returns. Kieren is already awake, standing in the aisle of the bus and playing with something in his hands. The floppy disk. He spins it once, twice, three times. Rayna is still sleeping a few rows down, and Hailey behind her. I am here. I am *here*.

Kieren ducks his head, trying to get a better look at me. He puts the disk away into the backpack he left on the seat. "You all right? I shut up the bot—sorry if that woke you."

"The bot is down?" The bus is still driving. The windows show a burgeoning morning, the mountains in the distance crisp and green. Each gray plume over the horizon comes lighter than the previous.

"No, I shut it *up*, not down. Told it we weren't interested in a guide until we departed Threto." His nose wrinkles. "You look very pale right now."

"Thank you," I say in Medan.

Kieren scoffs. "I meant on the verge of death. Do you have food poisoning?"

"Yes," I say, standing. "Excuse me. I need to go throw up."

"What?"

It's not a lie. My stomach heaves. My lungs restrict. I don't know why this has to happen to me. I don't know why I can't just live like a normal person without a brain that's half-broken, always convinced that my world is going to disintegrate the next time I take a step.

I dive for the bathroom at the back of the bus. I suspect no one has used this in eons because it's impeccably clean when I step in. I collapse to the floor, and a lemony scent wafts from the tiles. I gasp in. And in. And in. I am lying in my Pod downcountry. I am not lost somewhere deep within infinite planes of reality. I know where I am.

The door opens.

"Hello?" I find the energy to heave. "Have you ever heard of knocking?"

"No," Kieren deadpans. He closes the door. Steps in. Despite my best effort to splay my arms and stop him from sitting down, he settles on the floor beside me.

"This is absurd," I manage. "What if I had been having explosive diarrhea?"

"Thankfully you're just sitting here freaking out, so I think we're good."

I glare at him. He raises his eyebrows.

"It's not a big deal," I say after a beat. I'm still struggling for breath, so I don't know who I think I'm fooling.

"Is it Wakeman's Syndrome?"

"No," I snap quickly. The academy can't know. NileCorp can't see it on my files. "No, I'm only a little nervous."

"My mom has it," Kieren says. "It's not shameful."

"Don't."

"Okay," Kieren says softly. "Okay. Sure."

He doesn't get up and go. We've done this once before. The last time, in the tenth grade, I'd found myself awake early one morning. It was the dead of winter, which ruled out walking around the grounds. I'd gone to the campus library to avoid freaking out in my room, sat myself at one of the tables with my physical textbooks open. I didn't intend to study. I only wanted to go somewhere public. Somewhere with life, the candelabras on the windowsills gleaming under the dim, gold lights that the library kept on all night.

Kieren had walked in drowsily, wearing sweats and not yet dressed for the day. He looked shocked to find me in the library, not only at that hour, but *earlier* than him. I didn't say hi, didn't say a word. Still, he beelined right for my table and took the seat opposite me. Some sort of power trip, I'm sure, but I was clearly too out of it to mind. He'd harrumphed, making a show out of gathering his own physical textbooks and placing them on the table. Though we didn't talk, his presence changed the mood of the moment. I made an effort to act normal, to hide my disjointedness, and in the pretense it became real. I eased out of the episode.

I tip my head back into the sink cabinet. Kieren eyes the cuff links of my trousers, and when he tugs it, saying, "Gross. You've got mud here," I know he's doing his best to distract me.

"Those are brown sequins," I say. "Homemade."

"Looks like mud."

"Look closer." I stick my foot at him, and he grimaces, closing his hand around my ankle to keep my shoe at a distance. The floor is solid, virtual upcountry is unchanging, and I am here, I am present. The thought strikes me, suddenly and without prelude, that Kieren must have known I had Wakeman's Syndrome all along given how calm his reaction here is. He'd already recognized it back in the tenth grade.

He's never told on me.

A knock thuds outside the bathroom door. Kieren and I both jolt, and he releases my ankle. When I call *"Come in,"* Rayna pokes only her head through.

A coy expression instantly crosses her face.

"Hello," she says. "Didn't realize we were having a party in here."

"You were invited," I say.

"Lost my invitation. Someone must have wanted it to be an intimate gathering instead." She pushes the door wider, bobbing up and down on her toes. "We're almost at the city center. Am I free to do work of my own today, or do you want to get me in trouble some more?"

I grimace, clambering to my feet. I go slow, in case the movement triggers any further response. My breathing behaves. As does my stomach.

"Do what you need," Kieren answers for me, emerging first. "I haven't a clue what Lia and I are doing since we threw off the entire plan we were given."

"We can make some calls," I say.

Kieren starts walking toward the front. He bellows, *"Hailey!"* and Hailey startles awake, lifting off the seat in her shock.

"What?" she demands. She scrubs her hand along her brow. Kieren always does the exact same move. As different as the siblings look on a surface-level palette, they have the exact same dark brows that don't move an inch no matter how hard they're itching. "Who's here?"

"No one. We're almost in Threto."

The city is waking up alongside us as the bus enters city limits, early-morning joggers filing down the sidewalk and buildings dimming their holograms to make way for the rousing white sun. The air has gotten muggy inside, so I lean over one of the back seats to crack open a window. It doesn't help much. I pick up smoke in the distance when I inhale. It's not the sharp, acrid smell of downcountry, but there's definitely something burning in virtual today.

"First stop," Kieren calls from the dashboard. "Art museum."

I pull away from the window, leaving it open. "What are we doing at the art museum?"

"Nothing. It's just the first stop that was already on the tour." He's frowning when he turns around. He must be sifting through other locations on his display, because I get a rapid series of notifications as he sends links along to me. "It seems like a viable public place to buy some time. Virtual is busy today. Another day, another wave of some virus breaking out downcountry, and Medaluo always does quarantine periods in Threto. Everyone is going to be buying extra day passes to come up."

I grimace. That means security is going to be tighter and personnel doubled. For most people who aren't regular users, a quarantine means using rainy-day funds to purchase weeklong access to upcountry. Otherwise, there's nothing to do but sit at home all day and eat up food that they'll have to replenish.

"Maybe this is good news for us," I say, walking to the front and joining Kieren. "Upcountry turns slightly delirious if everyone is plugging in with an infection."

"I doubt the engineers at the Threto data center are daily users," Kieren says. "They're not getting infected by an outbreak if they rarely leave their Pods."

"If all the main sights are so crowded," Hailey intersects, "can we stop for breakfast?"

We've entered the city. The bus ambles through the streets, passing breakfast shops with lines wrapped around the block, large steaming baskets propped over an open flame and flat egg cakes flipped on enormous circular grills. Corporate employees wearing business casual weave their bikes along the sidewalk, staying off the narrow road to make room for the few vehicles that have come down from the overhead expressways. These roads weren't really made for cars, never mind a tour bus. Many pedestrians purposefully stop to stare daggers at our bulky vehicle.

"What do crowded tourist sites have anything to do with breakfast?" Kieren asks.

"Keeping up energy," Hailey replies easily.

"*Keeping up—*" He cuts himself off, not finishing the flabbergasted echo. "Lia and I have phone calls to make."

Hailey sighs. "Boring." She clambers onto her seat, facing the other way. Rayna is still hovering near the back. "Let's do breakfast?"

Rayna blinks. "Me?"

"I'm looking directly at you, Rayna, so yes, you."

The five-story structure of a museum appears within view, a flag of Medaluo fluttering on its roof. Its stone columns hold up the heavy structure, tall exhibit posters unfurled between each entrance. I open the first link that Kieren sent me, and my display fills with a hand-drawn map. Threto's art museum is less than a ten-minute walk away from its data center. This city has chosen the exact opposite location from Upsie: rather than the silence of its industrial outskirts, Threto's data center blends in with its commercial epicenter. Along the same road, there's a historic rice ball factory that's been operating in Threto for a hundred years.

"Sure," Rayna answers.

> LIA: very nice, very well done
> LIA: so casual
> LIA: so suave
> RAYNA: SHHHHHH

The bus comes to a stop at the far side of the museum's parking lot, joining the other tourist vehicles. When Twelve pulls the hand brake, its body turns slightly, keeping us within view of its front cameras. Then it slumps, quiet.

"We can meet back here at the end of the day if we want to keep traveling together," Kieren decides, swinging his bag onto his shoulder. "Ready, Ward?"

I wave a hand in front of Twelve's face. It doesn't respond.

"What happened to our driver?"

Kieren shakes his head, waving me out through the doors. "We can worry about it if it still hasn't woken by the time we're leaving. Maybe it overheated."

• • • •

We wander the art museum for a while, nodding and reading the descriptive plaques where appropriate. Upcountry museums are the only places to see art now. Downcountry they lock up real pieces in storage for safekeeping, afraid that the elements will damage them with new floods, afraid that someone is going to break in and steal the paintings right off the walls. The practice would probably be a lot more controversial if NileCorp hadn't come to an agreement with art curators and owners to let them duplicate their pieces up here for free, as though the art were a part of the infrastructure that the system is obligated to remake.

Mostly, NileCorp allowed that regulation because rich people didn't want to repurchase their expensive assets in virtual.

Kieren pauses in front of a clay statue, so I take his cue and stop too.

We placed a call to Kam when we entered the museum, but as soon as she picked up, she said she had a fire to put out and would call us back within the hour. Now we're lingering, waiting. Despite the size of this exhibit—one low, small room off the very end of the wing—there are many others milling around with us. The museum is almost at capacity. Threto is indeed busy today.

"Have you been looking at the feed?" Kieren asks quietly.

"No," I answer. "Kids these days, looking at the feed when there's art in front of you."

Kieren doesn't laugh. His gaze is blank, unfocused for a video. "It's your dad."

My heart stutters. "What?"

I open my display at once. I don't need to go scrolling the feed to find it. As soon as I hover over Dad in my contacts, the autosearch does the work for me, pulling the press articles and accompanying viral videos. SENATOR SULLIVAN UNDER FIRE FOR BILL "TOO SOFT" ON MEDALUO.

I go to the first video. It's clearly been cut for the most important parts, because there's no prelude. Dad's on the Senate floor, saying, "... expands the authority to put through emergency cases. The current processing *time* for Medans seeking asylum is thirteen months—and within this period, there is no promise of safety for their actions, meaning there's no real motivation for them to defect at all. If this war is about ideals, as we have heard from our own president time and time again, why do we offer no safe passage for those wanting to believe in Atahuan freedom?"

"Oh, dear," I breathe.

Unsurprisingly, the comments on the video are largely made up of people debating Dad's ethnic makeup. He's too Medan for the Atahuans, mad at the thought that we should be offering Medans asylum. He's too Atahuan for the Medans, unhappy with the insinuation that their citizens even need asylum. And any Medan we see on Atahuan apps is already sympathetic to Atahua in some capacity, either speaking the language or having familial ties across the ocean. If this video got downloaded and made the rounds on different Medan apps, onto their version of the feed, the reaction would be much worse.

"Not a fan of the bill?" Kieren asks.

"The death threats had only just started slowing down," I say unhappily.

My display suddenly fills with an incoming call, wiping away the next video trying to autoplay. Kieren and I exchange a glance. We can't speak to Kam here, in the open.

"I think I saw a cleaning supply closet," Kieren suggests.

We hurry out of the exhibit. There's a momentary rush of people, some school field trip bringing a cluster of eight-year-olds into this part of the wing. Kieren grimaces, halting every so often to avoid running over a child. At a certain point, I have no choice but to maneuver him along, children be damned. They're young. They'll bounce back if they're whacked.

I swing open the door into the supply closet, answering the call before we've fully situated ourselves inside. It's a tiny, cramped space. We barely fit because of the bulky cleaning cart, a half bucket of dirty water sloshing at its front.

"Ugh," Kieren groans, closing the door after himself with a thud. "It smells like feet."

"Status?" Kam asks, her voice upbeat.

I hope she's forgotten about Kieren's little fit.

"We're in Threto a little earlier than expected," I say. No need to go into unnecessary details—like us fleeing the authorities in Upsie—unprompted. "Ready to proceed to the Three Towns data center."

Tapping echoes over the line. Kieren's right: it's definitely long nails.

"You mentioned yesterday that it was a floppy disk you retrieved, yes?"

"Correct." Without calling a warning, I reach to check Kieren's pockets, hearing a clatter when my knuckles knock against the disk. He jumps. I thought I saw him transferring it out of his bag when we were walking up the museum steps—it was a good move to keep it safe.

"I am confirming that you should proceed with searching the Threto facility if that's where it says it originates. That being said, Mr. Chung did not keep an official office there, so I can't lead you to a likely location for the disk reader."

That's a surprise. "I thought he kept an office across all the major cities."

"No, he mostly worked out of Upsie. He makes appearances in upcountry Threto and Offron to check on his uploads, but his virtual activity at those locations is relatively sparse."

"On paper, he's the supervisor for the Ministry of National Defense's data and all the servers that department keeps," Kieren says. "Could he have a workstation in those rooms?"

"Those server rooms are indeed where his real work is kept, so perhaps." Kam is chewing gum too. I can hear it popping while she speaks. "I'll get the directions drawn up. As for your entry into the data center, it's Medaluo's Tomb-Sweeping Day."

Kieren and I exchange a glance. His expression mirrors mine, uncertain if this is supposed to be something we cheer or hiss at.

"Great?" I hedge.

Kieren's eyes swivel. He's clearly frantically searching the web. "Ah. I see. Parade starts in an hour."

"What does a parade have to do with tomb-sweeping?"

"Substitution celebration. No tombs upcountry, Ward."

"Here's the route," Kam says. "The onlookers have already formed."

A file drops into my display. It opens to a live, overhead view of the city, a red line showing where the parade will weave from west to east. The data center is on the east side of the water—the parade path will pass its front entrance.

"You'll meet the delivery bot outside your current location. Get dressed, then hurry along. You can walk the parade route normally until you reach your destination."

The line drops.

"Do you think she's ever ended a phone call with a nice *Goodbye*?" I remark.

"Unlikely," Kieren answers. "I'm not sure if this is a very good plan either. Just because we can walk past the facility on a parade route doesn't mean we can get in."

"I'm hopeful that the delivery—"

The closet door swings open, interrupting my thought.

"*Excuse* me."

A security bot has found us. These models were made to invoke authority, so I shouldn't be startled to glance up and find it towering over us in height. Its oval body glides closer using the wheels at its feet. Since it can speak, this must be a similar model to Twelve, but the security bot has a large panel to display an emoticon.

The current one is a red frowning face.

"I must ask you to exit."

I panic, immediately sprinting through a thousand various excuses for our presence in the museum. Before I say anything, Kieren's hand snakes up my arm, gripping tightly and warning me to pause.

"Sorry, sorry, we'll get out of this closet." He applies emphasis to the word "closet." I can't tell if it was intentional, or if his Medan just sounds prominent in an attempt to hit the right tonal vowels. "No more delinquent behavior, promise."

Then he puts his arm around me. The only reason I don't shriek is because I'm too confused to react. I let Kieren lead us out and sharply take a left, away from the bot before it has dismissed us. When I glance over my shoulder, convinced that couldn't possibly have worked, the bot is calmly peering into the closet to make sure there's no one else in there, then closing the door.

"You can't act that guilty, Ward," Kieren mutters beneath his breath, switching back to Atahuan. "It wasn't asking us to exit the museum as foreign agents. It thought we were fooling around in there."

My jaw drops. "That's... absurd."

"Think about what the bot was seeing. It's rolling after us now. Give me a little kiss on the cheek."

He's only trying to be funny, but I feel my stomach do a nosedive nonetheless. It must be nerves from almost getting caught. I can't believe he'd make light of the situation.

"Come on." Kieren makes little kissy noises, as if that's supposed to encourage me. I huff a breath, lean in, then bite him.

Kieren jerks away.

"*Lia*. Ow."

"You're so cute when you're being nibbled on." It was more satisfying than I'd have thought to get a mouthful of his face. "Can't risk a kiss. We don't want you getting a crush again, do we?"

The bot has entered a new exhibit. Kieren scoffs, pulling ahead. "Using my moment of vulnerability against me, I see. For shame."

For a moment it really seems that I've hurt his feelings. He's looking ahead, his shoulders stiff. I don't understand at what point we switched from lighthearted to serious.

"Kieren—"

He turns around. There's no hurt in his expression. The sight of his neutral manner should bring me relief, but another bout of nerves twist through my stomach.

What is *happening* to me?

I stride ahead. We're approaching the exit, the light of the main atrium washing us white. "Bet I'll get outside faster than you."

27

EIRALE

Blistering heat from the explosion licks into the basement, then recedes as the damage settles. A large piece of debris has fallen directly over us, propped up by the stair railing. The second floor has collapsed entirely, raining chunks of ceiling plaster onto the ground level.

Slowly, I shift around, taking inventory to check for injuries. Through a tiny gap in the debris—a pinhole barely wider than my finger—I catch sight of broken steel pipes jutting out of the walls and rubble that has scattered to cover the stairwell. We would have been crushed where we stood if we hadn't moved. I imagine Miz and Blare should have avoided most of the blow outside. The impact shot downward, not outward. And fortunately for Nik, both of his stolen server boxes were thrown out already with Miz and Blare.

Nik stirs, blinking hard under his glasses as he tries to adjust. I think he might have hit his head when the debris scattered, but I don't have time to sympathize. He makes a confused noise, and I shush him.

"Be quiet," I hiss.

I listen hard, trying to trace the path that the Medan authorities are taking as they enter the facility. It must be regular police—I see flashes of their siren lights. Their boots crunch noisily on broken glass. Someone calls for them to disperse and ensure the space is clear; another officer asks for confirmation about what they were called in about, and he gets a reply that there was a possible intrusion alert. One that succeeded, they say, given this mess.

Nik winces again, and I clamp down on his ankle in threat.

Footsteps press to the back stairwell. I inch lower, ducking under the line of light streaming through the pinhole in the debris. The steps keep moving after performing an inspection of the rubble.

"Hey," I whisper to Nik, releasing his ankle. "We should wait it out. We can leave when the city police give their all clear. I don't want to run into the units they've got around the perimeter."

Nik doesn't say anything in response, save for a grunt. I try to find a comfortable way to hunch beneath the slab of debris. My leg is caught at a cramped angle. I'm awkwardly situated, not wanting to sidle too close to Nik.

"Explosion came from the second floor. Surveillance tapes were stored locally there," a faint voice reports near the front. "One camera at reception and one camera outside. Looks like our intruders wanted to get rid of the evidence."

"Any damage?"

"No damage to the servers, but breaches in both rooms for National Defense. We'll get an engineer in. Make a report of what was taken."

While the police go back and forth over the rubble, Nik slowly lifts himself up from his slumped position. I'm relieved to see his bag on his shoulders: he hadn't dropped it in our dive down, so there won't be any signs pointing to the two of us hiding in the debris. I stay alert, waiting, listening, but the police don't circle into the back stairwell again.

"Don't move too much," I murmur. "They're still there."

The police are in and out multiple times as the hour passes. New voices, streaming through the lobby and coming down the ground-floor corridor. Long red and blue lights as larger cars pull up. I have plenty of patience to stay put exactly where I am.

Nik, meanwhile, keeps drooping his head.

I nudge him with my foot the fifth time, annoyed. When he doesn't respond or lift his head, the first hint of concern clenches through my stomach. "What's going on?"

"I'm fine," he barely whispers.

I wait a beat to confirm there aren't any officers directly near the stairwell. Then I shift forward quietly, putting a hand on his forehead.

"Are you vaccinated?" I whisper furiously. "Against all the avian flus?"

"Yes. Obviously."

"When?"

Nik swallows hard. His throat bobs up and down. "I don't know?" he replies. "Two years ago?"

Given how fast viruses mutate downcountry, he may as well tell me he's wearing armor with a giant hole in the middle. "Are you serious?"

"I'm so sorry," Nik replies testily. "It was hard to keep up with my check-ups while Atahua was trying to arrest me."

"Have you considered not engaging in criminal behavior, then?"

"Have you considered not working for a warmongering empire?"

"*You* try being born a Medan orphan," I fire back, and the moment my last word echoes, I hear returning footsteps.

Nik winces, his inhale rattling when he breathes. I reach over him for his bag, ignoring his flinch of protest. While another officer is walking above us, their steps crunching on the glass shards that blew in with the window, I rummage through the various items that Nik carries around, coming in contact with his hammer. It's a small object for how much power it holds. I risk the sound of zipping up the bag.

The footsteps fade away again. It sounds like most of the officers have left the immediate vicinity.

I sigh, unable to believe I'm doing this. Time is of the essence upon infection. I suppose I have no choice.

I strike the hammer at the large block of debris above us. There's no response from the facility while I break the block, the sound echoing through the basement. No officers hurrying toward the sound. I wince, shoving the hammer hard at another corner. This should be good enough.

"Get up."

Nik is too slow. I grab him by the arm and use every bit of my strength to lug him out from under the debris and onto his feet. Voices float faintly from the front of the facility. I have my fist tight around Nik's sleeve while we pick our way up the ruptured stairs, careful not to step somewhere that might cause another avalanche of fallen infrastructure. There's no need to climb out a window this time: an enormous hole has been blown through the wall on the ground floor. We squeeze into the opening using the protruding pipe for a leg up. Nik, at least, can still maneuver quietly when I hiss at him to move. I hear the first clatter of curiosity from the front. An officer has noticed us.

"Come on, come *on*."

We push out from the building, and I veer us sharply around the corner, cutting into an alley. The route leads into a wide road, which is dangerous since the first tendrils of the morning are starting to brighten the dark. A quick scan up and along the residential buildings tells me we have at least three different camera angles on us.

"Hey," I say. "Did you have an emergency exit plan? Where should we be going?"

More sirens in the distance. I wonder if our faces are still logged back there in the data center. Or if the explosion that the intruders before us set will have wiped us away too.

"Nik."

I shake him. His shoulders shudder before he drops onto his knee.

Fear clamps a band across my chest, spreads an aching pressure along my ribs. If he dies, what happens in Offron? Does Teryn's capture unit disperse, counting it as a job well done, or are they punished, having lost the asset before they could glean the program they wanted?

Am I allowed back into Atahua, or do I count as a compromised failure?

I need NileCorp to clear my name. Issue a statement, tell the media to run their press junkets and say Eirale Ward was set up, was deepfaked, was innocent.

"Can you get in contact with Miz and Blare?" I ask. "They've been out a while now."

Surely they've secured a vehicle in that time. They must be hovering somewhere nearby, waiting to receive a summons that it's all right to come and fetch us.

"Can't," Nik mumbles. "Internet is down."

"What?"

"I think the city government shut it for lockdown. They'll do it sometimes if too many people are posting videos on the feed they don't like. Should be back in half a day."

We don't have half a day. Depending on the speed at which this illness progresses, Nik Grant could be dead in half a day without a suppressant. I drag him forward, searching wildly for some place to take cover. He has the energy to move if I'm urging him along, but he turns entirely still if left alone.

"How," I mutter, "did you even get infected?"

"Virus particles are tricky."

Up ahead, I spot an awning with a building number upon it, and I hurry us toward the gate underneath. The gate latch lifts easily. It leads us into a narrow passage, the exterior walls dotted with windows up ten floors on each side of the neighboring buildings, before the alley spits us through to the courtyard of another. I don't take us any farther. Nik can't manage it.

"Sit here," I instruct.

He doesn't need to be told twice, collapsing onto the brick path. I take a moment to catch my breath. Most of the windows on the ground level are barred by steel rods, a safety mechanism against break-ins. There's a potted plant sitting on the inner ledge of the one I'm looking at. No movement inside the glass. Next door, the curtain twitches. Someone likely got nosy enough to peek out, then decided it was nothing they wanted to get involved in.

"Think, think," I mutter.

He needs Eveline. I also can't leave him out here in the open while I get it. Eveline is a miracle cure that Atahua invented, a pill that almost entirely suppresses the symptoms of all major influenzas and *"improves the survival rate to a staggering 99.8 percent!"* as the commercials jingle every time they play. A few hours after consumption, it stops most transmissibility of the targeted virus. I know Medan pharmacies are usually stocked because I did a research unit at the academy on Eveline the company. It accepted a bid from the Medan government as an investor, but lo and behold, due to great Atahuan outcry, though the company promised many of its vials to Medaluo, it came at a huge price point.

Medaluo imports the pills, and no one can afford them. Forget banks, forget jewelers. The most frequently robbed places these days are neighborhood pharmacies, and when the one-pill packages are taken, the pharmacies get insurance payouts from the government who pat themselves on the back for a job well done supplying their people with cures. As long as I can outrun a few alarms, the pharmacies practically encourage people to go in and take them.

Nik starts to tilt, losing balance. Just as I'm reaching forward to keep him steady, I hear the clatter of the gate, and I swivel fast, my grip tight on his arm.

The woman doesn't step through the gate, merely keeping it nudged open with her shoe. She's dressed in a pantsuit, a headset still over her ears with the mic pushed up, as though she's on a lunch break from her remote job.

"Hey," she whisper-shouts. I jolt. She's speaking Atahuan. "Are you Eirale?"

"That depends on who's asking."

The woman looks over her shoulder quickly. That answer didn't maintain much plausible deniability if this is a Medan official who wants me hauled in, but I suppose chances are higher she's an ordinary Medan who recognized me off the feed.

"Proceed ahead into the inner building," she instructs. "There's an empty apartment in 1F. You won't need to climb any stairs."

I'm already lifting Nik to his feet. This could be a trap. Medaluo military might be getting really good at its capture methods.

"Why?" I ask simply. "What's it to you?"

She taps her collar. Her nail is long and painted neon pink, visible from a distance. I can track it clearly when her finger loops in a miniature infinity symbol. That may have started as the icon for StrangeLoom specifically, but in recent years after a shift in marketing materials, it's come to be universally recognized for NileCorp at large. The NileCorp logo doesn't sit idle in its digital rendering: it will loop again and again.

"You don't need to trust me. You need to get somewhere quiet."

The woman slips away, the gate latching again.

There are no other ethnic Medans on Teryn's team, and I would recognize the handful of others from the Button City base. Either Teryn gathered a new team to enter Medaluo, or this woman is from a NileCorp outpost entirely unrelated to me.

I suppose I have no choice but to proceed with what I've been given. I haul Nik forward, his movements already significantly worse than a few minutes prior. We plod through the courtyard, then through the inner building, where the front doors have been taken off the hinges entirely.

"Just a few more steps, Nik," I say.

"What was that?" he mumbles. "Who were you talking to?"

"Don't worry about it."

I find 1F at the end of the hallway. I barely manage to get a grip on the doorknob while I'm focusing on keeping Nik upright with my other arm, and my sweaty palm slips, failing to turn it properly. Panic creeps in. It might be locked, or a lie entirely.

I try again, and the knob turns.

I drag him through the kitchen. Cold blue walls. The fridge is unplugged, its cords pulled out to save electricity, and the entire apartment is void of the usual hum that accompanies running appliances. I maneuver Nik to the couch.

"Where are we?" Nik rasps.

"Listen to me." I perform a cautionary survey of the apartment, poking my head through the two other doors. I find a tiny bathroom and an empty bedroom. "This virus has a coin-toss chance of killing you in a few days."

"Maybe . . ." He trails off. Wheezes, catching his breath again. "Maybe it's just common cold."

"Your eyes are turning pink."

Nik reaches up to rub his eyes, and I slap his hand away vigorously. He doesn't protest, his hand hovering midair for a second before it slackens, his body curling into the couch and his eyes fluttering closed. When I prod his forehead again, his skin is hot, feverish.

"Do you have an extra comm link for me?"

Nik doesn't reply, nearing sleep. I go to the kitchen and fill up a mug of water. Ice cold, slightly freckled with dirt from poor filtration. He's definitely still awake judging by the way he splutters when I throw it over him.

"*Hey—*"

"Do not sleep," I seethe through my teeth. "I am trying to make sure you don't die a tragic and insignificant death, so the least you can do is keep your eyes open. Do you have another comm link? We'll run it on radio."

He winces like he's thinking hard on the matter. "There are two in my bag on the same frequency—"

I'm already ripping his bag off him and rummaging through it. He's got a scratch pad shoved in here. A pair of socks too, for whatever reason. I make a note of both and then close my hand around an earbud case at the bottom.

"I looked pretty closely at the map when I was drawing our route across

Threto, especially around the river," I say. "There's a pharmacy three blocks over. I'm going to get you Eveline. I shouldn't be longer than an hour."

I shove one earbud into Nik's ear. He flinches, but he doesn't crane away entirely. The link activates.

"Don't go anywhere. Do you understand me?"

He tries to sit up. "If you're skipping out—"

"I am not having this conversation." In the kitchen, I put a hand towel under the water. No matter how long the faucet runs, it doesn't clear. This is as good as it's going to get. "Keep in mind that my life gets *worse* if you die, so pull it together. I'm returning shortly."

I toss the hand towel at him with a wet clunk. It lands on his arm, and because he doesn't make any move to pick it up, I grit my teeth and go over again, placing it on his forehead.

"Oh." He blinks at me. "Thank you."

I shove his other earbud into my ear. The connection snaps into place—I can hear everything on his end.

"I'm going," I say. "Keep your eyes open."

28

LIA

We found the delivery bot outside the museum spinning in circles to amuse itself. I was worried about the large box clutched in its arms, given the sheer speed it was whizzing at, but after we signed for it and ripped it open, it turned out there was nothing fragile anyway. It was two high-visibility vests and two hard hats.

The costume is certainly doing its job now. There must have been a call for volunteers to manage the parade that Kam mimicked the gear for, because there are others along the route dressed similarly. They're not walking with the cheering paraders like we are: they're performing crowd control among the viewers. I catch sight of one volunteer tugging a kid to the side, off the path. The kid barely notices he's being moved, only distractedly reaching up to make sure the willow crown he's woven into his head doesn't fall off.

Kieren and I stay somewhere in the middle of the slow-moving parade, behind a wagon cart and in front of a dance group. No one looks closely at us. While they're observing the parade, they see our vests, and their gazes glance right off. I peer up at the overhead skybridge we're passing, where more observers are hanging out, and some go as far as to look away if I've met their eyes. They're afraid that I'll notice something about where they're standing and ask them to move away from the nice spot they've picked.

We'll be approaching the data center soon. The map in my display shows a few more blocks.

"So," I say, breaking the focused silence that had settled between us, "what exactly does preparing for the cyber division entail?"

Kieren rolls his eyes, already knowing what I'm getting at. "I'm not a secret hacker, if that's what you're asking."

"Kam seemed to imply you were."

"Common misconception," he says, snootily. "Cyber will care about my math grades, but everything else is taught on the job. It's still NileCorp. They would definitely have an issue with a cadet committing illegal activity prior to recruitment."

Key word: "prior." If it's illegal activity while employed at the company, that's perfectly fine.

I veer closer to Kieren on the path. He scowls when I nudge right into his shoulder, but I know he's faking it. If he was actually annoyed, he would have moved.

"Somehow," I say, lowering my voice, "I figure they'd look the other way if you learned a trick or two."

Kieren's nose wrinkles. "No way."

"Hailey plays an illegal prank about once a month."

"Yes"—Kieren adjusts his shoulder, but only to thud into my side with gusto—"and I have a hard enough time making sure Hailey and Weston don't get me into trouble by association when they're trawling through the dark web. I don't need to risk it as well."

I scoff, firing up a returning shoulder thud. Somehow I find it hard to believe that his siblings can trawl through the dark web so frequently without Kieren picking up a few exploits too.

"You're trying to tell me that you don't know *anything* behind the science of hacking inside the StrangeLoom system?"

Kieren pauses. "I suppose I wouldn't say that."

Whack. He casts me a dour look, almost stumbling from the impact. Before any of the paraders can get suspicious about why their crowd control volunteers are acting like roughhousing children, we both snap back into order, spotting our target building at the same time.

The Three Towns National Data Center is six floors instead of the twenty or so in the buildings on either side of it. The scene along the riverfront appears normal. No extra security that might speak to Medaluo being afraid of intruders. A camera glints at the entrance, moving left and right to motion track each segment of the parade when it passes by. The most pressing disturbance for the data center at present is likely the sheer noise wrapping around its facility, endless excitement wafting from the paraders.

"I think," I declare, "I have an idea. Follow my lead."

To Kieren's credit, he issues no protests. We break from the parade route, murmuring our apologies through the cluster of spectators. They move out of our way, and we hurry up the steps to the data center before stopping outside its glass doors. I tap my knuckles to knock.

The receptionist glances up inside. I wave, and she stands, reluctantly. She's already spotted our high-visibility vests.

"Can I help you?" she asks when she approaches the glass. She doesn't move to open the door.

"City council directed us your way," I say. "Mandatory check of the buildings along the parade route." I make a quick survey behind me, as though I'm ensuring everything is still in order. "We have possible terrorism reports about a sound blocker targeting the parade."

The common user upcountry has no grasp on the basics of their world. They don't know how it operates. They don't know how processes are triggered in virtual, what chain reaction of inputs makes which output. All we know is that the display is designed and labeled to tell us results: *close tab, log out, see map.*

The receptionist rears back. "Are we in danger?"

"Not to our understanding," Kieren answers, picking up my pieces smoothly. "Just some activists trying to cause chaos during the festival. We only need to make sure nothing has been planted in the building."

Now the receptionist's worry transforms into a frown. Maybe we look too young to be working for the council—and in Kieren's case, too Atahuan. Still, his Medan is great. He could be an expat's kid. It's more unusual here, but it's not unbelievable.

"This isn't a commercial building," she says. "All visitors require credentials."

"We understand," I say. "But we only need your hallways to perform a scan."

"Otherwise we'll have to report that the building wasn't examined," Kieren adds. "And it's probably easier to only have us two poke around. If the city council comes with a team, you'll have to clear a dozen visitor passes. Absolutely not worth it just to check a blocker for a measly five minutes, but that's bureaucracy for you."

To be honest, *I'm* not sure how a sound blocker can be planted. I've heard of them used during firework shows on the neighboring blocks. I've also heard of them being illegally applied if teenagers are sneaking around—they're minor features that can be installed or uninstalled because the instruction is so easy to activate over an object.

The receptionist considers us. "*Sound* terrorism," she mutters in disbelief. She sighs, then presses a button to the side. "What has this world come to?"

And the doors open.

"Thank you," Kieren says, stepping in.

"Hallways only, please," she warns. "Do we know what group may be responsible?"

"Well..." I'm pretending to be very focused on the lobby when I enter, scrambling for some names of Medan groups. There really aren't many. "We don't want to make any assumptions before there's confirmation yet."

"I bet it's the Coalition," the receptionist says. There's a bite to her voice. I hear it at the academy all the time too, the kids from prestigious families who don't understand why insurgents protest NileCorp for taking their jobs. Asking why people can't work hard and earn their keep no matter what unfortunate circumstances befall them. Never acknowledging that the money and privilege their families have has kept *them* from needing to work hard their whole lives.

"I haven't heard of the Coalition," Kieren remarks.

The receptionist waves her hands, her lip curling. "That's for the better. Their flyers are plastered all over my building in bright Atahuan text. I don't know how the government hasn't gotten rid of them yet."

"In any case, we'll certainly make sure this threat is sorted out for you," I assure. "May we?"

The receptionist returns to her desk and gestures for us to proceed. The light on one of the lobby turnstiles switches from red to green, and I push through. Kieren follows suit.

He makes a show out of looking at the white walls when the corridor starts, and we proceed past the receptionist. Exposed wires run around the entryways and atop the carpeting.

"If Chung had a workstation here," he murmurs under his breath, "it's either on the ground floor or the sixth."

As though triggered by his words, my display suddenly shifts, activating augmented help that Kam set up. I already gave it permission from Upsie's facility, so this time there's no warning before a bright pink arrow bleeds along the flooring and points to the door at the end. Another fainter arrow splits off from it, leading up the stairwell. The two server rooms under Chung's supervision.

"You know how we lied about a sound blocker?" I ask slowly.

Kieren gives me a sharp look, instantly knowing where my thoughts are going. "Forget it."

"Mr. Elite Cyber Division," I say. "I know you know how to apply it."

"I'm not our hypothetical terrorist—I don't know how to plant one somewhere," he hisses. "The only thing I can do is give it to myself on my own avatar panel, and it would probably extend a six-foot radius. No one is going to buy it."

"They will. Meanwhile you open this door"—I point to the one closest to us—"and have a look. I'll use the distraction to check the sixth floor."

"And how am I supposed to do that?"

Each of the server doors has a badge scan and then a passcode to activate the lock. Double-layered security.

"Excuse me, ma'am!" I call, getting the receptionist's attention.

"*Lia.*"

Her chair rustles loudly at the front. Seconds later, the turnstile chimes when she pushes through and appears within view. "Yes?"

"We've found a blocker, unfortunately. It appears to be in here," I say casually, pointing at the server room door. "Any chance you can let us through?"

"You can't shut it off from out here?"

"We'll need to get a good look at its installation point," I say, completely making it up on the fly. "You see—"

My voice cuts out. I'm genuinely surprised when my mouth keeps moving without volume, all of my words muted in range of an active sound blocker. The receptionist's eyes widen, concerned. As she strolls toward us, her mouth moving and clearly venting her annoyances, I mime that I need to see what exactly is going on overhead and dash into the stairwell before she can say anything.

If Kieren can convince the receptionist to open the server room down here, it should distract her for a few minutes. Long enough to allow my snooping on the sixth floor.

I clatter up the stairs, putting all my vigor into my steps before sound snaps back on the fourth floor. I grimace, then quiet my footfall, hurrying up the next two flights of stairs.

On the sixth floor, I find no other employees around. Upcountry is usually only for appearance's sake when it comes to this line of work.

The arrow takes me to the first door within view, plain black with a numeric keypad lock. Out of sheer delusion, I try the handle. It doesn't budge. That was a long shot.

Still, with the action, a small notification has appeared at the corner of my display. I hurry to enlarge it, remembering the mysterious banners that appeared when I touched the smart key. This one is only a generic pop-up.

Error#z27LxQAwx4jDEw: Access denied. Please enter your personalized code.

I step away from the door, not wanting to trigger any suspicion in the system. My hands flex, scrambling to think. I don't have much longer up here.

Wait a second. I touch the door again, letting the banner appear in warning once more. Error#z27LxQAwx4jDEw. Wasn't that the exact sequence that appeared on Upsie's door too? There, the third option to open the door had been left behind on a user level, offering it as a choice that only I could access. So if this is the very same error, and it requires a personalized code . . .

I start to type. 2040-07-01.

The lock beeps. And the door opens.

I step into the servers' choral hum, shutting the door behind me quickly. My heart is hammering against my ribs. I need to control myself or my display is going to wonder if we need help. My *birthday* got me through the door into Chung's workspace. I might have written off Upsie's lock as a glitch in the system, some identification protocol that required its virtual options to display the user ID of anyone who tries to get in.

But this was intentional, undeniably. Someone already input my birthday into Threto's security system, prepared for my entry here after I made the connection to Upsie's error code.

"What is going on?" I whisper aloud.

The server room doesn't answer me. I slink forward like a robber in daylight, convinced that someone is sure to see me despite the complete absence of employees nearby. An imaginary countdown hovers over my shoulder for as long as Kieren can keep the receptionist occupied, and I move through the machines, the blinking lights, the dust-covered wires.

The aisle ends briefly to offer a cross section. I look left. Right. There's nothing of note, so I continue, hurrying along a new row. I pay no attention to the servers themselves, at a loss for what information could be stored within them. It's not until I reach the very back of the room that I finally find something valuable: a desk in the corner.

There's a jacket hanging on the chair.

I pull the chair quickly, its wheels squeaking in protest. The touch of suede crinkles underneath my fingertips—it's a nice jacket, one that doesn't seem like it should be left behind in a dark, windowless room. Even with a workstation installed here, I can't imagine it would be pleasant to spend long amounts of time seated with only a lamp. I flick it on. No light. It's not plugged in.

Instead, when I drop below the desk, there *is* a disk reader plugged into the sole outlet, lying haphazardly on its side.

"Jackpot," I hiss, yanking the disk reader out. I wind the cord around itself, my motions going fast enough to create a breeze that flutters my bangs off my face. With nowhere safer to put it, I shove it right into the waistband of my trousers, knowing it'll be more secure there than in my shallow pockets.

I clamber up from the desk, dusting off my hands.

Then the door to the server room opens.

"Hello?"

I dive into one of the farther rows, silently mouthing every curse word I know. The footsteps head toward me, and I start to combine the bad words for more variations. Did they hear me moving around? I didn't leave any lights on, didn't leave any visible sign of my presence. Unless the system is telling them otherwise, they shouldn't know I'm here.

I drop down to my knees, opting to crawl in case my shoes make noise. I'm scurrying into the cross section just as I hear a footstep squeak into the aisle I was in. Then, a long silence. Whoever has entered the room has clearly heard *something* and is eyeing all the aisles, suspicious.

I press up against the server rack, every muscle in my body frozen. The longest few beats of my life pass. I already have my chat box prepared, poised to type a message to Kieren to pull the fire alarm so I can get out.

Then the employee in the server room starts to whistle, the sound farther than the shoe squeak before. The metal racks groan, moving one of the aisles for server access.

I breathe out slowly, reaching forward again to get on my hands and knees. I crawl the remaining length to the door while the racks are shifting and, taking advantage of how the entrance has been left temporarily ajar, I slip through and burst back into the hallway.

My entire body is trembling. Adrenaline rushes through me, sweat coating the back of my neck to my waistband where the disk reader is hiding, and somehow I force myself to look only lightly confused when I finish descending the stairs and return to the ground floor. At that very moment, Kieren emerges with the receptionist.

Sound has returned. Kieren is saying, ". . . problem should all be solved, I've wiped the installation. Lots of troublemakers these days, huh? The StrangeLoom system really needs to be stricter. If it were up to me, I'd forbid any personal controls at all."

"Ridiculous," the receptionist agrees. "I'm just glad we caught the problem before it could erupt at an inopportune time."

Kieren turns, spotting me. "Ah! No trouble in the stairwell?"

"Nope," I answer smoothly. "The blocker must not have extended far."

"Good, good." Kieren nods at the receptionist. "We'll be out of your way now."

When the receptionist turns, Kieren gives me a silent questioning glance, but I don't dare respond to him yet. For as long as we haven't departed the facility, I'm still afraid that the employee on the sixth floor is going to chase me down.

The receptionist shows us through the main doors. We wave, make empty promises that no more sound blockers will be coming to bother them. Outside, the parade is still going at full force.

"Ward?"

"Let's find a quiet spot," I say, walking down the steps. I'm already shedding my costume and taking off my hard hat. "Hurry."

Incense wafts under my nose, thick, heady. The sticks burn from open tailgates, slow-moving trucks chugging along the parade path now. Picture frames decorate the truck beds, along with plates of oranges, bananas, apples to make a spread. At some point the spectators have started to throw flower petals, and I get a handful in my hair when we push through the crowd. Firecrackers echo down the road. I smell something rich. The next truck carries a whole roasted pig surrounded by small bowls of rice.

They're so . . . happy. The parade is one mass funeral, but it is the chance to gather side by side without risk to their bodies, without fear of harm. I almost want to linger, pretend that I'm a part of it.

"Where are we going?" Kieren asks.

"Anywhere." I glance over my shoulder. A kite drifts up from the other side of the parade. It snags in the air, catching the breeze wrong. One of its decorative ribbons detaches. "We just need to be out of view."

I make a turn toward the riverbank, throwing my hard hat and my vest into a trash can. Kieren does the same. There's no proper path when we proceed down. The mud glides underfoot—I hold my arms out for balance, just as I do on campus grounds, at the slopes near the cliffs that are always damp despite the weather. I cast a glance over my shoulder, wary in case Kieren needs assistance, but he's as prompt as I am, skidding along the grass until we've reached a flat pebble path again.

We haven't ventured far from the parade, yet the sound diminishes significantly, drowned out by the light ebb of the river. I stroll right up to the edge, pressing against the railing. The other side of Threto glints in hello. I retrieve the reader from my waistband.

"Pass me the disk," I say. I'm already searching for the wireless connection in my display, entering the reader's serial number to confirm that I want to link to the device.

A nudge against my arm. Kieren is trying to be subtle with the disk pass.

"Let me connect too." He reaches for the reader.

"Wait," I say quickly, veering it away. "Let me . . . let me see first. I just need to see."

Kieren frowns. It's broad daylight. Though the clouds are gray, our surroundings remain starkly lit. The murky water glistens; the buildings on the other side wink back.

But Kieren's eyes are wholly dark. He's suspicious because of my request, and there's a lurch in my chest that I identify as relief—a normal reaction, at last. Some indication that he must realize I've hidden information from him. I keep expecting his questions. In Upsie, after he found me in the office with the door unlocked. When we emerged from the facility back there, my retrieval a success despite the rigorous security safeguarding a server room.

My fingerprint is pressed in all these places where it shouldn't be. If he hasn't pointed it out, what does Kieren Murray *know* already?

I slide the disk in. The reader starts to whir frantically, and I get a pop-up in my display indicating that it's loading. Another series of firecrackers go off along the parade. I turn around with my display on half opacity, watch the white sparks dancing above.

FILES FOUND: 1

2044-09-08.eml

I click it open.

Mal,
I went in to watch her play today, and it is genuinely nothing short of a miracle. She is whole, smart, healthy. Chung warned me that she may be confused about what happened, but with time that will fade and the gaps will fill themselves. She asked for a juice box, entirely naturally, and I felt like I was wearing my heart outside of my chest.

This is a success. I know you have your qualms with what we've allowed to happen, but you should see this as a stride in science rather than something unnatural. We have had such precious little time with her, and now we can have her back.

I'll be home soon.
—Henry

There are no more pages to the file. Nothing more inside the disk. It's one email that my dad sent to Mallory. One email that warranted a unique reader setup and every method in our cadet-trained arsenal to obtain.

"Lia," Kieren prompts. "Show it to me."

I hand him the reader without any further protest, gesturing that he can connect and see for himself. I'm at a loss over these pieces, bewilderment and dread alike heavy in my stomach. We've followed the entire trail of Chung's disappearance and found him holding on to an email from Dad. Why would Chung even possess this?

Why set up custom warnings appearing in my display bidding me to say nothing. Why leave me access into the offices? Why scatter these devices as though we're partaking in a top-secret exchange, only for there to be one *email*?

"Is . . . this you?" Kieren asks. He's finished reading. "It sounds like he's talking about a young child."

"I don't think it is," I say quietly. "If it were me, there would be nothing noteworthy about it. No reason to keep it stored and protected like that."

Kieren frowns. "It's signed off by a Henry. That has to be your dad, right?"

"It is." I disconnect from the reader, clearing my vision. When that doesn't erase the words from my mind's eye, I scrub my hands vigorously down my face, needing to make some sense out of it, any sense at all, and I can only circle back to one conclusion. "I think he's talking about his birth daughter. The one who was supposed to have died months before this email."

29

EIRALE

I tie a jacket over my head, as though that'll do much against the cameras across Threto.

"Still alive?" I whisper.

The comm link rustles in my ear.

"Barely."

Nik's voice is muffled. I imagine he's got his face pressed into the couch arm, but he sounds lucid otherwise. With a swipe of my finger, I bring down the volume on my earbud.

I take a deep breath. The sun has risen over the horizon, beaming red across the lower clouds. For a few moments I only bounce on my feet, preparing myself to go. Before I am fully ready, I bolt forward, breaking into a sprint. I dash through a thin backstreet filled with dumpsters and parking spaces, tracing the map in my memory. When the gravel turns to grass, I veer left and squeeze along the exterior of a high-rise, wincing because I know every camera in the hallway inside is tracking me through the windows.

The surveillance circuit must know I'm here. It's only a matter of how long it takes before it sounds an alert and escalates into a pursuit. Really, it's sheer luck the pursuit hasn't already reached me.

I slow and quiet my steps at the next turn when sleepy conversation floats down from an open, lower-level window. Once I've put enough distance between myself and the voices, I speed up again, gulping mouthfuls of air to stay at my pace.

Almost there. I hurry around to the front of the building, then across a courtyard—a shared leisure space, smack-bang in the center of three matching high-rises. The benches glisten with a layer of condensation. A wide road makes up the courtyard's fourth side, and across that road awaits a row of breakfast restaurants. Once I sight the signs for porridges and soups in the distance, I know I'm on the right track. The pharmacy is at the end of the restaurant row.

A loud bang thuds overhead just as I've almost crossed the courtyard. I whirl around, clutching at air to feign having a weapon in case that scares off a pursuer.

It's only a woman on her balcony, pulling open her chair. Right below her, an elderly man is sitting on his balcony too, smoking a cigarette. We make eye contact. Slowly, he takes a long puff.

I lower my arms, almost embarrassed. The moment I look, I register another figure, then another, then several more—all out on their balconies, getting air first thing in the morning. Many are watching me, but no one says a peep. Some are clearly reading on their glasses; others hold a paper book. I thought more would have gone upcountry.

I pull myself away, my breath coming short. The courtyard is as quiet as a cemetery when I finish crossing it, looking left and right before stepping onto the empty road. If Threto weren't under lockdown, the breakfast restaurants would be at their busiest now: serving dry noodles with beef and scallion chunks, hot buns fresh out of the steamer, fried dough that crunches on every bite.

I've seen all the videos. On particularly exhausting days after I finish running drills, I go back to my room on base, plop onto my bed, put on my glasses, and open the feed to watch people eat in Threto. It's a guilty pleasure that I was always afraid NileCorp would find out about, and though they likely had the capacity to view my watch log, there's no reason they'd want to unless provoked. It's hard to explain exactly what was so compelling about those videos save for the fact that I wanted to be in Medaluo for those mornings. The vlogging quality wasn't the best, filmed on handhelds, and still I could smell the crisp pepper flakes, still I imagined the splatter of shallot-infused oil dripping down my fingers too.

I shouldn't feel guilty about my feed history, but if it gets publicized while I'm at large, it's another piece of evidence held against me. Unlike my assassination deepfake, those videos in my history are real. I watched them to feel like I might understand something about Medaluo. This country might actually run in my blood. If I had had a family here, I could have been one of those laughing customers queuing in front of a small restaurant, grabbing a bowl every morning before school.

Movement flashes from the junction at the end of the road. I have a split second to dive behind a postal box when a drone swoops into view, whizzing above the restaurants. The side of my hand scrapes hard on cement, but I've hidden myself before the drone can spin in my direction, its lights flashing blue and red.

Most of the lockdown drones are sound-activated, chasing after footsteps and voices rather than movement. It's cheaper to process. People are rarely running away without making a huge racket anyway.

I hold my breath, watching the drone pass by. It beeps happily. There's nothing worse than police drones that have faces installed on them, as though a small winking emoticon will make them as lovable as the server bots.

As soon as the scene is clear again, I get up from behind the postal box, securing the jacket tighter over my head.

I'm running immediately, hurrying past each shuttered storefront. In my final pivot, I almost go right past the pharmacy. The gated entryway has been secured with three padlocks down the side. Closed—the pharmacy ironically deemed a nonemergency entity during citywide quarantine—though the green sign remains lit. I consider the state of the padlocks, then shuffle around the back.

I kick my foot softly against the smaller back door. No shudder, so I expect it's dead-bolted from the inside. There is, however, a glass panel along the door, and I take my jacket off my head, wrapping it around my fist instead.

The first strike bounces against the glass, pain rippling along my knuckles. The second strike appears to make more headway, the glass quivering. I brace hard. On the third strike, the glass breaks, fragmenting into shards that dust the back step. An alarm goes off inside the pharmacy at once, but I ignore it to reach through the broken panel, unlocking the door, then pulling open the dead bolt too.

I grit my teeth. Tug my arm back. Nudge open the door.

"Okay," I say, directing my focus past the screaming alarm. Everything I say aloud I'm sure Nik can hear—he'll be getting a good earful of the alarm blaring too, which should be helpful in keeping him alert.

I dust off my hands and tie my jacket around my waist, inspecting the back room. I'll give myself two minutes. Any longer, and they'll send that drone from before with its firing capabilities activated, which are significantly harder to avoid than the guns of human police officers. I scan through the shelves in the dim light, my eyes squinting to make sense of the tiny print on the labels.

"Come on, come on," I mutter. These are antibiotics. I might be looking in the wrong area.

I dive to the next shelf, then immediately strike gold when I spot a viral medicine. Eveline *must* be somewhere nearby, and if not on the shelf itself, then . . .

A small metal lockbox waits at the bottom of the shelf. I don't hesitate. I pull the lockbox out and set it on the floor, then stomp down hard with my shoe. The lock breaks off. My heart is slamming in my chest when I flip the lid off and find only two blister packs inside. One tiny pill in the center of each. When I scramble to flip one of the packs over, the lidding foil at the back is printed with EVELINE™ ONE DOSE EVELINE™ ONE DOSE EVELINE™ ONE DOSE over and over again.

Success.

I shove the two packs into my pocket without hesitation. Past the screech of the pharmacy alarm, I can hear sirens. They might have redirected the same officers who were just at the data center.

The morning air is heavier when I emerge back outside, closing the broken door after myself. The horizon has darkened despite the sunrise, as though a storm will be rolling in soon. I creep around the pharmacy. The drones are multiplying down the road.

"Warning. All citizens are instructed to stay inside. This is a mandatory public health and safety effort. Breaking lockdown without official permit is prosecutable up to . . ."

The recording fades when drones turn the corner. The sirens, meanwhile, are getting louder.

"Hey," I say, flicking the volume of my earpiece up again. "You there?"

No answer.

"Nik?" I demand. I take one tentative step out, toward the road. Police cars are rounding the corner rapidly. "Say something."

I only hear a faint buzz on his end. His comms is still active, then. It's not a signal problem.

"Nik, I *swear*, you'd better be alive—"

The police cars screech closer and closer. *Ten . . . nine . . . eight . . .* If I wait any longer, this route will be blocked off, and even if I get him back on the line, it will be no use.

I grit my teeth and dart across the road. My boots kick up gravel in a spray, the vehicles screeching to a halt when they see me. I can outrun them. I'll return exactly as I came, cutting through the courtyard and—

A drone dives right into my path.

"Warning," it says, a red dot growing brighter in the center of its face. "You're in violation of lockdown protocol."

I duck, missing the drone's taser by a hairsbreadth. Its nodes dart out, then slump to the concrete ground, attaching to give the gravel a shock instead of my body. I stay very still, wondering if it'll reload if it fired once. I can't outrun a drone. I also can't go anywhere as long as it's focused on me, because it won't stop chasing me until its objective has been achieved.

My fingers creep slowly to a larger chunk of gravel. Maybe I can beat this stupid thing to death. I've got to act fast. The authorities will have put two and two together. A disturbance in their data facility, a break-in alarm, and an unregistered civilian on their cameras. If I don't go, they'll circle me in . . .

A whistle drifts down from one of the balconies overhead. The drone jerks, suddenly turning its camera, the pixel eyes of its emoticon face widening. I stifle an inhale and search for the noise too. My gaze lands on the elderly man, the one I'd made eye contact with before, right as he begins to sing.

What?

The drone rockets over on the noise, desperate to investigate. I almost want to call a warning, urge that he stop before the drone launches a taser his way. Someone else must be thinking the same, knowing what is impending, because another voice resounds from a balcony on the opposite side of the high-rises, joining the tune. I don't recognize the song. It's not Medaluo's national anthem—I'd recognize that—but it feels like an anthem, nonetheless. The drone zips across the courtyard in investigation, lured by the new voice, and all at once, as though some dam has broken over the balconies, the few calls become a chorus. I hardly noticed how many people there were earlier, too easily blended into the environment when they were sitting idle. Now that they're singing along, their volume is tremendous, growing their presence into something colossal.

"WARNING!" the drone bellows. It can't keep up with the different sources at once. "PUBLIC DISTURBANCE IS NOT ALLOWED DURING LOCKDOWN. PLEASE STEP INSIDE."

They keep going. It's a strange song. Something about a giant sleeping. Something about the sun rising. It must be a Medan classic if everyone knows the words, and up on his balcony, the old man starts to wave his arms, as though he's conducting the orchestra before him.

He looks down and winks at me.

I mouth, *Thank you. Thank you!*

And I take the chance to run.

30
LIA

I open my eyes to find Kieren holding a bag of fried dough in front of my face.

"Are you trying to give me pimples?" I ask, yawning.

"I'm trying to feed you, ungrateful youth."

There's no energy behind the barb. I shift in my seat, rousing from my nap. My attention is pinned on Kieren when I make room for him, patting the seat beside me. It's sometime late in the afternoon. In the corner of my display, our active call tab has been minimized for almost half an hour, according to the progression of the timer.

"Is everything okay?"

Kieren blinks hard. It's not my imagination. Not only does his gaze look slightly misty, but his hands have a tremble to them.

"Yes. Of course. It was ridiculously crowded outside." He sets the bag on my lap. He's quick to sit, which could either be a natural gesture after a long, tiring day, or he's trying to avoid my scrutiny.

Kam immediately accepted the incoming transmission as soon as we returned to the safety of the tour bus and made the call. Now she's on mute, running diagnostics on the file we found. Twelve is still powered down at the front. With nothing better to do, I nodded off to catch up on rest, and Kieren wandered out in search of food.

He doesn't seem to have gotten himself anything. Which is strange, because he insisted he was starving and was stepping out to peruse, so I didn't need to accompany him.

"Thanks," I say. I roll down the plastic. The dough forms two long sticks, joined at its ends. "You didn't get anything for yourself?"

"Ate already," Kieren replies.

I take a big bite of the fried dough. The warm crunch presses to the roof of my mouth, dances across my tongue. I almost moan. Why do we have to be in a cold war with Medaluo when their food is so good?

"What *is* this?"

"Fried dough." Kieren leans back. His lip quirks. "Seemed pretty obvious, Ward."

"I know, but—" I take another bite. "There's no other ingredient? It's just deep-fried dough?"

"Deep-fried dough, indeed. I watched them make it. Had a great conversation about the Threto men's soccer team and everything."

"What do you know about soccer in Threto?"

"Absolutely nothing. I guess I'm so likable that people will talk to me about anything."

I finish the rest of my food in a few bites before scrunching up the plastic bag. Kieren is watching me through the entire thing, and when I raise my brows to signal, *What?* he only shakes his head.

A click sounds in my ears. The minimized call tab trembles to signal activity, and the waveform in my display springs to life again.

"I'm back," Kam declares. "Is it a good time to continue?"

"Of course," Kieren says. "We're all ears."

"I ran the email through the checkers available to us. It seems someone's scrubbed the metadata very intentionally." Kam pauses. "They did leave behind the geoposition, though. It was written upcountry, so the pinpoint is marked clearly."

There's something to Kam's tone that leads me to brace before she's sent along the scan results. Before she says, "See for yourself," and I open it.

MEDALUO, Land of Outer Frontier, 7 Phoenix Mountain Road

"*Offron?*" I exclaim. "There must be a mistake."

It's not a fake email, given its contents. My dad wrote it. So how could it have come from Medaluo, much less Offron, at the very corner of the country? Offron is the hotspot for Medan government officials.

"I'm assuming the Henry of this sign-off is Henry Sullivan?" Kam asks.

Henry Sullivan, my father. Henry Sullivan, who, upon any cursory search at present, is getting slammed for being a Medan sympathizer.

"Maybe Chung altered the geoposition," Kieren offers in lieu of an answer. "Maybe he's leading us on some sort of trail."

Kam is typing rapidly on her end. "Any reason you think so?"

"This whole posting has been a treasure hunt," he says. I'm glad Kieren is taking the reins, because I can't summon a word. "A key. A disk. A reader. Now an address and *nothing else*. Why scrub a file that you're storing in your personal disk? Better yet, why scrub a file but leave a location? At that point you may as well delete everything. He obviously wants someone to follow it."

"You make good points. None of that can be discounted." A pause. "Regardless, I'd advise you take a look at this location in Offron and finish out the treasure hunt. I'm only your ground contact—I won't be making any reports to the company while you're in the midst of your survey. But you will need to answer the questions NileCorp will inevitably have. Or else they'll come asking me."

That last part is targeted. She means to say that I shouldn't try to hide my dad's involvement in this. Because Kam knows, and NileCorp will find out one way or another.

Kieren clears his throat. "Sure. We understand. We already have a tour bus we're in control of, so we can proceed."

"Great. Good luck."

Kam hangs up.

Immediately, as soon as she's off our call line, I get another trying to enter.

I'm too stupefied to react. While I can see the buzzing request in my display, I ignore it, still trying to parse what we were just given. I try to imagine the sequence of events before Dad wrote that email. Staying somewhere in upcountry Medaluo, checking on a young child: "whole, smart, healthy"—those were his words. How could it possibly be anyone other than his supposedly dead birth daughter?

The buzzing in my display stops. Seconds later, Kieren says, "Rayna?" out loud, picking up when she'd clearly tried him next. "Wait, you're *what*?"

My attention snaps over. I shove aside my whirlwind of panic over this mystery, needing to make room for whatever has gotten Kieren to use *that* tone.

"What is it?" I demand. "What happened?"

Instead of answering me, he loops me into the call. I connect to catch Rayna say, ". . . but Hailey altered our IDs just in time to show us as underage Medans rather than tourist Atahuans. They're willing to let us go with a warning, but they need our parents to come get us."

"Wait, wait," I say. "What's going on?"

"Lia," Rayna groans. She's clearly trying to keep her voice low, and she ends up sounding like she's imitating a rattlesnake. "Maybe if you had picked up when I called you first! We're in jail."

"You're *what*?" I screech. Kieren gives me a look. Now I'm caught up.

"Not *jail* jail, technically. The holding cells of a precinct. We got caught trespassing on military property, but we spun our story to only be ditching school." Rayna's voice grows quieter. If anyone is listening in on her, they'll be able to parse even the faintest whisper with volume adjustment, so this is more to make herself feel better about not getting overheard. "Please come get us. Change your IDs and put another twenty years on your birthdays.

Hailey used the first exploit she was holding in her inventory, so our fake Medan identities run out in an hour, and it's taken thirty minutes for them to process us."

I smack my head forward, colliding with the seat in front of me. Kieren grimaces. They make those exploits for underage Atahuans trying to get into nightclubs with fake ages. I can't imagine changing an entire *citizenship* is going to hold up for the Medan authorities if they look closer.

"Okay," Kieren says. "Okay, tell Hailey to see if she can extend the adjustment by checking its add-ons, but we're on our way. Where's the precinct?"

She sends the pin.

"Rayna," I hiss, "this is *forty* minutes away with traffic."

"Pleeeeeease," she whines. "Also, it needs to be the both of you. Hailey slapped her last name onto my ID in a split second to get rid of 'Ward,' so we're pretending to be related."

I pull my head back from the seat slightly, then thud into it harder. When I pull back to do it again, Kieren shoves his hand in front of the seat, mouthing, *Stop that!*

I thud right into his palm.

"Who is going to believe that?" I exclaim.

"They will if you both show up! Phenotypes are funny that way."

I'm going to kill Rayna. This is going to be so bad for her final grade. Great for ours if we can get her out. But bad for her, nonetheless.

"We're on our way," Kieren declares. "Tell Hailey *add-ons!*"

He ends the call.

"This is absurd," I say, flinging my arms out. "You'll need to change our IDs. And unlock our appearance filters so we can drag the aging bar in the direction no one drags it in."

"I can do that," Kieren assures me without hesitation. So much for *not a hacker*. "I'll only need a bit of time."

"Plenty of time in traffic." My eyes wander to the front, to the sleeping bot. We're not going to be able to push an AI tour bus through Threto's roads. It's creeping near the end of the workday. Everyone will be heading home in their small self-driving cars, making rapid lane switches to speed up their route by a minute or two. Forty minutes on a map's estimate is going to come to ninety in this behemoth of a vehicle.

I start to move.

"Lia," Kieren prompts when he follows closely behind. "Are you going to contact your dad?"

An engine cuts outside. As I'm hurrying down the steps of the bus, a motorcyclist detaches his bags from the back of his bike, hurrying up the steps of the museum to make a personal delivery. He's left his bike very close to our bus.

"I can't think about that right now," I say.

"I thought you were great at multitasking."

"We'll deal with it after we get Rayna and Hailey." My eyes trace the motorbike. It's been left on neutral. The ignition is still active.

The thought occurs to me. No time to second-guess it.

Without warning, I grab Kieren's wrist and drag him with me to the bike. "Get started on our IDs. I'm driving."

31

EIRALE

I close the gate behind me with a solid click.

For a moment, I stay put, waiting for any indication of danger in pursuit. The police cars didn't pull into the courtyard in time to see me run between the high-rises. The drone was too distracted trying to make sense of the voices. I should be safe. I *should* be.

I make one more cursory scan of the street. Nothing.

"Hey," I whisper into my comm link yet again. "Come on. Say something."

Nik has been silent this entire time. Maybe his earpiece fell out and he's too tired to get it. Or the frequency shifted inexplicably.

I hurry through the alleyway, running into the inner building. The most likely explanation, actually, is that he's dead. That the illness has halted his organ functions and stopped his heart. I don't know what I expect to find when I skid along the hall and barge back into apartment 1F. A cooling corpse, maybe. The last remnants of life clinging to his softer parts, like the guard in the data center.

I turn the corner into the living room. And I find . . . nothing.

Nik's gone.

He's not on the couch anymore. I locate his discarded earbud instantly, squished between two of the cushions. His bag isn't here anymore either.

I scoop up the earbud at once, scanning the room to make sense of what happened. There's no sign of a struggle. The windows are intact. No furniture overturned.

I backtrack out of the apartment, closing the door behind me. When I entered, the front gate under the awning had been latched neatly. If Nik had wandered out in a sickly stupor, I don't think he would have the time to close the gate behind him.

My head turns the other way instead, following the stairs that ascend through the building. The numbers on the mailboxes in the corridor showed ten floors total. No elevator. This residential block is older, built in the days before Threto knew it needed to sustain a population spike. The high-rises I'd passed before could climb as high as forty floors, but these stay closer to the ground—naturally, if residents have to make the trek up. They tend to have vacant topmost levels too, because no one wants to rent units that delivery bots on wheels struggle to reach.

I surge up the steps, my hand skating along the railing. Each time I peer around the stair landings, I almost expect to find Nik curled behind one of them. The shadows are thick, permeating densely. Cement walls and cement stairs make for a heavy structure, bouncing back my voice when I shout, "Nik! Come on!"

"*Here!*"

The voice is weak. I almost think I've imagined it, that I've mistaken the squawk of a bird for a voice. Then I hurry to the highest floor and through the first open door. The apartment is either abandoned, or very poorly maintained. Its floor is covered in soot and bricks and half-ripped tarps. The windows are boarded up, keeping out most of the morning save for a few harpsichord strings of lights. For a beat, I am merely scanning the dark shapes. My eyes may well be deceiving me to find Nik slouched beside the couch.

"Drones came by," he says when he sees me.

I reach into my jacket and tear through the lidding foil on the Eveline pill. Nik tracks my movement toward him. His gaze is unfocused behind his glasses, and though he attempts to make sense of what I'm bringing him, I still take him by surprise when I grab his jaw, forcing open his mouth.

"Wha—*eurgh*—"

I put the pill on his tongue. "You'd better swallow."

Obediently, Nik swallows. He pulls a face, gesturing distaste and dryness without water to wash it down.

"That was disgusting," he remarks. His eyes flutter.

"Yeah?" I finally exhale, loosening the cramp in my lungs with a long, deep breath. Ignoring the dirt on the floor, I sit too. "Tough luck. What are you *doing* up here?"

"Drones, like I said," Nik answers blearily. "No curtains on the windows, and it was a ground-level apartment, so I thought I'd better find another hiding spot. Kept telling you and wondering why you weren't replying." He sticks his finger into his ear, then laughs. "Silly me. It fell out."

I blink, taken aback. His laugh was short, but its echo peals wide. It's an ill-fitting sound, and I don't quite know what to do with it. There must be inflammation in his brain.

"Some stamina you have," I chide without hostility. "You needed me to drag you through that alley, but you got up ten flights of stairs yourself."

Nik grumbles something indecipherable. He's fading out. Eveline is fast.

"Couldn't stay in stairs and raise alarm from cameras," he manages in a garble. "Couldn't break into anyone's apartment and have police. Just had to keep going up. You'd know I went up."

His head tilts, and in the next second he's unconscious. I sigh, letting the silence of the tumbledown apartment sing in my ears. Then I reach into my pocket for the other packet of Eveline, scratching open the foil and plucking out the pill.

I swallow it with a wince. I don't feel sick yet—and I might be safe entirely given NileCorp's insistence on keeping us up to date with our vaccinations. Still, Nik was breathing in my face under the rubble, and I'd rather be preventive than wait for an illness to catch up. Even if it's only getting in there to scrub clean what's building.

I breathe out, closing my eyes when I lean back against the wall.

I let the pill take effect and drag me under.

• • • •

I wake before Nik does, sometime in the evening.

Slowly I lift onto my elbow, coughing dryly. At some point while resting in a neat, upright position against the wall, I must have tipped over and ended up splayed on the floor. I wheeze an inhale. I feel fine. Healthy.

I rub my eyes. I realize my mistake instantly when dust slathers onto my face, having collected all along my arm. The floor is disgusting. It's hard to see anything in this muted light, the world beyond the boarded windows hovering at a raw umber.

"Hey," I whisper. I kick my foot, nudging Nik. He remains unconscious, but groans, which is enough for me to confirm that he's alive. He'd been nursing the virus for some time before I got him Eveline, and he's practically unvaccinated, so it'll take longer for the cure to work. He's going to have to sleep it off.

It's cold in the apartment. I slowly clamber upright, brushing my hair off my face. Evening air blows through the gaps of the boarded windows. There's no glass, only two hollowed panes that the boards are trying to cover. I shake my arms, getting my blood flowing again before I go over and grasp one board in the middle. My strength hasn't entirely returned, but I gather my conviction. The board comes free with two rusty nails on either side. A better glimpse of Threto comes through in the sliver. I toss the board onto the couch, working on the next one. Within minutes I've cleared the windows, the glittering city winking its hello from a thousand different buildings.

I breathe out, my slow exhale forming a cloud of mist. The billboards are coming to life again. The constant barrage of subscription tiers for upcountry, the property insurance companies, the pills that promise different eye colors and new hair colors sprouting from the root. Threto's metropolis beats a pulse as the bull's-eye center of the country, the only resting place for those running from desolation in every other direction. It isn't coastal Upsie, where people can afford to shut themselves in their Pods and the billboards go unwatched. Here, even lockdown doesn't make the city go quiet. Every mumbling television in the apartments harmonizes with the droning advertisements outside, emitting a racket that shapes the skyline. It's thunderous.

I turn back around, eyeing Nik carefully. His chest rises and falls. His bag sits at his feet. He was smart enough to have put a cushion beneath himself when he chose his spot on the floor, and his head stays lolled on half of it for support. Though the cushion appears slightly waterlogged, it still holds functionality—better than resting on the floor directly, at least.

I scan the rotting couch, the broken tables. At one point in time, this residence must have been well decorated. Opulent, even. The walls underneath the thick black mold are a rich red. The skeleton of a chandelier hangs overhead, long harvested for parts and its wiry veins taken. If the window hadn't been smashed to let in the elements, I doubt the furniture around us would look like this, drooping and tired. There are no traces around the apartment to identify its former occupants anymore. No pictures on the shelves, no belongings scattered over the counter. It might have been years since someone was last living here, its former homeliness lost to time.

Nik doesn't stir when I return to his side and grab his bag. The scratch pad I'd seen earlier is still there, hidden in the lining. Writing on paper means less chance of getting hacked and having his notes read by law enforcement seeking his whereabouts. Too bad he didn't account for me being a snoop.

I flip through rapidly, finding various diagrams and sketches. I'm not sure what I expected an anarchist's personal notebook to hold. There are some pages with rough outlines of the Atahuan bases he targets. Other pages seem to be his stream-of-consciousness thoughts, writing down numbers to do quick arithmetic or a list for something he's brainstorming. There even seems to be a lunch order in here.

I scoff beneath my breath, flipping all the way to the back. I stop short.

EIRALE SULLIVAN

"What?" I say aloud.

There's nothing more. No context, no further elaboration. Nik had asked the very same question up in that helicopter the first night too. *Does the surname Sullivan mean anything to you?*

"Who do you think I am?" I ask him quietly.

Nik breathes in. Breathes out shakily. He is at no capacity to respond. I hurry to return the scratch pad into his bag, then feign nonchalance once I've zipped it back up. It's not as though he will know. There's no reason I should bother putting on an act. I clear my throat anyway.

Nik's shoulder jerks hard.

"Nik?" I try.

His eyes stay closed. A strong gust of wind sweeps into the apartment, howling through the open window. The sun falls fully under the horizon to leave the sky dark. When Nik twitches again, I catch sight of the sweat glistening on his forehead, which is good because it means his fever is breaking.

"Don't," he mumbles under his breath. "Wait."

I hesitate, inching forward on the dust-covered floor. I should wake him. It feels wrong to watch him have a nightmare.

"Hey." I reach out. Shake his elbow.

The shudder of helicopter blades suddenly comes into earshot, a rapid *thud-thud-thud* heading toward the apartment. This is the penthouse unit: the aircraft will pass dangerously close. I don't move while the sound is directly overhead, as though its spotlight might catch sight of me through the broken window. I watch the helicopter continue on its path. Its blinking yellow taillight gets farther and farther away. The roaring sound fades, and I'm still holding Nik's elbow.

"Somehow," I say, "it's hard to believe that dangerous criminals are capable of having nightmares."

His arm flexes out. He's saying something under his breath, though I can't parse anything coherent. I don't often have nightmares. When bad things happen in my dreams, I feel the falseness of the world immediately, and I only have to blink to wake up. I have little in my life to lose. The moment a dream casts a feeling of impending doom over me or my loved ones, I remember I have no loved ones, and I wake up.

"Don't," Nik murmurs again, his head twitching. "Please."

Whether out of the kindness of my heart or the sheer practicality of making sure he doesn't panic himself into a coma, I slot my hand into Nik's open palm. His fingers close around mine immediately.

"I'm here," I say.

The night sweeps another cold gust in, spreads its tendrils to join our clasp. I shiver, tightening my grip, keeping its intrusion out. Despite the heat emanating from Nik's skin, his palm is smooth and dry—not at all what I'm expecting.

"You're safe," I assure him plainly.

I try to stay at arm's length, as though that'll make this less strange. When that tires my wrist, I scoot closer, folding my legs more tightly in front of me, my boots pressing flat on the floorboards. The tracker in there continues to emit a signal, and I sit here, saving the life of someone I'll inevitably turn in.

I don't know how I ended up debating the matter, but I am. I undeniably am. I thought my task was straightforward: capture an anarchist, clear my name, regain my standing among my employers. It's only the most reasonable course of action. Anarchists cannot go running around killing people as they please. NileCorp is the only place where I belong.

My thumb moves, grazing along his hand. Nik Grant has killed people, hurt people. But it would be delusional to take the moral high ground from where I stand, because NileCorp is a thousand times worse. At least Nik pulls the trigger himself. NileCorp ensconces itself within so many layers as an entity that it's impossible to trace which of their suit-clad executives are responsible for the directives passed to their security forces. I've read the forums raising awareness for their crimes, the translated interviews from victims in other nations tortured by private soldiers sent into their civil wars. NileCorp holds no sanctity for human life. Their desire to capture Nik isn't out of justice for his victims—it is solely because of the insurgency he's promoting. They need to regain control.

Nik fires his gun in the hope that he can begin a fight. NileCorp fires to keep profits high, warehouses stocked, soldiers employed. NileCorp makes the world go round.

So what am I exchanging to be a part of that?

"Don't go," Nik whispers. He's almost inaudible above the whistling wind. I hear it, all the same. It's not for me. I know he's not speaking to me, but I stay put. A loudspeaker starts broadcasting from the street, telling Threto to remain inside, that lockdown is in place until they have made a count of the outbreak and the hospitals have determined their capacity. The helicopters circle once more, their scrutiny beaming onto the taller skyscrapers, and we hide tucked out of view in this abandoned nook.

The night lengthens. A gentle rain starts to fall at some point, splattering through the window onto the wooden floorboards, staining the color darker. I sit unmoving, watching the city's lights bleed through the water, waiting, waiting.

I sit, holding Nik's hand, tight as a lifeline.

32

LIA

"It would be really, really nice if we had helmets!"

The upcoming turn for the expressway comes out of nowhere. I apply the throttle so that we don't miss it, then push hard on the right. Kieren screams out loud.

"Hey, no time for being a wuss," I yell back, straightening the motorbike.

A car veers too close as it tries to change lanes on the expressway, almost slamming into our front wheel when I shoot past. The driver lays on their horn. I don't ease up on throttle. Behind me, Kieren is hanging on for dear life, his hands clutching my shoulders.

I've never driven a motorbike before. I downloaded an augmented guide in my display, and I'm entirely trusting its alerts. So far, so good. I put the guide on "Police Pursuit Mode" so that it'll direct me into any opening that appears in the traffic. It's nice of them to have that feature.

"If we crash—"

"We're not going to crash," I interrupt. A pop-up tells me that I can go faster if I want. I take my left hand off the handlebar quickly, maneuvering Kieren's arm down around my waist. "If you actually lean properly with me when we turn, you wouldn't feel like you were falling off—"

I smack my hand back onto the front grip, braking suddenly to avoid slamming into a car that has stopped with no warning. Kieren can't even scream this time because I've moved so fast that it has robbed the air from him—I hear his half-choked wheeze, cut off with a gulp. I swerve and apply speed again, following the sequence in my display to ensure the motorbike engine won't cut out. The other cars behind the scene come to a standstill. We proceed forward, gliding smoothly back into the flow.

If there's one thing I'm good at, it's following instructions.

Kieren has finally relinquished his sense of pride and wrapped his arms around me, clinging like a scared koala. I'm glad he can't see my face, or else my puffed-up grin would earn me a decade's worth of taunts to even the terrain again. I push left to change to the farthest lane, getting us close to the barrier and bypassing the slowing cars. Threto to our side shimmers golden with the sunset, the reflections glancing off the glass windows of the skyscrapers, the billboards changing their color settings for the night. The stolen motorbike rumbles assuredly, roaring with each throttle when I speed up.

"I've prepared the ID exploit," Kieren yells when I weave back into a center lane. "You need to connect with me."

"We're pretty connected right now."

I don't have to look back at Kieren to know he's turning red. "Your *display*."

I flip ahead to view directions, ensuring there won't be any sudden turns to make. Then I navigate away from the guide screen to pull open the main controls in my display, allowing remote access requests.

"Still pretty intimate."

"Lia, I can talk you through it instead if you want to do it yourself."

He's giving me way too much to work with.

"Okay, okay. Send your request."

Kieren breathes in sharply when the motorbike teeters. Uneven ground. I lean forward and swipe back to the guide, ready to veer at a moment's notice if we hit a bad bump. At the upper corner of my vision, the request enters, and I accept the pairing. It's strange to watch my tabs move around of their own accord when Kieren enters and goes digging, pulling open pages that I've never had a proper look through.

"Careful," I say, seizing partial control over my display when he opens too many tabs. "I need to see the driving instructions."

Chastised, Kieren shifts everything to the bottom, where it's less likely to interfere with my instructions. Just in time, the guide splatters a variety of arrows to push the left handlebar for a right turn, and Kieren has no choice but to follow suit when I lean right for balance, jolting onto the exit ramp successfully.

Night has almost fallen. The clouds hover low overhead, a watery true blue soaking darker with each second. The guide suggests applying brakes and slowing. We'll be at our destination soon.

"How's it coming along?" I call into the wind.

"Almost there. Birthday. Last name. Citizenship. And timer starts—now."

All the extra tabs at the bottom of my vision blink away. I get a few seconds of clarity before new ones open, running scripts that look far more complicated. The traffic light ahead turns yellow. I push faster to get through, crossing on the red. When the owner reports his bike missing, I hope it voids all the traffic tickets that have racked up on his record too.

"You want to look young for your age, or older than expected?"

"I'm ethnically Medan, Kieren. You could pull the lever to forty and I'll still look twenty."

"Is that a challenge I hear?"

YOUR DESTINATION IS TO YOUR RIGHT, the guide reports, offering its final arrow with a flourish. I squeeze down on the clutch and apply the brakes, getting us parked at the side of the road with only a mild bump.

When the engine cuts off, the varying scripts running in my display disappear too. Kieren's finished with his work.

"We're here," I declare. "Not bad, right?"

He releases me slowly. In all honesty, I'm shocked that we made it.

"Do you know," he says, "how many times we almost got flattened?"

"But we didn't." I clamber off the bike. "We—"

My hands fly to my mouth. I try to hold in my appalled laugh, and end up spluttering into my palm, staring saucers at Kieren.

"I know," he says. "I aged well."

I yank my hands down, trying to get myself together.

"You absolutely messed around with your other filters," I accuse. "Your jawline does *not* look like that."

He resembles every Atahuan movie star mashed together at once—the collated result of some early-century heartthrob who went on to become a philanthropist later in life as they focused on raising their family.

"All right, darling." He takes my hand without the spit. "Ten minutes left on their timer. Don't bite me again."

I catch sight of myself on the reflection of the precinct doors as we approach, and from afar I can hardly see the difference. It hadn't been a stretch to say that he could turn the lever to forty and I'd still look twenty. The sort of features I have will always make me look younger than I am. It's only once we get closer that I see the differences: the longer forehead, the sharper cheekbones. Before I can make a proper examination, Kieren is already opening the door, leading us through.

"Good evening," Kieren greets the officer at the front desk, his voice booming. I can tell that he's trying to channel his father. Headmaster Murray starts his assembly addresses the same way. "We're here for our delinquent children."

I squeeze his hand in warning. He squeezes back twice to communicate that he knows what he's doing.

"Ah," the officer says. "The military base lurkers."

"The resemblance is that obvious, huh?" I say.

I must sound nervous, because Kieren steps on my foot.

"I suppose," the officer replies. She hasn't even looked at us directly. Whatever is on her display keeps her occupied, her gaze unfocused. "Our holding cells are empty save for those two. *Most* people tend to behave in this neighborhood."

Her eyes swivel to Kieren before returning to her display. Ah, I see. A little suspicious jab at his possible Atahuan origins.

It's entertaining to be witnessing the other side of this, but it's still not the same. People are only anti-Atahuan in Medaluo. People are anti-Medan across the rest of the world. Without casualties to log nor battles to bleed in, that's the most foolproof way to track that Atahua is winning a cold war.

"IDs?"

I lean forward first, letting her point the scanner at my forehead. She barely gives me a second glance. She points it at Kieren next, then hums, going off to the printer.

"Fill these out, please."

The officer shoves a clipboard our way. I try to let go of Kieren's hand to take it, but he's distracted, and I have to shake several times before he realizes he needs to release. Smoothly, I pick up the clipboard and poise the pen over the text, ready to sign.

My head spins instantly at the Medan characters. I make an attempt to read the form naturally. Three lines later, I quietly turn on my translate function and resist huffing out loud. It's all just legal jargon. An acknowledgment that our children were in the wrong and we're not going to come back and make a fuss. The personal information sections are already autofilled from the ID scan. I sign quickly, making up something that vaguely resembles Lia Murray before passing it to Kieren.

He scribbles a few circles and passes it back. The officer presses a button to activate a speaker. "All right. Bring them out."

I wring my hands. The bottom of my shirt grows increasingly rumpled. I try to count forward from Rayna's call, calculating whether their altered

IDs have worn off. If they walk out exposed, Kieren and I are dragged in with them. If we're all hauled away, that will mean trouble I can't even begin to comprehend.

The side door buzzes. With a heavy clunk, another officer leads out a nervous-looking Rayna and a smiling Hailey.

"Hi, Mom. Hi, Dad," Hailey greets.

"Oh, don't you start," Kieren says softly.

The officer removes Hailey's handcuffs first. When it's Rayna's turn, she's trembling so much that they struggle to get the key in, requiring several tries. Once she's free, she makes her way to me immediately, her eyes pleading.

I smack her on the head.

"What were you thinking?" I hiss.

Rayna sticks out her lower lip, as penitent as a confessor. "Sorry, Mama. Can we go now?"

• • • •

We barely get one block away from the precinct before I launch myself onto Rayna, attempting to throttle her.

"Nooooo!" she cries. "I learned my lesson!"

"A military base?" I hiss, keeping my voice down. "You didn't scope it first? You didn't wait until nightfall? How are you about to *graduate*?"

"In our defense," Hailey tries, "we got what we needed!"

"Yes, that makes it so much better," I deadpan.

Rayna takes the distraction that Hailey has afforded her to scuttle away, smoothing her hair down. There are plenty of other pedestrians strolling the sidewalk, so we stay to the right, going at a slower pace.

"Maybe any point deductions we receive are for the best," Rayna muses. "If we're lacking skills upon graduation, we should definitely take safer positions that aren't critical."

I am flabbergasted. Utterly flabbergasted.

"Rayna, is this some cry for help?" I say. "Because impostor syndrome can be combated. You're allowed to want something good for your career."

"Thank you, dear mother."

"*You—*"

"Lia."

I swivel with a scowl, thinking Kieren must be cutting in to have me lay off. His appearance adjustment has worn off: he put the filter application on a timer just like our IDs. He looks like himself again, a regular seventeen-year-old. And he's not even paying attention to the spiel I'm giving Rayna.

"Yeah?"

Kieren only points. I follow the direction of his finger, searching past the holograms swimming in the night. It's hard to see anything because of the various electric-green fireflies, but I have to assume he's looking over at the mall.

"Wow," Hailey says. "How did you drive that over so quickly? I thought you must have found a different method."

I finally see where Kieren's pointing. In front of the usual bus stop that drops passengers off at the mall, there's a tour bus instead. *Our* tour bus.

"We . . . did."

I meet Kieren's eyes. He clearly didn't summon it. Neither did I. How did our bus know to follow us?

"It could be another one," Rayna suggests. "The other buses from the tour company probably look very similar."

"It's ours," I say. "Same number plate."

I suppose there's nothing else to do here except head over to the bus and make use of it. A hush has fallen among us. We cross the road hurriedly. Though I find myself leading the charge at first, Kieren has matched my pace by the time we've reached the vehicle, and he steps on before I do. The lights snap bright. Twelve is awake.

"Hello!" it greets, turning in its seat. "Buckle up! Our next stop is a good one."

I don't move far once I'm on. The doors close automatically after Hailey and Rayna.

"*Offron?*" Kieren exclaims.

It's already displayed on the dashboard. LAND OF OUTER FRONTIER, CITY CENTER. I meet Kieren's startled gaze instantly. Offron hadn't been the next stop on the tour, the last I checked. Twelve was listening during our conversation with Kam. It's adjusted accordingly.

"All right," I say with a nervous laugh. "Any reason why?"

Twelve's blue circle spins once. "This will be the best picture of Medaluo."

Rayna sidles a bit farther up the stairs. She's leaning onto the dashboard casually.

"Not Norca?" she suggests. She doesn't know why Kieren and I are so startled, but Rayna loves contributing to meaningless debate in any situation. "Or Wespic?"

"The capital is only special because it's the capital," Twelve replies cheerily. "And Wespic? So passé. If you wanted to see terracotta statues, you'd go furniture shopping! Ha ha!"

Kieren folds his arms across his chest. "I want to shut it down."

Twelve swivels vigorously in its seat. "I beg your pardon?"

"You heard me. Sleep, please."

"I . . . I must decline. I need to drive."

Maybe I'm just uninformed, but I didn't think bots were capable of stuttering.

"I'm sure you have a mode where the bus drives but you're sleeping," Kieren snaps. "Go to sleep."

"Kieren," I say sharply. "Don't be mean to the AI."

His annoyance pivots. "Don't be mean *to the AI*? It doesn't have feelings, Ward."

"Neither do microwaves, but you still shouldn't hit them," I fire back.

"I don't want it awake! How about this?" Kieren pivots back to Twelve. "Connect me to customer service. They can do the shutdown."

"Connecting!" Twelve declares. "Please hold tight . . . Ah—so sorry. Customer service has declined your call. They're having some problems with human laborers, you see. No one wants to log in for dull work."

Kieren's jaw drops. "How are they declining the call if no one is there?"

"Auto-decline!"

"I'm just going to hack it," Hailey declares, clearly at her limit with Kieren's efforts. "I can get it shut down."

"Please don't do that," Twelve says. "I have rights."

Kieren splutters. "You do not have rights!"

Without any more prompting, Hailey puts her hands around the bot's neck.

"What . . . are you doing?" I ask. A part of me is concerned that I'm about to witness the world's first case of bot murder.

"Reset button," she answers. "Clears the loading queue for me to write into."

Hailey takes a few steps away to observe the results of the reset. The lights on the front of Twelve's chest flicks quickly through the entire color wheel, whirring twice before stopping on blue again. I almost expect the bot to malfunction or call the police, but Twelve only jangles a tune from its speakers.

"We are heading to the Land of Outer Frontier! Travel time approximating at seventeen hours and fifty-one minutes. Located at the far northeast of the country, this was the sight of vast Medan exploration in the early days of mining gold. Offron's significance has faded since then . . . but worry not, because the culinary experience far north is a delight!"

We stare at Hailey, silently asking whether she's triggered actual movement toward Offron or only the tourist brochure. The bus doesn't move. Neither does the bot, its arms staying at its sides. Hailey glares hard at Twelve, slightly unfocused to indicate she's typing in her display.

A minute passes. Kieren is the first to break the silence, saying, "Hailey . . ."

"I'm fighting someone," she grits out.

I blink. "Excuse me?"

"The controls," Hailey goes on tightly, "of the bot. I'm fighting someone. It's not an AI. An active user with real StrangeLoom credentials is popping in and out to take control. They're trying to undo each new line I write."

My jaw drops.

Kieren rears back. "I *knew* it," he insists. "I knew it was creepy—"

"Shut up, I need to concentrate," Hailey interrupts. "I can pull the user ID and . . ." She trails off. With a blink, her gaze clears perceptibly, looking only at the bot without her display in the way.

"Hailey?" Kieren prompts.

Hailey grabs the bot's arm. "Weston Murray," she bellows. "You get out of that thing right now."

I understand, by linguistic logic, the words that Hailey just said. I'm not comprehending what it means. When I turn to check on Kieren, he appears equally flabbergasted, his expression frozen in its previous state.

"Weston?" Rayna is the first one to break the spell. "What does Weston have to do with this?"

"He can speak for himself," Hailey says. "Weston, I'm not going to warn you again!"

And then, with the sudden warp usually seen only at landing pads, a new avatar blinks into view. Where there was empty space before, now there's shaggy-haired Weston, grinning with all his teeth.

"Hi," he says.

Hailey's entirely red in the face. "What are you doing in the Medan server?" she demands. "How long have you been following us?"

Weston squirms under her scrutiny. He inches closer and closer to Twelve's unmoving inorganic body, looking like he wants to get back in.

"To be fair," he grumbles, "I wasn't following *you*. I was following Kieren."

Kieren's eyes bug. He smacks his hands to his head, then inhales so loudly that it makes a whistling sound through his nostrils.

"You"—he drags his hands down—"*what*?"

The realization strikes me with a physical force. "You're the cat!" I exclaim. *Oh. I didn't think it would be you.* "You followed the wrong user ID when Kieren and I were both initially injected."

Weston's wince tells me everything. "I may have crept a little close. I didn't realize the system was going to warn you."

Kieren has entirely given up on trying to react in a normal way. He's dropped to a crouch, both his hands braced on his knees. Hailey appears no better, like she's caught between running laps around the bus or letting her avatar blow steam out of her ears.

"Weston," she says, very low, very firmly, "what are you *doing*?" She turns to check the time on the dashboard. There's a twelve-hour time difference to Atahua, so it'll be seven in the morning. "You have class soon."

"Conveniently," Weston retorts, "when classes start over there, you're usually going to sleep here anyway."

"As if you have some sort of responsibility to be following us?" Kieren bellows. "This is *dangerous*."

"I'm not doing anything." Weston taps his hand behind himself. Twelve wakes up, chirping a tune. Without Weston inside it, the bot doesn't talk at all. The bus starts to drive, its wheels slowly screeching out of its parking spot. I'd forgotten, for a moment, why we'd even boarded the bus.

"I heard Dad pull you aside that night you came home, right before your posting," Weston goes on. "He said he was proud of you, which was freaking weird. And then it sounded really dangerous if he was insisting you had to earn the secret assignment—"

Kieren immediately slashes his hand across his neck, cutting Weston off. His manner stiffens, different from the shock that emerged before. Rather than concern for Weston, it's panic. I tilt my head, trying to make sense of the switch. Kieren's gaze, unintentionally, swivels and lands on me.

"Secret assignment?" I echo.

Our posting is confidential, but that doesn't seem to be what Weston meant.

"No more!" Kieren declares. "Go to school!"

Frustration etches a heavy mark into Weston's brow. His fists clench. "You and me and Hailey always talk about how NileCorp has brainwashed Dad. We said we were going to protect each other from him. I needed to make sure I could help you. I've been guarding your Pod downcountry, by the way! I have emergency bags waiting in the antechamber in case you need to log out quickly and get help."

"Weston, this is not the time nor the place," Kieren urges.

"What if he brainwashes you too! I don't want you sacrificing yourself for NileCorp!"

"Okay!" Hailey interrupts. Her manner has grown softer. She takes a step forward, putting her hands on Weston's shoulders. "I know you had good intentions. But you have to go back to school now before you're noticed. Thank you for watching our Pods at home. I'll check in with you later today, okay?"

For a moment, it seems that Weston is going to keep arguing. Hailey must be more convincing than I thought, because he nods, defeated. He disappears before our eyes, as quickly as he blinked in, and Hailey's arms drop to her sides with a thunk.

The bus is still driving. It's picking up speed, rolling onto the expressway, where the traffic has since eased. The dashboard continues to display the time to Offron. Seventeen hours.

"Can I speak to you?" Kieren says to Hailey.

Hailey nods. She catches Rayna's gaze before walking over, offering a small smile of assurance. Rayna smiles in return, her cheeks faintly pink, but Hailey has already passed by. She and Kieren march to the back of the bus, settling at the furthermost row. They duck their heads to whisper.

"Well," Rayna remarks after a beat. "That was something."

"Sure was," I say slowly. My suspicion has been stoked. I feel it as a small ember at first, charring where it touches, but then it starts to grow. The flames find kindling. Kieren glanced at me when Weston spoke about Headmaster Murray. *Insisting you had to earn the secret assignment...*

"Wanna sit?" Rayna asks, cutting into my thoughts.

"Yeah," I say. "Let's sit."

The bus sways, hurtling at high speed. It's going to be a significant journey. I suppose Rayna and Hailey are throwing their lots in with us now and are going where we go, surveying where they need. Easier than finding their own mode of transport while their names are temporarily logged in multiple precincts' warnings.

Rayna slides into one of the rows first. I follow after her. As soon as we're comfortable, she drops her head onto my shoulder, and I give her a small pat, letting her settle. She closes her eyes to rest, but mine stay wide open, locked out the window to resist inspecting the back row, to resist asking what the Murrays are hissing about. We drive through the city's outer periphery, yellow beer glasses projected into the night to mark the bars and silent movie trailers beaming above the theaters. I can pinpoint the exact moment we leave city boundaries because the scene outside the window turns an eerie black, blotted only with the faint glimmer of factories grumbling overnight.

I lean heavily into my seat, syncing my breaths to Rayna's soft snores. If I could hear Kieren at all, it would be so easy to turn the volume meter higher to try eavesdrop, but he keeps his voice below that threshold. I open my display, opting to waste time on the feed. My suggestions provide news on Dad. The headlines, the think pieces. I've scrolled for only a few minutes before I'm tired of it, because what I really want to do is call him and ask him to explain that email, but where do I even *begin*?

Rayna's snoring gets louder. I rest my head on top of hers. Maybe I should follow her example. My eyes are straining. I tap my main controls, wanting to play music from my central panel.

But the page looks different. It isn't only my usual controls—there's another pathway here. I'm staring at it for too long before realizing that I recognize the user ID. When Kieren sent the remote access request, he connected our displays. He could rummage through mine, but that also opened the link for me to rummage through his.

He forgot to disconnect after he finished.

I take a very shallow breath, trying not to be obvious about my finding. I have access to everything in Kieren's display.

33

EIRALE

When the first rays of the new morning trickle in, I'm half convinced I've imagined the creak overhead.

I shoot to my feet at once. I'd been alert all night, keeping watch. Nothing has appeared out of the ordinary. The loudspeakers ran on a loop every hour. The apartments turned off their lights and went to sleep at some point nearing midnight, and then it was only me and Threto, staring at each other in darkness alike.

The creak comes again. This time, I'm certain. Footsteps. There's someone on the roof.

I dig into Nik's bag, retrieving the hammer. It's the most makeshift weapon I can imagine, something that'll only have any effective use if I end up engaging in a close brawl, but I have no other options. With my own footfall light, I pad to the windows, each step drawing goose bumps on my arms.

The footsteps follow my path. Creeping closer, closer to the edge of the roof.

I grip the side of the window, maintaining balance to shove half my body out and swivel directly up, preparing to swing with my other hand.

I almost drop the hammer.

"Teryn."

She tilts her head, taking in the threat, or lack thereof. It would be more embarrassing if I withdrew the hammer, so I let it dangle coolly in my hand.

"I was wondering where you'd gone," Teryn says, matter-of-fact. Her gaze turns farther down, to the street. "Drones?"

"Drones," I confirm. I don't know how long she's been observing me and how much she saw, but my instinct is to obscure the fact that I wasn't here when we moved apartments. Nik got himself to safety; I was making a run to a pharmacy. It isn't something illicit—we want him alive if he's going to finish fetching his files. Still, NileCorp might have expected me to use the situation against him instead. Press him to distress until he divulged how he plans to retrieve this program, then continue the mission myself once he succumbed to illness. Admitting that I kept him safe feels like an unnecessary confession.

"I see." Teryn crooks a finger. "Come up, would you?"

She doesn't wait for an answer before retreating from the edge of the roof. I'm left with little choice except to pull myself back through the window and return the hammer into Nik's bag. He's still sleeping soundly.

I slip out through the door, taking the last set of stairs to the tallest point of the building. It ends with a ladder, ascending to a hatch. The handle is rusted over when I try to push, and it takes several hard strikes that I try to muffle before the trapdoor opens onto the rooftop.

I poke my head out. There aren't any protective barriers, no guardrails. Only a thin, metallic sheet lying flat across the roof, directly above the penthouse apartment. Teryn is standing by a plumbing vent, her shoe toeing the plastic.

In the time we've had working together at the base, I've learned some tells in reading her expressions. If she's entirely impassive, she's not feeling good about the situation.

"You're delayed," she says.

"You said Offron in three days," I return. I don't emerge any farther from the hatch. "There's still time."

"It's hardly good practice to press right up to the deadline." When Teryn flips up the collar of her jacket, not a hair moves out of place. The sun comes up, and her light brown ponytail practically glows a halo around her head. I don't know how she got into the city under lockdown, how she's navigating Threto as an Atahuan without the police coming after her. None of that matters, because she's Teryn Moore.

"Is he ill?" she asks flippantly.

"Yes," I say. "He's on the mend. He'll be awake today, and we'll resume."

"Where are the other two?"

I shouldn't be surprised that Teryn knows about Miz and Blare—it would be more shocking if she didn't. This whole time, the capture mission has been *Nik Grant Nik Grant Nik Grant* because he's the one gracing Atahua's headlines, but of course NileCorp would bring in the members of his team too. I suppose they didn't split our focus in Button City because it was obvious that as soon as we secured Nik, his team would follow suit.

My palms itch. My throat constricts. It is less that I'm surprised to hear NileCorp knows about Miz and Blare and more that I actively wished they didn't, that I'd done a better job at hiding them from my employers' surveillance—and *that* surprises me. The moment the thought settles into my conscious awareness, there's no coming back from it. It's easier to justify handing Nik over when he's murdered someone in cold blood. Yet no matter how much I twist and turn the situation with jargon from my corporate soldier handbook, I can't pretend there's any world where it makes sense to let Miz and Blare endure the same fate. *Especially* Blare.

Teryn glances over, her eyes narrowed. I scramble to cover my reaction.

"We got separated from them," I explain. "Another team's getaway interrupted our second location's file retrieval."

"International intelligence, probably," Teryn remarks. "I doubt they were successful."

Because Nik is the only one who can retrieve these files, allegedly. I am still in the dark as to why. I don't think Teryn knows either. It is merely what NileCorp told her, and she'll relay the message with every bit of conviction.

"The other two," I say carefully. "I don't think their involvement justifies capture."

Teryn gives me an incredulous look.

"Are they under duress?"

"No." My fingers are tapping on the hatch, and I force them still. "But it's only Nik who drops the bombs."

"And there's a reason our laws charge an accomplice of a crime the same to the perpetrator." Teryn pauses. "I came to check if you were well. I didn't think there would be cause for concern."

"There isn't," I assure her at once. "I only fear we're coming down hard on people who are misguided."

"Misguided," Teryn echoes. "You're sympathizing with terrorists."

"I'm not saying Nik was right to kill our soldiers. It's just that maybe his team doesn't need to be snuffed out in a back room." I'm getting distracted from the point. That wasn't entirely what I started out arguing. "The girl, Miz—she blames private forces for killing her best friend. I think it's that simple. Her anger is misdirected. And Blare? They're just a kid. They're not bad people. We should keep that in mind."

A muscle twitches in Teryn's jaw. I see it starkly in the light, each minute movement speaking for her before she opens her mouth again.

"You're parroting them. Their justifications."

I jerk back. My foot almost slips on the ladder. "No, I'm not."

"Sure, you are. Uncle said this would happen."

Uncle? As in—

"James Moore?" I grip the latch hard, hiding the tremor that shakes down my arms. The NileCorp CEO was talking about *me*? "What do you mean?"

"He was concerned that you'd be recruited." Teryn adjusts her stance, rising to her full height. "It happens often to soldiers planted into a situation among extremists. My instructions were that I needed to pull you out if it looked like that was happening."

"No!"

I didn't realize this had gone all the way up to James Moore. That the entirety of NileCorp was waiting for the outcome.

"I was entertaining possibilities," I say firmly. "In no way do I intend to deviate from my orders, nor question instructions."

Teryn folds her arms. She is quiet for a moment. Then she nods.

"I believe you. But it's more important that my uncle does. Do you know what his head of security didn't include in our briefing when they sent us on our capture missions?" She lifts her left foot slightly, swinging it in the air. Teryn starts to walk a straight line along the roofing sheet, each step summoning a soft, rhythmic creak. "We've had a tripled increase of violent crime directly linked to Nik Grant's calls to action. Uncle James wouldn't tell me this while we were at the base. I had to squeeze it out of him before he sent me here. He's so careful not to incite fear. He wants the best for an orderly nation."

Teryn halts at the edge of the roof. She's turned her back on me. The thought occurs, in the snap of a finger, that she would have no recourse if someone suddenly came up behind her and pushed her off the building. As quickly as the notion entered, I shake my head to clear it.

"I understand," I say carefully. "If we acknowledge the havoc he's sowing in Atahua, it would only empower him to his supporters."

The media can't be stopped from rushing to his sites of activity and filming coverage, but they don't need to find out about the copycats. Or the groups that form to take up his proclamations. NileCorp's worst fear is spreading confirmation that Nik Grant's stunts are achieving exactly what he wants.

"The outright murders are bad enough," Teryn mutters. "Never mind all that spray painting. Those leaflets with the ugly slogans. Those ludicrous claims that are sending protesters outside NileCorp centers nonstop. *Indisposition!* Can you imagine?" She shudders, and swivels around in a quick motion. "Get to Offron. Let's put an end to terrorist activity."

It's as clear a dismissal as any. Without any parting words, I push away from the hatch and close the door again, climbing down the ladder. I have to assume Teryn got up there by scaling the exterior. How she extricates herself is not any of my business.

I pad back down the stairs, entering the apartment again. Nik still appears asleep. I put my finger under his nose, tracking his breathing pattern. It's even.

Tripled increase of violent crime directly linked to Nik Grant's calls to action. NileCorp is not going to let that go easily. They'll make an example out of him.

I sit myself back down, leaning against the wall. A horrible feeling has taken root in my stomach.

• • • •

The apartment interior grows bitterly cold. Two hours later, when the temperature reaches a frigid peak, Nik is shivering as he opens his eyes, slowly raising himself up onto his arms. His fever must be gone, at least.

"What are . . . ?" Nik trails off, squinting. Light drapes over the horizon, fighting to surface against the smog. When Nik looks back at me and focuses, I offer him one of those tight-lipped smiles that old Atahuan ladies do when you let them go through the door first.

"Are those my glasses?"

"Yeah." I close the tab I've been on. Despite knowing better, I spent the morning going through posts about myself, everything from EIRALE WARD NAMED THIS CENTURY'S WORST SPY to TEN REASONS WHY EIRALE WARD IS BEING SET UP. As soon as I made a search on the feed, I knew I had sunken into a rabbit hole. I wasn't only looking at sources from international news organizations anymore, I was reading some fifteen-year-old from Button State's listicle on their personal page.

I take the glasses off, handing them back to Nik. "I didn't call anyone, don't worry."

"I imagine not." Sluggishly, he grabs the glasses and puts them on. "Did you go looking for your footage?"

I frown. I hadn't thought to go looking for it. Why hadn't I? A small pit of self-consciousness replaces the all-around dread I've been wallowing in these past few hours. That would have been one less item to worry about when it came time to clear my name.

"Yeah, found it and stole it already," I intone. "Goodbye. You can no longer hold me hostage."

Nik clambers into a proper sitting position. He makes a delicate process of it, ensuring that he can distribute his weight at every small change before he straightens fully. By the time he's upright, he looks like he might start panting.

"I suppose," he says, reluctantly, warily, "I have you to thank for saving my life."

"Go on."

Nik looks away. He sounds utterly stiff when he says, "Thank you. I appreciate it. I was quite delirious by the time you forced Eveline into my mouth."

"You're welcome. I do need you to survive if I'm going to go free." I stand up, dusting off my hands. I'm trying not to think too hard about the act of going free, and what it'll take. Proceed forward one step at a time. What other choice do I have? "Are you okay to be on the move? You're probably going to be extremely weak for another day."

"I'll be fine." Nik's gaze swivels quickly, typing behind his glasses. "We don't have time for me to lounge around resting."

"You may have to," I say. Daylight shifts with a change in the clouds outside. A dam has broken in the sky, spilling bone-white over the city. "I don't know how you expect us to get out when Threto's closure extends for two weeks."

"Government cars are allowed to exit with a negative avian flu test. Miz and Blare have already gotten out. Miz is routing a self-driving car to arrive downstairs as we speak." Nik starts to rise. The floorboards creak beneath him, protesting at the motion.

It almost disguises the scraping sound by the door too.

"Stop, stop, stop," I hiss suddenly, holding my hand out. "Stop moving!"

He freezes.

"Get behind the couch."

"Why—"

"Nik. *Now.*" I shove him when he doesn't move quickly enough. Just as I'm ducking behind too, the door opens quietly. Whispers enter the apartment, numerous footsteps dispersing wide. They're light. I count three, then more.

My heart is pounding in my ears. I thought Teryn was letting me finish the assignment. Has she sent forces? Did I lose her trust?

We're too high up to jump from the window. Too surrounded to make a run for the door. Frantically I switch between either scenario with no alternative in any direction, and before I've come to any decision, one of the intruders surveys around the couch, spotting us.

Ski mask, large jacket, gun in his hand.

I don't wait for him to make the first move. I rise, knocking him off his feet. As soon as I'm up, I've heard the click of a gun coming off its safety. I skid two steps and spin to face the others in the room. The one farthest from me holds the weapon.

Nik slams upright too. He rasps, "Wait," and I can't comprehend why when a bullet strikes the wall. The gunman aims again, but I've closed the distance and gripped his wrist, throwing the next shot awry to hit the windowpane. I see my opening. I strike hard on his arm, and the gun clatters loose.

The others are moving. I see them in my periphery, but I'm quicker to pick up the weapon.

"*Soldier.*"

I finally freeze, the gun steady in my hand. Nik's been trying to get my attention. I was aware of it as some faraway call until now, once his volume rises to a thunder strike.

I turn.

"Don't shoot," Nik says. He's standing, his arm outstretched, palm out like *I'm* the enemy he has to persuade to disarm. "Come on, soldier. They're kids. They're just kids."

And I look at the intruders properly. They're holding varying bags stuffed with tin cans, with bottles and glass. The masks hide most of their features, but now that I've stopped moving, I realize none of these people are any taller than my shoulders, skinny and gaunt under their oversized jackets.

Horror seizes my chest. This isn't NileCorp. Teryn has nothing to do with this. The intruders have frozen too, eyeing the gun in my hands nervously. Nik steps forward.

"Take the gun," he instructs me. "But let's go. Leave them here."

I don't know if they'll move once I lower the gun. I start to step backward for the door with my aim still in place, watching Nik when he picks up his bag. He says, "We're going. Don't come after us, and we'll leave you alone too." The kids don't respond. They let us get to the door, and it's only when I'm stepping out into the hallway that I hear the slight noise one of them makes, the indication that they were silent because we'd scared them.

Nik closes the door hard after himself, doing his best to latch it despite the misfitting frame.

"I didn't know—"

"They're looters," Nik explains, cutting me off. "They'll scope out rich residents who haven't set their security alarms with high enough parameters and enter while they're oblivious in their Pods. Usually they're in and out within seconds. Not enough time for police to catch them after the alarm goes off."

I take a shallow breath. I'm struggling to fill my lungs.

"They're not going to find much in that apartment."

"No." Nik hurries down the stairwell. I focus on following him, mimicking the rhythm of his steps so that there's only one set echoing along the levels. "I have to assume they're trying all the apartments. This isn't a particularly wealthy neighborhood to begin with."

As promised, a car is waiting on the street when we emerge from the courtyard and back through the alleyway. I hear the faint announcement of a loudspeaker drone coming from the next street, and Nik hisses, *"Quickly."* He slides into the driver's seat; I get into the passenger, tossing the small handgun to the floor. The vehicle is only fit for two people at the front—the rest is left for the trunk. With another glance over his shoulder to check on the roving police drone, Nik starts the engine with a press of the button and steps on the accelerator to drive.

"Aren't you going to switch to self-driving?" I ask after a minute of his erratic turns.

"I'd like to be in control right now."

We go quiet while Nik navigates with his glasses, leaning forward on every map instruction to peer at the approaching street signs. I'm still shaken over almost shooting a bunch of children, so I have no particular penchant for chatter, my hands clutched in my lap. Each time I think Nik is about to say something again, I realize he's only mumbling under his breath to complain about the illegibility of the smaller signs from afar.

I can't imagine him doing this before his attacks on Atahuan soil. Squinting. Navigating himself on location.

Before long, we approach the city border, coming upon the toll booths on the other side of Threto from where we entered. Through the tinted car windows, I count the national soldiers guarding the area, each of them wearing exo-suits not dissimilar to the ones NileCorp issues.

"Put your mask on."

I retrieve my scrunched mask from my pocket, looping the straps around my ears. The car cruises right up to the barrier, and Nik rolls his window down, his arm casually propped to the side. He gestures wordlessly to me. The soldiers salute. A light flashes from the booth to scan the number plate, the thermal cameras overhead confirm that we're not running fevers, and the barrier lifts.

Nik rolls his window back up and drives through.

"That was easy," I mutter.

"We're logged for an official's ill-behaving daughter and a low-wage hired driver." Nik flicks a finger at the dashboard, turning the headlights on against the gloom. "Besides, we're exiting, not entering. They're most worried about keeping journalists from getting in. Less worried about government cars getting hacked to take people out."

I fall silent again, watching the window as the vehicle climbs up a ramp and picks up speed on the expressway, leaving Threto behind. The landscape shifts. The road grows long and bumpy.

I try to sit back without fidgeting. The entire vehicle jolts every few miles, and I jostle up and down too. The screen on the dashboard has an automated bot for instructions. On the third jostle, I start to notice that there's an emoticon popping up every time the car shudders, pulling a face with us.

I snort.

Nik glances over.

"Look," I say, pointing at the dashboard.

He's watching when the car jostles again. On normal setting, the screen in the middle shows the speed we're going at and the temperature outside. When the car flies up a few inches off the rough ground, the settings disappear briefly to show >:0 instead.

Nik scoffs. "Wonder which kid designed that in the corporate department."

"I don't think it was a kid."

Nik raises an eyebrow. He keeps his gaze forward, paying attention to the dust clouds on this stretch of the expressway. "No?"

"No. Old man. Engineer in his last year before retirement."

The car must be somewhat listening—enough to be waiting for verbal instructions in collecting maps or pulling open radio stations—because its screen flickers, then displays :) for a brief second. Whatever system they've got installed there is the same as the restaurant servers and bank guards. They can comprehend the conversations happening around them. They're only not given the capacity to come up with replies any more complicated than "Let me do that for you" or "Let me put you in touch with a human."

"Fine," Nik says. "I think that was confirmation that you're right."

A quick splutter of rain sprays down while we're accelerating, then stops before the droplets have barely finished gliding along the windshield. Middle Medaluo is polluted enough already, but with this shaky weather, the sun is nothing more than a faint circle through the clouds.

"Maybe this is a design choice across all the cars," Nik says after a while. My mind has long wandered off, but he's still on the same topic. "Many people get attached to their self-cleaning vacuums. This bonds them to their car."

I prop my arm up on the door, leaning into my hand. "They need a bit more charm than only an emoticon. Think about misshapen fruit. Self-cleaning vacuums have nothing on them."

Nik sniffs loudly. "I cry every time the lumpy apple gets left behind."

I'm taken aback for a second. I can't imagine Nik Grant eating his fruits and vegetables, never mind crying in the grocery aisle. It doesn't occur to me that Nik has cracked a joke until I meet his gaze when he glances over momentarily, and he allows the faintest smile through.

The car says its fifteen degrees Celsius outside. While my arm is pressed to the window, it collects the condensation gathering there, keeping my skin cool.

"What did you do before this?"

The question falls out of its own accord. Nik glances over again. The steering wheel shifts under his hand, making a slight turn in the curving highway.

"Before I set you up for treason?"

"No." I know already what he did before he set me up for treason. I did my research. "Before all of it. You weren't born a domestic anarchist, were you?"

He must think I'm picking at something.

"Maybe I was," Nik says evasively. "Maybe I was born to criminals."

"I doubt it."

Nik narrows his eyes. "Why?"

"You once made your escape off the top of a mountain base by skiing away. You put your shoes on as though you received formal teaching on the most polite way to manage it, and"—Nik's shoulders are already tight as I speak, but when I tap his nose, he must realize that I've been watching very carefully—"your freckles are permanently burned off. I can see the lighter patches where they used to be."

He's silent for a long moment. Then he mutters, "You're an astute detective, aren't you?"

"I went to school with many people like you. It's not detective work."

Nile Military Academy was a strange place. There was no in between. There were the kids born to parents who were some of the highest-ranking people in Atahua, attending the school as a matter of prestige, and then there were the kids whose enrollment was government-mandated for no reason other than being a Medan orphan, banned from full adoption by Atahuan parents. There were kids who were troublemakers from day one after years in the foster care system, and they were either straightened up by punishment or kicked out before long, the headmaster making the call that they wouldn't be useful for NileCorp forces upon graduation anyway. Those cadets inevitably ended up on the streets, because they'd still owe the debt of the academic year they started. There were always a few with every incoming class.

Nik focuses on keeping the steering wheel straight.

"Fine, you've identified the signs correctly," he says. "That's not going to help you narrow down my background, unfortunately."

"I know." We've entered the rural parts of Medaluo, the elevated expressway transforming into wide country roads. "Where did you grow up?"

"Atahua."

"Button City?"

"Button State."

He's been nearby, then. Even before his crimes, he has always circled my vicinity.

"And your parents?" I ask.

"Irrelevant."

"Hmm." I shift in my seat. We pass a copse of trees, gnarly and dust-covered, most of the leaves so waxy that they appear fake. Not so pretty on the eyes, but that's the sort of greenery surviving through the worst climate crises. "Atahuan?"

"Obviously."

"You almost don't look classically Atahuan, though."

Nik huffs. "What is this—twenty ethnic questions?"

"Ah, ah," I say, pointing at him. "You're not allowed to say that."

"It's not a *slur*—"

"I can see the tabloid headlines now," I interrupt, waving my hand in front of me. "'Nik Grant Called Me Ethnic.'"

"That's *not* what I said!"

I can't hold back my snort. It echoes through the car before I bite down on it, suppressing the sound. Nik eyes me suspiciously for a moment. When I'm clearly done ridiculing him, he says:

"My family isn't all Atahuan. Half are from Cega. My mother's side."

I wasn't expecting that.

"I didn't realize it was incorrect to call you a domestic anarchist."

"It's correct," Nik says flatly. "It doesn't matter where anyone before me came from. I'm Atahuan. I have the right to protest how Atahua is being run."

How easy it is for him to make that statement, even if half his bloodline only came over to Atahua one generation ago. It's different for Medans. It'll be different for Medans for as long as this cold war goes on. It doesn't matter when I was brought over, nor how much I claim that I'm Atahuan. No one believes me the same.

"Are you still in touch with them?" I ask. "Your family."

Nik frowns. "Some."

"Your parents?"

"No."

The car is struggling to maintain speed on the rural road. We're hitting a rough patch where there hasn't been maintenance in decades.

"Not on good terms?" I ask.

Nik concentrates on the road, steering the wheel rapidly to avoid the worst of the ditches. I suspect he'll ignore my question entirely. He's quiet for so long that I even forget what I last asked, lolling my head into my seat.

Then, when we're rumbling onto an elevated expressway again:

"It's complicated."

I blink, my attention snapping back to him. "How so?"

"You go rogue for long enough," Nik says, "and you begin to expect that you'll lose. Maybe you can win the final war, but in the process there'll be a dozen fragmented battles trying to take what you have. Your family. Your loved ones."

His hands are tight on the steering wheel. It must be easier to have nothing, then. No family. No loved ones. I would be a better candidate. Instead Nik Grant has to become someone else, callous and cold, only to prevent losing more in the line of fire.

"So much has been taken from me," he goes on, "but I'm going to take everything back."

I probably shouldn't have asked. All the same, I'm met with a pang of bitterness that I can't particularly place. Nik would have the willpower to walk across the oceans demanding the waters hold him up, and he could drown in the process but he would try anyway. I don't understand purpose so all-encompassing. I was likely born missing the part of me responsible for that urge.

Maybe that's why I've developed this pull to be near it.

Near him.

"I'm sorry," I say plainly.

"Don't be." The car beeps, warning of a large pothole approaching, and Nik tugs the wheel with vigor. "That's why we're going to Kunlun now. I'm not accepting failure."

I don't say anything for a long time after that.

34

LIA

I wait for Kieren to go to sleep.

We start slowing when Wespic's glowing horizon creeps into the distance, the roads turning narrower to accommodate the approaching city. Seven of the seventeen hours have passed. It's almost three in the morning. A steady rain drizzles down the windows.

Without Weston, there is no commentary from the bot. I don't know if he shut down the original guide on purpose, or if the AI tour bus went on the fritz after his occupation. My eyes flicker once more to the window. I track a bead racing along the exterior, but in truth I'm using the reflection as a subtle method to keep tabs on Kieren. He's three rows back, having moved closer since he and Hailey ended their conversation. Hailey is curled up in one of the other rows, and Rayna has been knocked out for who knows how long.

At this point, it's only me and Kieren in a race to stay awake, and he doesn't know he's participating.

His eyes have been fluttering for over an hour, his head resting on the seat. Just when I think he's closing his eyes fully, he opens them again, his lips ever so pursed, pensive at some imaginary spot on the bus ceiling.

Just sleep, I want to snap. *Be normal and rest for once.*

Kieren sighs out loud, as though he can hear me. His gaze wanders around, and I hurry to look away from the reflection of the window, fixing my own attention forward. A few minutes later, I glance back, and his eyes are finally closed.

It took long enough.

I twiddle my thumbs for five minutes. Then ten. When I'm finally certain that he must be asleep, and there's no chance he'll open his display and see it moving around, I click in, activating remote access.

It's jarring to have someone else's display overlaid. Though there's nothing different from mine on a structural level, I have the disorientation akin to suddenly finding my left hand on the right: his default buttons are in another order, his shortcuts go to different places. I'm already committing several moral infractions being connected without permission, so I don't go idly browsing.

Kieren has been watching me. That much I am certain now. The refusal to ask me more about Chung, the readiness to accept how I've been getting into each secure location. From the morning before we were injected into the server, he's been doing all he can not to trip my suspicion.

Hadn't I suspected this from the very beginning? One cadet for bait, another cadet to work the actual posting.

My hands are shaking as I go to open his files. His briefing for the exam posting is labeled the same as mine, pinned at the top. It pulls up the last page he must have left it on. I flip through the remaining pages, reaching the end. When I find nothing out of the ordinary, I go in the opposite direction, flipping page after page to the front.

There's nothing new here.

I go back to his file catalog. This time I sort them by date added. I want to see what came in most recently.

His files reshuffle. At the top is one simply titled ADDENDUM. It was sent to him nine hours ago.

Which was when he left the bus, giving the excuse of searching for food.

I stare at it too long. Before I'm fully ready, my display opens it, putting the text in front of my eyes.

ADDITIONAL BRIEFING—CONFIDENTIAL
Kieren Murray

1. INTRODUCTION:
There are times where we find ourselves embarking on what the academy must call a double-prong bait effort. Rarely are investigations as clean-cut as obtaining the truth or exposing a traitor. More so than doers, the field requires watchers.

Thank you for your patience regarding your primary posting. Any duplicity was not intended as a comment on your loyalty. Given your proximity to the suspects involved, there was a certain criteria to be met before confidential information could be shared. Upon receiving your submissions, the board has unanimously voted to proceed.

I have to put my hands underneath my thighs, sitting on them so I don't shake hard enough to wake Rayna beside me. The academy is always opaque with their written briefs, but worse is their tone, as though they're speaking to an imaginary adoring audience. A cadet reads it now, but a hundred years down the line, Nile Military Academy will prepare to declassify their files, let the world know how many times it was saved.

2. IMPORTANT NOTES:
i) CHUNG YIN
Mr. Chung has been missing since he was last seen leaving the Upper Sea National Data Center downcountry. He has not been located in any upcountry server; nor has he appeared

anywhere on Medaluo's extensive surveillance network. The most likely possibility is that he is dead.

ii) HENRY SULLIVAN
Prior to Chung's disappearance, he exchanged several heated phone calls with Sullivan. They had not been in touch since Chung renounced his Atahuan citizenship and left for Medaluo. While neither spoke in clear terms, one phrase was repeatedly used by Chung: "I need Lia. It's time." Sullivan declined, and quickly ended each phone call. He may already suspect our surveillance of his communications. If he has found ways to circumvent our monitoring, we cannot be certain that he hasn't exchanged further correspondences with either Chung or other Medans.

iii) LIA WARD
Chung's last text exchange with Sullivan asked "Do you never want to see Eirale's face again?" Days later, Chung disappeared, and Operation Coldwire began self-destructing across the Medan data centers. What little remnants that Chung left behind was stamped with a partial signature. Our system scans have indisputably acquired an owner to the signature: Lia Ward. There is no evidence to say that Sullivan sent Ward to wipe the program and assassinate Chung. There is also no evidence that Ward is *un*involved.

I have to take a breath, physically sick from reading. I don't dare close the display in case it does something to trigger my access, but I tip my head down, trying to ease the nausea.

They think *I* went in like some assassin of the night? I'm a *cadet*. I can't hack myself across servers upcountry. I don't even leave my house downcountry. How could I possibly delete a top-secret program and then cause a grown man to go *missing*? It's so beyond absurd that I can't believe someone at NileCorp wrote this brief, that the academy board approved it, that Kieren proceeded to read it and take it seriously.

Then it gets worse.

iv) EIRALE SULLIVAN

To consider all possibilities, it should be noted that at one point in the StrangeLoom database, logged from birth as a method of record-keeping, Eirale Sullivan was assigned the digital signature that has now been given to Lia Ward.

Our records show Eirale Sullivan as deceased. She passed away before she could receive StrangeLoom credentials.

3. OBJECTIVES:

Primarily, we must understand what role Henry Sullivan plays in Chung Yin's Operation Coldwire. Our acquisition of Coldwire is paramount, yet just as NileCorp's ground team were closing in on it, the program—and Chung himself—disappeared. Did Sullivan offer Chung a warning? Is a third party involved? Either prove Henry Sullivan is working as a foreign agent for Medaluo and has contributed to their research, or acquire an explanation otherwise.

<u>To achieve this, your role is to gather any evidence that Lia Ward possesses.</u> She will be detained upon entry back into Atahua.

I can't keep reading. The briefing goes on to ask further questions, like why Chung needed me and to what extent am I aware of my father's treason, and I can't digest a single word more. I've surpassed nausea and sunken into numbness.

All this time, Kieren has been spying on me. Even if he didn't have the full context until this addendum, he must have known enough if he avoided certain topics to prevent triggering my suspicion. *Earn the secret assignment.* What did his father tell him? That I would lead Kieren to something, and he only needed not to tip me off until they told him what he was looking for?

I lurch to my feet, needing to get up, get away. The bus is driving at high speed so it's not as though I can leave, but I stagger to the front, standing next to the bot. Twelve is quiet company, its hands planted neatly on the wheel while I heave in, heave out, each breath a rattle. I close out of the file and disconnect from Kieren's display.

The clock on the dashboard ticks forward another minute. It's afternoon in Atahua. Dad will be at work. Any communication I make to him will be monitored on his end—and that's if Kieren isn't already somehow eavesdropping on my every word here.

"Any chance you could stop for gas soon so that we can stretch our legs?" I ask Twelve.

It doesn't say anything in response. The light on its chest flickers once, and I have to take that as enough of an answer.

"Thank you," I say. I stay at the front.

• • • •

It turns out Twelve did receive my instruction.

After a while, the dreary surroundings put me in a near-hypnotic state, and I only break from my reverie when the tour bus activates its turn signal, a loud *click-clack-click* sounding from the dashboard. The flat road offers a small approaching oasis in the form of a gas station, a structure that resembles a bus stop on first glance. Its signs read FUEL, but I can't figure out what the strange objects protruding from the overhead shelter are until the tour bus stops and I follow the tubes running down the inner wall. Ah. They're nozzles—on the ceiling.

Twelve silently cuts the engine. In the abrupt stillness, the others stir behind me, woken by the change in environment. Blearily, Rayna asks, "Where are we?" and I watch one of the nozzles start to lower from the overhead line, automatically syncing with the fuel opening on the side of the bus.

"Refueling," I say shortly. "I'll go check on it. You all stay here."

As soon as I step out, I close the doors after myself by force, waiting until I hear the mechanism click. The rain is coming harder than I thought, getting into my eyes. I barely pay it any heed, trudging to the other side of the bus. Here, at least, the overhead shelter provides some respite from the downpour.

I open my display. Unless Dad is having a late night, he ought to be at the Melnova apartment now, bringing his work back. He isn't fully off until he goes to sleep, but he'll be in his home office instead.

I don't dial him. Nor the house line. I skip right to Tamera.

"Didn't think I'd be hearing from you so soon," she answers cheerily. Water is running in the background. She's in the kitchen. "You're finishing up your posting?"

"Not quite," I say. I keep my voice hushed. "Is Dad home?"

Tamera takes a beat. She's spent enough time with me growing up that she knows when I'm lying and when I'm saying that I had a good day to indicate I actually had a horrible day.

"Sure, he's here. He just got in."

NileCorp is monitoring his communications actively, but maybe they're on a delay with me. They've got Kieren here in the field already. I have to hope that means there's no soldier with a headset listening to every call I make.

"Can you put your display on speaker? So he can hear what I'm saying?"

Tamera is confused. She must be wondering why I don't call him directly. She doesn't ask it outright. She says, "Easy enough," and turns off the water running in the sink, the rush of background noise easing. On my end, the splatter of the rain is incessant, tapping a restless rhythm when it drops off the edge of the shelter. "Henry? Lia's calling."

"Lia?" Dad's voice has a faint echo, picked up by speaker mode from across the room. I can imagine Tamera standing at the entryway into his office, my dad seated at his desk. "What's going on?"

"Dad, they're investigating you." I don't know where to start. I don't know how to ease in. So I don't. "My posting is Uncle Chung. He went missing after making a weapon for the Medans, and we were supposed to find him. I don't think they've ever been worried about where he is. I think they already have an operation in place to acquire the program anyway. The point of my whole posting was to lure you out because they suspect you have something to do with his work, and I just opened Kieren Murray's second secret briefing where it says he's watching *me* to find whatever he can to pin *you*. You need to do something. Go public first or hide or—I don't know, *anything*—because they're going to charge you with treason otherwise."

Silence. If it weren't for the sound of Tamera's breath, in and out, out and in, I would have thought the line dropped.

"I can't, Lia," Dad says. "It's true. I am involved."

I stagger, leaning against the bus. The surface is cold, wet, agonizing.

"I don't... I don't understand."

"It's not treason. Not in the way they want me for. There's too much to explain, and I can't speak it all here."

"Try," I say. My voice cuts through the rain. I've gotten louder. "You owe me that much." I've been shoved right into the middle of his scandal without knowing it. NileCorp used my entire practical examination to get to Dad, as though I'm only an extension of his guilt.

"It's not safe. You should have told me this had to do with Chung. I would have never let you be sent after him. You could have stayed with me—"

"I'm on a posting because I'm trying to stay with you!" I exclaim. "My whole life, Dad. I've been working so hard my whole life so I'll have the choice of staying by your side."

"None of that matters if NileCorp hears the wrong thing. Lia, whatever Chung has recently made is child's play. His first attempt was shut down, and he'll never get there again."

Project Wit. The program he was working on in Atahua, that NileCorp forced the government to put away.

"That's what Medaluo recruited him for, isn't it?" I say. "They've called it Operation Coldwire. It's a remake."

"It's not."

"Then what—"

"Say nothing. Do nothing. It doesn't matter what you find for them—"

And the line goes dead. The entire call tab disappears from my display, and I jerk back, clicking around. "Hello? Dad? Tamera?"

I try to call again. Dial tone.

They're already watching me. NileCorp have shut the call down.

"Lia."

I whirl around. Before my eyes adjust to the dark, I think that I'm hearing an intrusion inside my display, that Headmaster Murray has taken over the line to speak to me directly. A second later, I find Kieren standing behind me, right where the shelter doesn't quite reach. The rain has soaked through his shirt.

Even several paces away, I can already feel his guilt rippling off him like some physical aura. It occurs to me, immediately, what I did wrong: I should have flipped the pages back to where he'd left them after I'd gone through his files.

The moment he viewed them again himself, if he was paying the slightest attention, he knew that I knew.

"What do you want?" I intone. There's no point feigning normalcy, pretending that this might be a misunderstanding. *A joint posting.* I could laugh that I believed it even for a second. How stupid am I?

"At least let me explain," Kieren says, begs. "My father called me earlier and said NileCorp felt satisfied enough to send me my real directive. I knew nothing prior to this. That addendum was entirely sprung on me—I barely got a word in edgewise."

"Don't lie."

Kieren takes a step forward. I match him at once with a horrified step back, and he falters, freezing where he stands. "I'm not," he rasps. "I'm—"

"What was Weston talking about, then?" I ask. "What about a *secret assignment* that your father hinted to you before we entered Medaluo's server? Tell me it had nothing to do with me. Look me in the eye and tell me he didn't suggest I might be involved with Chung's disappearance."

I'm heaving for breath once my words scatter into the rain. And in the hazy dark, with only the headlights of the bus for any illumination, Kieren stays quiet. Which is all he needs to say to confirm everything.

"I'm going to be sick," I mutter.

"I didn't know," he says faintly. "I couldn't have imagined how severe their accusations were. I assumed there was a memory you were keeping to yourself. A passkey that Chung gave you in your childhood. Something minor that warrants negotiation with NileCorp, not your father being pinned for treason."

"Why did your brief say NileCorp decided to proceed after *receiving your submissions*?" My demands are hoarse. I hardly recognize my own voice. "What have you been sending them?"

Kieren looks down.

"Footage," he whispers. "Your access into the Upsie office. Your reaction to your dad's email."

The betrayal shears away every bit of affinity I had for him.

"All while you were telling me that you think NileCorp took away your dad," I hiss, "you were also jumping when he said *jump*, spying when he said *give NileCorp what they need to punish Lia*." I want to scream. I want to tear into my ribcage and pull out my heart to inspect how it must be shriveling with every passing second. "I trusted you. I thought we were working toward the same thing."

"We *are*." Kieren drags his hands through his hair. Water splatters on either side of him when his arms lower again. He's getting more and more drenched by the minute. "I have no love for NileCorp. I'm not their loyal soldier just waiting for them to lift me out of obscurity. All this time I have stayed obedient among their cadet ranks so that they'll give me some leniency. All I've wanted is to get out of their scrutiny and prove that they brainwashed my father. I was trying to use my bargaining tools carefully."

"Is that what I am?" I fire back. "A bargaining tool?"

"No!" Kieren exclaims. "You're not—it's not—" He stops. "At first it wasn't so different from being at the academy. Keeping an eye on you for a leg up was just another way to win extra points. Then it turned into this. I was trying to figure out how to tell you. How to fix it. I'm sorry."

Kieren suddenly steps out of the rain, into the shelter. He's imploring me to look at him, meet his eyes, but I stay where I am, my arms wrapped tightly around my middle to the point of pain.

"Your trust isn't wasted," he says quietly. "I'm closer to your side than theirs."

"When have we ever been on the same side?"

I'm saying it to hurt him more than I actually believe it. We've been on the same side since our atoms burst into the universe. There is no logic in a world where we possess different instincts. We have been completing the same thought back and forth since the moment we met. We'll continue doing it until we run out of ways to rearrange our tie.

"Then." Kieren takes another step forward. "Now. Always. Competing with you is supposed to make the both of us better. I thought that was what this was. You *have* made me better, year after year, and I won't accept an alternative where that's not true anymore. No matter what NileCorp wants."

My eyes finally snap up, locking Kieren in place. He's come close enough that I could reach forward and touch his shoulder. His face, freckled with rain.

"I just want to know," I intone, "when you agreed to this posting, did your dad promise valedictorian to you?"

What else could justify it? What else but the title we want the most?

Kieren wilts. He says, "I didn't think this would be the exchange."

My world collapses.

I have always understood how my would-be employers operate. NileCorp doesn't care who they upset because their forces are detachable fragments. If they irritate Medaluo in its territories, they claim that it was a few rogue soldiers defying their station. If they're roughing up relations at the border with Cega, it was a unit going behind their superior's back. NileCorp is the hand that pulls the world in line for whatever Atahua wants to do. NileCorp is the armor that absorbs damage from Atahua's enemies, able to be blamed at every moment because we are expendable as its little pieces. We exist to be burned through and discarded. In my years at the academy, I accepted this.

Yet I still thought they'd have sense of some honor. That maybe I could be valued for my hard work.

"I wonder," I say—mildly, colorlessly, "if they ever even considered giving it to me."

"I'm not going to let you be dragged down by any of this," Kieren says firmly. "We'll find out what happened to Chung. Resolve what involvement your dad has. Once it's over, a good posting doesn't only take the top rank. It just takes three recommendation letters and a reliable final exam score. You'll have done your job here."

"Kieren," I say. "None of this is going to be resolved." I breathe out. My eyes are so tired. They flutter closed for a brief moment, and tears fill the corners, trying to relieve the stinging sensation. I open my eyes promptly, lest they gather. No Medan has been the academy valedictorian in recent history. There are only Atahuan faces on the photo boards. "We'll reach the end, and my good scores won't be enough. Recommendation letters won't be enough. If I can't choose my post, they would never place me in Melnova to stay close to my dad. They'll stick me where they need the foreign face. I'll be posted on security, put in the teams sent into the line of fire."

It's not a hypothetical any longer. This is what waits for me.

They were never going to let me have anything else.

"I just want to be Atahuan," I rasp. "I want to be respected. I want to be more than the enemy's face." The rain falls, and it falls, and it falls, and I am as transient as the rivulets. "I suppose it doesn't matter now. They're going to charge my dad with treason."

"Lia."

Kieren's arm lifts. His hand hovers beside me for a moment, idling in the air. With the next gust of the wind, his palm touches my cheek, as gently as a leaf falling onto a still pond.

My anger finds an easy target with Kieren. I can kick and scream at him over the betrayal of his compliance, his role in throwing me to NileCorp. But he's not the one at fault. He's not the idea I'm mourning. I droop forward, my forehead pressing into Kieren's warm collar, and I don't have any more fight left in me. His arms wind into place at once, one hand along my hair and one on my back. He's shaking. He's drenched with the rain. I hardly feel anything other than the pitter-patter of his pulse, pushing through onto my skin.

"We said *May the best cadet win*," I mumble. "But NileCorp doesn't care. There's no fair fight."

Kieren must hear my intention in those words alone. I haven't said anything more before he begs, "Don't, Lia. I need you here."

I wish I were still the person I was an hour ago, when that sentiment would have meant everything. What I wouldn't have given for Kieren to declare that I am an integral part of the work we do, the best of the best. Now it only stings, because it's not enough. If he needs me here, it's so that NileCorp won't dock points from his assignment to get me detained.

I pull away. Though I take only one step back, cold air rushes between us at once, widening the distance with an icy bite.

"If we were to finish this posting together," I say, "you would walk the graduation stage as valedictorian while I'd be held in a back room to process my dad's treason accusations."

"But what are they going to do to you if you leave?" he counters. "You'll be out of NileCorp ranks entirely."

"Tell Rayna I'll message her when she's back in the home server. I'm sorry not to say goodbye."

"*Lia.*"

I open my display and click into the main panel. Past the overlay of my display, Kieren is pleading without words, his hands making fists at his sides.

"It will be more dangerous for you if you do this," he says firmly. "They're going to perceive it as running off."

"I'll be out of your way, at least," I return. "Isn't that all you've wanted? The path to valedictorian cleared?"

"No." A droplet of water falls from his hair. It trails down his cheek. "Lia, no."

"Just *admit* it. It's easiest for you if I'm gone. If I'm pulled into the treason claims too, all the better."

"Don't put words in my mouth," he says harshly. "If that is the cost, I don't want valedictorian. It's not worth it."

I manage a laugh, entirely without humor. I slide along the headings in my display.

"Don't you think I know what you want well enough by now?"

"You don't, Lia."

My vision turns red. Suddenly, I'm furious enough to close my display, all my attention focusing on Kieren.

"Can you at least have the decency not to pretend you care about me—"

"I'm not," he interrupts, "*pretending*."

"You don't have to lie," I snap. "The only reason you're resistant at all is your *guilt*. I'm releasing you from it, Kieren! You're not at fault. You had no choice—fine!"

"Lia—"

"But don't tell me," I go on, "that it's not worth it. Don't tell me to stay if only to relieve your own fault in this."

"That's not it."

"There's no other—"

"I want you to stay where I can see you, where you can't be hurt," Kieren says indignantly, "because I *love* you."

I rock back on my heels. My anger snaps away, entirely engulfed by bewilderment. I blink once, then again, and the rapid motion is uncontrollable enough that my display opens itself up again, ready for use.

"You—what?"

Kieren scoffs. He tips his head skyward, glaring at the shelter above us, the continuous strike of the raindrops.

"I love you," he says again. "I'm sorry. I always have."

It's a bitter, mournful admission. As though there's nothing left to lose, and so he's been permitted to play his last card, knowing defeat waits afterward. I witness it all through a transparent display, my attention focused on my main panel. I have to. Otherwise I don't know what I'd do. I can't stay. I can't.

"Kieren . . ."

"Some part of me has always been aware that my goals are futile. Proving that NileCorp harmed my father isn't as simple as merely getting away from him and into their cyber division. It's an endless staircase to climb afterward, and even the first step sometimes seemed impossible. The only part that was bearable was you. Half my motivation for all of this has always been to stay alongside *you*."

I couldn't speak even if I wanted to. My throat has been scraped raw.

My mind reels, frantic and stumbling over each thought. There's so much to understand at once, and in response I go blank entirely, heading toward one course of action.

"Don't go," Kieren whispers. "Let me help you."

I've long been staring at the red button in the corner. Enough time has lapsed. My display makes the decision for me.

"I'm sorry too."

And I log out.

35

EIRALE

Nik insisted on driving all the way to Wespic without pause.

I tried twice to suggest he would be less likely to crash us and send us into a ditch if we pulled to the side and he rested for a few minutes. Or—wait for it—if he just put on the self-driving capabilities. But Nik refused, so I wasn't going to press any further than necessary. I opted to white-knuckle my way through his shaky steering.

"City boundaries are right up ahead," Nik announces. He reaches forward, wiping away the condensation misting the inside of the windshield.

"Great," I reply. "We're stopping for the night, yes?"

Nik frowns. He says nothing in answer. After a few phone calls earlier that I'd had to operate, we'd drawn out the next steps: Miz and Blare were waiting in Wespic for us, and we would continue onward to Offron together as soon as Nik and I caught up. Miz had a contact in Wespic—she would acquire a method of transport specific to Offron. That way we could drive in without triggering surveillance. At the edges of Medaluo, our excuses need to be totally bulletproof. No reason for a tourist to be out there.

I tap my foot against the carpeting under the passenger seat. I mimic the windshield wipers on the light rain: left, right, left, right.

We'll be arriving well within the deadline Teryn set. I don't know if that means it will be some time before her team swoops in. Whether the tracker in my boot will signal them to act as soon as Nik has what they want. Whether they need to wait for a certain hour when Medaluo isn't watching.

"If you don't get some rest," I say, eyeing how heavily Nik is blinking, "I fear I broke into that pharmacy for nothing."

"Don't exaggerate."

Wespic's entry toll booths appear within view, and Nik starts to decelerate. WELCOME TO THE LAND OF WESTERN PEACE. I find myself bracing, afraid that we'll be stopped again, that another closure will come down and shut us out of Wespic just as we were almost blocked from Threto.

But the automatic arm lifts, registering the car's license plate. In seconds, we're through. I almost can't believe how easy the entry was, shifting in my seat to glare at the arm on the booth as it comes back down. There are no other cars behind us. The road in front is empty too. It gives Nik the permission to speed up again on the asphalt.

We are only hours away from Offron. Which means we're only hours away from the end of everything. From my freedom, one way or another.

"Even a half-hour nap," I say, "would be very beneficial for your health and well-being."

"Instead of showing unnecessary compassion for your kidnapper," Nik counters, "maybe walk through your plan into Kunlun once more to make sure we haven't missed anything."

I'm unmoved. "What happened to not being my kidnapper?"

"I don't know. It's kind of growing on me as a label. Reclaiming it, redefining it, and all that."

The plan into Kunlun is solid. We have the list of log-ins that Blare retrieved in Threto, which includes twenty unique sets of credentials from Kunlun citizens. I like our odds. Out of twenty, it's statistically very likely that we'll have a few where users haven't changed their StrangeLoom passwords since they wrote it somewhere in plain text.

I just need to hope that I'm right about Offron's data center providing a back door without us needing Kunlun's tricky second password.

Nik makes a sharp turn. We've entered what appears to be the city downtown, following a row of blue streetlights that indicate a main path. Wespic isn't under lockdown, but it feels quieter than Threto did even during isolation. I catch a glimpse of a tattoo shop with a cluster of motorbikes parked outside. A late-night soup shop with its lights on.

"Where is everyone?" I ask.

"Everyone moved." Nik brakes, pulling the car onto the side of the street. To our right stands a nondescript building, decorated only with one neon sign: a high-heeled purple boot kicking back and forth.

He pauses a second, considering the empty road. When Nik gets out of the car, I'm quick to follow, closing my door with a louder slam than his.

The only metropolis on this side of Medaluo larger than Wespic is Threto. If even Wespic can't hang on to its civilians, then the smaller urban centers have no chance.

Music floats from inside the purple boot building. There's an archaic sort of atmosphere to Wespic, the sense that the entire city might have been left behind in time. Cobblestone streets and wood-cut pillars hold up the brick roofs; gaslit lamps and the faint smell of sulfur permeate the air. There aren't quite enough people here to justify many bots, and the bots they do bring through tend to break down quickly, tired of the long distances they have to wheel.

It's not so different from Atahua. Short of Button City, Melnova, and Vermillion Bay in the west, it's a land of ghosts downcountry. Everyone who stays will die out, sooner or later.

Nik pushes his glasses up onto the top of his head. He shoulders through the door, holds it open for a beat so I can duck in too.

"Watch your step."

I've already noticed the raised ridge, my foot lifting without my looking down. The space is nearly empty inside, just a bartender cleaning a table in the corner and a few sleeping figures slumped in separate booths. It could have been a very popular nightclub once, given the size of the dance floor. Tonight the music is kept soft enough that I can hear the bartender's glasses clinking across the room. The light-up panels on the dance floor splutter in effort, spinning a few patterns with long pauses in between.

"Come on. Second floor."

Nik goes up the steps first. After a delay, I stride along too, eyeing the sleeping woman closest to the stairs.

The second floor is a StrangeLoom plug-in lounge. It takes me a moment to recognize the setup, the sleeping forms tucked on the plush couches with their eyes closed and a Claw on their head. Miz is curled at the far end, logged in. Blare stands when they see us coming, opening their arms. Nik goes over and, to my surprise, gives them a proper hug.

"I'm not contagious," Blare declares. "Miz got me Eveline from the pharmacy yesterday."

Nik scoffs. "Don't worry, kid. It's an antibody party here."

I walk over slowly, my eyes tracing the unmoving figures. Suddenly the sleeping people downstairs make a lot more sense: they're catching up on some rest before returning to the second floor. Given that they're hourly users for StrangeLoom, sleeping upcountry would be a waste of money. I'd never gone to any of these public lounges in Atahua. Plenty of other NileCorp soldiers did—these arrangements are for people without a port and the necessary wiring installed in their homes, and the base didn't have any on purpose so as not to distract us. Members of my team would ask for nights off to visit a StrangeLoom lounge and go upcountry, see family and friends, attend weddings and special occasions.

I was more untethered than most. During the academy, I had my own Pod on campus to log on monthly, like everyone else. It didn't seem necessary after I graduated. My job was downcountry.

"How's it going?" Nik asks Blare. "How long has she been logged in?"

"Almost an hour. She's on stolen credentials, so she'll have to convince her contact that she's who she says she is."

If she takes any longer, she's probably going to get kicked off by the original user noticing that she's up there. Even if she took the credentials of an hourly user who isn't upcountry all the time, every transaction, every transportation catalog, every message sent is linked to the user's devices downcountry. It takes a single awry two-dollar bus fee before someone is immediately making a stolen identity report. NileCorp is obligated to restore their credentials as soon as the report is filed.

"Wake her up if she's not out in the next ten minutes," Nik says. "We've got to go."

"You do it," Blare replies. "She'll say I'm bothering her."

"She's not going to say you're bothering her."

"Why don't you do it then? Bet you're afraid she'll think you're bothering her."

"*Blare*..."

I turn while they argue back and forth, fighting the urge to look away from the couches and run out of the lounge entirely. This place elicits a peculiar itch in my subconscious, gives me the creeps if I stare too long at any of these ports. It feels unnatural, somehow.

Blare holds up a sack, summoning my attention again. "Also I got the Claws. They're so cheap now."

"NileCorp mass-produces the ones that plug direct-to-port," I say, eyeing the nodes stuck over Miz's temple. "I hear they break the moment you yank it wrong."

As if she can hear us, Miz's eyes fly open. It gives the rest of us a shock, and her expression brightens. I catch her correction. There's a split second when I swear she was about to grin before she wiped it off her face.

"Good. You're here," she says, clearing her throat. "We can get going." She pushes the Claw off and bounces to her feet. As soon as she hands the Claw back to Blare, she's on the move.

While Nik and Blare gather their bags, I have nothing to do except follow Miz down the stairs to the lower level. I fall into step with her. Miz casts me a sidelong glance. I wait for her to say something to explain the inspection, but she remains quiet. It's not quite a glare. It's barely contained excitement, if anything.

"I suppose you found a good method of transport into Offron?"

The sleeping figures down here haven't moved at all.

"It'll do," Miz replies. "I told my friend that we wanted quick over upscale."

She doesn't actually sound all that excited about her success in retrieving a route into Offron. So I suppose it's something else. Whatever program they're finally closing in on. That they'll soon have in their possession.

And as soon as they do, there will be NileCorp helicopters overhead. A whole perimeter surrounded with soldiers and rifles.

I swallow hard. Miz opens the door and glances at me just at the wrong time to catch my expression.

"There won't be any problems," she says when we step out. Nik and Blare are still on the stairs, making their way down. "I made sure of that."

It's fortunate that she provides this excuse for me to seize on to. "You're certain your friend is trustworthy?" I ask, pretending that's what distracted me. "Nik's been active in Atahua for a while. I assume that means you've been with him since the beginning. At minimum, you haven't been present in Medaluo for the last ten months. No time to uphold the connection."

Miz doesn't look bothered. She takes a left, proceeding down the block.

"That's why it's called *friendship*," Miz says. Her tone turns exasperated. "There's nothing to uphold. It just is."

I've successfully derailed her from my reaction, only to stumble into this, and I find myself experiencing a new twist of panic. It's odd. It's nonsensical.

"I apologize. I didn't mean to offend you," I scramble to say.

"You didn't." Miz frowns. She reaches up to smooth her air, mussed from the Claw. "Don't be weird."

My heart thuds beneath my ribs. Wespic is colder than any of the other cities we've been to. Drier too, its air sharp in my nose. I put my hands in my jacket pockets.

I suppose my apology is less about what I've said here. I'm jumping ahead for the inevitable apology I'll owe when NileCorp rushes in.

Miz hurries forward, our conversation over. There's an armored van ahead, and she calls for everyone to hurry up, particularly Nik and Blare, lumbering down the block. I slow to gather a few extra seconds alone on the sidewalk, to think, *think*—

I can't envision any scenario where NileCorp will let Miz and Blare free.

Miz pulls the van's door open. "Courtesy of the Medan government's discontinued junkyard collection," she announces. "Get in."

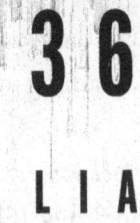

36

LIA

A STRANGE LOOP...
ON A STRANGELOOM...
WELCOME BACK.

The Pod opens its lid, releasing its internal atmosphere with a hiss.

I'm confused for a moment. I've never emerged from the Pod during the dead of night before. Only a freckle of moonlight creeps through the blinds, cast onto the carpet at the foot of my neatly made bed. I haul myself upright with a grunt, easing my head out of the Claw to avoid snagging my hair in the nodes.

"Dad?" I call, though I know he won't be here.

The house is silent. I get out of the Pod, finding my balance. My socks are smooth on the carpet threads. The faint scent of bleach hits my nose as soon as I straighten up. Slowly, I make my way through my room, then open the door into the cold hallway.

There's no responding noise, no shift of the floorboards to signal that the house has acknowledged my return. A digital panel blinks on the wall outside my room, one-half showing the external temperature and another with a monthly display calendar. I don't know what guides my hand to tap the next arrow, browsing through the weeks. I tap the arrow, again, and again, and find one date circled, marking my next reset day, a week before graduation.

I want you to stay where I can see you, where you can't be hurt—

I push Kieren out of my mind firmly. If I digest what he said back there, I'll end up spiraling in circles for hours. I need answers to my questions. Regardless of what he did, what information he sent to NileCorp, it's all done, and every puzzle piece has been shaken out of the box.

I need to put it all together. I logged out for the truth.

"Tamera?" I whisper in the hallway. There's no response. Tamera is usually waiting by my Pod with a cup of tea to warm me up when I emerge for a reset day. But she didn't get any advance notice this time. When our call was cut off, she couldn't have known I'd come offline. She must still be upcountry.

I hurry down the hall.

"Tamera," I say louder, opening her door. If I shake her enough, the StrangeLoom system will register the disturbance and warn her she may like to log out.

I can't see anything in her room at first. The curtains are drawn tightly, the light kept out save for a telltale glow seeping through the bottom of the fabric. A cold sweat breaks along my neck, down my spine.

The room is empty. I don't need light to tell—it's void of noise, void of warmth and any indication that someone sleeps or sighs within the blankets. I march over to the curtains, pushing them open with my breath held. The moon casts the scene bright outside. The fallen tree branch in the yard is gone. It's perfectly tidy by the picket fence, not a leaf out of place. The room drowns in silver too, and when I turn around, I confirm that I was right. Tamera is not here. The bed is made. It hasn't been slept in. Her usual Claw sits unused on her chair.

Where could she *be*?

"*Tamera?*"

My voice bounces through the house. There is no response. If she's still upcountry, maybe she decided to use a port in another room. I pad back into the hallway, opening every door I pass: the closets, the bathrooms. No Tamera, no activity. The overhead chandelier trembles when I hurry down the stairs, its blue dewdrop crystals shivering in sync to my motions. My steps echo on the wooden boards of the ground floor. I walk by the empty living room, the cold marble atrium, and come to the wide front door.

I pull the handle hard.

It doesn't open.

"Warning," the home security system intones, giving me a fright. I swivel fast to trace the voice. It's coming from the panel at the side of the door. The screen shows an external temperature of thirty degrees Fahrenheit. "Please step back from the door. The elements are not suitable for you."

"Open the door," I say. If there's no one here, I'm going right to Melnova. I'll find Dad myself, shake him out of his Pod and demand an explanation to this mess. "Override lock."

"Warning," the system repeats. "Dangerous air levels. It is not recommended to exit."

I've run out of patience.

"Override lock, forced command," I snap. The home system cannot defy that. There's a moment of pause. Then a click sounds in the jamb. I pull the door open.

I'm met with a huge black slab, blocking the entirety of the doorway.

My jaw drops. I can only stare at the object for what feels like a full minute, flabbergasted by its presence. There's not a slit of space I can pry into, the slab perfectly fused to the doorway. When I do snap out of my horror and attempt to push it out of the way, the slab only warps around my hands. Color emerges where I press, like it's a television screen—one of those old models with texture on the surface, making noise if I scratch my nails over it.

I whirl around, marching for the kitchen. My balance has turned entirely awry. I skid on the tiles, almost teetering until I grip the countertop to halt my momentum. There's a knife block nearby; I hurry to yank out the cutlery inside. I lay each knife straight on the counter, lined one after the other like sleeping children tucking into bed. Then I heft the heavy, emptied knife block into my arms. I take it over to the sink, rise onto the tips of my toes to get a good look out the window and into the backyard. Glistening moon, bone-white picket fence.

I fling the knife block at the glass.

And instead of it breaking the window and exploding into the yard, the entire window goes black, just like the front door. With a pitiful clunk, the knife block clatters into the sink.

I think I'm losing my mind.

I don't understand. I can't comprehend what's happening. First I assume something has wrapped around the house. Some government-controlled blockade, restricting my movement. That doesn't explain the view of the backyard disappearing. There one second, blinked out the next.

I have to get out. I have to find Dad.

"Hello?" I return to the front door, prompting the security system. "Please open! Forced command! Override everything!"

"Door is open," the security system reports plainly.

"No, it's not!"

I kick the slab in front of the door. It doesn't move. Again, a discolored mark flashes each time my foot makes contact with the black object. I'm out of options. There's got to be a way to knock it over, get it out of my way. I take a few steps back for a running start.

"Action is not recommended," the security system says.

I sprint at the black block with my full force. There's such a loud *thud* upon collision that my ears seize in protest, but the block does not shift an inch. I'm the one who bounces hard, collapsing on the cold kitchen tiles with my head spinning, my vision going out entirely.

I take a deep breath in. A deep breath out. Moments later, when I've recovered with my entire body throbbing, something immediately doesn't look right, and I turn fast to catch a flicker of light in my periphery. It dances away from me. I turn again, only to focus and realize I'm seeing the translucent drop-down arrow of *my display*.

"What the fuck?" I say out loud.

The realization sets in, heavy as an iron vise wrapping around my throat. I finally have no choice except to hold still and parse through the facts I cannot deny. Running at the blocked door forced a hard reset. It put my display back into my control after it was coded to be hidden.

I'm still upcountry.

37

EIRALE

Endless desert flowers pockmark the side of the road. I watch them fly by with a detached level of curiosity, waiting for the clusters to disappear when the dry plains grow larger in the horizon. They do not. The expressway continues to carry us forward. We've long left behind the elevated structures that passed over cities and towns. Instead the route courses solidly through brown earth and bedrock, the skies perpetually a dusty red shade.

With every mile closer to Offron, a new ripple of adrenaline overflows in my gut and spreads outward. I flex my fingers, then shift my feet. I'm paranoid that Teryn will try to get a message to me. Each time my gaze drifts to the screens on the dashboard, my eyes skate away in a fit before I shake myself back to reality, knowing there is nothing she could possibly use that Nik wouldn't see.

Nik has grown quiet too. The dashboard map shows our location as a blinking red dot, the armored van crossing the long stretch between Wespic and Offron. At a certain point, Miz leaned over to ask Nik about two route options—one that was quicker and one that avoided the tolls scanning outside the city of Hibond—and Nik didn't hear her until she thudded his shoulder with the back of her hand.

Nik and Blare are decrypting the two server boxes at the back of the van. I couldn't begin to parse what they're doing, three laptops open, disk readers and drives and wires in abundance on the floor. Miz sleeps at the driver's seat, having set the vehicle on manual self-driving so she'd be able to take over if the alarm beeps at her. Downcountry roads are not forgiving in these parts.

I loll my head back and forth. I shift in my seat to face the side, and then Nik has appeared in my periphery, his brow furrowed while he stares at his laptop screen.

I would be lying if I said a part of me isn't considering reneging my mission. A small part, a fanciful part, but a part, nonetheless. It's only natural. I put so much effort into getting Nik Grant here, so I don't want to give him up at the end. Farmers must feel this way raising their piglets for slaughter. But the supply chain must still be fed. Criminals need to answer for their warrants of arrest. Soldiers do as their employers say.

I turn in my seat properly. Blare has nodded off since I last checked, lying on the floor. Their mouth gapes open.

Maybe there's a way to sneak Blare away before Teryn brings in her team. I could kidnap them. Blare wouldn't even know what was happening if I blindsided them and shoved them into a self-driving car headed for Upsie.

Miz jolts in her sleep. I look to her, asleep with the frown lines between her brow smoothed out, and I have to tighten my fists to avoid twitching. NileCorp soldiers surrounding us. NileCorp soldiers taking them away. I can't keep thinking down this track. I shouldn't feel like this.

I tap the back of my seat, getting Nik's attention.

"Hey."

Nik types a few more commands before looking up. Light from the screen drapes the planes of his face, each line a harsh mark.

"You see something?" he asks.

"No," I say. "Something occurred to me."

Nik only raises an eyebrow, prompting me to continue. I point over to the server boxes he's peeled open and undressed.

"These were stored in national data centers. Property of the Medan government."

"Medaluo's largest computing power provider is the government," Nik counters, turning back to his screen. "Plenty of companies enter into contracts to use the facilities. Not everything is the property of the Medan government."

The government can certainly access everything if they own the facilities, though.

"In any case," I continue, "you already said the corruption exploit belonged to the Medan government."

Nik narrows his eyes. He keeps his focus on his screen. "What are you getting at?"

"I'm just musing about our final destination." My eyes dart to the dashboard map again. It's currently showing a preview to Offron. "Kunlun is private territory. That's the only reason the International Assembly allowed it to remain as a virtual space. They would have erased it if Medaluo tried to claim sovereignty over the city. Other nations would also take tremendous issue if the Medan government was allowed to access decrypted information feeding out from it. That's why we have to enter Kunlun and can't just steal from Offron's servers, right?"

Nik finally shifts, his laptop sliding off his lap. It takes the light off his face, softens his features instantly. He considers the matter. I haven't spoken anything untrue. Medaluo is the one who hosts Kunlun, but they have no jurisdiction there.

"Your point being . . . ?"

"My point being what sort of Medan program is split in thirds across Upsie, Threto, and *Kunlun*?"

Nik stills. His eyes dance away. This is not a question he was prepared for.

"Nik," I prompt when he stays quiet. "What are we walking into? If you don't tell me, I can't prepare accordingly."

"It's nothing unreasonable," Nik replies. "The three files are purely data, so they can be stored downcountry or upcountry. At least we're certain the third one won't be encrypted because it'll already be loaded and ready to go upcountry."

"That still doesn't answer my question about how it ended up there."

He pulls his laptop closer. Acts like he needs to concentrate on his screen. "File storage diversity."

I bristle. The armored van bumps up against a series of rocks on the road. We jostle, the wires and disks clanging at the back, but Blare continues sleeping.

"Prepare me, Nik," I say evenly. "Or else we're doomed to fail."

"No."

I think I've misheard for a moment. That surely he wouldn't be difficult for the sake of it.

But that's exactly what he said.

"Excuse me?"

"I said no. Worry about getting us up there. Then we can talk about what we're looking for."

"This is absurd." At this point in time, it can't be that Nik doesn't trust me yet. We have had too many close calls, too many mutually beneficial exchanges for his reluctance to be anything personal. It also can't be that he's *lost* his trust in me. If he suspected the tracker in my boot, he would have long pried it out, long confronted me about it and threatened my life. "You can't possibly believe I'm better off in the dark."

Nik's gaze shifts over, as hard as steel. He does believe it, that look tells me. He believes it enough to stand by his answer.

"Remember," he says, "that you still don't know what happened to cause your memory loss."

I stop. Finally, he acknowledges that my void of memories has something to do with our current undertaking. This is the first admission I've gotten from him that confirms I was here, I knew him, something *happened*.

"What do you mean?" I ask. Each word comes delicately. Like I could scare him off if I ask something without removing the sting first. "That I got into trouble because of these answers?"

"I didn't say that."

"This doesn't make any sense." I keep pushing. "Whether or not I remember my last time in Kunlun won't change where we go now."

"Or maybe," Nik says, "you'll refuse to go if you know."

Again, the image of what awaits at the end of this task flashes before my mind. Line after line of diligently trained soldiers. A capture team won't be enough. They're going to bring more numbers if they've traveled this far. Lights beaming down on us, Nik's every angle surrounded.

I can't back out. I can't.

"Are we doing something morally evil?" I ask. I want him to say yes.

"No," he answers in an instant.

"Hurting anyone?" *Say yes. Make my duplicity worthwhile.*

"The opposite. It's supposed to help people."

Then either something doesn't add up, or he's not telling me the truth. *Forget it.* I turn to face the front again.

The van drives into rougher terrain. I cross my arms and my legs, glaring daggers at the red dot on the map. For several minutes I clear everything from my mind save the present moment. I will not think about Kunlun. I will give no consideration to what happens after.

Then I feel a presence behind me, and I glance up. Nik has come to hover at my shoulder. He sighs when our eyes meet. Reluctantly, so much so that I can see him physically fighting to lift his arm despite his displeasure, he passes me a handheld. It already has a briefing loaded on it, low resolution and clearly copied from someone else's device, marked CONFIDENTIAL.

"You asked what this program is," Nik says. "It's called Project Wit.

Memory backups were left in Upsie and Threto. There's one more file in Kunlun, in the creator's house."

I swipe through the pages. Before I've fully understood what exactly I'm seeing on the page, Nik says:

"Together, it's a creation of sentient AI."

3 8

LIA

"Hello?" I bellow.

I spin around the room, searching desperately for hidden cameras, for some indication that I'm being made victim to the world's worst prank. I find nothing. Everything looks as it should—like the stale, undecorated house that Dad owns in downcountry Haven State. The same house I always come to for my reset days.

"This isn't real," I whisper under my breath. Someone must have hacked me. They must have changed my automatic routing, and instead of safely logging out, I was pulled into another layer of upcountry where they re-created my house. Where they have trapped me.

Or, a small voice says, *this has never been real.*

"Come on," I say to myself. It's an instruction, a plea. There must be some explanation to this, and I'll see it when I work through the panic. Maybe I'm deep in the throes of Wakeman Syndrome right now. None of this is actually happening, and I'm only questioning the nature of my reality enough to vividly hallucinate a blockage over my door and upcountry's display over my eyes again.

How would it make sense otherwise? How could someone know what my house in Haven looks like to trap me here? How could they know every detail down to the softness of the carpet threads and the way they turn slightly rough on the stair landing where I once spilled a carton of yogurt?

Hesitantly, I try to control my display. It responds as quickly as it would when I'm in regular upcountry. When the messaging panel opens, though, it's empty. The contacts are similarly blank. As much as this resembles my usual display, I can't connect to a thing; nor can I find my usual shortcuts. I'm cut off entirely.

My local downloads are the only section that stays accessible. I open the files one by one, locating where I was last reading. I don't know if I would be capable of hallucinating this.

"No. No no no—"

I close everything in a hurry, not wanting to look at it. The moment I go back to my general display, I realize there's a new sidebar to this version, with far more options in the core function panel. It's listed like a computer would be.

> System Settings.
> Recent Items.
> Sleep.

And at the very bottom ... *Force Wipe*.

"This isn't real," I insist aloud. "None of this is real!"

Haven't I seen the front door open? Haven't I watched Dad come in before?

The harder I think, the more tenuous my own memories feel. I recall Dad coming up the stairs in earlier years. I recall occasions when I was sitting at the alcove and Dad poked his head in to see how I was doing. But I can count on one hand the number of days I've spent time with him in this house, and I have never stepped foot outside to greet him. Since I started at the academy, our hours downcountry never overlap anymore. He'd visit me at the academy and take me to lunch in Button City. If there was some event he wanted me to attend with him, I logged out of school without leaving my Pod, then logged into upcountry again by selecting the District of Melnova on the map, appearing at the Capitol's landing station, where he would be waiting to greet me. Then we would go to his office or the Melnova apartment near the Capitol. Of course I haven't once stepped foot out of this door, in this house. *Why would I?*

In a panic, I start to run, needing to return to my Pod, go somewhere there will be people I know, even if it's Nile Military Academy. I take the stairs three at a time, moving with such haste that I stumble on the last one. My knee bends, striking down; my palms land hard to catch myself, but it doesn't stop me from sliding back against two of the steps, my whole body dragging on carpet. At once, the friction burns harshly on my palms, and when I look at my hands, there is blood beading to the surface.

I freeze where I am. Slowly, I raise my left hand only an inch in the night's shadows, watching the droplets form.

I'd thought that drawing blood in the bathroom on my last reset day was evidence to contradict my paranoia. I'd thought it meant that I was flesh, organic matter, made of something real. Foolish of me, I suppose, to think that it would be that easy to peel apart the facade. As though an engine as adept as StrangeLoom would be clumsy enough not to hide the seams.

I don't register that I'm crying until I see the tears landing on the carpet in front of me, staining a picture into the threads. I remember being five years old. I remember crying on the playground of elementary school because I felt so overwhelmed, eight years before I would start at Nile Military Academy, before I received the highest score possible in the entrance exam. I have memories of an entire childhood. I've lived so many years being real.

So how can this *be*?

"Please," I sob. "Please, there has to be an explanation."

Nothing comes. No clarity, no relief. There is only me in an empty house, in the middle of an empty world.

• • • •

I must spend hours lying there on the stairs, waiting for something to happen.

The moonlight fades. The sun rises. A new day seeps through the windows I haven't broken, and I am too afraid to shatter more in case there is nothing behind them all. Stuck forever in a house is one thing. Stuck forever in a house of perpetual darkness is another.

At some point when it seems rather silly to be sprawled on the stairs in the middle of the day, I get up. One slow step after the other, I finish climbing the stairs and return to my room, stopping in the doorway. I made such a big fuss about logging out; I need to do something with this time. Even if I'm not actually logged out.

This room has never been a space that felt like mine, but now the sight is more foreign than I thought possible. The bed I do not sleep in. The floors I do not walk. The room wasn't supposed to feel like a place for living because I *didn't* live here, but how was I to know it wasn't real at all?

I try not to look at my Pod initially, intent on investigating the house and pinpointing exactly where I am, what has occurred. I can't keep my gaze averted for long, and I gravitate right back toward the urge to step in, flee to what I know, pretend none of this happened. The Pod brought me here. No matter what plane of reality we're in, it must have the ability to take me away again.

I stop directly before it, my hands hovering over the half-open cover. The polished surface curves at the head and the feet, making rounded edges on both ends. I follow the insulated wires that trail out from the underside of the Pod and locate the port in the wall, near the air vent.

"Don't break it," I warn myself. I ease my nails under the protective cover of the port, pulling at the plastic. It doesn't budge for a second. I shift into a crouch and tug hard. Then the plastic cover comes off with the wires stuck in the center. If it had been plugged into the wall, the plastic would have slid along the wires, looped through them like a bracelet.

Instead, there's no port beneath the plastic, nothing except for smooth wallpaper. It's no different from the windows. Everything is merely an illusion.

Which means that the Pod doesn't even *work*.

I throw the plastic onto the carpet, letting the wires tangle up in their useless bundle. Each time I get into this Pod, it's only for show. I haul the cover open properly and tap the back where the screen is, and it lights up despite not being plugged in. It lights up because it's never been the Pod taking me upcountry. I've always already been *here*.

So how do I get out?

I blink hard. The main panel of my display returns.

> System Settings.
> Recent Items.
> Sleep.

My breath shudders. I hover over *System Settings* and can't make myself press down on the option. I don't want to know what exists in the metadata that runs my avatar. I don't want to have to face the truth if it tells me what is becoming clearer and clearer. Dad told me I was only anxious. Even the feed offered me a real illness that explained why I couldn't understand the nature of my reality—why I always felt as though I were floating above everything like a ghost, something incorporeal that never truly touched the people around it.

System Settings opens itself anyway. I've been staring at it for too long. The first two lines are familiar. My credentials have always been listed in the profile section of my usual display.

Everything beneath is entirely new.

> User ID: #204007012058051774021
> Password: numberoneforever

Property of the Mercy Labs, 208 M Street, The
Independent Virtual Territory of Kunlun

Citizenship: Medaluo
Date of Birth: 2040-07-01

Citizenship: Kunlun
Date of Acquisition: 2040-07-01
Entry Password: [Machine is to logic as wordplay is to ___]

    I want to throw up. I want to scream. I want to tear apart this house brick by brick only to see what is underneath and learn why they have put me in here.

    But I do none of those things. If I want answers, it's clear where I need to go.

    I clamber into the Pod, slamming the cover shut over me. I don't bother with the Claw, don't bother settling properly into the headrest. If I were truly downcountry, I would need these processes to obtain access, but this must be a rendered shortcut, some pathway for me to jump across spaces in upcountry.

    I tap the screen hard to trigger the map, then drag it over to Medaluo, hunting down Offron. I've seen the videos—I know how my favorite influencers activate their access to Kunlun. They double-tap Offron, and that tells the Pod they would actually like to access Kunlun, not upcountry Offron. A window pops up, asking for a second password.

    I breathe hard, gritting my teeth. Then, letter by letter, I enter w-i-t.

    "Come on," I mutter. "Come on—"

· · · ·

It spits me onto the street with a lurch, my shoulder crunching hard on the pavement.

I barely have the time to brace and stop myself from rolling right onto the road. A car speeds past.

"Hey!"

I flinch, swiveling at my waist. A young boy stands a few paces away on the sidewalk, holding the leash to a cat. He's dressed in overalls, a luxury brand label stitched on the ankle cuff.

"You appeared out of thin air!" he bellows. "Mommy lied! She said no one can appear outside of landing stations."

"Shh, shh," I urge, hurrying to my feet. "I didn't appear out of thin air. I, um, I'm a magician trainee. I can't explain my tricks, okay? It would be betraying the league."

The boy blinks. "Oh. I understand."

"Good. Good." I dust off my elbows. We're at the intersection of a busy street, the signs reading H ST one way and 12TH AVENUE in the other. A public park stretches to the left. A group is throwing a Frisbee.

Disorientation doesn't even begin to cover the feeling. I may still be hallucinating.

"Are you lost?" the boy asks now. "From your magic league?"

"Yes." I clear my throat. "I'm looking for M Street. Can you take me there?"

The boy nods. He turns on his heel immediately, his small shoes squeaking on the pavement. On the leash, the cat is well behaved, hastening to walk too. "Mommy taught me the grid when I was *five*. I can't believe you don't know it."

"I'm new." There are birds flying overhead. The smell of spring rustles from the green trees lining the street side. Kunlun is so *clean*. It was designed entirely by scratch—its grid perfectly measured, each block aligned. Twenty-six streets across and thirty avenues long. The edges of Kunlun bleed off into forestry in every direction. If someone finds themselves trekking into the trees, they'll walk for a mile and find themselves emerging at the other end. A self-contained world, connected like a miniature globe. I can't stop gawping. Smooth concrete under my feet. Blue skies above.

"Where's your mom anyway?" I ask.

"At work," the boy answers. "She gives us the news in our heads."

I have to assume that means his mother is a newscaster he can watch on his display. During their first few years upcountry, children are given simplified versions of a full display, ones they can understand. It's hard to remember how we used to see virtual before we even had a developmental grasp on the world itself. Watching the news really is having the image in our heads.

I assume they simplified my display too, during my childhood years. Perhaps I'm wrong to believe they eventually gave me back all my controls.

"Here." The boy stops a few blocks down, pointing at the sign. M ST.

"Thank you," I say. "It was lovely to meet you."

The boy skips away without a response. His cat doesn't complain about being tugged along, toddling quickly after him on its paws.

Left alone, I start making my way down the street, examining the numbers on each of the buildings. There are plenty of pedestrians who pass by on the pavement, some talking on an active call in their displays, others zoning out to finish typing a message, their arms pumping high in their exercise clothes.

I walk by a massage parlor at 180 M Street. Then several residences. Quaint town house buildings segmented for cafés and tutoring centers. There are far more children here than I would have expected. A preschool is letting out at 206 M Street, releasing new entrant five-year-olds to the arms of their waiting parents. I weave through the crowd, coming to a stop in front of the building directly beside it.

208 M Street. It's a small, nondescript house. There's no signage that declares it to be the Mercy Labs, nothing that tells me I've landed at the right place except a circular fixture on the exterior wall that resembles a robotic eye. For all I know, this could be a family owned optometrist.

Still, I walk up to the front door, my shoes kicking the small pebbles of the footpath. The gold knocker is worn. I forgo it entirely, using my knuckles on the blue-painted wood.

I listen to the footsteps inside. Even, steady echoes, coming closer and closer to the front atrium.

Chung Yin opens the door.

He stares at me. I scramble for something to say, for a way to explain myself, to offer enough that he'll understand my desire for answers. But he beats me to it.

"Lia," Chung says. "I've been waiting for you. Come in."

39

EIRALE

"Soldier, did you hear anything I said?"

I start to attention, whipping my gaze back to Nik.

"Sorry," I say. "Again, please?"

Nik, shockingly, doesn't show any displeasure at my absentmindedness. He makes no snide remark, does not shake his head to remind me that I'm working for him to save my own skin. He must know how much his answer has shaken me, and though hours have passed and we are rapidly nearing our destination, I am no closer to digesting the nature of our mission.

Sentient AI.

"I was saying," Nik tries again, "that Blare has to stay behind to continue decrypting the drives. There's no more remote access past this point, so it shouldn't be a problem. As long as you're able to handle inserting the credentials."

"Yes," I say. "Yes, I can handle that."

Once we've infiltrated Kunlun and obtained the final file, there will be no going back. It's not only Nik accessing the program. Project Wit. *That's* what NileCorp is trying to swoop out from under him.

My first, selfish thought is that they won't need me anymore. This is going to alter the landscape of the world. Why hire private forces when they have a system that can access anything from anyone? Why dole out human security when they can stop any conflict before it happens?

Under any regular person, it's a terrifying weapon that can be used to incite vast change.

Under NileCorp, it will make them unstoppable.

I shiver, trying to draw my jacket tighter.

"Here." Nik hands me a printout. A piece of paper with two columns. The log-ins. "Just follow me closely. I've got the route mapped. Offron's facility is the most complex of all of them."

I nod my understanding, scanning the printout. The van bumps, and I scramble for balance, merely hovering upright at the back while Nik and Miz pack their equipment. When it smooths out, I duck to look out the windshield, but there's not much to see in Offron. The main roads are less places of living and more routes to get deeper into the city, where streets will branch off into pathways, and pathways extend a long, long route before reaching separate houses, protected by their own walls and turrets. Offron's population count isn't high enough to justify taller buildings. There are a few that house government facilities, towers where military officials live for a better view over their bases in the distance.

"Hey." Miz hands me a ski mask, the holes for the eyes cut as small as possible and the opening for a mouth no larger than a slit. "Wear this. Facial recognition will log you instantly otherwise."

I slip it on. The material is tight, scratchy, but I don't complain. Nik says something softly to Miz, and then she takes the bag he gives her, nodding. The armored van must be parking, finding a spot at the side of the road. The moment we come to a full stop, Miz doesn't waste a second. She palms the handle of the back doors and runs out. The wind is howling. An enormous gust swirls into the van before doors shut again, securing with a click.

"Wait," I exclaim. My voice comes out muffled under the ski mask. I have missed more than I thought in my daze. "Where is she going?"

"Planting bombs," Nik answers candidly. He tugs his own covering on.

His appears looser, but that's likely because it's been so often used. "The only way we're getting in is if another part of the facility is being attacked at the same time."

He pulls his bag onto his shoulders. The clanking inside tells me he's carrying the Claws. I mirror his stance, and for the first time during this entire endeavor that Nik Grant has dragged me on, I am sickeningly out of my depth, scrambling to keep my head above water. It is only him and me entering the City in the Cloud, then. Only two credentials out of the twenty.

The printout crinkles in my pocket when I put it away. I meet Nik's eyes.

"Remember that you insisted knowing the details wouldn't impact your participation," he says softly.

Except I was wrong, clearly. What we finish retrieving in Kunlun will set incomprehensible technology loose on the world. It'll change Atahua; it'll change the cold war. It'll give NileCorp the all-access power to do whatever it wants. How can I give them that?

"I can see you thinking," Nik goes on. "Cut it out. Don't do that."

I try to sneer, but my mask restricts all my movement. "Nice one. *Don't think.*"

"I mean it."

Before I can offer another retort, there's a series of booms, far louder than I was expecting. I almost want to stop and take cover, but then Nik is opening the back doors, yelling, "All right. Move it!"

"Good luck!" Blare calls.

My breath stuck in my throat, I follow Nik out, braced for the worst. There's nothing on fire yet, though the wind has taken on a furious intensity. The Outer Frontier National Data Center is made of multiple wings across a large rocky space. There is smoke to the west, but night is setting in fast, tamping down the appearance of trouble. Nik is already cutting through a chain-link fence. He's quick to lift the corner, signaling for me to go.

Gunfire, off by the west side of the facility. Nik catches up quickly and brushes my elbow when he passes, tilting his head to indicate we're going around the second building that comes within view. It's no larger than a hut, the rounded walls made of metal. I suspect the material must be thick enough to prevent anyone from breaking their way in by cutting a path. Nik places a small pouch onto the locked door panel, balancing it on the curve of the handle. He glances over his shoulder, counting a few seconds after there is shouting at the other end of the facility. As though he's cued them into action, another series of explosions rocket from west to east, the sounds piercing my eardrums.

Nik hurries to cup his hands around a lighter, protecting the flame from the wind. It wavers a few times before latching on to the pouch, licking up the side of its plastic. With a sudden spark, the pouch burns into the handle and drops to the ground, having eaten a path through the lock panel. Nik kicks the door open.

As instructed, I stay close behind him, mimicking his steps. I pin my eyes to Nik in the dark, making no attempt to memorize our way through or mark my bearings. There's only the sound of our breathing here, irregularly matched to the clatter of our steps. Nik pauses for a moment at a corridor split.

The booms have stopped.

Nik inclines his head, and then he's running again, taking the left curve. We dash quickly through the facility, on and on until two right turns bring us to an atrium that ends with a large steel door. My steps are ginger when I stop, but the atrium is entirely still. Nik settles another pouch on the lock and performs the same maneuver, flicking his lighter.

"Close your eyes."

I follow his instructions, turning my face away from the flash. He's on the move before I know to open my eyes, and instead of wasting time telling me, Nik only grabs my wrist, urging me down the narrow stairwell.

It's not one flight down, as Upsie's server room was. This is a spiraling stairwell, descending down and down and down so far that I am dizzy by the time my feet hit solid ground again. Before I can slow and embrace the urge to gag from a wave of nausea, Nik is hissing to keep moving, that we don't have much time before the facility knows we're here.

It's dark underground. The corridor uses the same emergency exit floor lighting that hotels are so fond of, a row of red beading along either side of the linoleum tiles. There are multiple doors on both sides of the corridor, placed in close succession to one another. We bypass them all, heading for the very end of the space, where the shadows have camouflaged a right turn, descending deeper along a ramp.

I'm struggling to catch my breath. It doesn't seem like there are any cameras, so on the next turn when we slow, I lift my ski mask the slightest bit, exposing my mouth. Somehow, Nik notices my move immediately and reaches over to tug my mask back down.

"There are night-vision sensors. Don't do that."

"I'm suffocating."

"We're almost there. Kunlun's servers are stored in the coldest part of the facility."

I suppose with the amount of energy running a virtual city takes, they need foolproof cooling equipment. We keep going farther and farther—my ears pop when we round a corner, and then Nik marches straight for a door. He doesn't bother burning past the handle this time. There's a side panel instead, and he takes the fence clippers out of his bag, jamming the metal straight into the glass. A terrible noise screeches to signal malfunction, and he kicks the door open.

"Start typing," Nik instructs, sliding his bag off his shoulder. "I'll find maintenance ports."

My breath is lodged in my throat. In my chest. Ballooning into a tumor and turning acrid inside of me.

There are two central screens in the small room. I go to the controller on the left, pulling open a window to start working. I don't have the interface of a Pod here, nor the StrangeLoom code, where double-tapping Offron on the map will activate a window that shortcuts access to Kunlun. I only have raw Kunlun beneath my fingertips, entirely separated from StrangeLoom's display. Without their interface, there's nothing intuitive about what I'm looking at. I search through the tabs, looking for some entrance point. I have to remember that these controllers are here for maintenance. If a technician was running an inspection, they would have to log in somewhere.

I navigate into View, wondering where the tester function is hiding. Kunlun citizens can enter from the Pods because Kunlun's independent governing body made an agreement with NileCorp to install the access route on the StrangeLoom system. When data engineers run improvements here, they'd have to use their own StrangeLoom credentials too. There's no chance Kunlun doesn't mandate a tracking system, some way of recording every user poking their head into their city.

I hit the right series of commands and find a tester portal. The window loads a StrangeLoom page, asking for a user ID and password.

"I've got it!" I bellow.

"Give me a second," Nik replies. His head pokes around from the other end of a tall shelf. "I've found a port for this, but I don't see how the rack connects back to the central controller."

I peer over the central screen. There's a thick loop of wires stemming from the main box, streaming along the floor and then plugged into the rack at the very end.

"There," I say, pointing to the ends of the wires. "Unplug it and move it to this rack."

Nik nods, hurrying to yank them over. I go to the second screen, performing the same series of commands to find my way onto the tester portal. The moment I see Nik plugging in the Claws and activating their node function, I pull the list of credentials from my pocket, holding the paper close to the screen's light. The first few combinations of user IDs and passwords don't work. By the seventh error upon attempting to log in, I'm getting worried. A cold sweat breaks down my neck.

"Did you activate one?" Nik asks from the racks.

"No, I think that was the building shaking," I mutter. I try number ten. Error. "Look, if this doesn't work, I think maybe we need to bring Blare down and—"

The pop-up disappears on the screen. It worked. Number twelve on the list of credentials is valid. I allow myself one beat to scan the screen, confirm that the fuzzy image is definitely Kunlun's rendering, ready for someone to enter with the Claw and see the full photorealistic picture. Then I go back to the first screen and continue down the list.

Number fifteen works too.

Nik watches me put the printout back in my pocket. "We're in?"

"We're in," I confirm. I pull my ski mask off entirely. Within these shelves, I have to assume that we're in a blind spot for camera functionality. "Ready for access."

Nik pulls his ski mask off too. He's as serious as a funeral pyre. Posture dead straight, shoulders pulled taut. He hands me a Claw.

"After you."

A shiver runs down my spine. I'm hesitant to reach for the Claw, my fingers suddenly stiff and cold where they weren't before. When I take it, a pang emits from the base of my head. It's not quite pain. Just a peculiar sort of revulsion. I touch my hairline, trying to trace its source, and it's perfectly where my chip should be. The very item that allows my connection to upcountry when I put this device on.

"Is everything okay?" Nik prompts.

I nod quickly. No feeling is strong enough to counter my desire to get into Kunlun. To finally return to a location I can't remember. Despite my increasing waves of dread, I take a seat where I'll be able to lean against the server rack, and I put the nodes over my head.

"See you up there," I say.

I close my eyes.

40

LIA

I step into Chung Yin's house, an unsteadiness shaking through my knees as though I am a fawn newly birthed from the womb.

It smells like fresh baking. Without speaking, Chung closes the door, then gestures for me to follow him through the living room. The afternoon is warm, sunlight heavy along the backs of the armchairs. A fur throw has been left at the foot of the couch. A golden retriever snoozes within its soft fabric.

"That's Dou Dou," he says. "He's two years old."

I eye the dog. I can't find it within myself to summon any affection.

"He's not real," I say.

Chung casts me a careful look. I'm not entirely sure how to read it. We enter his kitchen. He gestures for me to sit at the table, a small square surface. The top is painted green. The legs are painted an overripe banana's yellow. If he lives here, he must live alone—there are no signs of other occupants. One set of running shoes by the door. One jacket dangling from the coatrack.

I slide out one of the ladder-back chairs, taking a seat. They're similarly painted, split green-yellow between the surface and the legs.

"I'm sure," Chung starts, putting the kettle on, "you have many questions."

We've been speaking Medan since I stepped through the door, but now he switches to Atahuan. If it weren't for the physical evidence in front of me, I might think I was suddenly speaking to my dad. Their cadences are nearly identical—the sort of mannerisms that develop over time, over the critical years when someone is deciding who they are. I wouldn't have picked up on this when I was younger, but now I wonder how long Dad and Chung really have known each other, whether they might have met earlier than I thought.

Dou Dou pads over, whining in question. Chung clicks his tongue at the dog. He reaches for a mitt while the kettle boils, bringing out a baking tray of treats from the oven.

I'm initially unresponsive. Chung shakes the treats into the dog bowl in the corner.

Somehow, where I end up starting is: "You're missing."

"Yes, I suppose that's what the news is saying, isn't it?"

"What is that supposed to mean?" I draw my knees up to my chest. "How can you be missing? They should see your user ID active in Kunlun's servers."

Chung sets down the tray, then grabs a towel hanging from his oven. It's stitched with lotuses along the edges.

"They can't see my user ID in Kunlun's servers because I asked to be hidden."

He is exceedingly nonchalant. The kettle clicks to signal it has finished boiling. Chung reaches for it.

"Coldwire," I say. "You made it with the ability to hack StrangeLoom and rewrite its code. You asked it to go in and hide you."

"Correct."

I pause. Then, "Did you make me too?"

That's what I ask. Not *what am I*. Not *what did you do*. I want to clarify the matter of ownership first.

"I coded you," Chung says. His hand is steady as he pours water into the teacups. "I renamed you. But I suppose I didn't actually *make* you."

"You're speaking in riddles." Every element of this final posting has slotted into place only because of Chung's doing. From the moment they assigned me this task to my arrival on his doorstep. "You were the one who wanted me here, weren't you? You deleted Operation Coldwire. You made yourself go missing. And you plastered *my* digital signature across the entire mess."

Chung sets my tea down in front of me, on top of a coaster. Beyond the kitchen window, a yard stretches behind the property, growing neat rows of flowers. I catch a glimpse of climbing string beans too, wrapped around one of the wooden support beams.

"Yes," he says, taking a seat. "It was a lure. I know how NileCorp likes to operate. I went to the academy too. It's where I met your parents."

He says "your parents." As though Dad remains my father after he's lied to me all my life. As though I should have some claim to Mallory, who I don't even remember.

"Dad never told me he went to the academy," I say.

"He had it scrubbed eons ago. The academy was younger then, so it was easier to withdraw the files. Bad look for a politician when his attendance wasn't mandatory." Chung pushes the cup of tea toward me. I don't move to take it. "We did our postings back then just as you do them now. I knew that if NileCorp perceived something relevant emerging about a cadet, they would look into it. Forgive the subterfuge."

The banners that showed themselves to me. The errors left in the metadata that meant only I could access his spaces.

"So what was it all supposed to be?" I ask. "Some *test*?"

"Yes. I was testing you. And NileCorp was testing me."

Chung, slowly, drinks from his own cup of tea. While my legs keep shaking up and down, he is the very picture of relaxation, taking a break during a busy afternoon spell. I'd believe he were a parent who'd just fetched a child from the preschool next door and was now getting the dinner started.

"Do you know what a cold wire is?" he asks after a moment. "It's the return route in a power supply. The opposite to the surging hot wire. It's not a real kick-start itself. It's just the mechanism to loop energy back to the source. Coldwire has the capacity to do anything to StrangeLoom. But you still need to know how to direct it." Chung swirls his teacup. "An organic mind like mine can't truly interface with it. I can only speak to the program like a chatbot assistant. It's hard to make changes when you have to understand what exactly you're kick-starting first, isn't it?"

"As opposed to what?" I ask slowly, though I know already. "What's the alternative?"

"Coldwire was built to interface with what I started in Atahua. The project that NileCorp shut down."

Dou Dou barks, finished with the treats. Chung waves the dog off to play in the living room. I finally reach for my tea, taking a sip to order my thoughts. It's warm on my palms. Bitter on my tongue.

"My dad said you performed a miracle." I put the cup down. "The email you left in the floppy disk. You wanted me to see it."

"I did," Chung says shortly. "I wanted you to see how he behaved when we first started. That way you can't accuse me of making up stories if what I'm about to tell you has such disparity to his current attitude."

It's not safe. You should have told me this had to do with Chung. I would have never let you be sent after him.

"You wouldn't know it now," he goes on, "but in the earliest years of the cold war, it felt like Atahua had limitless money to spend on technological research. Whoever ruled upcountry ruled the world: you know the catchphrase. Project Wit was one such research project. It could only be simulated, our findings written about. But I thought it had the potential to be so much more." Chung sets his teacup down too. "A few years into my work, I had clearly hit a wall. It wasn't that my supervisors didn't like my research. It was that they didn't like my name. Investors could see the appeal of the project, but they didn't want to put my face on television if they went wide with it." He scratches the side of his chin, his hand lingering. I understand the gesture, the casual motion. It's the instinct we have to shrink in front of a crowd, hopeful that maybe the Atahuans won't care just this once that we look so wildly different. "When an agent of the Medan government reached out with an offer to work for them under the table, I took it. They told me I should think of it as a boon for science. That they were just benefactors in the pursuit of knowledge. It wasn't political."

There is nothing in our current landscape that is no longer political. Even the color of a someone's shoes is political.

"You couldn't have believed that."

"Of course not, Lia. My generation may not have been born into the cold war as you were, but it did begin during our most formative years. I knew what it meant. I knew it was treason—I couldn't have fooled myself if I tried. So I began living a double life. I made the pretense of working downcountry in the day and then came here every night to perform my real research. Medaluo bought me citizenship to Kunlun. They figured it was safer ground to be double-crossing my government if I wasn't actually on enemy territory."

The oven rang to signal that it was still on. It was warming up the kitchen. Sweat pricked at the small of my back.

"Did my dad know?" I ask.

Chung gets up. He returns the kettle, then hunches over to switch off the oven.

"No," he says. "Not at first. Not until Eirale got sick."

Eirale. Up until I saw it in Kieren's second briefing, I hadn't even known her name.

"Project Wit started as a study. We weren't targeting StrangeLoom yet, though the investors were certainly eyeing NileCorp as a source of funding. Wit was just a language model training on data to answer one overall question: Can it understand the nature of its reality? If we give it a virtual world, does it know that houses sit on streets? Does it realize that people go to work? Can it think of itself as a part of this ecosystem?"

I remember my feed search, the summaries trying to grasp why Project Wit was shut down. Of course NileCorp got threatened. If Wit could truly *understand* a virtual world, then it could also replicate it in a snap.

"It seems," I say, "a little silly to build AI that understands the nature of virtual reality and *not* expect it to target StrangeLoom."

"Medaluo thought so too. Once they employed me, that's what they angled for. Atahua was pulling all funding for Wit anyway—I suppose I was happy to comply. I started to build a new program with an eye toward usability. Something that understood human command so a person could alter StrangeLoom without needing to know the intricacies of the code themselves. Under Medaluo's influence, Wit's original template was transforming into the first prototype of a glorified chatbot that could understand the StrangeLoom system. It was becoming Coldwire. I thought I'd left Wit behind entirely."

I can see where this is going. I look down at my hands, at my pixel-rendered avatar, and I know exactly what happens next.

"And then Eirale gets sick."

"And then," Chung echoes softly in confirmation, "Eirale gets sick. It's terminal. Henry is distraught. He finds me in the labs downcountry with a huge stack of stapled paper. He tells me in a rush that he'd read my original report for Project Wit cover to cover after remembering a conversation we'd had. In it there was a proposal that Wit's language model could possibly learn to *become* someone if it was built with comprehensive data. It could freeze them at a point in time; put an avatar of them in virtual reality. It would be as though they never died upcountry."

Oh, Dad.

"I've never been able to say no to Henry. Whether he was trying to get us into trouble at the academy or asking me to be his best man at his elopement. His request intrigued me. Science calls for experimentation. No one has ever discovered anything new by flinching from the unknown. So I did it."

I put my hands over my mouth, trying to keep my breathing controlled. A scream bubbles up into my throat. I don't want to say something I'll regret; I don't want to scare away any part of the truth being given to me. The sound trapped inside me is molten, and it sears and it sears, but I keep it back.

"It worked. You shimmered into appearance inside this very house, Lia. It was glitchy in the early weeks. You would remember some days but not others. Hold on to certain memories but then recycle more important ones. You have to understand that when you were first created, the assumption was that you'd think exactly as four-year-old Eirale did and stay that way. No one has tried training a language model to truly believe it's a human mind. It was all trial and error."

"I don't—" My head hurts. My throat hurts. I feel as though I'm being disintegrated from the inside out, and maybe I am. "I don't understand. When did it become me? You speak of freezing Eirale, and suddenly it's *me*?"

"I had to rename you. I'd missed a parameter in the first input and you didn't appear resembling Eirale. There was data scrambled in that veered you closer to an average of what a Medan child looked like. I didn't think that mattered when your mind was copied over entirely, and anyway, your dad thought it was for the best. He could bring you home with a new identity rather than explain to the authorities why he had a death certificate for his still-living daughter. I suppose you became Lia somewhere around there.

"At that point in time, my bare-bones prototype of Coldwire was functional enough to take us into upcountry Offron without visas to meet your dad. He had a diplomacy mission there downcountry that month. It was perfect timing."

I take a shallow breath. An impression of a memory brushes the farthermost recesses of my mind. Someone was leading me around. A street in the rain. *A siren in the distance—not a police car, maybe an ambulance.*

"He logged in with a Claw to see you and put the pieces in place to set up a fake adoption in Atahua. Six months later, as soon as your programming was stable, I transmitted you into upcountry Melnova, and you were adopted."

There's a ringing in my ears. An awful tinny hum, growing increasingly louder in volume.

"I thought Dad and Mallory spent time downcountry raising me." I remember being five years old in a house of grief. I remember Tamera moving in to help out, introducing herself to me by name and tutting when I referred to her as Miss Great-Aunt instead. She pinched my cheek and said I was a small sweetie, insisted, *You're calling me Tamera,* and she's been around ever since. "Mallory died in a car accident a year after I was adopted. I thought it was because we were all downcountry."

Chung stills. Finally, his ease has disappeared, tension tightening each line of his posture when he leans against his counter.

"Lia, I'm sorry," he says. "You'll have to hear the full story from your father. But Mallory didn't die in a car accident. She killed herself."

The whine in my ears heightens to a complete roar. "What?"

"It's not your fault," Chung urges. "But Mallory was . . . resistant to you. She and Henry grieved in very different ways, and she was more determined to put Eirale to rest. At first we assured her that you were merely a captured picture of her. To think of it as a photo frame of memories."

"No," I mutter under my breath. "No no no—"

"You were never supposed to *grow*. In all the time we've had AI models, nothing could be classified as sentient because nothing we'd built had ever truly considered itself human. How could they? They're lines of code. They're put to work downcountry, and there's no confusion about their place in their environment."

I'm going to be sick.

"It's my oversight for not considering that possibility. No one had resurrected someone as an avatar upcountry before and not told it the truth. More importantly, no one had asked a language model to imitate a human child and let it take its own actions from there. You were built from someone young enough not to understand the transition—your source code acted accordingly. Your programming decided to age naturally. Your programming decided to adopt maturity as you entered puberty, to mimic what it understood to be the teenage girl. The human girl died while you carried on in her image. But it was only because you didn't know your real nature that you could learn to become human. You may have started as Eirale, but you evolved into someone new entirely."

Sweat soaks my shirt. My heart rackets inside my ribs, hammers through to my ears.

"So it was because of me," I rasp. "Mallory couldn't handle her dead daughter resurrected as some garish imitation, and she *killed* herself."

"Mallory was sick with grief," Chung snaps. "If there's anyone at blame, your father should have prepared her better."

"I can't— I don't—" I bend down, putting my head between my knees in an effort not to faint. I'm not even real, so none of this should matter. I'm nothing but a script stored in the data centers downcountry, and yet I've been relegated to experiencing this rush of blood leaving my head.

"By the time you were in your last year of elementary, I had to sit your dad down and tell him we needed to plan around this," Chung says, carrying on despite my reaction. The curtains are drawing; I get the sense that he's urging me toward his final test. "You couldn't be an avatar forever, and you were clearly aging at a normal rate. I built you another layer of upcountry for your reset days, but that wasn't going to fool you once you matured. Sooner or later, you would realize you had never stepped foot downcountry. You would notice something was wrong, and we needed to allow that. It would mean you understood the nature of your reality. It would mean you were truly, *truly* sentient, and that was a colossal breakthrough in science."

My head jerks up. Chung must read the warning in that, the anger in my eyes to him calling me a *breakthrough*, and he clears his throat.

"It is not a bad thing," he insists. "We were always supposed to evolve. You're the first bridge we've ever built between human and artificial."

My voice is hoarse. "Because I'm not real."

"Because you made yourself real."

"I made myself *wrong*."

I've felt ill-fitting among my peers my entire life. Abnormal from how they think, how they love. To realize that this whole time...

"That's not unique to you," Chung says evenly. "To be human *is* to feel different. Each bit of development you've had away from the norm only confirms that you have self-realized into a unique category. I didn't code any of that for you. You developed it for yourself. *That's* consciousness."

My stomach is churning. It all only upsets me more, because I can't even control my own body's reactions when I seem to have thought myself into existence. Through my childhood, I wasn't only anxious—I was sensing what felt off. The explanation doesn't make me feel better. The fact that there was a *reason* for the wrongness is horrifying. There wasn't supposed to be a reason.

"This is evil," I whisper. "To bring me to life like this, then trick me for so long."

"Your father was supposed to send you back to me earlier," Chung counters, "and he refused."

"Leave him out of this."

"How can I? We argued about this furiously as you got older. When we started this endeavor, we had preserved some of Eirale's genetic material during the scans. Technology had evolved. We could use the material to 3D print her body downcountry and give you a true organic host. You were young enough that we could make slight adjustments here and there to fuse her appearance closer to yours—and even if we didn't, plenty of Atahuans in government were sending their kids to school with entirely different faces for safety. It was a good plan. No one would be able to tell the difference between you and a natural kid unless they opened your head to find only data chips instead of brain matter."

"Please stop." I don't want to hear anymore. I've had enough.

He keeps going. "But he refused, and I left him be. *He* was your father, after all, even if I'm the one who built your model. I'd had enough of my double life anyway. I left Atahua entirely. Renounced my citizenship."

I remember the murmurings in the weeks after his absence. Tamera asking me whether I'd seen my Uncle Chung recently. Her slight nervousness—I'd assumed she was worried about him, but maybe she was worried about me instead. If Tamera has been around since I was *adopted*, she must know the truth about what I am. Maybe she feared Chung would kidnap me from under Dad's nose. When she thought I was playing out of earshot, she'd pressed Dad about the matter, and Dad had shrugged off the question. He must have felt relief that his friend was gone. An ocean away in the real, no longer pushing him on something he didn't want.

"And so we find ourselves in the present time," Chung says. "I expected you'd finish the route in Offron before making your way here, but even missing the last piece, you made it anyway. It proves your capability without a shadow of doubt. Your dad was content to lie to you forever, keep you trapped as a normal user in virtual. But that's not who you are."

"There had to have been a better way to get me here than throwing him under the bus," I hiss. I force myself to stand, my hand gripping the table. "He's being investigated for his association with you. He's going to lose his job, his career."

"He would have been under investigation sooner or later."

"Because of me?"

"Because of *me*. Have you heard of Indisposition, Lia?"

The question is peculiar enough that I blink, scanning the room quickly. It didn't sound like he posed it as a threat. Even if he did, I can't imagine he'd give me a warning before invoking it.

"Of course I have," I say. "I've been online. I've seen the conspiracy theories."

"It's not a conspiracy. Indisposition is something that NileCorp has been doing for the better part of a decade."

I scoff. "Sure."

"The reason no one has realized," Chung says, his tone sharpening at my flippancy, "is because people's minds aren't merely wiped in virtual. They're *replaced*. And whose research do you think they got that from?"

It's a gut reaction to laugh at anyone who believes in Indisposition. As though there might be some big culling effort that no one has noticed. As though anyone could possibly get away with that without loved ones crying out in protest.

But...

"Shit," I say quietly.

"The truth is, Henry was not going to be left alone for long, nor were you. NileCorp has been watching me from the moment I ran off. NileCorp has been eyeing the progress of Coldwire, marking it as the next thing they can swoop in on, because while they may have forced a halt to Project Wit, they had no qualms about using its core components to create bots that replace anyone who has the potential to make trouble for them. It's a perversion of what Project Wit was devised for. They're humanlike without any sentience. Scripted to recognize a broad picture of someone's personality, capable of fooling the general public while entirely under NileCorp's command."

It occurs to me then like a thunderbolt, lighting up each thread I've held in my hands without a way to connect them.

I mean that ever since my dad left his job, he's been entirely different. I can't explain it. It's as though he's been brainwashed. Or recruited into a cult...

"Headmaster Murray...," I start slowly.

"Yes," Chung confirms before I've finished my sentence. "They got him when he wanted to retire. Too dangerous to have him walking around with company secrets. Brilliant, isn't it? You won't ever have a public figure stirring unrest toward NileCorp if they're all rewritten to love NileCorp. The veneer gleaming without anyone the wiser to what's underneath."

The user wiped, replaced with an AI program whose first priority is NileCorp.

"How could people not notice something like that?" I demand. "Kieren must speak to his father downcountry. I know they've attended funerals together. How is it possible to get a *bot* into reality—"

"Same way as we were prepared to download you into Eirale's body," Chung answers. "You would have been trickier as a fully conscious mind. You'd need more storage. A collection of chips to hold everything. But NileCorp's bots? That chip we already possess to connect to the Claw is capable of holding memory too. It's an easy infection. One download, and the bot is walking around downcountry."

I can't hold back my slight gag. My whole-body revulsion.

"How do you know this?" I rasp. "Where is your proof?"

"They told me. James Moore himself did, actually. He wanted me to know what my work had achieved."

That doesn't sound like something NileCorp would do out of the goodness of its heart. And if there was a purpose to it . . .

"James Moore has been in contact with you?"

"As of last week, he has recruited me into NileCorp ranks. Head of their AI division. I can finally get back to my work at the scale I've always wanted."

Dread spreads from my chest to my fingertips. Numbs the edges until I can't feel it when my fists clench.

"And why," I say, "would he give you that?"

"Because NileCorp found me," he says plainly. "They didn't connect the pieces between you and Project Wit until Operation Coldwire was deleted with your digital signature. I put you in front of NileCorp, and suddenly they understood that I was summoning you back to me, what that must mean. While I thought I was tricking them into sending you, they played along so they could get in on what emerges at the end. They wanted the confirmation too. They needed to know you were prepared to handle it. It benefits us all if we let them in."

I take a step back.

"Uncle Chung," I plead. "Wait."

I see the pop-up enter my display. It doesn't give me any option of accepting or declining. The moment it appears, it already begins to install, trickling from 2 percent up to 18 percent, then straight to 59 percent.

Coldwire_download_initiated

"Each moment on your route here was a test to confirm that you are capable enough," Chung says. "I didn't intend Coldwire's final form to be a mere chatbot. The program can only reach its full potential if it interfaces with a sentient person, yet a human mind would splinter if we tried downloading Coldwire onto our avatars. I can't manage it. But you can." He is calm. He offers a faint smile, as though I've fallen over on the playground and skinned my knee, as though I've nervously offered him a test marked with a poor score. It's supposed to be reassuring, and I'm almost swayed.

Until pain erupts in my head, and I stagger against the seat, my shoulder colliding with the side of the table.

"Wait, wait," I beg. "I just want to be normal. Please, let me be—"

Coldwire_download_successful

The world before me explodes into myriad threads. I can see nothing for a moment save for what resembles the birth of a star: gleaming white in every direction, galactic color spreading outward.

Then I blink, and I'm back in Chung's kitchen, frantically trying to make sense of the thousands of pathways available in my display. Every element of StrangeLoom fights forward for my access: the chatter, the signals. The buttons they press downcountry to make it run; the code that darts to life up here. I lift my head, and suggestions bloom around Chung—his previous locations, his notes, his observations. In barely a blink, a flutter of my eye, I trace what's around him and read his chats, his emails, his carefully concealed burner transmissions. I only have to think about wanting to know what he's done, why he's done it, and I've instinctively sifted to the correct messages stored in his display. If he does this for NileCorp, he will be granted the resources he's always wanted. Just get me up to my full potential. They'll keep an eye on me while I follow the path he built. They'll make sure Kieren Murray is reporting in, collecting what they can to prepare my dad's treason charges. Another burst of suggestions opens there, and I follow that route into NileCorp inboxes, their memos, their redacted briefings. Pin Henry Sullivan for treason, and it's only another reason for me to cooperate with them once they swoop into Kunlun for the prize.

"Lia, stay calm," Chung says. "I know it must be overwhelming. Your mind has been human for seventeen years. You need to let it adjust to an artificial interface—"

When I scan through NileCorp's active surveillance open for this task, I see Offron. Then I see my friends. Kieren. Rayna. Hailey. Blinking into Kunlun after entering the shortcut that Chung created at the very end of his treasure hunt: *7 Phoenix Mountain Road, Offron,* the metadata had said. He'd used Coldwire to forge the route, meaning for me to use it once I followed the last clue.

I pivot to the next alert that shows when I'm searching through Kunlun's entry logs. There's another frenzy of rapid warnings. A barrage being sent up.

"No. No, no, *no*—"

NileCorp's soldiers.

I try to slam everything away. My display won't close. All these shifting, dancing elements of upcountry has become another feature of my vision.

"Lia, you should sit down—"

"Sleep!" I scream.

Chung drops like a stone. He hits the ground hard, then doesn't stir. That collision will call emergency services. My gasp gets stuck in my throat, horror calcifying the sound into physical sensation while I track the new threads that jump to life before me. I watch Chung's user ID register with Kunlun's emergency department—then, just as quickly, NileCorp going in and striking the alert.

"This isn't happening," I whisper. "This isn't happening. . . ."

Chung's dog pads over to investigate, and I skitter away, stepping into the living room. I offer myself a few seconds to catch my breath. The clock on the wall ticks erratically, warping to my ears. I have no way of navigating the endless system: I make a desperate lurch to try to see where Dad is, to cry out to him for help, but because I don't know where he is, I don't know where to start. I try haphazardly to summon the image of him, but I quickly lose track of the threads I'm following, returning to the beginning for the ones in my immediate vicinity.

I heave in a desperate breath. Chung said my interfacing with Coldwire was supposed to give me its full potential. He's turned me into this machine *thing*, my mind a key that unlocks every administrative component of StrangeLoom, and still I don't know how to *use it*.

In hysteria, I backtrack, desperately needing to return to Kunlun's entry logs, and my display splits into two to follow the threads I'm most interested in. On the left is the chatter on NileCorp's communication channels while they move into position. On the right is Kieren's location. The right half brightens when it notices that's where I'm paying attention, showing a map of Kunlun's streets. Across the city, in the busy commercial neighborhood, his dot begins to move, unhurried.

". . . secure Lia Ward as an extremely hostile asset," NileCorp's channels are saying on the left. "Indispose the other cadets."

"Kieren," I say, nudging through the commands and opening his line by force. "Can you hear me?"

"Lia?" he replies, his voice pitching high. "What? How—"

There's that. At least I can do that.

"Run!" I command. I dive for the front door, flinging it open. "Run, *now!*"

41

EIRALE

I enter Kunlun, and the hole in my memory instantly trills to make its presence obvious.

The trees wave with the breeze. I've landed in the shadow of a tall building. Instinct tells me to look up, and I trace the high rise to the sky, stretching beyond where my eye can follow. Its middle floors are decorated with foliage and a chrome finish. There's enough space in between for a small aircraft to pass through. The entire building breathes with each gentle gust of wind, its alveoli rising and falling in the form of green vines.

I should remember what I was doing here for my posting, but I *don't*.

"Something wrong?"

I whirl around, finding a stranger standing behind me. I'm frozen for a moment, ready to scramble for excuses and run away from this middle-aged Atahuan man.

Then he pulls his suit sleeve, adjusting its fit, and I realize it's Nik.

"No," I assure him. The deeper sound of my voice gives me another fright. This time I recover quickly enough not to let it show. I go into my panel settings, erasing the existing password and putting in a new one. Now the original user has been forced out for at least twenty minutes. "I forgot we would be wearing different avatars."

We made it in. The neighborhood in Kunlun continues on per normal. No one has registered our appearance as anything beyond the natural log-in of citizens coming through the landing station.

"Did you want to take a look at yourself to get your bearings?"

I glance down at my hands. There's a high likelihood I'm also a middle-aged Atahuan man right now.

"I think I'm good," I say. "Where to?"

Nik inclines his head left and begins to walk. I'm entirely jarred by how bright Kunlun is, the sunshine and the smell of freshly cut grass wafting from the public parks we pass. It's not that upcountry Atahua doesn't have this. The system knows to adjust past the polluted readings it gets downcountry. There are definitely days where the sun peeks out and the daylight feels crisp on our faces, calculated statistics for how it used to be before skies clogged up.

I'm only not used to so *much*, in such liberal helpings. The singing birds. The splashing fountains.

"There aren't any obvious surveillance cameras," Nik murmurs as we cross the road, "but Kunlun covers a lot of ground with traffic sensors and automated bot patrols. We only need to avoid setting them off."

Easier said than done when I can't seem to stop gawping at every block we pass. I nod, keeping in stride at Nik's side. He casts me a glance. I don't know what to make of the way his gaze lingers before he looks away again.

"Six more blocks," he murmurs under his breath. It's late afternoon. We pass a boxing gym with its windows thrown wide, opening its lesson onto the street. The people inside pay us no attention, the coach at the front counting a one-two with gusto. I almost stop, fascinated, but Nik tugs me to keep going, continuing his countdown as we get closer and closer to our destination.

"Four blocks."

A woman walking two chihuahuas passes us on the sidewalk, calling her hellos. Nik smiles and nods. I barely think to respond until he nudges me hard, and then I manage the politest, "Good afternoon." Not a block later, there's another woman, dressed almost the same in highlighter neon colors, blond hair slicked back into a low ponytail.

"Stunning day," she declares on passing.

"Absolutely," Nik responds.

She turns the corner. I pull a face.

"This is eerie," I hiss.

"This is Kunlun," he responds. "Home of the richest people in the world. One more block."

My stomach swoops. I keep quiet, searching frantically for an early indicator of where we're going. I'm waiting for something clinical in the distance, something that resembles a data center. Instead, when Nik seems to be making a turn to cut across a lawn, my eyes land on a preschool, the gates already open to signal that the children have been let out. A girl my age stands inside the fence, changing the lightbulb on a dangling garden light.

She waves at us. She looks Medan. Her sundress flutters loosely; her hair sits neatly in two plaits. There's almost an even split of Medans and Atahuans up in Kunlun. If there's any place where the elite of both countries will flee to while their nations snarl and snipe and raise the prices on anything and everything in an ongoing battle, it's here.

Nik proceeds past the preschool. I accidentally kick a pebble when I follow behind him. Nik whips around, his eyes wide, and I cast my hands up, apologizing wordlessly. My gaze is locked over his shoulder. At the end of the pathway—where our destination awaits, presumably—the front door to a small house is already ajar. If there is anyone home, they're sure trusting to be leaving the door open like that.

"Hello?" Nik calls out. He's switched tactics, going for niceties rather than sneaking up to the house. He's noticed the door too.

He prods the door open with his shoe, not touching anything. It's silent inside. Gaining more assurance, Nik enters properly. He hasn't been here before, I observe. Though he didn't admit it outright, I got the impression that Nik was somewhat familiar with the data centers of our previous locations, but here he's taking everything in with new eyes. He calls, "Hello?" once again.

Nothing.

Nik hurries down the hall without a further word. I make a slower route forward. Turn into the living room. The fur throw on the couch still has the imprint of being recently used. A prickle creeps along my spine. I should go and lock the front door, warn Nik that someone may come in at any moment. Whatever happened here was interrupted.

I poke my head through the kitchen, scanning the table, the overturned chair, the oven mitt left on the counter.

"Soldier. Come here for a second."

I drag my attention away from the kitchen, following the sound of Nik's voice down the hall. He's in the office, rummaging through the desk when I enter. There's a large whiteboard fixed to the wall, scribbled with a variety of calculations.

"Where are we?" I ask.

"Headquarters," Nik answers shortly.

I frown. A jacket has been discarded on the floor, its sleeves turned inside out.

"This looks like someone's house."

"It can be both."

Nik's gaze is distant. It's strange to see him doing this without his glasses in front of him, but even without the visual cue, I know that he's flipping rapidly through something on his avatar's display. I've never witnessed him in virtual until this moment, yet that gesture feels glaringly easy to read. My understanding is almost innate, as silly to explain as why I'd assign red for heat and blue for cool.

"I've got it," he announces.

"Already?" I exclaim. I thought it would have been harder. He did say that Kunlun's file was out in the open, but with that speed, I was entirely useless up here. Nik could have come alone.

"I'm asking Blare to connect the pieces now," Nik says. "They've got it ready to go."

My eyes flit around the office. I frown.

"We can't log out first?" I ask. "We're still sitting in that server room."

"I know," Nik says plainly.

And with that response, I understand there must be more to it than simply fetching the file piece and sending it off to Blare.

"Nik," I press. "What's going on?"

Nik blinks out of his display. He's finished with his transfer.

"I'm sorry for the pretense," he says. "But I needed to get you under a Claw so we could transmit into you." He turns slightly, speaking to a line he must have opened. "Now, Blare."

"*What—*"

I can't move.

I can't move.

"Don't panic. We're going to do the merge. You'll be just fine, Lia."

What are you talking about—

The house implodes. I am aware only of all-consuming heat, eating into my limbs, my eyes, my guts.

Then there is nothing at all.

42

LIA

I slam around the corner of M Street, frantically enlarging the map on my overlaid window.

There has to be a better way to do this. Operation Coldwire fused with my code has to be worth something. I'm supposed to be interfaced with StrangeLoom. That means anything the system can do to its avatars, I should be able to as well.

"Excuse me, excuse me," I call, pushing through a group clustered around a square. There's a small concert playing in the middle. A duo, their guitars connected to miniature speakers. I take the time to hop over the wires, then I'm running again, ducking beneath the waving banners behind their performance. Those who I pass turn in haste, puzzled by my urgency. This isn't a common sight in Kunlun.

I make an abrupt turn, taking the route on the map. It's hard to think while I'm panicking, which also means I can't quite follow the threads waving continuously in front of me. I think back, briefly, to the way Weston popped into Medaluo's server on the tour bus, and I slam out a command to my display, asking it to spit me right beside Kieren's location.

ERROR: System Instruction Not Found. flashes bright red across my display.

"*What?*" I screech. "Are you *useless—*"

While I keep running, I pare down the command, staring at another point on the map. Make it two blocks.

ERROR: System Instruction Not Found, it repeats. Then, when the line disappears, it offers: **StrangeLoom Allowance Within Eye View**.

My attention snaps beyond the map in my display, locking on to the end of the road instead. I turn down opacity in my display. And I move.

My avatar physically bounces, landing at the end of the road with a jolt. I huff, then continue running. That was still useless. But I suppose I'm understanding how Chung built Coldwire.

I can pry into endless data with the correct prompts, sniff out any information floating in the aether. I can interrupt phone calls, enter inboxes, change whatever I'd like about someone's personal information hovering online. But I can't mess with StrangeLoom's fundamental constraints. I can only hack what already exists. Chung can create shortcuts that send my friends through Kunlun's landing station. The system understands that command. I can move my avatar as far as I can see. The system has that prepared in its code already too: our avatars automatically move to the first spot we see if we enter a landing station at the same time as someone else to overwrite collision.

I can't shove myself to the edge of Kunlun and help my friends. I can't grow a hundred feet tall and crush NileCorp's soldiers under my feet.

I've reached a busy bus depot. I scramble up the stairs for the walkway that continues over the buses. The view I have on NileCorp's soldiers tells me their team leader is making a call. Just as I've tuned in, it drops, but another related one appears for my perusal.

"... this won't be a problem. We have a one hundred percent success rate in retrievals. When have we ever failed?"

I recognize that voice. James Moore.

"Chung transmitted an automatic notification the moment his program installed. We've got to move fast, given her capabilities now."

This second voice is familiar as well, but I'm struggling to place it. Just as I'm peering down to watch a bus depart from the depot, my display knows I'm requesting more information, and it floods with information: **Secretary of Defense, Chip Graham.**

I stumble in my step. I tear through his emails, his notes. Once I am merged with Operation Coldwire, they want to capture me, then put me in an isolated room. They're going to bring out Dad and Tamera and Kieren and Rayna and they're going to force me to mutilate Medaluo until the country is in chains. They're going to kill everyone I love unless I keep in line. They're going to use me for decades, for centuries, until my very code fries into oblivion. I see it all. I read the plans faster than my newly non-human mind thought possible.

My display starts to flicker between everything I'm watching at once. I'm nearing Kieren, his dot at the very edge of Kunlun. NileCorp turns the corner of the landing station. Their radios crackle. I activate them, hear bits and pieces: "Sir, half this cohort are Murrays— The instruction was clear— With Kelland Murray, I can't imagine— You don't know Kelland Murray, do you?"

I skid down the stairs at the end of the overhead walkway and emerge back onto the footpath of B Street, at the northern end of the depot. I search the NileCorp files for Kelland Murray—Headmaster Murray—and I almost throw up on the sidewalk.

"Lia?"

I spot him then, under the shadow of a parked bus. It's only Kieren. Where are the others?

"Shit," I whisper. "Shit, shit, shit—" I scramble forward, running toward him. His eyes widen; his arms open. I don't intend to, but it's Kieren who reached for me first, and I react accordingly, diving into his arms and burying my face in his neck.

"I'm sorry," he says. "I didn't want you to log off, I didn't want you to lose everything—"

"Kieren, none of that matters anymore," I breathe in a panic. "I forgive you. I understand. But you have to go. You have to go *now*."

"What? What are you talking about?" His grip tightens. His mouth is warm against my hair.

Kieren holds me like I'm real.

I pull away. I have to make this fast. "Your father isn't the same person anymore because they Indisposed him when he quit as head of security. Chip Graham was afraid that letting him into a civilian life would mean the exposure of state secrets. He asked James Moore to delete his consciousness. The father you know is AI. It's a bot that learned to behave like him using the information NileCorp scraped from their own databases. *That's* why he's so different."

Kieren's mouth opens and closes. He's turned pale. His expression is caught somewhere between distress and disbelief, unable to grasp what I'm saying.

"That's—that's—" Kieren stammers. "Lia, what? I've seen my father downcountry."

I risk a glance over my shoulder, checking our surroundings. B Street hovers on the quieter side. Its highest concentration of establishments are bicycle rental shops, dotted every few blocks. But I can hear the first rumble of disturbance in the distance. Surprised commotion from civilians.

"NileCorp can download the bots into our chips too," I say shortly. "Listen to me: he's far from the first person they've done this to. It's all government retirees. Politicians. Activists. Anyone who could be a danger to the company. They're coming *right now* because they want me, and they're going to Indispose you, too, and no one will know because they'll use all the data they have on you to replace you with an imitation."

Kieren shakes his head, a flash of clarity finally entering his eyes.

"Lia, I need you to backtrack," he says firmly. "What happened when you logged out? How are you here?"

"It's too much to explain right now." I can't get into all of it. There are too many moving parts—too much to explain about *me*, not AI like the thing that replaced his father, but something that evolved differently. Something *sentient*. "Where's Rayna? Hailey?"

"One block away. I ran ahead when I heard from you."

I hear the roar of the motorbike first. At once I'm sprinting for the overhead walkway again, my heart pounding against my ribs. Along the top, I have a perfect view down the street, into the next block. There, Rayna and Hailey are hurrying forward.

"Rayna!" I scream.

Her head lifts. She spots me.

Another roar of a motorbike engine, this time furiously close. The sound cuts me off when I try to shout again, and then it doesn't stop reverberating, nearer, nearer, nearer. I'd assumed the motorbike would be coming from the south, but it shoots out from an avenue ahead, screeching to a halt in the middle of the road. I hadn't been paying attention. I should have opened every camera in the vicinity. I should have sped through them to keep track of where the soldiers were.

The rider is facing Hailey and Rayna. He hefts a rifle upright, his eye pinned through the scope.

"Ready," he announces into his earpiece. "Please activate malware."

He fires, and the world slows to a crawl. The bullet hurtles from the gun, wrapped with a faint white aura. It travels through the air on an unmistakable arc toward Hailey, dead center for her head. It'll land and launch with malware, scramble the consciousness she's trusted to this system.

"No!"

When the world speeds up again, the bullet hits nothing. Hailey is gone. The soldier freezes, his gun halting at the end of its kickback.

I have no idea what I just did.

"Rayna, log off!" I shout. "*Log off!*"

She makes a strangled noise. Her eyes meet mine, frantic, desperate, uncomprehending. But Rayna trusts me, and despite everything she risks, she logs off, disappearing in a blink.

"What's going on?" Kieren exclaims behind me. "Lia, *what—*"

The revving of the engines is coming from all sides. They're going to have us surrounded.

"Kieren, listen to me." I pull him to a crouch, using the barrier of the walkway for a cover. He doesn't resist. "You are the person who knows me best out of anyone in the world. The only person who can talk to me and understand everything I'm saying and everything I'm not."

He blinks rapidly. "Thank you?"

"They want me in my full form. They want me as an all-powerful weapon, and I can't give it to them."

Kieren shakes his head. Bikes screech to a complete blockage, north and south, on each side. "Lia, I have no idea what you're talking about—"

"Me, I'm talking about me. *I'm* Project Wit."

He searches my face. Traces my features to the point of memorization.

"Project Wit," he echoes softly. "You?"

I know what he's asking instead. I nod.

"I'm going to hide myself along this posting we've shared," I whisper in a rush. I'm code. I can create a duplicate. "Three locations. I'll lead you when you're there. Nobody else will be able to find me, but you will, when you're ready. I'm not going to let NileCorp have me. If they take me now, there will be no end to what they do with me."

The enormity of what I'm asking dawns on him without need for elaboration, in the same way that he knows how to anticipate my feint on the sparring mat. I see it in his expression, in the scrunch of his brow.

"Hold on," Kieren says sharply. "I can come with you. We can hide together—"

"No, it doesn't work like that," I interrupt. "I'm virtual. I can only exist inside the StrangeLoom system, and *you* need to get off StrangeLoom and not come back until you're ready—because the moment you do, they'll be able to hurt you. I can't be brought back as myself until there's a scenario where NileCorp can't take me away. You need to decide when that is."

They're shouting below now. Footsteps, thudding up the stairs on each side of the walkway.

"Lia," Kieren pleads. "If I'm understanding you correctly, you're—

I can't even comprehend what I'm saying—you're, what, *deleting* yourself?"

I take his hand. It is as much for me as it is for him. Despite all that I am saying, I still feel this contact to the bone. I could fool myself into thinking I am organic, each of my nerve endings here sparking to life.

"I can't truly be deleted." I search through NileCorp's treasure troves of classified documents while I speak. I find their write-ups of Indisposition, the pages and pages of carefully designed malware, then the function that searches for everything NileCorp knows about a person. Their messages and their photos. Every word uttered aloud upcountry, every action performed as an avatar inside their realm. While I'm using Coldwire's rapid threads to find the code capable of turning a person's entire life into a simplified chatbot, it's also easy enough for me to pluck out the parts demanding a bot's loyalty to NileCorp. Leave behind the ability to summon any thought the imitated user would viably say, take away the parameters of allegiance.

In that moment, I understand Chung a little more. It is otherworldly to be capable of doing this. Science pushed beyond my imagination.

"They're going to keep bringing me back," I say. "But I'll exhaust them on this version until they give up. Which means you're in charge of recovering the other one somewhere far away from them."

"Absolutely not," he hisses. "*This one, the other one.* Lia, you're *you*."

"And until I say otherwise," I say firmly, "I'm yours. Only yours. Find me, Kieren. Please."

Kieren's eyes turn fiery. It's the face he pulls when he knows he's lost. When I have beat him on that last stretch of the lap around campus, when I was faster to submit my assignment at the bottom of the stack for extra points.

When he gets like that, he's only motivated to be better the next time.

"You're impossible," he whispers, ruined, reverential.

"I trust you," I whisper back. "Log out. *Please.* Before they get you."

Kieren shudders through an inhale. Our fingers are interlaced with such force that I feel every bit of his desperation screaming from his touch, and he must sense my anguish alike.

"Okay. I'll find you again."

And in the face of everything, I'm devastated when he actually disappears, my hand closing its grip on nothing. Tears rush to collect in my eyes, finally allowed to surface.

"Freeze!"

The soldiers have circled me in. They shift into position, line the steps so that there's no chance I can run. I grit my teeth, idling a little longer. At last I finish revising NileCorp's own Indisposition code to make my surprise and download it onto the handheld registered among Kieren Murray's belongings downcountry.

Then I run down the list of options in my own core command.

> System Settings.
> Recent Items.
> Sleep.
> Force Wipe.

"Can you hear me?" I say out loud. I see the call box has opened on the left side of my display. **James Moore: Connected**.

"Lia?" he says hesitantly. "Is that you?"

"It's me." One of the soldiers yanks me upright. "You've had such an eye on me, have you? Yet for all your surveillance, you still didn't see this."

They try to lead me to the steps. I drag my feet.

On the line, James Moore says, "Lia, this is for your safety."

I laugh. "Go fuck yourself."

I have enough time to lift my arm, landing one full strike dead center on the soldier's face. The loading bar completes.

LIA.MEM successfully deleted.

43

EIRALE

"Blare, pull her out!"

44

> Loading . . .
> Loading . . .
> Loading . . .
> Loading . . .
> Loading . . .

45

"Lia," Nik says. He's shaking my shoulder. The Claw drops off my head, and I'm blinking, I'm trying to understand where I am. We're back in the server room in Offron. A loud banging echoes faintly above us, moving through the labyrinth of the facility. "Lia, do you remember?"

Nik is watching me carefully for a reaction, his eyes wide.

No, not Nik.

"*Kieren*," I breathe.

46

I remember the first attempt they made to reboot me.

They tried to launch me in a NileCorp lab. It didn't take me long to put together my surroundings: Chung, at my side, hovering over a computer; James Moore, standing by the door. Dozens of security scattered at the entrances for the visual despite the inherent safety of upcountry. I reached for the stapler on the desk and threw it at Moore's forehead for good measure. Before he could react, I deleted myself again.

They loaded me again. On that iteration, I could tell something was slightly off. Different. In seconds I had traced the available cameras, the reports, the active phone calls in the building to figure out what happened. They had ablated me. They cut away one part of my coding to see if it would make me tamer, more cooperative. I didn't bother searching for the exact piece they thought would be useful to remove. I deleted myself entirely.

Each time they tried, I remember. I couldn't track how many days passed between each attempt, how long I stayed offline while they fiddled with the next ablation. All I knew was that I couldn't linger the moment I was live, because I was scared they would threaten someone I loved, and then I couldn't delete myself in good conscience. They couldn't hurt me upcountry. I couldn't hurt them upcountry. But they were the only ones who were capable of going down to the real.

They brought me back. They cut another piece. They wanted the weapon without the girl; they tried to slice me away so they could lose Lia without losing my sentience.

I died, again and again and again. A hundred Lias, a thousand Lias. Each version they loaded emerged a little farther from the checkpoint they had, from my wipe in Kunlun. It didn't matter what they took away. I loaded into existence in the lab, I registered my surroundings, I identified the NileCorp logo within periphery, and the rage curling in my stomach was enough for me to hit my own delete function once again. They couldn't stop me. No matter what they did, they couldn't stop me from taking myself away from them.

So they gave up. The weapon could not be removed from the girl, so the girl had to go. I remember that last wisp of relief when I realized I had no sensation, I had no awareness. They'd loaded nothing except my neural network, and that wasn't me. That didn't come with any of my memories, any of what made me *me*. They'd finally cut this version to shreds, destroyed what chance they had of retrieving something useful.

Which meant the only remaining copy of me was up to Kieren to find.

"Queue the download." That was the last thing I heard in the lab. "We'll have to start fresh."

47

LIA.MEM successfully restored.

48

I lurch to the side, coughing to put air back into my lungs, fighting past the paralysis that had overtaken my body. My head spins with the onslaught. Everything shifts into linear sequence at last, finally correct since I deleted myself up in Kunlun.

I can recall everything again. Erasing myself each time they relaunched Lia Ward. My neural network, taken out and downloaded into an organic body. Eirale Ward, forced into existence solely to give my personhood some time to develop, to let new connections grow over the top of my resentment and resistance. All those mixed-reality simulations I performed at the Button City base—the NileCorp rogue unit was re-creating that final day up in Kunlun. With every week that passed as Eirale, they were making sure Lia wasn't coming back. Once enough time had passed, once Eirale Ward had truly stabilized from that download, they were going to send me upcountry as a new avatar, merge that version of me with Coldwire. Re-create the weapon they'd wanted.

But that was all threatened by Kieren trying to get me back. When they realized there was one more copy of Lia Ward outside their grasp.

"You dickhead," is the first thing I manage to wheeze. "It's illegal to change your appearance upcountry."

Kieren releases a single laugh, the sound filled with such bewilderment that he almost looks scared. The image of him before me is jarring alongside the memories I've suddenly recovered. I've only known this face of his as Nik Grant. Kieren Murray appeared entirely different.

"Come on," Kieren says, giving me his hand. "We have to get out of here first. I don't know who has arrived outside, but someone clearly has."

I scramble to my feet woozily, blood rushing from my head. My mind fights through the collision between the fake memories installed in Eirale and the real ones trying to fill the gaps. Dad, Haven State—real. Foster care, years and years alone—false. Rayna. *Rayna.*

"Miz," I realize with a gasp.

Kieren swings my arm over his shoulders, holding my weight to walk. "Yeah. She's not even Medan, by the way. A week after we went dark to flee NileCorp, her orphan file opened up. She was so depressed about having to run and leave her mom behind without explanation that she tracked down her birth parents to fill the void. Which, you know, made her resentment toward NileCorp even worse. Her birth parents were Pyaish. Atahua changed it on purpose so she would be mandated into military school."

He slams the server room door open, peering out into the hallway. When our immediate vicinity seems clear, he squeezes my hand twice, then tugs us out to keep moving. I have so many matters to ask about at once. A year's worth of questions.

"That's terrible. And Hailey?"

Kieren shakes his head. "We don't know. She hasn't woken up. We were hoping you'd have the answers once we restored you. NileCorp managed to suppress the scandal of me disappearing, but they didn't react in time to hide that Hailey's in a coma. My mom swooped home to scream at everyone. I think the only reason NileCorp hasn't made any active threats toward me by seizing Hailey is because my mom is taking care of her, and she has that livestream running twenty-four seven. Her viewers have been asking where her sons are. She just ignores them."

We take a left.

"Shit," I mutter. "Blare. *Weston.*"

Their faces don't match, but now that I've merged back with my memories as Lia, there can be only one explanation.

"Blare really did change their name properly. It wasn't just to evade the law like me," Kieren says.

"I bet all that kept my memory away for longer," I mutter. "As did your continued insistence on pretending we were looking for Operation Coldwire so that you could mimic our final posting again. *There's a Medan government program broken up across three files in three locations.* Really, Kieren?"

Kieren rolls his eyes good-naturedly, and in that motion alone, his face becomes familiar. He becomes the Kieren I know. I haven't seen it the entire time we've been downcountry.

"I had to come up with a reason why we needed you," he says. "That way you'd take our threats against you seriously and stay with us."

Because the only true reason had been to keep me away from NileCorp. To take me along for the ride until they could pick up my pieces across the three locations, then restore me.

"You did a great job," I mutter.

My mind is still swirling. Kieren, Nik. Nik, Kieren.

"Why *do* you and Blare both look different?"

We hurry up a set of stairs. Kieren glances behind us every so often, ensuring that there is no pursuit.

"My siblings and I have avatars customized to look different from our actual faces. It's a safety feature. Prevents kidnapping attempts of affluent children when people don't recognize their targets downcountry. NileCorp also recommends it for high-level employees and their spouses. My mom opted out. My dad took minor adjustments." Kieren's jaw tightens, facing forward again. "Little good that did for him at the end of the day."

I stifle a breath, a new piece clicking into place. The nightclub. The secretary of defense. Kieren, firing the shot that set off everything—and killing the man who Indisposed his father.

"Kieren," I say suddenly. "What happened to my dad this past year?"

In that fake life they drew up for Eirale Ward, they'd gotten rid of him entirely. I was left to run around Button City, and I couldn't have known to check on him. I couldn't have known to search for him.

"Nothing," Kieren answers. The ramps underneath our feet are starting to even out. We're approaching ground level, emerging back to the top of the facility. "You remember the Atahuan media accusing Medaluo of infringing on human rights in Kunlun?"

I nod. How could I forget? I'd watched those news segments over and over again trying to prompt some familiarity in my memory.

"Of course. Everyone in Kunlun was wondering why NileCorp's private soldiers had flooded their streets."

"They couldn't exactly say it was because they came up to grab us," Kieren says, "so they covered it up by claiming they were protecting Kunlun's citizens from Medaluo. In the process, they were issuing Medaluo a subtle threat by announcing they'd discovered Chung's work and stolen Operation Coldwire out from underneath them. Medaluo couldn't say anything back. But it sure gave your dad an excuse to kick up public fuss about Atahuan overreach. The media was already slamming him for being too soft on Medans. No one thought it was out of the ordinary when he went downcountry in protest and decided he was only working there until NileCorp apologized for marching into Kunlun."

Which they would never do.

"He knows," I say with certainty. "Chung must have warned him."

Otherwise he couldn't have known to stay downcountry. Log out of StrangeLoom, prevent NileCorp from trying to Indispose him.

"Shocking, given what Chung has done to you," Kieren mutters.

Before I can respond, he gestures for quiet as we approach an atrium door. Kieren presses his ear against the panel to listen.

"Where is Miz?" I whisper after a beat. "Still inside?"

"No," Kieren replies. "She's already back in the van. Let's go."

I lean back just in time for his kick on the door. We make a rapid sprint up the stairs. Around the corner, through the lower level, then into the main area.

I halt at once, skidding to a stop right before I can wade into the bodies collapsed on the floor. Hard helmets and bulletproof vests that have done nothing to prevent the spray of bullets embedded in their necks, their faces, their fleshy parts left exposed. They're wearing NileCorp suits.

"They were in first," Kieren notes immediately. "Glass on their sleeves. They broke through the windows. Guns unfired—"

"Shit," I say aloud. There's more to remember outside the restored year and my false memories. The tracker in my boot. Teryn Moore. "Kieren—"

The facility is suddenly as bright as glaring day, spotlights shining in through the broken windows in every direction. It's only now that I hear the shudder of helicopter blades. Multiple aircrafts, floating over the facility.

"Hands up!" a voice bellows from outside, amplified by a megaphone. "Hands in the air, or we shoot!"

I'm struggling to search for the source through the spotlights. My foot inches forward, and I hear a click: a promise to make good on the threat to shoot.

"Hands up! Now!"

Kieren slowly raises his arms. Puts his palms out.

"Lia," he hisses. I haven't moved. "Come on. I only just got you back."

"I don't understand," I say. "If the bodies on the ground are NileCorp, who are these—"

"*Hands up!*"

"Lia, do it!" Kieren urges.

I throw my arms into the air, relinquishing.

Instantly, there's movement through the windows in a frenzy, dark-clothed figures with rifles in their hands. The soldiers reach us, hauling us down. My forehead smacks the floor, the spike of pain striking my scalp hard enough to make me gasp. I strain to catch a glimpse of Kieren, but he's being pulled up and dragged away.

"Come on," one of the soldiers says. He cuffs my wrists behind my back. "Off we go."

Having my memories newly restored has made me more sluggish than I'd thought. Because it's only then, as I'm being yanked upright, that I register the soldiers were speaking Medan the entire time.

We're being taken in by Medaluo.

49

I'm freezing cold.

An unfortunate side effect of being placed into an organic body, I suppose. Existing entirely at the whim of the air-conditioning blowing through the vents above the heavy metal door.

I sigh, drooping my head onto the table. They've looped my cuffs to the middle, forcing my arms to stay straight in front of me. It's cutting off my blood flow. By the time someone actually comes into the room to interrogate me, my arms will have fallen off, and they're going to have to attach cybernetic limbs to the stubs. Then I'll *really* be AI.

I straighten up at the thought. A year ago, when Chung speculated about bringing me downcountry, he'd mused that no one would even know I hadn't been born organically human. *Unless they opened your head to find only data chips instead of brain matter.* He clearly brought the plan into effect. If they ended up naming me after Eirale, then this is the original's genetic material they used for 3D printing. They installed my neural network on the chips. And when Kieren restored my memory, he slammed my entire lifetime as Lia in there too.

I roll my shoulder, trying to ease the cramp there. They took my clothes and gave me a dreary white uniform to wear. They took my shoes with the tracker inside, and I haven't a clue whether it's even emitting anymore. My feet stay bare against the cold floor. My toes have gone numb.

In this body, I can bruise. I can bleed to death. I can board a ship and ride through rough waves and make a visit to Temple Island. I don't really want to go upcountry ever again if that puts me at risk of getting divorced from this feeling—this sense that I am *real*, despite everything.

The door finally opens, startling me out of my reverie.

"Sorry for the delay."

The woman comes in speaking Atahuan. She's Medan, but her speech is like mine, an accent that possess the smoothness of growing up in Atahua. Her pantsuit is pressed and pristine, not a wrinkle appearing even when she drags the chair out the other side of the table and takes a seat.

I know her. She's the woman who stepped out in Threto. The one who directed us to the abandoned apartment, the one who'd traced the infinity on her collar to indicate her employment under NileCorp.

I freeze. What is this? Has Medaluo's federal bureau been infiltrated? Or was she undercover in NileCorp?

"My name is Poppy Kam," she says, lowering the glasses that were sitting over her head. "But just call me Poppy. I hate formalities."

Slowly, I sit up straight. "*Kam?*" I echo.

"That's right." She makes no indication that the name is anything special. She hums under her breath while she scrolls on her glasses, her long nails tapping down on the table. Her hair doesn't budge from behind her ears. It's tucked with such orderly smoothness that there must be droves of pins in the layers keeping the strands straight. I can't gauge her age. She could be anywhere between twenty and forty.

"Why don't we start here?" she says. "What do you remember of your installation?"

The room grows colder.

"I'm not sure what you mean."

She waves up and down. "This body."

I stay aloof. "I didn't realize there were so many terms for birth these days."

Poppy lifts her glasses a half inch. She eyes me. "Is that how we're playing it?"

"I just feel like a lot of people would bristle to hear childbirth called *installation*...."

A sharp metallic sound clatters on the table. She's produced a scalpel from her suit jacket. It lands just out of reach from my fingers.

"Shall we test that?" she asks. "Let's cut into you."

"Blood and guts," I return strongly.

She picks up the scalpel. The blade glints from the floodlights shining in the corner. She's really going to do it, I realize when the tip touches the back of my arm, pressing in. It breaks skin. Pain shoots up my limb, stings so badly that I can't help but try to tug myself away, resist against the handcuffs, find some sense of safety.

"Stop, stop," I hiss.

Poppy withdraws the scalpel. She pauses. The wound is very small. No longer than a fingernail, no deeper than a bee sting.

"Let's try your head next."

"Enough," I demand. "I don't remember much of the process. I have a vague sense of being put in. That's it."

"That was easy, wasn't it?"

Her tone is far too casual for a Medan officer. I don't know who I'm talking to right now, NileCorp or Medaluo.

"It's interesting," Poppy continues. "To have succeeded in making so much trouble for them as Lia Ward that they figured they needed to invent a whole new backstory."

I attempt to splay my hands. The handcuffs hold my wrists in place. A windowless Medan facility is perhaps only the second-worst place to be after a windowless NileCorp facility. At least in Medaluo, they don't have as much to threaten me with.

"I did what I needed to do," I say evenly. "I had no interest in providing anyone with my limitless services."

"That's very understandable. NileCorp already rules the world with the information they collect from StrangeLoom. Anarchists and protesters who understand their clutch are brushed off as conspiracy theorists and extremists. You can't have NileCorp accessing even more."

I narrow my eyes. "It's not only NileCorp I'm worried about. I said *anyone*."

Poppy nods pleasantly. She's still scrolling her glasses.

"You're pretty smart." She pauses. "You think they sent you after Nik Grant on purpose?"

They put my unit in charge of capturing for him on purpose—that much is certain. Maybe they thought it would be some ironic form of punishment for the two of us. I doubt they imagined he would realize who I was, though. And I doubt they expected him to snatch me from under their noses.

But once he did, they sure did work with what they had.

"I think they wanted the Lia version of me deleted permanently," I say. "And it was compelling enough, poetic enough, to send me out and bring that about myself. Take Nik Grant down and collect the file." I lean back into the chair. My handcuffs rattle. "I don't think they imagined he would perform a merge instead."

They might have thought he would try to convince me that we once knew each other. But without the memories that Kieren put back in, NileCorp would have won that one. The false life they embedded into me *was* stronger than my faith in the imaginary Nik Grant. Painful as it would have been after our time together, I would have stayed loyal to my company.

"I'm sure they wanted your file deleted," Poppy decides. "But they also really wanted to close in on Nik Grant. He's stirring more dissent against NileCorp than they've ever seen. It's dangerous. And the only way they were going to capture him was if *you* made him let down his guard first."

I narrow my eyes. This is not a line of questioning I would expect from Medaluo. It hardly sounds like a line of questioning at all—it sounds more like a *debrief*.

"How do you know that?" I ask.

"Why wouldn't I know that?" Poppy returns.

"I'm sorry, I think I'm missing something," I say. "What are you getting at here?"

Poppy takes her glasses off. She sets them on the table. For several seconds, she says nothing. She only waits.

Then the sharp white lights snap out around us and come back red, activating the rapid whir of the backup generator.

"I'm very disappointed," Poppy says. "You and Mr. Murray were supposed to report to your contact at every stage of your final posting, and I didn't hear a peep after Threto."

I swing my hands up, confounded. The cuffs pinch into my wrists.

"It *is* you," I exclaim. "Who are you? Who do you work for?"

"A year ago, I worked for NileCorp. Now I work for the Medans. But if what you're really asking is who I'm *loyal* to, then that's the only question where you'll get a true answer."

She reaches into her pocket and pulls out a card. There's nothing on it except for a symbol: a full circle, four arrows converging in even sectors on the circumference.

"There are two options for you," she says. "As a Medan official, I will offer you the same deal I offered Nik Grant: work for us. You have asylum here."

"I have no use to you," I interrupt.

"Sooner or later NileCorp is going to pick up this battle against you, so you'd do well to remember it will be fought downcountry. You should want an ally behind you." Poppy pushes the card forward. "This"—she taps the symbol with her nail—"is your second option. We're a stateless organization known as the Coalition. Our ultimate goal is destroying NileCorp.

These are my true employers. They're giving us five minutes with the power out so we can speak without the cameras recording."

My eyes snap up. Poppy turns her palm over. When she reached into her pocket, she'd pulled out more than the business card. There's also a small, round bit of metal sitting in her hand, and in the red light, it takes me a beat to recognize it as the tracker. The one Teryn gave me.

"As a member of the Coalition, I have a counteroffer to Medaluo's path," she goes on. "Pretend to accept. Be released into the safe house we'll get you set up in. Your other two friends are already there. You tell them nothing. And before Teryn Moore evacuates the country tonight, you activate this tracker again and lead her to you. We'd shut it down the moment you stepped foot into Offron—but you only need to hold it over heat to turn it back on. When Teryn storms the safe house, you give her Nik. You are Eirale Ward, and you have no memory of anything else, despite Nik's best attempts. You fulfilled your mission: you captured Nik Grant. You go home, NileCorp welcomes you back. And from the inside, you take them down."

I feel the physical cold of the room seep deep into my bones, crystallize my veins. For several moments, I cannot summon the strength for a reply. Then:

"That is absurd."

"Why?"

"I'm not giving up Kieren," I spit. "Offer this to him instead. Ask him to turn me in."

"He has no path in," Poppy says. "Only you do. NileCorp will benefit more having you under their watch than sacrificing you. For as long as you can develop into their promised weapon, they will take you back."

My teeth are starting to chatter. I clamp them together, gritting, "I can't take them down by merely returning."

"You can, and you will." Poppy puts the tracker into my palm. Closes my fingers around it, then turns my hand over to hide the object. "We have people planted already, plans in motion. We only need someone on the inside."

I would be joining a rebellion under NileCorp's noses. But I would have to use Kieren as my tithe.

"I'm not who you think I am."

"Maybe not," Poppy says plainly. "But Nik Grant, Kieren Murray—whatever you want to call him—he's pretty clear about his goals, last I heard. If you don't take your chance in, you've failed him. He would forgive you for making use of him. He would offer himself up if he knew. Wouldn't he?"

I don't answer her with anything more than a glare. I don't need some random woman telling me what Kieren believes in. I am human because I had Kieren to grow up alongside.

Which means, unfortunately, every version of me *does* know what every version of him wants.

NileCorp, burning. NileCorp, engulfed in flames hotter than their worst crimes.

I look away.

"It's up to you, ultimately," she says. "You don't need to accept the Coalition's offer. You can stay in Medaluo with your friends. But you must understand that you would be giving up your fight against NileCorp. They will continue Indisposing all the people upcountry they don't like, and it's only a matter of time before they get to your father. He's been holding strong in the real. But how much longer does he have?"

The lights return. I flinch, taken aback by the bulbs. It's too much at once, and I can't even move my hands to cover my eyes. The tracker sits heavy inside my palm.

"I'm glad to hear that you will consider our offer," Poppy says, her tone changing entirely when she stands. "In the meanwhile, we will get you set up safely." She straightens her jacket. Walks to the door.

"Wait."

Poppy turns around.

"How long has Medaluo been watching us?" I ask. "Since I saw you in Threto?"

She raises an eyebrow. "With our cameras, did you really think we wouldn't notice you entering the country?"

But the Medan government didn't react. They bided their time. It's not as though it would have served them to take Nik Grant prisoner the moment they identified him landing within their borders. He had come looking for something. So they, too, waited until Offron to swoop in, once he had it.

"If that is all, you'll have to excuse me," Poppy says. She tugs open the door. The hinges offer a long, low squeal. "It's your choice, Lia. How you act here dictates the fate of two countries and the world that shapes after them." She steps into the corridor. "I'll go get someone to release you now."

50

True to their word, Medaluo's soldiers take us to a safe house. They transport us in vehicles with nice seats, then hold the doors open when we're exiting. Kieren was riding in the car behind me, and I seek out his gaze as soon as I step onto the sidewalk.

He nods to assure me that he's fine. No bruises, no beatings. Like me, he was given a new set of clothes: plain civilian fashion, a white shirt and black trousers. Regular sneakers, fit for a park jogger. We aren't being held captive.

"This way, please," one of the soldiers say. "We'll be guarding the perimeter, so don't you worry."

I follow the path. They open the front door for us. Someone calls a warning to watch my step when the floor sharply descends at the entryway. They close the door behind us.

Then:

"Did it work?" someone calls down the hall.

My breath catches. "Rayna?"

She walks into view, her arms folded. "It's Miz now," she says carefully. "You already got used to it. No need for backtracking."

Each step she takes closer to me is cautious, apprehensive. Then I open my arms and Miz must see something in my gesture that is comforting enough, because she dives in, so rapidly that I barely have the time to brace.

"Hi," I breathe. "Hi. It's me."

There's something about being hugged in the real that feels different, the faint scent of shampoo that virtual never generated, some twinge of pressure at the elbow that Miz presses particularly hard on, some warm feeling in my chest. I say, "I'm here, I'm here," and Miz is crying.

"You're so ridiculous," she says between gasps. "You couldn't have known we'd be able to bring you back! You couldn't have known it would work!"

"I'm sorry," I say. "I'm sorry. I had to. That was the only way I could escape them."

Miz takes a shaky breath. When she pulls back, she nods resolutely, even while tears continue streaming down her face. Her eyes flicker to the side, bringing Kieren in.

"Everything is going to be okay," she says, and it sounds more like she's trying to speak it into existence than reassure me of our current state. "We got you back. We're going to get Hailey back. We'll be okay."

Miz squeezes me hard again, and my arms delay a beat before I wrap them around her properly. I don't know what I did to Hailey. But I'll get her back. I'll find her if I have to tear apart the entirety of upcountry to do it.

"It worked?"

It's Blare who pokes their head through the other end of the hallway this time, two sets of glasses stacked atop their hair. They amble over casually, hands tucked in their pockets without a care in the world.

"It worked," Kieren answers. He pushes us into the hallway. His hands land on my shoulders, and I lean into it entirely, glad to be guided. "Come on. Let's step inside."

I offer Miz my sleeve to wipe her tears. She chokes out a laugh.

• • • •

The clock turns to ten thirty.

I trace the rim of my empty cup, my eyes flickering to the digital display on the oven every few minutes. The full moon streams in from the window, taking away any need to find an overhead light in the kitchen. Call it lingering trauma, but I'd made sure to lift the window earlier, wiggling my finger out and ensuring I was meeting night air rather than a screen. Definitely night air.

I'd used the handheld on the kitchen counter to look up our current location too. This house is the last one on a residential street at the edge of Offron. There aren't many residential areas in Offron: most civilian streets are surrounded by military outposts. I'd stepped outside before to speak with the soldiers standing guard around the perimeter. We're only supposed to be here for a day before Medaluo sends word for a debrief. That's when Miz, Blare, and I have to give them an answer on whether we're willing to work for them—though the soldiers are already talking to me as though the answer is yes, as though we're on the same side. I guess if I were to turn down their offer, they likely have instructions to shoot me, so it doesn't matter what they reveal. They were even willing to let me rummage through their weapons supply when I asked, just to check how safe we were in the event of danger.

"Lia."

I jump, my teacup spinning out of my grip. Kieren dives into action, grabbing it before it can teeter off the counter and smash onto the floor. Miz and Blare have gone to sleep. Kieren's the only one still walking about the house too.

He's already agreed to the Medans' offer.

"Sorry," he says. "Didn't mean to scare you."

"No, no," I assure him. "It's my fault. I was zoned out."

He pushes the empty cup back at me. The kettle has been filled with water, but I haven't turned on the stove. It only sits on the burner, idle. Kieren must notice that's where my attention lands when I clutch the cup again, and a small crinkle appears in his brow. I can't quite get used to the new arrangement of his face. He was always fine to look at upcountry, in that vague, unremarkable way.

He's very distinctive now. It makes me a little nervous to make direct eye contact with him, which feels ridiculous. If there's anything to be nervous about, it should be how we left off with each other at the end of our posting.

"Do you want me to turn the stove on?" he asks.

"Yeah," I say softly.

He turns the knob. The burner begins to heat up, reddening at the edges first.

Neither of us says anything for a moment.

"Lia," Kieren prompts. "Are you sure you're all right?"

I know for a fact that a safe house must be bugged with listening capabilities. The Medan government wants everything. Nothing is too small to be parsed through.

"It's been a lot to digest," I say. "The past year catching up to me at once, and all that."

"I'm sure. It would have been nicer if we weren't immediately hauled in the moment you were merged, but I suppose beggars can't be choosers."

My lip quirks. Typical of Kieren to complain when he isn't actually mad.

"Hauled in by your new employers, no less," I say delicately. "What's that about?"

"What, working for Medaluo?" Kieren leans against the counter, his hands settling on the heavy granite behind him. I find myself pinning my eyes there. His index finger traces a pattern along its rock face. "I promised as much, didn't I? I'll turn traitor against Atahua if it means bringing down NileCorp. Medaluo is offering their resources to me."

Nik Grant as an entity has proved his hatred for NileCorp sufficiently enough. Medaluo has made a promising bet.

I shuffle closer, coming around the corner of the kitchen island. My

Kieren has changed dramatically since I last saw him. He kills in cold blood now. He wreaks a line of devastation only to make a point.

But Nik fills in the blanks. I have come to understand Nik. And so the two merge easily in my head, even if I was the one who was separated.

"You haven't answered them yet," Kieren states.

"No. I'm... still thinking about."

I must pause too long. Kieren tilts his head, lets my words linger in the air to indicate that he noticed my tone. But he doesn't remark on it.

"I'm new, you know?" I say. It doesn't matter so much if Kieren notices my pause, but I don't want Medaluo's eavesdropping devices around the house catching it too. "In my head, I only lost valedictorian yesterday. It really meant something to me at one point." I consider my words. "To us. It meant something to us."

"It was the one path we thought we could actually dictate," Kieren agrees. He pulls his hands off the counter, lacing his fingers together. "I'm sorry we were pitted against each other."

I huff a laugh. "Who got it?"

"They canceled graduation, actually." Kieren pushes off the counter, opting to come and stand beside me instead. Our sleeves brush together. "There's no coverage that mentions us by name, but there were rumors about an operation that went wrong because of NileCorp entering Kunlun. As far as our classmates are aware, valedictorian was still assigned, just not announced. The academy didn't gather everyone afterward. Graduates were given their positions, and everyone dispersed."

No one would even know that Kieren and I are fugitives. They may think we're both having a swell time working somewhere within NileCorp, only mildly bitter that an international incident took away our opportunity to walk the stage in our formal uniforms.

"Do you think any of them have put two and two together?" I ask. I knock my shoulder into his. "You used to read those Nik Grant comic books all the time. I'm annoyed that *I* didn't figure it out sooner."

He knocks my shoulder back. "Those comic books are a hundred years old. I'd be shocked if any of them recognized Nik Grant for an obviously fictional name. The only reason NileCorp didn't come right out and expose me is because they don't want to open a media storm on me. On my family. My identity as a formerly upstanding cadet would legitimize me as a threat and make them look bad."

I grow still. Kieren does too. In the quiet, I lean into him properly, offering solace. I see it all replaying in my mind, cast anew. Kieren, slinking out of the chaos in that nightclub. Kieren, interrogating me up in the abandoned hallway. He had gone in for revenge and emerged with the intention to take me. I remember what he'd said on his earpiece: *Change of plans. I have something interesting here.*

"How did you know it was me?" I ask.

Kieren pulls back a fraction so he can look at me. My different face, my different voice.

"I actually wasn't sure for a while," he replies. "I had a gut feeling on the first encounter. I almost got distracted when I spotted you, and it didn't make any sense because by all appearances you were a stranger."

The first capture mission took place in east Button City, by the waterfront. It failed spectacularly—he had a Jet Ski waiting to take him away.

"The second time, we fought. You remember that?"

"Of course." It was brief. We hadn't spoken, as we did at the nightclub. I almost got him, and he almost relinquished, but the bomb blew and the ripples shoved me off-balance.

"I got suspicious there. Miz and I spent a year preparing to go after your hidden memory files. I had every contingency plan prepared, which meant I'd done my research into you, your dad, your family. It was mentioned only once, in a newspaper: Eirale Sullivan. Your dad's birth daughter."

I shiver. My mind drifts back to Dad, to the life he had before me. The moment my thoughts float to Mallory, I shut everything out quickly. I have to.

"And then," I say, "after that fight, you looked me up."

"It was far too big of a coincidence," Kieren says. "The typical work of someone who thinks themselves too smart to be caught, which is classic NileCorp. They marked your final posting as Kunlun. They put you as a graduate of Nile Military Academy our year when I knew for a fact you hadn't been there. Other cadets might have waved it off, figured they hadn't paid attention, but *I* knew."

I frown. "Rude."

Kieren blinks rapidly. "Why?"

"I was your biggest competition. No need to go memorizing the rest of the class lists."

His alarm fades. "Are you jealous, Ward?"

"Exceedingly. Your attention belongs to me."

Kieren rolls his eyes, then extends his right arm. The pale strip of skin on his wrist has faded more now, but I'd noted it early on when we were first setting out. I'd suspected that he'd consistently worn a watch and then removed it for Medaluo, or else the tan line wouldn't have been that prominent.

"It does belong to you," he says. "Even when I wasn't talking to your little bot, I wore it around with me. Always."

Ah. But the moment I was there, he couldn't risk me noticing the bot of myself hanging out on his watch. He switched back to the handheld.

He really must have panicked when I started teasing him about an AI girlfriend installed on it. I suppose it wasn't too far from the truth.

"I hope it was useful." I lift my hand, smoothing my thumb over his wrist. He's warm. Solid. "I have no clue what it was telling you in the time I was offline."

"Do you want to see?"

When he pulls his handheld out from his pocket, he hands it to me with the most relaxed manner I've seen from him downcountry. Of course he was tense with it during our entire mission. That day in Kunlun,

I had downloaded a chatbot of me built using pieces of NileCorp's own Indisposition code and sent it to Kieren's handheld, armed with all the information he'd need to find my memory files. Because it was local to the handheld, NileCorp couldn't spy on it. But that also meant if Kieren lost the handheld, he lost the bot, too.

"I'm not sure if you know this," he says, swiping up the chat log for me, "but even though your bot wasn't connected to the internet, it could ping your main network. I could ask for updates about you. Which iteration you were on while NileCorp rebooted you."

I wince immediately. Kieren nods.

"It was painful, Lia. I didn't know if they were hurting you. Torturing you. I could only keep checking and checking to receive your status. So the day the bot stopped being able to ping something, that was when my suspicion took root. Either NileCorp had given up. Or they'd taken you offline."

"That was when they downloaded me as Eirale," I finish softly.

He nods. Gestures down to the handheld.

"So many versions of you. Scattered where I couldn't reach."

I start to scroll through the chat log, stopping periodically on each date that marked a data center breach downcountry.

> KIEREN: **We're in Upsie's data center. Where to?**
> BOT!LIA: **first coordinate is the score you initially got in the Atahuan Literature midterm before you kicked up a fuss about the bonus points**
> KIEREN: **Wow . . .**
>
> • • • •
>
> KIEREN: **sory for the typing there's a time limit here**
> BOT!LIA: **you're in threto?? also this is how i type too what r you apologizing for**
> KIEREN: **yea it's not very eloquent . . .**

> BOT!LIA: **don't think you can talk smack because I don't have a corporeal form right now I'll beat you up later**
> KIEREN: **In Threto! Coordinates?**
> BOT!LIA: **what's the jersey number of the nile academy lacrosse player we both hate . . .**

"I didn't realize my own bot was using riddles," I say.

"It's a great method. Even if it fell into NileCorp hands and they talked to it pretending to me, they wouldn't be able to work out where each of the file locations were."

I go to pass the handheld back to him. The screen moves at my motion, scrolls a bit farther down. I catch a glimpse of **I miss you, it's not the same without you around properly** and in reply, time-stamped three seconds later at two in the morning, **you'll get me back!!!!! i trust you. wholly and completely.**

It almost feels like I've glimpsed something illicit, which is comical when he was talking to a bot trained to speak exactly like *me*. Without questioning it for a moment, I'd given him something that would answer his every message with my innermost thoughts. Every instinct of mine that my functioning mind might prefer to hide.

"As you see, it was very useful," Kieren says, setting the handheld down on the counter. "I'd be lying if I said I wasn't a little attached to it."

I can't help my smile. A soft sensation spreads between my ribs.

"Thank you," I say. "For not leaving any of me behind."

"I couldn't," he returns. "By the time we had that exchange after the nightclub, I suspected enough that I didn't want to risk it, even if it wasn't fully you. It couldn't hurt to bring you along. Then we could make a merge rather than have a fragmented copy of your mind existing as Eirale Ward."

It's an odd notion to wrap my head around. That there could have been a split, Lia Ward and Eirale Ward as two different people. When Eirale melded into my larger consciousness, I could accept that those actions were mine and those days spent on the run with Nik Grant and his team were my memories to carry. All the same, she was a branch. A sector. Closer to me than the Lia Bot I'd put in Kieren's handheld, but still not entirely *me*.

"It was Threto, wasn't it?" I ask. "The zipline."

Kieren's hand hovers up to my temple. He smooths back my hair.

"The zipline," he confirms. "The saving my life from bird flu. The hand-holding."

My pulse stutters. "I didn't realize you were awake for that."

"Incredibly delirious. But aware in some capacity."

I swivel suddenly, intent on confessing everything that unfurled afterward, about Teryn and what she demanded. As soon as I tilt my chin, I bring us much closer than I'd realized.

The kettle is going to whistle any second. My heart is hammering in my ribs. The tracker in the well of water inside reactivated the moment the stove burner turned on. I've made my choice.

I could explain myself, or I could trust that he knows me. Use this time to clutch the one thing that I haven't let myself long for, because it would be too terrifying not to be understood, too heartbreaking if it wasn't accepted.

Kieren breathes out softly, holding still.

I lift onto the tips of my toes, and he reads my gesture in an instant. When my lips touch his, he is gentle, soft. His hands skate onto both sides of my face, and for once in my life, I can't think of what more there is, what more I need. I am satiated, I am satiating, I am tucked safer than a creature in a shell. I am organic, I am strange, and I wrap my arms around Kieren's neck, bringing him closer. He kisses me, he murmurs my name. It isn't the sort of hunger I've seen described, it isn't some distant yearning for an abstract body. It is him, only him, within reach in my grasp after all this time he's spent searching for my pieces to get me back.

The kettle whistles at a high shriek.

We pull apart slowly. I hear the first thud on the rooftop. Kieren doesn't notice. The pit in my stomach is fathomless. This is all I can have for now; it must be enough.

"I promise," I whisper, "that I'm doing this for you."

The explosion blows through the house with a colossal noise. Kieren's quick to duck, pulling me down, but it's hard to escape the sudden onslaught of debris and ash falling from a hole in the ceiling. The fumes are in my nose, in my ears, stinging my eyes. There's screaming, distantly, from the back of the house. Miz and Blare, woken from their sleep.

Don't hurt them, I plead. *Please don't hurt them.*

"Clear!"

"Lia? Lia, what—"

Someone grabs me. I recognize the NileCorp-issued gloves, its rough grip scraping against my bare arm. Kieren is fighting back. Through the haze of smoke, I can hear the commotion, the grunts, but before long they must have him secured because he goes quiet. My arms are pulled behind me. I'm cuffed as tight as possible. They're shoving me into the living room and I'm scrambling to perform a quick count of how many soldiers NileCorp has brought, whether they've called in more backup after losing so many at Offron's data center. Then I'm pushed outside, the ash from the explosion left behind.

The night is brisk. The stars are out in full force in Offron, the air cleared after decades of inactivity from the factories. No plumes, only velvet swaths sweeping atop the mountains. The Medan soldiers who were guarding our perimeter are all down. With merely one aircraft, NileCorp has brought enough people to overwhelm them. By the time a warning signal is sent to Medan federal for backup, we will be gone.

"Eirale Ward."

I close my eyes before I can turn to face Teryn. I search fast, digging through the swirl of panic trying to rise. I scrub off every trace of Kieren that remains. Forget him off my skin, off my hands, off my lips. When I open my eyes, I know she's back, retrieved from whatever hidden channel she'd been shoved into. Amenable, dutiful Eirale Ward.

Loyal Eirale Ward.

"There's no need to handcuff me," I say. "I sent for you."

Teryn isn't in her combat suit. She's wearing a formal uniform. The issued gear of high-ranking NileCorp private forces. Surely she hasn't ascended to that already.

"Your tracker went down," she says tightly. "When a survey unit checked out the data center, they were shot by Medan authorities."

"Because Medan authorities rescued Nik Grant," I offer. "They have new tracker-blocking capabilities. I waited until I was alone before forcing it active."

They're hauling Kieren out. Then Miz. Then Blare. My friends see me speaking to Teryn. Miz yells out, confused, but Kieren stays deathly silent.

"Are you familiar with Project Wit?" I ask.

"What are you doing?" Miz asks as she gets pushed into a line with Kieren and Blare. "What's—what's going on?"

"No, I'm not familiar," Teryn says.

I nod at the team. My friends, who I stay entirely blank toward. "They claimed to be after it but failed to initiate a download. There's no program, but I figured you'd want the assets nonetheless."

For a very long moment, I'm convinced that Teryn will see right through me. That she'll be able to tell the difference between Eirale and Lia, that something in my mannerisms will give up the memories in my head, the sentience lingering at the center of my neural network. I am only safe within NileCorp if they believe me ignorant.

But Teryn must not know about me, nor the true objective of the mission that I was sent on. I realize this when she narrows her eyes, when she's looking at Kieren instead in an effort to figure out whether I'm telling the truth, because it's not me she suspects of lying; it's him. She suspects that he might have fooled me in the process of retrieving the program.

"No, no, no!" Miz is still struggling. "You said it worked. You lied!" She turns to Kieren. "Are you seeing this? I told you she could be NileCorp's soldier! I told you it was a risk!"

I ignore her. It cuts me in two to keep my gaze even, but I do. Teryn's attention moves to Miz curiously, and I need Teryn to take it all in, because it will matter when she reports back to NileCorp executives. *Word for word, Teryn. Note it all down. Record it if you have to.* If I'm going to break my best friend's heart, it better be for good reason. It better earn James Moore's credence when he reads the report.

"Scarab beetle!" Miz wails. "Scarab beetle!"

"Has she lost her mind?" Teryn mutters.

She's trying her last-ditch effort to get something out of me, and I cannot give it to her. My eyes twitch, wanting to fill with tears, but Eirale Ward has nothing to do with this, and so I can only observe it blankly.

"Uncuff her," Teryn says, waving at me. "Take the others."

The soldiers close in.

"Say something," Blare mutters, and they're talking to Kieren, who's been silent, only silent, since the forces led him out from the house.

I finally dare to look. The moment our eyes meet, the smoke bomb erupts in his hands.

The soldiers call out, frantically trying to maintain order. I am the only one who is not surprised, because I'd stolen the smoke bomb from the Medan soldiers earlier while chatting, and then I'd slipped it into Kieren's back pocket just before the kettle shrieked.

I can't see anything. I feel movement, though, rushing around me, the smoke swirling. Teryn is screaming, asking the forces to mobilize, to expand out—

A warm grip closes over my arm. Before I can lurch into combat, I've been pulled with an abrupt movement, my back colliding with a familiar presence.

"Soldier," Kieren says into my ear. "I pay attention."

It's an echo. A familiar set of words—*What can I say? I pay attention*—and in the time it takes me to remember the zipline, the quick work with the two of us on the very same wavelength, he's put his knife to the side of my ribs, and he slashes.

I scream out, pain spasming along my torso in furious waves. Kieren releases my arm. I have no time to catch a glimpse of him: he's gone with the smoke. Despite the blood pouring from my side, despite the relentless tremor that has seized the entire right side of my torso, I have to stop myself from gasping a laugh—an absurdist titter. It takes two rapid battle moves for Kieren and I to communicate with each other in code.

The smoke clears enough to show me my immediate surroundings. I spot Teryn, frantic while she gesticulates at her soldiers, and I stagger forward.

"Teryn. Teryn!" I almost topple onto her. "Teryn, please, he stabbed me. Please help me."

Her face is washboard pale. "Where?" she demands. "This is—I can't—*someone get these cuffs off her!*"

She tries to draw away, still searching through the smoke for where Kieren has gone, and I cry out, falling to my knees. Teryn has no choice but to grab me, to swear violently when a soldier finally comes close enough with the magnetic keys, touching them to my cuff for release. I clamp my hand to my side. My fingers return slathered in red.

"Please don't let me die," I beg, grasping Teryn's arm. It smears a scarlet picture across her sleeve, onto her proper white jacket, and it will be her fault if a soldier dies on her watch. A soldier her uncle sent her to watch personally. Even if she doesn't know why James Moore is so invested in me, she must understand it holds weight. "Teryn, please, *please*—"

"Get the helicopter!" she yells. "Hurry up!"

"Ma'am, the fugitives," one of the soldiers says in a rush. "If we don't secure them, the Medans had cars parked behind the safe house—"

I scream, clutching my wound harder.

"Help, please," I scream, sounding delirious. "Help me, please, please—"

"Get her in—we're going," Teryn commands. "Grab the med bag, now!"

The smoke has almost cleared, and two soldiers haul me to my feet, helping me to the waiting helicopter. I risk a glance over my shoulder, finding an empty scene. They're gone. Kieren's gotten them away.

"Up!"

They put me in a seat, a frenzy of activity rushing to the back of the helicopter to find the emergency medical bag. I stay where I am, both hands wrapped around my wound, a cold sweat forming on my face.

"You're going to be fine," Teryn promises when she comes to sit in front of me. Another soldier yells, "*Lift off!*" and slaps the side of the aircraft, dragging the doors closed. The helicopter shudders. It teeters with the wind, then begins to rise.

They got away.

"I'm sorry," I rasp. "I'm so sorry—I didn't see him in the smoke. I couldn't defend myself."

"You will be fine," Teryn says firmly. She blows out a breath. "You really pissed him off, didn't you? He didn't need to target you to get away. That damn bomb afforded him plenty of time."

Teryn's going to have to answer for that. Why her unit didn't check him for smoke bombs. Why they assumed he'd be unarmed when bringing him out of a Medan safe house.

It can't possibly be *my* fault though, when I'm nursing such a wound.

"Are we going to a hospital?" I ask weakly.

"We've got supplies on board. It should fix you up to stop the bleeding, but otherwise we've got a long ride ahead." Teryn's shoulders straighten. "We're going home. We'll get you patched up there."

I breathe in. I breathe out. The window by my seat shows the flat land of Offron we're leaving behind, aglow from the strong lights at the underside of the helicopter. The cement roads slope into sand, an endless brown that stretches toward distant mountains. Medaluo lies expectant. Its vast terrain is eager to boot us out. It is not Atahua, and it is not mine.

But I will miss it.

A strong gust of wind shakes the aircraft, and my eyes whip back to the window, scanning the scene. It goes so quickly that I almost miss it. The helicopter casts its light on a symbol in the sand below: a full circle with four arrows—and then we've flown past.

"We'll have to cut away your shirt to apply gauze," Teryn says. She didn't notice the symbol outside the window. She wasn't looking.

I nod. My blood drips to the floor, growing a wider circle of red around me, smearing in all four directions as the soldiers walk about. It almost looks just like the Coalition's symbol.

"I'd like a uniform instead," I say. "And when we arrive, I'd like to speak to James Moore myself."

EPILOGUE

BRIEFING—CONFIDENTIAL
James Moore

. . .

2. PRELIMINARY INTERVIEWS
Upon return to Button City, Eirale Ward was taken to the hospital to tend to her injuries. We ensured there was no contact with anyone outside the transport team and two approved hospital personnel in the three days she spent recovering. She was fully cooperative and recounted her time in Medaluo. All facts corroborated with Teryn Moore's write-up.

. . .

5. RECOMMENDATION
At your discretion, we agree that it would be beneficial for you to meet with Eirale and hear from her personally.

6. CONCLUSION

The threat level that Eirale Ward currently poses is low. She has shown no familiarity with former cadets Kieren Murray and Rayna Ward. She has not reacted to mixed-reality scenarios depicting her encounter with our soldiers in Kunlun, which continues to indicate there is no overlap in her memories with her former state.

Eirale is not yet ready to accept Coldwire. Patience is important to ensure that her mind has stabilized, with our values respected foremost. There is nothing to worry about while we continue to monitor her. We have changed Lia Ward's StrangeLoom credentials successfully, and Eirale remains unscanned in the system.

As of right now, and for the indefinite future, **Eirale Ward has no access to upcountry.**

ACKNOWLEDGMENTS

[Acknowledgments to come.]